VESPERTINE

MARGARET ROGERSON

SIMON & SCHUSTER

First published in Great Britain in 2021 by Simon & Schuster UK Ltd

First published in the USA in 2021 by Margaret K. McElderry Books,
an imprint of Simon & Schuster Children's Publishing Division,
1230 Avenue of the Americas, New York, New York 10020

1 3 5 7 9 10 8 6 4 2

Simon & Schuster UK Ltd
1st Floor, 222 Gray's Inn Road
London
WC1X 8HB

www.simonandschuster.co.uk
www.simonandschuster.com.au
www.simonandschuster.co.in

Simon & Schuster Australia, Sydney
Simon & Schuster India, New Delhi

A CIP catalogue record for this book is available from the British Library.

HB ISBN 978-1-3985-0794-4
ANZ & IN PB ISBN 978-1-3985-0854-5
eBook ISBN 978-1-3985-0796-8
eAudio ISBN 978-1-3985-0797-5

Printed and bound by CPI Group (UK) Ltd, Croydon, CR0 4YY

MIX
Paper from
responsible sources
FSC
www.fsc.org   FSC® C020471

TO EVERYONE WHO WOULD RATHER SIT
IN A CORNER PETTING THE DOG THAN
MAKE CONVERSATION AT A PARTY:
THIS ONE'S FOR YOU.

ONE

If I hadn't come to the convent's cemetery to be alone, I wouldn't have noticed the silver gleam of the censer lying abandoned at the base of a tombstone. Every novice and sister carried one, a thurible on a chain to defend ourselves against the Dead, and I recognized this censer by its shape and its tracery of black tarnish as belonging to Sophia, one of the youngest novices, brought to the convent only last winter. When I crouched down and touched it, the metal still felt warm. I had to press my wrist against it to be sure, because my scarred hands weren't good at telling temperature.

I knew right away that Sophia hadn't dropped it while climbing trees or playing among the tombstones. She wouldn't have burned incense unless something had really frightened her; even children knew that incense was too precious to waste.

I straightened and looked toward the chapel. A bitter wind whipped loose strands of my braid around my face, lashing tears from my eyes, so it took me a moment to locate the ravens sheltering beneath the eaves, huddled against the mossy gray stone. All of them were black, except for one. He sat apart from the rest, nervously preening his snow-white feathers, which the wind kept ruffling in the wrong direction.

"Trouble," I called. I felt in my pocket for a crust of bread. As soon as I held it out, he launched himself from the roof in a wind-buffeted flurry and landed on my arm, his claws pricking through my sleeve. He tore apart the bread, then eyed me for more.

He shouldn't be alone. He was already missing a few feathers, cruelly plucked out by the other birds. When he'd first come to the convent, they'd left him in a bloody heap in the cloister, and he had almost died even after I'd taken him to my room in the dormitory and pried his beak open every few hours to give him bread and water. But I was an older novice and I had too many responsibilities—I couldn't watch over him all the time. Once he'd healed, I had given him to Sophia to look after. Now wherever she went, Trouble followed, especially indoors, where she had a habit of upsetting the sisters by hiding him inside her robes.

"I'm looking for Sophia," I told him. "I think she's in danger."

He fanned out the feathers on his throat and muttered to himself, a series of clicks and grunts, as though thinking this over. Then he mimicked in a little girl's voice, "Good bird. Pretty bird. Crumbs!"

"That's right. Can you take me to Sophia?"

He considered me with a bright, intelligent eye. Ravens were clever animals, sacred to the Gray Lady, and thanks to Sophia, he knew more human speech than most. At last, seeming to understand, he spread his wings and flapped to the tumble of earth and stone that shored up the chapel's rear wall. He hopped along the length of a slab and peered into a dark space beneath.

A hole. Last night's storm must have eroded the chapel's foundation, opening an old passageway into the crypt.

He looked back at me. "Dead," he croaked.

My blood ran cold. Sophia hadn't taught him to say that word.

"Dead," Trouble insisted, puffing his feathers. The other ravens stirred, but they didn't take up the alarm.

He had to be mistaken. Blessings reinforced each stone of the convent's walls. Our lichgate had been forged by holy sisters in Chantclere. And yet . . .

The passageway yawned beneath a fringe of dangling roots. I had approached it without thinking. I knew what I should do—I should go running back and alert Mother Katherine. But Sophia was too young to carry a dagger, and she'd lost her censer. There wasn't time.

I unhooked the censer that hung from my chatelaine. Gritting my teeth, I forced my clumsy fingers to open the tiny hatch and fumble with flint and incense. The scars were the worst on my left hand, where the shiny red tissue that roped my palm had contracted over time and pulled my fingers into permanent claws. I could close them into a loose fist, but I couldn't open them all the way. As I worked, I thought of Sister Lucinde, who wore a ring set with an old, cracked ruby. The ring had a saint's relic sealed inside, whose power allowed her to light candles with a mere gesture.

Finally, the spark caught. I blew on the incense until embers flared. Then, wreathed in smoke, I stepped into the dark.

Blackness swallowed me. The smell of wet earth closed in, as smothering as a damp rag clapped over my nose. The opening's thin, watery light faded away almost at once, but like all girls taken in by the Gray Sisters, I possessed the Sight.

Strands of light swirled around me like cobwebs, their ghostly shapes resolving into a contorted face, a reaching hand. Shades. Groups of them congregated in places such as these, drawn to graves and ruins. They were a type of First Order spirit, frail and nearly formless. Their fingers plucked at my skin as though searching for a loose thread to unravel, but they posed little harm. As I hurried past, the smoke that spilled from my censer mingled with their translucent forms. Sighing, they dispersed along with the incense.

Shades were so common that Trouble wouldn't have paid them any mind. Only something more dangerous, a Second Order spirit or higher, would have caught his attention.

"Sophia?" I called.

Nothing answered but echoes of my own voice.

The wavering ghost-light revealed niches filled with yellowed bones and scraps of decayed linen. Nuns were traditionally interred in the tunnels surrounding the crypt, but the age of these remains surprised me. They looked centuries old, crumbling and clotted with cobwebs—older than the Sorrow, when the Dead first rose to torment the living. If this section of the tunnel had been sealed off at some point in the convent's distant past, it was possible a spirit had risen from one of these piles of bones and haunted the catacombs for years without anyone knowing.

A sound shivered through the passageway's thick underground silence, almost too soft to identify. A child's sob.

I broke into a run.

The shades whipped through me, each touch a sudden shock of cold. My censer banged against my robes until I wrapped the chain tightly around my hand. I drew it in front of my face in the defensive position taught to me by Sister Iris, the convent's battle mistress.

A glow bathed a bend in the tunnel ahead. When I rounded the corner, my stomach turned to stone. Sophia had climbed into a niche to hide, her face buried in the knees of her robes. Hovering just outside, a ghoulish form peered in at her, the crown of its bald head visible over a hunched and knobby spine. A shroud flowed weightlessly around its cadaverous body, shining with an unearthly silver light.

For a heartbeat, I stood frozen. The last seven years melted away and I was a child again. I smelled hot ash and burning flesh; my hands throbbed with phantom pain.

But that had been before the Gray Sisters found me. Before they had saved me—and taught me that I could fight back.

I slid my dagger from its sheath. The spirit whipped around, alerted by the whisper of steel against leather. It had the hollowed face of an emaciated corpse, its lips shriveled back from an oversized set of teeth that took up nearly half its skull, bared in a permanent grimace. There were no eyes above, only empty sockets.

Sophia lifted her head. Tears shone through the dirt on her cheeks. "Artemisia!" she yelled.

The spirit's form blurred and vanished. Instinct saved my life. I turned and swung the censer, so when the spirit reappeared a handspan in front of my face, the incense held it at bay. A groan shuddered from its jaws. It flickered out of existence again.

Before it could re-form, I lunged forward and threw myself in front of Sophia's niche, already swinging my censer in a well-practiced pattern. Only the most powerful spirits could pass through a barrier of incense smoke. To reach Sophia, it would have to fight me first.

I knew what it was now. A common Second Order spirit called a gaunt, the corrupted soul of someone who had died of starvation. Though known for their speed, gaunts were fragile. A single well-placed blow could destroy them.

I raised my dagger. Gray Sisters wielded misericordes: long, thin blades designed precisely for such a strike. "Sophia, are you hurt?"

She sniffed loudly, then said, "I don't think so."

"Good. Do you see my dagger? If anything happens to me, promise me you'll take it. I hope you won't have to, but you need to promise. Sophia?"

She hadn't responded. The gaunt reappeared near the bend in the tunnel and flickered closer, zigzagging an erratic path toward us.

"I promise," she whispered.

She understood the danger of possession. If a spirit managed to gain control of a person's body, it could break through barriers designed to repel its kind, even walk among the living undetected for a time. Luckily for most people, only the Sighted were vulnerable to possession. Otherwise Loraille would have been overrun by the Dead long ago.

Another flicker. I sliced my dagger through the air just as the gaunt materialized in front of me, its bony hands grasping. The consecrated blade etched a line of golden fire across its shroud. My breath stopped as the fabric dissolved into vapor, laying bare the unharmed sinew beneath. I had only caught its sleeve.

Its hand closed around my wrist. Splinters of cold shot up the nerves of my arm, wrenching a cry from my throat. I struggled to free myself, but it held my wrist fast, captured in the space between us. Past its clawlike nails, its face swam into focus: drawing closer, the huge jaws parting as though breathing in my pain, sampling the taste. Any moment now my numb fingers would no longer be able to grip the dagger's hilt.

Deliberately, I dropped it. Sophia screamed. As the gaunt's attention caught on the glint of falling steel, I grabbed my censer in my bad hand and drove it upward into the spirit's chest.

It looked at me in surprise. Then it coughed up a trickle of smoke. I thrust the censer higher, barely feeling the metal's heat. The gaunt shrieked, an eerie, echoing sound that sent a shock wave of cold through the tunnel, stirring the brittle bones in their niches. It arched its spine and clawed at its chest, its form blurring in every direction, violently shredding apart, until it suddenly exploded into wisps of glowing fog.

Sophia's uneven breathing was the only sound as the tunnel darkened. I knew I should say something to reassure her, but I could barely move for the pain in my frozen wrist. It was coming alive again in waves of pins and needles, and there were already lines of bruised-looking purple where the gaunt had touched me and blighted my skin.

"Artemisia?" Her voice scratched like a mouse behind a wall.

"I'm fine," I said. I hoped that was true in case I needed to fight again, but I doubted I would. A single gaunt might escape Mother Katherine's notice, but she wouldn't fail to sense the presence of more. I turned to Sophia and let her climb down into my arms. "Can you stand up?"

"I'm not a baby," she protested, brave now that the danger had passed. But as I poured her onto the ground, she abruptly seized my robes, jolting a stab of pain from my wrist. "Look!"

Light seeped into the tunnel ahead, throwing a crooked shadow across the wall. It was accompanied by the sound of hoarse, indistinct muttering. Relief flooded me. I knew of only one person who would be wandering down here talking to herself.

"Don't worry. It isn't another spirit. It's just Sister Julienne."

Sophia clutched me tighter. "That's worse," she whispered.

As Sister Julienne shuffled into view, still muttering, her face hidden by draggled waist-length hair lit white by the lantern, I had to admit that Sophia had a point.

Julienne was the convent's holy woman. She dwelled as a hermit in the chapel's crypt, watching over the holy relic of Saint Eugenia. Her unwashed robes reeked so pungently of sheep's tallow that my eyes began to water at her approach.

Sophia stared, eyes wide as saucers; then she knelt and scooped up my dagger, silently pressing it into my hand.

Sister Julienne didn't seem to notice. We might as well have been invisible. She shuffled past us, close enough that her hem trailed over our shoes, up to the niche that Sophia had just vacated. I strained to make out what she was mumbling as she poked the disturbed bones back into order.

"Heard it down here for years, moaning and wailing . . . finally quiet now . . . Sister Rosemary, wasn't it? Yes, yes. A hard year, a terrible famine, so many dead . . ."

My skin prickled. I didn't know of anyone named Sister Rosemary. But I suspected that if I checked the convent's oldest records, I would find her.

Sophia tugged on my robes. She whispered in my ear, without taking her eyes from Sister Julienne, "Is it true she eats novices?"

"Ha!" Sister Julienne exclaimed, wheeling on us. Sophia started. "Is that what they're saying about me now? Good! Nothing better than a nice, tasty novice. Well, come along, girls, come along." She turned and began to shuffle back the way she had come, the lantern swinging in her wrinkled hand.

"Where is she taking us?" Sophia demanded, following reluctantly. She still hadn't let go of my robes.

"We must be going through the crypt. It's the safest way back to the chapel."

Truthfully, this was only a guess, but as Sister Julienne took us through a series of doors fitted into the roughly hewn tunnels, it seemed increasingly likely. I was sure of it when we reached the final door, a heavy black monstrosity of consecrated iron. The lantern's light leaped over its banded surface as Julienne opened it and ushered us inside.

The air eddied with ribbons of incense smoke, so thick that my eyes stung and Sophia coughed into her sleeve. We had entered a stone chamber, pillared and vaulted. Robed statues stood in the archways between the columns, their hooded faces shadowed despite the candles that guttered at their feet in puddles of dripping wax. Sophia peered around suspiciously, as though searching for a cauldron hidden in one of the corners, or maybe the gnawed bones of past novices scattered across the floor. But the flagstones were bare except for the holy symbols carved here and there, their shapes worn nearly invisible with age.

Sister Julienne let us gawk for a moment, then impatiently beckoned us onward. "Touch the shrine now, for Saint Eugenia's blessing. Be quick about it."

The shrine dominated the middle of the crypt: a white marble platform with a life-sized effigy of Saint Eugenia lying atop the lid of the sarcophagus, her beautiful stone face serene in death. The candles arranged around her body cast a shifting glow over her features, lending her a faint enigmatic smile. She had died a martyr at fourteen years of age after sacrificing herself to bind a Fifth Order spirit to her bones. The spirit was said to have been so powerful that it burned her entire body to ash except for a single joint of her finger, a relic that now rested inside the sarcophagus in unseen splendor. It wasn't like the minor relic in Sister Lucinde's ring, useful for lighting the occasional candle. It was a high relic, wielded only in times of desperate need.

Solemnly, Sophia stepped forward to touch the effigy's folded hands. The marble was shinier there, where countless pilgrims had touched it over the past three centuries.

Sister Julienne wasn't watching Sophia. She was watching me, her eyes glittering through a tangled curtain of hair. "Your turn. Go on."

Sweat itched beneath my robes from the heat of the candles, but the chill in my wrist intensified as I neared the shrine, its pain throbbing in time with my heartbeat. Bizarrely, I didn't want to touch the effigy. The closer I got, the more my body tried to strain away from it without my permission; even my hair felt like it was trying to stand on end. I imagined this was the way most people felt at the idea of touching an enormous hairy spider, or a corpse. Meanwhile, here I was experiencing it instead at the idea of touching a holy shrine. Maybe there was something wrong with me after all.

The thought drove me forward like the punishing sting of a whip. I stepped onto the dais and planted my hand on the marble.

I regretted it immediately. The stone grabbed hold of my palm as though it were coated in birdlime. I felt a sudden, stomach-lurching plunge, and the crypt fell away into darkness. I saw nothing, heard nothing, but I knew I wasn't alone. I was surrounded by a *presence*, something vast and ancient and hungry. I had an impression of feathers shifting in the dark, less a sound than a sensation—the stifling weight of imprisonment, and a devouring, anguished fury.

I knew what this presence was, what it had to be: the Fifth Order spirit bound to Saint Eugenia's relic. A revenant, one of only seven that had ever existed, each now destroyed or imprisoned by the long-ago sacrifices of the high saints.

Slowly, I felt its regard turn in my direction, like a beacon sweeping through the dark. Terror squeezed my throat. I tore my hand from the sarcophagus and blindly stumbled away, nearly singeing my sleeve on the candles. Light and sound flooded back. I might have fallen if a bony grip hadn't caught my shoulder.

"You sense it." Sister Julienne's voice rasped in my ear, puffing sour breath against my cheek. "You feel it, don't you?" She sounded eager.

I gasped for air. The crypt's candles burned on uninterrupted. Sophia was watching me in confusion, beginning to look alarmed. She obviously hadn't felt anything when she'd touched the shrine. I had long suspected, but now I was certain—what had happened to me as a child had damaged me somehow, left an empty space inside. No wonder I had such an affinity for spirits. I had a place carved out for them already, waiting to be claimed.

I stared grimly at the floor until Sister Julienne released me. "I don't know what you're talking about," I answered, so clearly a lie that heat crept dully to my face as I spoke. I moved away and took Sophia's hand. She looked genuinely frightened now, but when she clutched me back I realized with a pang of gratitude that it was Julienne who was scaring her, not me.

"Suit yourself," Sister Julienne muttered, shuffling past us to open another door, beyond which lay the stair to the chapel, spiraling upward. "But you can't run forever, girl. The Lady will do what She wants with you. She always does, in the end."

TWO

News of the gaunt traveled quickly. The next day everyone was staring at me, trying to get a look at the blighted marks on my wrist. Mother Katherine had ordered Sophia and me to the infirmary after we'd come into the chapel, but little could be done for blight; it healed on its own over time, slowly fading to yellow like a bruise. I was given some tinctures for the pain and didn't take them. I told no one what had happened in the crypt.

Life went on as usual, except for the staring, which I hated, but I was used to it. I'd grown skilled at avoiding it by taking convoluted routes through the narrow cobbled paths that wound between the convent's buildings while I went about my chores. Sometimes the other novices shrieked when I appeared, as though I were skulking around specifically to frighten them—I was used to that, too.

But I couldn't avoid them forever. We trained in the cloister's enclosed courtyard three times a week, Sister Iris watching us like a hawk as we practiced forms with our censers and daggers, and there were daily prayers in the chapel. Then, every morning, the lichgate opened to admit corpse-wagons into the central courtyard.

For the past three hundred years, the Gray Sisters had carried out the sacred duty of tending to the dead. Souls that failed to receive the necessary rites would eventually corrupt and rise as spirits instead of naturally passing on to the afterlife as they had done before the Sorrow. When the corpse-wagons arrived, the most decayed bodies were rushed to the chapel's ritual chambers, where they vanished beyond a consecrated door curling with smoke. Less urgent cases went to the fumatorium to be washed and wait their turn.

The fumatorium was named for its perpetual fog of incense, which slowed the process of corruption. The lower level, where the bodies were stored, was built underground like a cellar, dry and cool and dark. On the aboveground level, large clerestory windows filled a bright whitewashed hall with streaming shafts of light. We attended weekly lessons here, in a long room filled with tables that bore a strong resemblance to the refectory where we ate our meals. I kept that comparison to myself, however, because the tables were laid with corpses.

I'd gotten a young man this week, perhaps eighteen or nineteen, only a year or two older than myself. A faint odor of putrefaction hovered beneath the smell of incense seeping up through the floorboards. Around me, some of the other novices were wrinkling their noses and trying to persuade their partners to handle the more disgusting aspects of inspecting the bodies. Personally, I didn't mind. I preferred the company of the dead to that of the living. They didn't gossip about me, for one thing.

"Do you think she'll pass the evaluation?" Marguerite was

whispering, or at least thought she was. I could hear her from two tables away.

"Of course she will, but that depends on whether they'll let her take it," someone else whispered back. Francine.

"Why wouldn't they?"

I opened the dead man's mouth and looked inside. Behind me, Francine lowered her voice further. "Mathilde snuck into the chancery last week and read Mother Katherine's ledger. Artemisia really was possessed before she came here."

Several gasps followed this pronouncement. Marguerite squeaked, "By what? Did it say if she killed anyone?" Multiple people hushed her simultaneously.

"I don't know," Francine said, once the noise had died down, "but I wouldn't be surprised."

"I bet she did kill someone." Marguerite's voice throbbed with conviction. "What if that's why her family never visits? Maybe she killed them all. I bet she's killed lots of people."

By now I had heaved the corpse over—difficult, without a partner—and was examining his buttocks. I really didn't want to listen to this. I wondered what I could say to get them to stop. Finally, in the profound silence that had followed Marguerite's speculation, I offered, "I would tell you how many, but I wasn't keeping count."

A chorus of shrieks erupted behind me.

"Girls!"

Everyone stopped screaming at once, except for Marguerite, who let out one final wavering bleat before Francine clapped a hand over her mouth. I saw that happen because I had looked up to watch Sister Iris swoop down on us from the other end of the hall. She looked straight-backed and severe in her plain gray robes, unadorned aside from a silver oculus pendant at her throat and a small moonstone ring that glinted against the dark-brown skin of her hand. Sister Iris commanded universal fear and respect among the novices, though by our age there was an element of pageantry to our terror. Most of us had figured out that she was a benevolent force despite her stern mannerisms and eviscerating glare. She had once stayed up all night in the infirmary when Mathilde had fallen gravely ill with sweating sickness, mopping her brow and probably threatening her not to die.

She turned that glare on us now, lingering on me for a few additional seconds. She liked me, but she knew I was responsible for the screaming. I almost always was.

"May I remind you all that a priest is arriving from Bonsaint in one month's time to evaluate each one of you for admittance into the Clerisy. You may wish to use your time more wisely, for you will not," she said pointedly, "receive a second chance to leave Naimes."

Looks passed between the girls. No one wanted to stay in Naimes and spend the rest of her life tending to corpses. Except for me.

If I was selected for a higher education by the Clerisy, I would have to talk to people. Then, after I completed my studies, I would be ordained as a priestess, which would involve talking to even more people and also trying to solve their spiritual problems, which sounded horrific—I'd probably make them cry.

No one could deny that I was better suited to the life of a Gray Sister. Administering death rites was important work, more useful than idling away my life in a gilded office in Bonsaint or Chantclere, upsetting people. Then there was the other duty of the Gray Sisters, the one I looked forward to the most. They were responsible for investigating reports of children with the Sight.

I rubbed the scar tissue on my hands, conscious of the places where I felt no sensation. It was like touching leather, or someone else's skin. If someone had looked harder, found me sooner . . .

I doubted it would be difficult to fail the evaluation on purpose. The priest could hardly drag me out of Naimes by force.

Sister Iris was watching me as though she knew exactly what I was thinking. "I see you've finished examining the bodies. Artemisia, tell me your conclusions."

I looked down. "He died of fever."

"Yes?"

"There aren't any marks on his body to suggest a death by injury or violence." I was conscious of the other girls watching me, some leaning toward each other to trade remarks. I could guess what they were saying. Commenting on my stony, unsmiling expression, my flatly emotionless voice.

Little did they know that this was better than the alternative. I had once tried smiling in a mirror, with profoundly unfortunate results.

"And?" Sister Iris prompted, sending a look at the novices that quieted them at once.

"He's young," I went on. "Unlikely to have experienced a paroxysm of the heart. He would be thinner if he'd died of a wasting disease or the flux. His tongue and fingernails aren't discolored, so poisoning is unlikely. But there are broken veins in his eyes, and his glands are swollen, which indicate a fever."

"Very good. And what of the condition of his soul?" The whispering had started up again. Sharply, Sister Iris turned. "Marguerite, would you care to answer?"

Marguerite's cheeks flamed red. She wasn't as pale as me, but her fair skin could display a spectacular variety of colors—generally shades of pink, but sometimes an impressive purple flush, and occasionally an interesting greenish cast, when something I said to her almost made her throw up. "Could you repeat the question, Sister Iris?"

"What manner of spirit would this man's soul become," Sister Iris said in a clipped tone, "if the sisters did not purify it before it succumbed to corruption?"

"A shade," Marguerite blurted out. "Most souls turn into First Order spirits, no matter how they died. If not a shade, then—" She cast a panicked look at Francine, who avoided her eyes. She hadn't been listening, either.

I shared a room with Marguerite in the dormitory, which was so cramped that our hard, narrow beds nearly touched. She signed herself against evil every night before she went to sleep, eyeing me meaningfully the whole time. Truthfully, I didn't blame her. Mostly I felt sorry for her. If I were someone else, I was sure I wouldn't want to share a room with me, either.

Lately, I felt even sorrier for her than usual because I didn't think she was going to pass the evaluation. I couldn't imagine her becoming a nun, and I had an equally difficult time envisioning her as a lay sister, shouldering the convent's never-ending burden of washing, cooking, gardening, and mending. But if she failed, those would be her only two choices. The Lady had granted her the Sight, which meant a life dedicated to service. None of us could survive without the protection of the convent's lichgate, or the incense and consecrated daggers provided to us by the Clerisy. The risk of possession was too great.

Sister Iris had her back to me. When Marguerite's desperate gaze wandered over in my direction, I raised a hand to my forehead, miming checking my temperature. Her eyes widened.

"A feverling!" she exclaimed.

Sister Iris's lips thinned. She cast me a suspicious look. "And to which order does a feverling belong, Artemisia?"

"The Third Order," I recited dutifully. "The order of souls lost to illness and plague."

This received a curt nod, and Sister Iris moved on to questioning the other novices. I listened with partial attention as they described causes of death: exposure, starvation, flux, a case of drowning. None of the corpses provided to us had died violently; those souls could turn into Fourth Order spirits, and they got whisked off to the chapel immediately.

It was difficult to conceive of a time when Fourth Order spirits weren't the most dangerous threat in Loraille. But Fifth Order spirits had been orders of magnitude more destructive. During the War of Martyrs, the seven revenants had raged across the country like storms, leaving entire cities lifeless in their wake. Blighted harvests had blown away as ashes on the wind. There was a tapestry in the scriptorium that depicted Saint Eugenia facing the revenant she had bound, armor flashing in the sun, her white horse rearing. It was so old and faded that the revenant looked like an indistinct cloud rising up over the hill, edges picked out in fraying silver thread.

I could still feel its hunger and fury, its despair at being bound. I imagined that if I listened closely enough to the stillness that yawned beneath the convent's mundane everyday bustle, past the muffling hush of shadowed corridors and ancient stone, I would be able to sense it festering in the darkness of its prison.

"Are there any questions?"

Sister Iris's voice snapped me back to the present. We were

about to be dismissed. As everyone else drifted toward the door in anticipation, already beginning to murmur among themselves, I heard myself ask, "What causes a soul to become a Fifth Order spirit?"

Silence descended like an axe. Everyone turned to look at me, and then at Sister Iris. In all our years as novices, this was something no one had dared to ask.

Sister Iris pursed her lips. "That is a fair question, Artemisia, considering that our convent is one of few to house a high relic. But it is not an easy question to answer. The truth is that we do not know for certain."

Whispering started up again. Uncertain glances traveled between the novices.

Sister Iris didn't look at them. She was studying me with a slight frown, as though she knew again what was on my mind. I wondered if Sister Julienne had revealed to anyone what had happened in the crypt.

Her expression gave no clue as she went on. "It is, however, beyond a doubt that no more revenants have risen since the Sorrow, Goddess have mercy." She sketched the four-point sign of the oculus on her forehead, a third eye that represented the Lady and Her gift of Sight. "The scholar Josephine of Bissalart believed that their rising was tied to the cataclysm that brought about the Sorrow— the Old Magic ritual performed by the Raven King."

Everyone stopped breathing. All of us knew how the Sorrow had happened, but it was a topic rarely discussed and therefore carried an air of the forbidden. When we were younger, a popular dare had involved sneaking a history book from the scriptorium and reading the passage about the Raven King aloud in the dark by candlelight. For a while, Francine had had Marguerite convinced that speaking his name three times at midnight would summon him.

I was sure Sister Iris knew about all this. She sternly finished over the renewed whispering, "The ritual shattered the gates of Death and reordered the laws of the natural world. It is possible that some souls were uniquely corrupted by this act, resulting in the creation of the revenants. Josephine was correct on so many other accounts"—here she pinned the whispering novices with her gaze—"that I trust we need not fear a recurrence, particularly not while you all proceed in a timely manner to your afternoon chores."

Weeks later, I sat watching my breath plume white in the cloister, the chill of the stone bench seeping through my robes and into my thighs. Dozens of other novices my age surrounded me, their nervous chatter filling the predawn gloom like early-morning birdsong. Some of them had traveled from as far away as Mont-prestre for the evaluation, the straw of wagon beds still clinging to their hair. They gazed around in awe at the cloister and stared at the ruby on Sister Lucinde's finger, most likely wondering if it was really a relic, as their neighbor had claimed. Most of the northern convents were so small that only their abbesses wore a relic, and then just one; Mother Katherine wore three.

Marguerite sat hunched beside me, shivering. In her effort not to sit too close to me, she was nearly falling off the bench onto the ground. I'd moved over earlier to give her more room, but I didn't think she'd noticed.

"I've never killed anyone," I offered. That sounded less reassuring out loud than it had in my head, so I added, "Or seriously hurt anyone, either. Not permanently, at least. I assume they've all recovered by now."

She looked up, and for an awful moment I thought she might actually try to talk to me. I wasn't prepared for that. To my relief, the priest arrived then; brisk footsteps sounded against stone, and our heads craned to watch his dramatic figure striding down the center of the aisle. I glimpsed an imperious sweep of black robes and a flash of golden hair before he disappeared with a swirl of fabric into the evaluation room.

As soon as the door closed, the pious silence that had gripped the cloister dissolved into giggles.

"Girls," said Sister Lucinde quellingly, but a great deal of stifled noise continued as the first novice was called into the room.

The giggles stopped for good when the girl emerged only a minute or two later, white-faced and bewildered. Sister Lucinde had to take her by the shoulders and steer her in the direction of the refectory, where pallets were being laid out to accommodate the visiting novices. As she stumbled away, she buried her face in her hands and began to cry.

Wide-eyed, everyone watched her go. Marguerite leaned toward Francine, seated on the bench opposite us. "Don't you think that was fast?"

It was fast. She hadn't been in there for long enough to answer a few cursory questions, much less take an evaluation. It was as though the priest had been able to judge her aptitude at a mere glance. Out of sight, my hands curled into fists.

Dawn light crept into the cloister as the benches rapidly emptied, its pink glow seeping down the courtyard's stone walls, flashing from the windows and glaring in my eyes. By the time the light flooded across the tamped-down grass where we practiced our forms, less than a quarter of us remained. The last novices filed out one by one until only Marguerite and I were left. When Sister

Lucinde called her name, I tried to think of something encouraging to say to her, but I wasn't good at that at the best of times. I was still trying to think of what I should have said when the door banged open less than a minute later, and she rushed past me where I stood waiting, her face crimson and streaked with tears.

Sister Lucinde looked after her and sighed. Then she nodded to me. As I stepped over the threshold, my eyes struggled to adjust to the room beyond. It seemed dark indoors now that the sun had risen, even with a fire crackling in the hearth, stiflingly warm, and a few lit tapers scattered around, throwing shivering reflections from mirrors and polished wood.

"Is this the girl?" asked a silhouette in front of the fire.

"Yes, Your Grace."

The door's latch clicked. Sister Lucinde had shut me inside.

Now I could see better, well enough to make out the priest. His pale, austere face floated in darkness above the high collar of his severe black robes. He was tall, his posture immaculate, his sharp cheekbones casting his cheeks into shadow. His gaze had already returned to Mother Katherine's ledger, its worn pages cramped with records of each girl admitted into the convent. Without looking up, he gestured formally at the empty chair in front of the desk. A ring flashed on his hand, set with a large onyx gemstone.

"Sit, my child."

I obeyed, grateful for my perpetually blank expression. I was used to being called "child" by white-haired Mother Katherine, but the priest couldn't be any older than twenty, almost of an age with us novices. That explained the giggling.

He looked up. "Is something the matter?" he inquired, in a cold and imperious tone.

"Forgive me, Father. You're the first man I've seen in seven

years." When he only stared at me, I clarified, "The first living man.
I've seen plenty of dead ones."

His eyes narrowed, taking me in afresh, as though I were something unidentified that he had just scraped off the bottom of his shoe. "The correct way to address me is 'Your Grace.' I'm a confessor, not an abbot." The ledger snapped shut with a clap, sending dust motes swirling through the air. "Artemisia," he said, disapproval clear in his voice.

"It isn't my birth name, Your Grace. Mother Katherine chose it for me when I arrived at the convent. It's the name of—"

"A legendary warrior," he interrupted, looking slightly annoyed. "Yes, I am aware. Why didn't you provide your birth name?"

I didn't want to answer. I wasn't prepared to tell a stranger that I didn't want my name because the people who gave it to me hadn't wanted me. "I wasn't able to," I said finally. "I didn't speak for more than a year after I came here."

The priest leaned back, studying me unreadably—but to my relief, he didn't ask any more questions. Instead, he drew a silk handkerchief from his robes, which he used to select a small, intricately carved wooden box from a stack on the side of the desk. He briskly slid it between us, as though wanting to get this over with as quickly as possible, and I saw my reflection ripple across the mirrored inlay on its surface: white as a corpse, a draggled-looking black braid draped over one shoulder.

"You may find the evaluation's format strange at first, but I assure you, it's a very simple process." His voice sounded bored, tinged with irritation. "All you must do is hold your hand over the box, like so." He demonstrated and then withdrew, watching me.

I didn't understand how this could be a real test. I suspected he might be mocking me. Warily, I extended my left hand, ignoring the way his gaze sharpened at the sight of my scars. As my fingers neared the box, the air grew colder, until suddenly—

I plunged into cold water, bubbles exploding from my throat in a soundless scream. I choked on the stink of river mud, desperate for air, unable to breathe. Slippery waterweed tangled around my ankles, drawing me downward; and as I sank into the depths, my pulse throbbed in my ears, growing slower and slower. . . .

I yanked my hand back. The torrent of sensation faded immediately, replaced by the cheerful crackle of the fire and the warmth of my dry robes. I focused on the desk, willing nothing to show on my face. The box contained a saint's relic. I could almost picture it inside: an ancient, moldering bone nestled in a bed of velvet, seething with ghostly energy. I guessed that the entity bound to it was an undine, the Second Order spirit of someone who had drowned.

Now I understood. We were being tested on our ability to sense relics. The priest had been able to eliminate the other girls so quickly because to them the box seemed completely ordinary, just as most people touched Saint Eugenia's shrine and felt only lifeless marble. No wonder that first novice had looked so confused.

"There's no need to be afraid. It can't hurt you." He leaned forward. "Just hold your hand in place, and tell me what you feel. Be as detailed as possible."

Now he seemed tense with suppressed energy, like a well-bred sighthound trying not to show its excitement over the presence of a nearby squirrel. I thought back to his exchange with Sister Lucinde and felt a quiet knell of foreboding. He seemed very sure now that I was worth his time, though he hadn't before, not when I had first sat down.

Slowly, I stretched my hand over the box again. This time, I was able to keep the room in focus as the undine's drowning agony lapped against my senses. "I don't feel anything," I lied.

"Nothing? Are you certain?" Out of the corner of my eye, I saw him brush his fingers across his onyx ring. "You can be honest with me, child."

"I—" That was all I managed to get out before I snapped my mouth shut on the rest. I had almost told him the truth.

Worse, I would have enjoyed telling him the truth. A reassuring warmth filled my stomach at the thought of doing what he wanted, of being virtuous and good—and obviously, that wasn't like me at all.

The ring's stone glinted like a beetle's shell in the candlelight. The polished black gem dwarfed even Mother Katherine's large amber cabochon. Earlier, he had called himself a confessor. A cleric's rank was determined by the type of relic they wielded, and each granted a different ability depending on the kind of spirit bound to it. It wasn't difficult to guess what power this one commanded.

Careful not to let my understanding show, I met the priest's eyes. I had never liked doing that; it didn't come naturally to me. I hated trying to figure out the unspoken rules about how long you were supposed to look and how often you were supposed to blink. I always got it wrong. According to Marguerite, I tended to overcompensate by staring into people's eyes too directly, which made them uncomfortable—only she hadn't put it in those words, exactly. She had been crying a lot at the time.

"I'm certain," I said.

Impressively, the priest didn't react. If he was surprised or disappointed, I couldn't tell. He only said, "Very well. Let's continue." He moved the first box away and slid a different one across the desk.

This time, when I put forth my hand, a miasma of sickness enveloped me: the smell of stale sweat, sour breath, and unwashed linens. My breath rattled in my chest, and a foul taste coated my tongue. My limbs felt weak, as brittle as sticks arranged beneath a heavy coverlet.

Third Order, I thought. Most likely a witherkin—the soul of someone who had died of a wasting disease.

Unlike the revenant in the crypt, it didn't seem conscious of its imprisonment. Neither had the undine. That would be a useful observation to share with the priest, I caught myself thinking; he might be impressed by my insight, my ability to sense a Fifth Order spirit. . . .

I pinched myself on the thigh. "Nothing," I reported flatly.

He smiled, as though my uncooperativeness pleased him. When he slid a third box toward me, I thrust my hand over it quickly—and paid for my mistake.

Flames roared around me, licking at my skin. Embers swirled through the suffocating, smoke-filled darkness. And there was the familiar heat, the pain, the stench of burning flesh—the mindless terror of a death by fire.

I flung myself away from the desk. When my vision cleared, I found that my chair had skidded an arm's length across the floor, and my fingernails were sunk into the wood of the armrests.

"An ashgrim." He rose from his seat, his eyes glittering with triumph. "The same type of spirit that possessed you as a child."

The smell of scorched meat still lingered in my nose. I locked my jaw and sat in defiant silence, my breath shuddering in and out. He couldn't claim that I had passed the evaluation if I admitted nothing.

"There's no need to pretend, Artemisia. I know everything about you. It's all right here in the ledger." He came around the desk to stand above me, his hands folded behind his back. "I will admit, I initially had my doubts that your story was true. Most children don't survive possession, especially not for the length of time described in your entry. But those who do are often known to demonstrate an extraordinary talent for wielding relics. Terrible though it is, being forced to practice resisting a spirit's will at such a young age does yield results."

When I refused to meet his gaze, he sank down on his heels, putting our faces level. I saw for the first time that his eyes were a luminous shade of emerald-green, the color of stained glass pierced with light. "You sensed that it was afraid of fire, didn't you?" he breathed. "That was why you burned yourself. It was your way of subduing it, preventing it from harming anyone else."

Before, I had mistrusted the priest. Now I despised him: his beautiful face, his uncalloused hands, every inch of him unmarked by hardship—exactly the type of person I never wanted to become.

He didn't seem to notice the intensity of my hatred. He wouldn't; I had been told that all my facial expressions looked more or less the same. When I still didn't answer, he gracefully rose and paced back to the desk, his black-robed figure straight as he began to pack the relic boxes in a satchel.

"Nearly anyone can master a relic binding some common First or Second Order wraith. The sisters are proof enough of that. But your talent is in a different realm entirely. I have no doubt that you are destined for great things. In Bonsaint, you will be trained to wield—"

"I'm not going to Bonsaint," I interrupted. "I'm going to stay in Naimes and become a nun."

He stopped and stared at me as though I'd spoken gibberish. Slowly, a look of astonished disgust crept across his features. "Why would you ever want such a thing?"

I didn't bother trying to explain. I knew he wouldn't under-stand. Instead, I asked, "To be accepted into the Clerisy, wouldn't I need to have passed the evaluation?"

He gazed at me a moment longer; then a condescending, almost bitter smile tugged at his mouth. "The sisters warned me that you might deliberately try to fail. The true test wasn't your ability to read the relics. It was whether you were strong enough to resist mine." My eyes went to his ring. "A relic of Saint Liliane," he explained, with another brief, unpleasant smile. "It binds a Fourth Order spirit called a penitent, which grants me the power to draw truth from the lips of the unwilling, among . . . among other things." Briskly, he tightened the satchel's buckles and turned to leave. "Fortunately, the matter isn't up to you, and the Clerisy must be alerted as quickly as possible. I will have the sisters collect your belongings. We leave for Bonsaint tonight."

"No." I watched him pause with his hand on the doorknob. "If I'm able to resist your relic, you can't force me to tell the truth. How will you prove to anyone that I passed?"

He had gone very still. When he answered, he spoke quietly and with deadly calm. "It would be my word against yours. I think you'll find that my word is worth a great deal."

"In that case," I said, "I suppose it would be embarrassing if you brought me all the way to Bonsaint, only for the Clerisy to discover that I'm completely mad."

Slowly, he turned. "The sisters will confirm your soundness of mind. In writing, if necessary."

"Not if it's a new development. Everyone already knows there's something wrong with me. It wouldn't be hard to pretend that the shock of confronting an ashgrim during your evaluation was the final straw." I lifted my eyes to meet his gaze. "Alas, it seems that the reminder of my past simply proved too much."

I wondered how long it had been since someone had last defied him. He flung the case aside and took several great strides toward me, his eyes like poison. I thought he might strike me. Then he visibly mastered himself.

"I take no pleasure in this," he said, "but you leave me without a choice. Know that this is for your own good, child," and he clasped his hand over his ring.

At first I felt nothing. And then I gasped. A crushing pressure gripped my heart, my lungs. After a dazed moment I realized it wasn't a physical force but an emotional one, a despairing, ruinous guilt. I wanted to collapse to the floor in misery, to weep and beg the priest for forgiveness, even as I knew I was undeserving of redemption—undeserving even of the Lady's mercy.

The penitent.

I clenched my teeth. I had resisted his relic before, and I could do it again. If he wanted me to crawl on the ground and repent, I would do the opposite. Painfully, I stood, fighting against every joint; and then I lifted my head to meet his eyes.

The relic's influence evaporated. He stumbled a step back, grasping at the desk for balance. He was panting, regarding me with a look I couldn't interpret, a lock of golden hair fallen loose over his forehead.

There came a loud pounding on the door. Before either of us could react, it swung open, flooding the room with daylight. The person who stood on the threshold wasn't Sister Lucinde, but rather a terrified-looking young page, clutching a folded missive.

"Confessor Leander," he stammered. "Urgent news, Your Grace. Possessed soldiers have been sighted in Roischal. Your aid is requested—"

The priest recovered enough to yank the parchment from the page's hands. He unfolded the letter and scanned its contents, then clapped it shut again, as though whatever he'd read had stung him.

I had never heard of Clerisy soldiers succumbing to possession. The priest's face had gone bloodless white, but not with surprise, or even shock; he looked furious at the news. He breathed in and out, staring straight ahead.

"I am not finished with you," he said to me. He ran trembling fingers through his hair to put it back in order. Then, in a swirl of black robes, he stalked out the door.

THREE

one of the sisters said anything to me, but they had to know I'd done something, even if they didn't know what. I kept my head down for a few miserable days, dazed with lack of sleep and dreading going back to the dormitory.

Marguerite had a wealthy aunt in Chantclere who sent her letters and drawings of the city's latest fashions, or at least used to—the letters had eventually slowed and then stopped without explanation. For years, she'd kept them tacked to the wall above her bed so she could look at them every night. I returned to our room after the evaluation to discover that she had torn them all down. Standing in the pile of crumpled parchment, she had looked at me with accusatory red-rimmed eyes and declared, "I would rather *die* than spend the rest of my life in Naimes."

Over the next couple of nights, her weeping kept me awake until the bell rang for morning prayers. I tried talking to her once, which turned out to be a terrible idea; the results were so harrowing I slunk off to spend the night in the stable, grateful that I couldn't inflict emotional trauma on the goats and horses—I hadn't managed it yet, at least.

Then more news arrived from Roischal, and no one was thinking about the evaluation any longer, not even Marguerite. As the first cold rains of winter seeped into the convent's stones, whispers filled the halls like shades.

Everything would seem ordinary one moment, and then the next I'd hear something that tipped me off-balance: novices in the refectory, heads bent together, whispering fearfully about a sighting of a Fourth Order spirit—a rivener, which hadn't been seen in Loraille since before we were born. The next day I crossed the gardens where the lay sisters were tearing up the last shriveled autumn vegetables, and I overheard that the city of Bonsaint had raised its great drawbridge over the Sevre, a measure it hadn't taken in a hundred years.

"If the Divine is afraid," whispered one of the sisters, "shouldn't we be, too?"

The Divine of Bonsaint governed the northern provinces from her seat in Roischal, whose border lay only a few days' travel to the south. Kings and queens had once reigned over Loraille, but their corrupt line had ended with the Raven King, and the Clerisy had risen from the Sorrow's ashes to take their place. Now the divines ruled in their stead. The most powerful office was that of the Archdivine in Chantclere, but according to rumor, she was nearly a hundred years old and rarely extended her influence beyond the city.

Newly ordained, the current Divine of Bonsaint had once traveled to our convent on a pilgrimage to Saint Eugenia's shrine. I had been thirteen then. Locals had turned out in bewildering numbers to see her, strewing spring wildflowers across the road and climbing the trees outside the convent's walls for a better view. But what had left the greatest impression on me was how young the Divine had looked, and how sad. She had seemed subdued on her walk to the crypt, a lonely figure lost in splendor, her attendants lifting her train and holding her elbow as though she were spun from glass.

I wondered how she was faring now. As far as I could tell, the worst aspect of the unfolding situation in Roischal was that no one knew what was causing it. Spirits hadn't attacked in numbers like this in well over a century, and in the past it had always happened in the wake of obvious events like plagues or famines or a city ravaged by fire. But this time there wasn't a clear reason, and even the Clerisy didn't seem to have an explanation.

The day that disaster reached Naimes, I was on my way back from the convent's barnyard, hefting an empty bucket of slops. After an incident in the washing room when I was eleven, the sisters didn't entrust me with any chores that might injure my hands. That day, I had scalded myself with lye and not told anyone—at first because I hadn't been able to feel it and then because I hadn't seen the point. I still remembered how, when at last someone had noticed the blisters, everything had gone quiet and the sisters had given me shocked looks that I didn't understand. Then one of them had shouted for Mother Katherine, who had taken me away to the infirmary, her touch gentle on my arm. Ever since, I had been assigned work with the animals.

Beside the plot where we grew our vegetables, our convent had a small ornamental garden. Roses bloomed there in the summer, their overgrown blossoms nearly burying the garden's half-crumbled statue of Saint Eugenia. This time of year, the hedge around it turned brown and the leaves began to fall. Thus I caught a glimpse of someone inside as I passed. It wasn't a visiting pilgrim; it was Mother Katherine, her downy white head bent in prayer.

She looked frail. The observation swooped down on me without warning. Somehow, I hadn't noticed how old she'd gotten—it was as though I had wiped the dust from a painting and seen it clearly for the first time in years, after ages of simply forgetting to look.

"Artemisia, child," she said patiently, "are you spying on me? Come here and sit down."

I abandoned my bucket and joined her on the bench. She didn't say anything else or even open her eyes. We sat in silence, listening to the breeze rustle through the dry leaves and rattle the hedge. Dark clouds scudded above the convent's walls. The air smelled heavy with rain.

"I've never sensed them," I said finally. "Your relics."

She held out her hand. The gems shone against her papery skin: a tiny moonstone almost identical to Sister Iris's, a cloudy sapphire with a chipped facet, and the largest, an amber oval that captured the light, illuminating small imperfections within. They were mere decoration for the real treasures: the relics sealed away in compartments beneath. Cautiously, I touched the amber and felt nothing but a smooth, ordinary stone.

"The spirits' auras become dimmer when the rings are sealed," Mother Katherine explained. "This doesn't affect our ability to draw them forth, but it makes the relics much more comfortable to wear."

She was regarding me with one keen blue eye, and at that moment she didn't seem frail at all. I remembered little of the night of the exorcism, but I would never forget the feeling of her prayers tearing through my body, drawing the ashgrim forth in a wrathful whirl of smoke and silver embers. The sisters later told me that it had taken all night, and when she had finished, she hadn't reached for her dagger. She had merely lifted one hand and destroyed it with a word.

"A tooth of Saint Beatrice," she went on, tapping the moonstone. "This is the relic I use to sense nearby spirits. It may only bind a shade, but I find it is often the humble relics that prove the most useful." Next she touched the chipped sapphire. "A knucklebone of Saint Clara, which binds a frostfain. It has weakened over time, but its power does help ease the chill in my bones on cold winter nights, and for that I am very fond of it. And this one . . ." She ran her fingers over the amber stone. "Well, let's just say I can no longer wield it as I once could. I'm afraid that when the relic's strength outmatches the person wearing it, there is a danger of the spirit overpowering its wielder. Have I satisfied your curiosity, child? No? If you wish to learn more, these are all things that you can study in Bonsaint."

She said that last part pointedly, with a twinkle in her eyes.

It was a waste of time trying to hide anything from Mother Katherine. At first that had terrified me. I had been convinced that if she could see into my soul, she would decide I wasn't fit for the convent and send me back home. But she hadn't, and then one day a skittish goat had come to the barnyard, beaten by its former master. After I finally succeeded in coaxing it to eat from my hand, she had asked me if I blamed the goat for all the times it had bitten me and whether I thought we should give it back. I'd gotten so angry I had almost bitten her in turn. Then she had given me a knowing smile, and I hadn't been afraid of her after that.

Now I felt a hand on my braid, stroking it much as I had once patted the goat. I wasn't sure I liked it, but I also didn't want her to stop. "I don't believe you would have found Bonsaint as terrible as you imagine," she said. "But if you wish to stay in Naimes so badly, perhaps that is the Lady's will. She may well need you here instead of there."

I opened my mouth to deny this, but Sophia's shouting interrupted me.

"Mother Katherine! Mother Katherine!" She was pelting across the garden, her robes rucked up around her knees. "Artemisia," she added, skidding to a halt beneath the arbor. Trouble's beak poked from the folds of her robes.

Mother Katherine made a show of taking in the dirt and scratches on Sophia's brown legs, her lips pursed to hide a smile. "Have you been climbing again, child? You know that is not allowed."

Sophia looked unrepentant. "There are soldiers coming up the road," she gasped. "Can I help Artemisia tend to their horses? I can carry buckets of water, and straw to rub them down. And bring carrots—" She stopped at the look on Mother Katherine's face.

"Are you certain of what you saw? Soldiers? How many?"

Sophia gave me an uncertain glance, as though I might have an explanation for Mother Katherine's sudden urgency. "They have armor on," she answered, "and there are a lot of them—enough to fill up the road. Stop that," she said to Trouble, who was worrying at her robes with his beak. Then she released him with a shout, falling back from his beating wings.

"Dead!" he cawed, wheeling above us.

The rest of the convent's ravens erupted from the rooftops in a thundering black cloud. "Dead! Dead! Dead!"

Mother Katherine was standing, touching her moonstone ring. "Sophia, Artemisia, into the chapel. Now!"

I had never heard her use that tone of voice. The shock of it propelled me from the bench. Sophia's trembling hand sought mine, and we ran.

The chapel's bells had begun to ring, the space between each toll clamoring with the harsh cries of ravens. Sisters joined us on the path leading to the central courtyard, where everyone was streaming up the cobbled hill to the chapel, clutching their robes against the wind. The air carried by the storm smelled of damp earth, and around me the sisters' faces were blanched with fear.

The moment Sophia and I reached the chapel, gloom swallowed the convent. A sudden needle of cold stung my scalp, then my cheek. Dark spots bloomed on the cobblestones.

"Go," I said, releasing Sophia's hand. She tried to argue, but a sister took hold of her and dragged her inside, lifting her from the ground when she struggled.

I clambered onto the tumbled stones of the ruined inner wall that had once surrounded the chapel, dragging away handfuls of ivy until the lichgate came into view below. It was twice a man's height, its black finials rising skyward like a row of spears. Figures milled on the other side: shying horses, the bulky shapes of armored men.

I had never seen soldiers before. Boys with the Sight were raised in monasteries, and most went on to become soldiers or monks. Only some, like the priest, rose high within the Clerisy's spiritual ranks.

A curtain of rain swept forward, hammering mist from the cobblestones, but I didn't move. I watched through a blur of rain as one man threw a rope up over the finials and yanked on it to draw the loop taut. His movements were jerky and strange. Behind him, a horse whinnied shrilly, struggling to free itself; it had been tied fast to the ends of the ropes. And more horses ahead of it, forming a chain.

I barely felt the downpour soaking my robes. What I was seeing didn't seem possible. Surely, I thought, the consecrated iron would hold—but the lichgate was meant to protect us from spirits, not the brute strength of living men.

There came a distant crack, and the horses lunged forward. The lichgate groaned. Its finials warped, bowing outward. At first I thought the gate would resist, that it would bend but not break, but as its shape deformed, there came an agonized shriek of metal, and it twisted free from the hinges securing it to the wall. It toppled forward in one piece, like a lowered drawbridge. Within seconds its bars were trampled into the mud.

Soldiers poured into the convent. They set upon the granary, their swords hacking and battering with inhuman strength. The door splintered. As they rushed inside, one man paused to look toward the chapel. His eyes shone silver through the rain.

"Everyone is accounted for, Mother Katherine." Sister Iris's voice, behind me.

Heedless of the cold rain trickling down my back, I clung watching as though I had rooted to the stone. A gentle grip took my arm and drew me away. Down from the wall, into the chapel. Mother Katherine.

We must have been the last to enter, because the doors groaned shut behind us and the floor shuddered as the heavy bar fell into place. The pounding of the rain receded to a muffled drumming. The chapel's warmth enfolded me, but gooseflesh still pricked my body. Mother Katherine surveyed the huddled mass of girls and women, faces ashen, wet hair plastered down.

"The soldiers are possessed." My robes dripped onto the carpet. "Aren't they?"

She squeezed my arm. "Wait here. I will have need of you."

I obeyed, gripped by a sense of unreality as she herded the youngest novices toward the altar, then instructed the lay sisters to pray and light incense. Led by Sister Iris, the Gray Sisters drew their daggers and formed a defensive line. I didn't think it would help much. The sisters weren't equipped to battle living thralls, Clerisy soldiers wearing armor and wielding swords.

In my mind's eye, I saw the pews hacked to kindling. The cloth torn from the altar, flames licking at its fringe.

Mother Katherine returned holding a lit taper. She briefly shut her eyes. Then she nodded, confirming something to herself. Sorrow shadowed her face as she passed me the candle. "Artemisia, I have a task for you. You must descend to the crypt and alert Sister Julienne. She will know what to do."

Wordlessly, I set off along the aisle. A numb blankness filled my mind as I hurried past the tall stained-glass windows adorned with images of spirits and saints, their tranquil faces downcast. Somewhere, a young novice wept and a sister tried to comfort her. Whispered prayers rose and fell around me.

"Goddess, Lady of Death, Mother of Mercy, give us strength. . . ."

"Our flesh may be weak, but our hearts are as iron in service to Your will. . . ."

"Lady, do not forsake us. Please, do not forsake us. . . ."

My candle's flame stopped wavering and stood perfectly still. All around the chapel, the rest of the candles did the same. Hairs stood up on the back of my neck. The Lady was listening to our prayers.

But that didn't mean She would save us. She couldn't—She relied on mortals to carry out Her will in the physical world. Whether we lived or died was up to us, and maybe She had come so we wouldn't die alone.

I reached the banded door set into the wall of the transept. As I lifted my sodden robes to descend the stairs, I felt a dull throb of hope in my chest. Mother Katherine must be planning to call upon the relic of Saint Eugenia. Sister Julienne—had she been trained to wield it? I had never paused to wonder whether her life of privation and solitude was in pursuit of a higher purpose.

Underground, the prayers faded along with the distant pounding of the rain. Smoke swirled from the depths to twine around my shoes, eddying with every footfall. My steps echoed from the walls.

"Sister Julienne?" I called.

A faint, sucking gasp wafted up the stairwell like a draft.

I raced around the final bend—and froze. The lid had been shoved from Saint Eugenia's sarcophagus. A soldier lay slumped against it, a sister's misericorde protruding from his throat, the wound bubbling forth a pink froth of blood. Dead, or dying. How had he gotten inside?

The collapse. The opening had been filled, but the foundation was still awaiting permanent repairs. The rain must have washed the passage out again.

Another gasping breath disturbed the crypt's silent, stifling air. I rushed around the slab to find Sister Julienne sprawled on the flagstones, clutching a small jeweled box. As I bent over her, she struggled to open her eyes. Blood had soaked through her robes, leaving them a sheet of shining crimson.

I dropped the candle and pressed my hands to her stomach, where the sword wound gaped. Hot blood welled between my fingers. "Stay awake, Sister Julienne. Just a little longer. I'll bring the healers." Even as I spoke, I recognized the futility of those words. No healer could help Sister Julienne now.

Her eyes sprang open. Swiftly as a striking adder, she seized my wrist. Her fingers were deathly cold. "Artemisia," she rasped. "Take the reliquary."

The box. I forced myself not to recoil. Its gilded surface sparkled with opals, fiery glints of color showing through the smears of blood. "Take it where?"

Her clouded eyes sought mine, wandering and unfocused, as though she saw through me to another plane. "We have guarded Saint Eugenia's relic for three hundred years. It cannot fall into the grasp of the unliving. They know that the revenant cannot be freed, only destroyed. Thus they seek to destroy it. It is our greatest weapon, and without it we have no defense."

"I don't understand," I said. "Should I take the reliquary to Mother Katherine, or do you mean that I should—run, escape with it from the convent?"

"No," she croaked. My shoulders slumped with relief. I couldn't imagine fleeing, abandoning Sophia and the others to die, even if staying here meant dying with them. But what she said next dashed my relief on unforgiving stones. "I pass my duty on to you, Artemisia of Naimes. You must take up the relic of Saint Eugenia. This is the Lady's will."

The crypt suddenly seemed far away. Black spots swarmed my vision, and ringing filled my ears. "I haven't been trained," I heard myself say, my voice eerily calm to my own ears. "I don't know how."

"I'm sorry," Sister Julienne whispered. Her eyes sank shut. "Goddess have mercy on us all." Her hand slid from mine to fall limp on the ground.

For a long moment I couldn't move. My thoughts turned gray and crawling. Then I remembered everyone in the chapel above, afraid, waiting, helpless. I doubled forward, bunching handfuls of my robes in unfeeling fingers.

I wasn't in the habit of praying alone. I recited the sisters' prayers out loud every day along with everyone else, but that was different, easier than coming up with my own words. I could barely talk to people; trying to talk to a goddess seemed like a bad idea. But I needed to know.

Lady. Please, if this is truly Your will, give me a sign.

Two things happened at once. There came a knock of metal against stone, and something cool and hard touched my knee. The reliquary had tumbled from Sister Julienne's slack grip and had fallen against me, candlelight glinting in the opals' depths.

Simultaneously, barely an arm's length away, the soldier's corpse exhaled. Mist poured in streams from his eyes and nose and mouth, gathering into a shape that hovered in the air above him. He had died, and the spirit that had possessed him was exiting his body. As soon as it re-formed, it would attack.

I had no more time to think, to hesitate, to doubt. The Lady had answered me—not once, but twice. Swallowing back bile, I took the reliquary and pried its latches open.

FOUR

For a heartbeat, nothing happened. The inside of the reliquary was lined with crimson velvet, so old that it had worn smooth and dark in places and reeked suffocatingly of dust. Saint Eugenia's finger bone was slotted into a groove in the velvet, blackened as though by fire. I saw no evidence of the revenant bound to it, and more unsettlingly, felt nothing.

I was starting to wonder whether there was something I was supposed to do, a ritual to perform or a blessing to recite, when mist boiled upward from the bone and my world exploded into pain.

Sometimes, I sat on the dormitory's roof before dawn to watch the bats return from the countryside. They roosted in the chapel's bell tower by day, and just before sunrise they descended upon it in enormous flurrying clouds of black. That was what it felt like to take the revenant into my body—as though its essence funneled into me in a whirling, shrieking cloud, flashing dark behind my eyelids and battering the inside of my rib cage with a thousand wings. It was too much. I couldn't contain it all.

A scream tore from my throat. Convulsions overtook my body. Through red streaks of agony, I felt my spine arching and my heels gouging the floor. Inside me, something howled, and my own thoughts disintegrated before the onslaught. My fingers twitched, then curled into claws.

I hadn't thought it would feel like this, like being possessed again, a thousand times worse than the ashgrim. I remembered what Mother Katherine had said in the garden. I wasn't a match for a high relic; the revenant was trying to overpower me.

I couldn't let it. I forced a resisting arm downward inch by inch to reach for my misericorde. I wrenched it free from its sheath and pressed the flat of the blade against my wrist.

My skin sizzled where the consecrated metal touched. The dagger fell from my nerveless fingers and I collapsed, relieved, as the revenant's power shrank back. But spasms still racked my body, and I couldn't do much more than twitch and gasp against the flagstones.

That was when I heard the voice.

"Get up, human." The rasping command came from everywhere and nowhere, slithering between the spaces of my thoughts. *"Do you want to die? Get up!"*

I wondered if I had lost my mind. Spirits weren't supposed to be able to talk. Even while possessing me, the ashgrim had only expressed itself through simple urges, flashes of rage and hunger that I'd barely been able to tell apart from my own desires. Most of the time, it hadn't even felt like a separate entity. But I remembered, touching Eugenia's effigy, how different the revenant had felt compared to the less powerful spirits—

"If you don't get up, I will make you. I'll tear your mind apart, if that's what it takes."

Yes, it could speak. I heard myself laugh, a horrible mirthless croak.

"What's wrong with you?" the voice hissed. *"Are you mad? That's just what I need, a deranged nun for a vessel."* And then, *"Move!"*

From somewhere inside me, the revenant *pushed.* I rolled over in time to see a spirit's ghostly claws rake through the air where my face had been a moment before. Instinctively, I reached for my misericorde.

"No," said the revenant. *"Not that. Take the dead soldier's sword."*

The sword lay within reach. Staggering upright, I eyed the heavy length of steel. "I've never—"

"That doesn't matter. Pick it up. Now!"

I wasn't about to start taking orders from a spirit, but I sensed movement nearby and knew I couldn't hesitate. I lunged for the weapon, only to stumble an extra step forward when it proved impossibly light in my grasp, almost weightless. Normally my hand's weakened muscles wouldn't be able to grip something this heavy securely enough to use it in combat, but that didn't seem to impede the revenant.

"Turn," it commanded.

I pivoted, trying not to overbalance again. The spirit flowed toward me as a boiling mass of vapor, becoming more defined the nearer it grew. I made out a lopsided face, the features melted like wax, its eyes febrile sparks of light in sunken sockets. A feverling.

"Swing."

Unearthly strength coursed through my body. The sword traced an effortless arc, steel flashing in the candlelight. It felt so easy that at first I thought I had missed. Then I saw that the feverling hung sliced nearly in two, only a few wispy filaments of vapor connecting its halves. And its face—I had never seen a spirit look afraid.

"Again."

One final swing, and the feverling shredded away to nothing. Satisfaction coiled through me, like a cat licking its whiskers after a kill. I clenched my hand on the sword's hilt. That feeling had belonged to the revenant, not me.

"Perhaps you aren't as useless as I feared. Still, there's something strange about you—you're listening to me, for one thing. . . . Oh, what's this?"

Sister Julienne's blood pooled at the corner of my vision, shining crimson. I looked away, but it was too late. Everything I saw, the revenant also perceived through my eyes.

"A dead aspirant? What does that make you?" An astonished pause. *"You don't have any training at all, do you?"*

"Be quiet." It hurt to speak, my throat raw from screaming. I rested the sword's point on the ground and bent to retrieve my dagger.

"I doubt you even know how to dismiss me back into the relic," it went on, incredulous. *"Do you have any grasp of the danger you're in, human? It's only a matter of time before I possess your body and take it on a long, merry—"*

Its voice cut off with a hiss. I had slapped the dagger against my arm again, raising another welt. In the merciful silence that followed, I tasted a coppery tang in my mouth. When I swiped a hand across my lips, my fingers came away freshly gleaming red. I must have bitten my tongue while convulsing.

The blood looked unnaturally scarlet, almost pulsing in the crypt's shifting candlelight. It wasn't just mine; most of it belonged to Sister Julienne. As soon as I had that thought, my vision tunneled, and a rush of vertigo swept through me, turning my knees to water.

Weakness wasn't an option. Taking measured breaths through my nose, I sheathed my dagger and tucked the reliquary beneath my arm, making sure it was tightly latched as I set foot on the stairs. Though the revenant's presence had receded, I still felt it evaluating me, circling my defenses like a fox around a henhouse. The moment I let down my guard, it would try to possess me again. That was assuming it got a chance.

"What happens to you if I get killed, revenant?"

"Nothing," it replied, too quickly.

"You go back to the relic," I guessed. "If that happens, you'll be helpless, and the spirits attacking us will destroy you. To be able to protect yourself, you need to keep me alive. That's why you helped me."

"Why do you care, you horrid little nun?" it snapped.

"Because you're going to keep on helping me," I said grimly. "You don't have a choice."

Halfway up the stairs, I could hear the prayers again, muffled by layers of stone. Another few steps, and there came a scream, a splintering of wood. I took the rest of the stairs at a run.

When I burst into the chapel, I was met with a scene of disarray: novices weeping, Sister Iris shouting orders to the nuns. She stood guarding Mother Katherine, who knelt at the altar, deep in prayer. The doors still held, but barely; as I watched, a new sliver opened in the wood, bitten through by a blade.

Sister Iris turned as she heard me enter, her expression relieved for the instant it took her to take in my appearance. Then she definitely stopped looking relieved.

"Artemisia? Where is Sister Julienne?"

I was bleakly aware of how I must look, dripping with gore and clutching a sword. I bolted the crypt's door and held out the reliquary. "Please keep this safe."

The blood drained from Sister Iris's face. "Oh, Artemisia."

I couldn't bear the look she was giving me. Would she believe me if I told her I wasn't possessed? I didn't know. Wordlessly, I turned from her and walked down the center of the nave, between the pews, conscious of how the prayers and weeping silenced as I passed. I caught a brief glimpse of Marguerite, her mouth hanging open. Ahead, the door shuddered with continuous battering strikes. A crack appeared in the bar.

"Revenant," I said, ignoring the stares this earned me, the frightened whispers. "Attend me."

"I'm not your servant," it hissed. Then, grudgingly, *"There are dozens of thralls outside. Be ready."*

Another blow shook the doors. Then they burst open in an explosion of flying splinters.

So many men. A tide of them, stinking in their mud-spattered chain mail, eyes shining silver with ghost-light. To them I must have seemed an easy target, standing alone in their path. My drab gray robes did nothing to distinguish me from the other sisters. I felt the wind blow a mist of rain across my face as they came for me.

The revenant tugged on my arm, like a puppeteer tweaking a string. I lifted it, palm upraised. Power roared up within me like a wildfire, consuming, unstoppable. A *push*, and the soldiers halted as though they had slammed into an invisible barrier. A *twist*, and every last one fell to his knees, seizing. Their mouths stretched wide; a torrent of vapor poured from them as they jerked and trembled and at last slumped unconscious to the floor.

I swayed forward as the last of the revenant's power funneled out of my body. The ground pitched beneath my feet, and dark spots bloomed across my vision. I caught my weight on the sword, its point sunk into the nave's carpet.

The evicted spirits roiled above the soldiers in a writhing, disoriented mass. Some of the men stirred and groaned. Alive, but in no condition to join the battle.

"They're at their weakest now. Stop dawdling and destroy them before they regain their senses. Or is my power too much for you, nun?"

In answer, I stubbornly hefted the sword and staggered forward. A flash of startled approval came from the revenant. Strength surged into my limbs, quickening my steps to a run. My sword sang through the air, effortlessly cleaving the nearest spirit to ribbons just as it began to take shape.

"On your left!"

I swung around, intercepting a gaunt that had flickered into existence beside me. Its claws brushed my cheek, but the touch left only a faint chill in place of the searing cold of blight. A second stroke reduced it to tatters.

The revenant must have sensed my surprise. *"I can protect you from blight, as long as I'm not trying to do too many other things at the same time. But that's all. Swords, arrows, axes—anything that belongs to the physical world can still harm your pathetic flesh vessel."*

It was probably telling the truth, but I felt unstoppable. Spirits fell before me like wheat to a threshing. The exertion filled me with an awareness of every heartbeat, every breath that expanded my lungs, the charged smell of rain and stone from the storm outside. Even the sticky heat of the sword's leather grip felt new and wondrous. I had never realized what a miracle it was simply to have a body—to be alive, to *feel*.

The revenant. This was the revenant's pleasure coursing through me, sharing my human senses.

Motion flickered at the periphery of my vision. The sisters had joined the battle, their daggers flashing like quicksilver. Now that the soldiers had fallen, they were able to fight.

More thralls crowded the chapel's doorway. I turned to face them. The revenant's power welled up again in my outstretched hand, and this time I was prepared for the push, the twist, the emptying rush of its force flung outward. I barely stumbled as I pressed forward, weaving around the men's unconscious bodies strewn across the floor.

A strange ripple in the air came as my only warning of something amiss. Then an unearthly wail filled the chapel, and pain split my skull. I doubled over, the sound grinding relentlessly in my ears. Through a haze of agony I saw the hangings on the walls billow in a ghostly wind. The flames of the candles blew sideways, and then they snuffed out. Sisters fell clutching their heads.

A pale shape rose from the muddle of spirits, veiled in silvery radiance. Diaphanous garments swirled around its slender form. Though it had a coldly beautiful face, its eyes were terrible, stark and staring with rage. The cry that poured from its lips stretched on and on without breath.

"A fury," the revenant hissed, sounding as distressed as I felt. *"Your head—I had forgotten—"* Pained, it broke off. A whisper of numbing cold traveled up my spine. The throbbing in my head grew bearable, but my dread didn't ease.

I had never expected to see a fury in my lifetime. They were Fourth Order spirits born from victims of murder. In our history lessons, we had read about a single fury decimating entire companies of soldiers during the War of Martyrs, incapacitating dozens of men at a time with their paralyzing scream.

The fury raised a delicate hand and pointed toward the back of the chapel. Faster than I could react, the mass of newly expelled spirits streamed past me, re-forming into recognizable shapes as they boiled over the pews. Gaunts flickered ahead of the pack, darting here and there as they sought paths between the curls of incense. I started after them, but my muscles locked. The revenant was straining against me.

"Leave them. The fury is their leader. It's a more important target."

"But—"

"Can you fight in a dozen places at once?" it snarled. *"Destroy the fury, and the rest will follow."*

The revenant was right. The sisters wouldn't be able to defend themselves until the fury's cry ceased. But I physically couldn't make myself turn my back on the novices. Only Sister Iris and the lay sisters remained close enough to the altar to defend them. Sophia had found a candlestick and was clutching it as a weapon, her face screwed up with pain. Any moment now the spirits would find a way through the incense, and there were so many—

I had forgotten Mother Katherine. Serenely, she rose from her position kneeling at the altar and touched her amber ring.

For a disorienting moment, it seemed that two figures occupied the space where she stood. There was Mother Katherine, white-haired and frail, and there was also a hulking, armored shape looming above her, its shoulders bristling with broken spears and arrows. It held a giant notched broadsword, which came swinging down like an executioner's blade.

When the weapon struck the floor, a shock wave rippled outward from the point of impact, violently tearing through the first spirits it encountered and flinging back the rest. A gaunt shrieked as it struck a hanging censer and dissolved within the smoke.

"Have you seen your fill? Move!"

I was already turning, running. The fury took no notice of me until my sword whistled toward it. Then it pinned me with its wrathful gaze and shifted just enough that the blade harmlessly soared past, biting deep into the wood of a pew instead. I planted a boot on the armrest and wrenched the sword free.

"Behind you. Wait—cover your eyes!"

Just as the revenant shouted its warning, the fury's wail intensified to a deafening shriek. I flung a protective arm in front of my face as the chapel's windows shattered inward, filling the air with glinting shards of colored glass. A bright line of pain sliced across my neck; another scored my ankle below the hem of my robes. When the wail cut off with a final wretched sob, someone was screaming.

I recognized the voice. Sister Iris.

The fury looked hungrily toward the altar. In a flash it plunged away, swooping up the nave. I pursued it, broken glass crunching beneath my shoes. Wind-lashed rain gusted across the aisle, clearing the air of incense smoke. Mother Katherine had collapsed beside the altar, and Sister Iris held her, frantically touching her face.

"My reliquary," the revenant hissed.

The reliquary lay on the floor, unguarded. That was the fury's target. But all around it sisters were fighting for their lives. Some had already fallen, nursing blighted wounds, as others defended them from multiple spirits simultaneously.

The revenant didn't see any of this, I sensed—its attention was locked on the reliquary as though nothing else existed. Nausea clenched my gut at the writhing turmoil of its emotions. Saint Eugenia's relic was at once its ancient, hated prison and its only fragile protection against oblivion.

I flung myself into the fray. My sword felled one spirit after another, but there were too many. I couldn't reach the fury, now circling above the altar, covetously eyeing an injured girl who lay curled on the floor below, her chestnut hair spilled across the carpet. Marguerite. Weakened, she had become an ideal target for possession.

In my head the revenant spat, frantic: *"The moment the fury possesses that girl, it will use her body to destroy my relic."*

I cut down a feverling in my path. Through clenched teeth, I said, "Then don't give it a chance. Force it from her body, like you did before." Nearby a sister cried out, mobbed by several spirits at once.

"It will resist. We've lost the advantage of surprise—this time it will sink in its claws." Panic scrabbled at my ribs. I couldn't tell the revenant's rising desperation apart from my own. *"Give me more control, nun. Let me end this. I have the power; you only need to let me use it."*

Out of the corner of my eye, I watched Sophia swing her candlestick at a hovering spirit. The metal wasn't consecrated and had no effect except to draw the spirit's attention. It was a frostfain, icicles hanging like a beard from its rime-encrusted face.

If I unleashed the revenant, I wasn't sure I could subdue it again afterward. But I was out of time. I had no choice. Above my head, the fury was gathering itself to pounce. The frostfain was reaching for Sophia.

"Do it," I said, and threw aside my sword.

The revenant's elation tore through me like an inferno. Silver hazed my vision. I felt a spreading at my back, the lifting and unfurling of a great pair of wings. Every face, spirit and human, turned and beheld me with fear.

Ghostly flames licked over my body. There came a pulse like a wingbeat, and the silver fire roared forth, blazing across the floor, over the pews, up the walls, dancing cold across the beams of the vaulted ceiling. The sisters cried out and shrank back as every spirit flared bright, like scraps of paper igniting in a pyre. And then they snuffed out, consumed, as the revenant howled and howled.

It wasn't finished. The flames licked higher. I felt the ghost-fire spill out the broken windows, across the convent's grounds. I felt it tearing through the crypt, through the winding tunnels of the catacombs, devouring every lingering shade in its path. I felt all those things as though the fire had become an extension of my own body.

And I felt life. The grass, the trees as the flames swept outward, the soldiers unconscious on the floor, the nuns cowering in front of me. Even the worms and beetles that crawled unseen beneath the soil. Hunger yawned inside my chest. I could consume them all.

No. That was what the revenant wanted, not me. "No," I said out loud.

The ghost-fire vanished. In the darkness that followed, I dropped to the floor in agony. The revenant thrashed inside my body like an animal in a cage. My fingers tore at my own skin, at the carpet, at the broken glass surrounding me. I surrendered control of my left hand to focus on my right and reached down to draw my dagger. I gripped it with all my strength.

"I won't go back," the revenant hissed, its spiteful voice laced with venom. *"Do you know what it's like, being trapped in a relic for hundreds of years? I'll kill every wretched nun in this place before I let them put me back! I'll make them regret the day they imprisoned me."*

Inch by agonizing inch, I pulled the dagger to my breast. I felt the revenant's awareness latch on to the weapon. Scornful, it laughed.

"That won't work again, nun. This body is mine. All you can do now is delay me, and whatever you try, it will hurt you as much as it hurts me—"

The dagger pressed against my skin, a bright, chill point. The revenant froze.

"You won't," it said.

I pushed. Blood trickled wet down my stomach.

"You're bluffing."

I had studied anatomy under the Gray Sisters' tutelage, and knew exactly how to angle the blade to drive it up between my ribs and into my heart.

"Stop that," the revenant snapped, exerting itself on my arm to no avail. *"I said stop!"*

"You won't possess me." My voice barely sounded human. "If I have to take my own life to stop you, I will."

"You idiot! You have no idea what you're doing. If you die while I'm still in your body, our souls will become entangled—you'll be imprisoned with me in the reliquary!"

"Then I pity you, revenant."

"What?" it seethed.

"You'll be trapped with me forever. After a few days, you'll beg for your relic's destruction just to get away from me."

"You're insane!" it howled. It lashed out with renewed fury, but I knew that I had won. I grimly held on as it railed against its fate, its deliberate struggle giving way to frenzied clawing, clawing and shrieking, wordless in its rage. And as my consciousness faded, I gripped it tightly and bore it down with me into the dark.

FIVE

I burned with fever. I had been split into two halves, and both were trying to devour the other. I twisted in sweat-dampened sheets, seeing the faces of nuns warp above me, my body shoved down again and again by their restraining hands. Prayers stung my ears; incense scoured my lungs like poison. My mouth was pried open and a bitter syrup poured down my throat. After that I fell still, my thoughts lurching strangely to and fro.

I loved the nuns, but I also despised them. There was something terrible about being their prisoner. They would lock me in a dark box and leave me there forever. Sometimes they would even pray about the Lady's mercy while they did it. Wretched nuns! All I cared about was not going back into that box. I would do anything, anything . . .

"I'll do anything," I moaned aloud. "Please."

Sister Iris's face hovered above me. There was a cut on her

forehead, which made me think about shards of glass flying through the air. How long ago had that happened? The cut was already scabbed over and beginning to heal.

"I know, Artemisia," she said, brushing a sweaty lock of hair from my face. "Remain strong. Help is on the way."

Part of me clung to those words fiercely while the other part thought about biting the nun's hand. She moved away before I could decide. Soon I was given more syrup and no longer had to think about anything at all.

As the battle raged on inside me, time lost its meaning. Sometimes the world was dark. Sometimes it was light. But eventually I noticed something different: a sense of movement, a jolting and juddering, my head swaying against a padded surface that felt too flat to be a pillow. Horses' hooves clattered in my ears, and the space around me gave little squeaks of wood and metal and leather as it bounced and jostled around.

The hot, stifling air couldn't belong to a wagon. A carriage? I tried to focus, but my thoughts slipped from my grasp, slimy and elusive. The syrup's taste still coated my tongue, and I was already drifting away.

Later, I was woken by shouting.

Consciousness returned in a slow trickle of sensations, each one more unpleasant than the last. My head pounded. My skin felt greasy and itched beneath my robes. The carriage jerked along at a slower pace now than before, queasily bumping over every rut and rock on the road. I blinked until an expanse of dark, cracked leather swam into focus in front of my face. It smelled musty with age and incense. Under that there was another, fainter smell, like old meat mixed with dirty coins. Blood.

Four long gashes scored the leather, as though someone had clawed through it with their fingernails.

"Stay back!" a man's voice commanded. "Clear the road!"

I shot fully awake, my heart hammering. I recognized that voice.

When I dragged myself upright, there came a heavy clink of metal and a drag against my wrists. Looking down, I discovered that I wore iron shackles, their cuffs engraved with holy symbols. The thick links of the chain attached to them lay coiled at my feet.

I was in a carriage, but not a normal one. It looked like the inside of a confessional booth. The tall, narrow walls were lined with tarnished metal, stamped to give the appearance of ornate molding, and the single arched window to my left was set with a perforated screen, a somber red glow filtering through. Locks covered the door on the carriage's opposite side. The chain's slack fed into a winch sunk into the middle of the floor, which I guessed could be tightened to restrain me.

I knew what this was. A harrow, a type of carriage that had been popular over a century ago, designed to transport people who were possessed—usually the most dangerous cases, in which a divine was needed to perform the exorcism. I knew about harrows only because I had seen illustrations in the scriptorium's books. I hadn't known that any still existed.

The revenant must still be inside me, even though I couldn't feel it. Perhaps the harrow had driven it into hiding.

I breathed in and out, fighting the nausea brought on by the harrow's relentless heat and motion. Then I eased myself to the window and peered through the screen. I almost jerked back when I saw the crowd outside, dozens of people, hundreds, all standing along the side of the road staring, their faces dirtied by travel and drawn with fear.

After a moment, I relaxed slightly, realizing that they couldn't see me through the screen. They were only staring at the harrow as it went by. But my relief proved short-lived as I took in the children's hunger-dulled eyes, the mud coating the wheels of the over-burdened wagons, the dead mule that lay in a ditch, buzzing with flies. Smoke gusted past the screen, streaming from incense burners fixed to the harrow's roof. The setting sun lit the smoke pink and soaked the crowd in ominous shades of crimson, throwing long shadows across the rutted field beyond.

As I watched, a woman drew her child toward her body and signed herself. A dark blighted mark stood out vividly on her arm.

These people must have fled their homes, which meant we were probably traveling through Roischal. There had been stories of families abandoning their villages, fearful of spirits and possessed soldiers, but in however much time had passed since the attack on Naimes, the situation had clearly gotten worse.

Lifting one of the heavy manacles, I pushed up my sleeve. The weals left by my dagger's consecrated steel had healed to pale pink-ish stripes. I'd lost a week, at least.

"Clear the road!" called the voice again. "Let us pass by the authority of Her Holiness the Divine!"

I shifted until the speaker came into view, riding ahead of the harrow on a magnificent dapple-gray stallion, his black robes untouched by the filth.

The faces turned his way reflected both fear and desperate hope. My attention caught on a man arguing with his family. I willed him not to do whatever it was he was thinking of doing, but then he stumbled out onto the road, jogging to keep pace with the stallion. He looked dirty and unkempt beside the rider's austere magnificence.

"Please, Your Grace, we've been driven from our homes—and we were turned away at the bridge at Bonsaint—"

The tall, golden-haired figure turned slowly to look down at him as he rambled on, unaware of the danger.

"We're traveling north. There's word of a saint in Naimes. They say she carried the relic of Saint Eugenia into battle and defeated a legion of spirits . . . and that she has scars, that we will know her by her scars. Please, is it true?"

Instead of answering, the rider made a subtle motion with his hands. The man toppled to his knees as though felled by an axe. In the crowd, someone screamed. As the harrow drew closer, I saw that the man's face was contorted with guilt and anguish, and he was clutching helplessly at the pebbles on the road. "Forgive me," he gasped over and over as the harrow rumbled past, spraying mud on him with its wheels.

The priest had changed since I'd last seen him. His pale, imperious features had frozen to the cold hardness of marble. He rode stiffly, as though he were favoring an injury beneath his robes, and dark shadows bruised the skin beneath his eyes. Saint Eugenia's relic hung from a chain around his neck, the reliquary's opals sparking fiercely in the fading light.

The man on the ground hadn't recognized it. He'd had no idea that the relic was right in front of him or that the person they sought was chained inside the harrow, heading past them in the opposite direction.

By chance, the priest glanced toward me, and our eyes met through the screen. His hands tightened on the reins. Without expression, he spurred his mount onward out of sight.

Confessor Leander. That was what the page had called him. I couldn't forget what he had said right before he'd used his relic on me. It was the same thing I would have tried to convince myself about the shackles, the harrow, the locks on the door. *This is for your own good.*

"Revenant," I said into the dark. Again, nothing answered.

I'd been trying for hours. Night had fallen outside the harrow, and finally we'd passed the last of the wagons, only that hadn't necessarily been an improvement—the abandoned villages had come next, their rooftops black against the darkening sky, the doors of houses hanging askew on their hinges, and the streets littered with refuse and occasionally bodies. I knew the priest had to have seen them too, but the harrow never slowed down.

No one was going to bless those bodies. Soon their souls would rise as spirits.

With that I knew for certain that whatever was happening in Roischal, the Clerisy couldn't stop it. Perhaps they'd sent soldiers to help at first, but the soldiers had only gotten possessed and killed more people, which meant more spirits, then more soldiers to fight those spirits, then more thralls. Everything was going to keep getting worse.

"Revenant," I tried again.

Silence.

Eventually, we stopped to change out the horses. I didn't see much, because shortly after the harrow came to a halt, a torturous grinding sound vibrated through the walls, announcing the tightening of the winch. Once the chain had been pulled taut, tugging me down to the floor, someone shoved a chamber pot and a tin cup of water through a slot in the bottom of the door. I made use of them both and then nudged them back toward the slot with my shoe. The hand that retrieved them was gauntleted with consecrated steel. Moments later, we started moving again.

I pushed aside my physical discomfort and closed my eyes, trying to concentrate, which wasn't easy with the way the harrow slammed over every rut in the road, rattling my teeth and bouncing the chain. I focused on remembering what the revenant had felt like—the roiling darkness, the seething anger, the prickles of annoyance and grudging approval—the heady rush of its power flowing through me.

There. A presence lurked deep inside my mind, like a drowned thing floating in the water at the bottom of a well. It wasn't moving. Carefully, I imagined doing the mental equivalent of poking it with a stick.

"Stop," the revenant hissed feebly. *"That hurts."*

My eyes flew open. "What happened to you?" I demanded.

"You did," it answered. *"But right now . . . the shackles you're wearing. They're Old Magic. Designed for me . . . for revenants."*

Terror lanced through me. Pulse racing, I lifted the heavy, clinking shackles and studied them in the orange light that juddered through the screen, cast by a lantern swinging outside. Slowly, my heartbeat calmed. The revenant had to be confused. The shackles did look old, but the engravings . . .

"Those are holy symbols," I said.

"Suit yourself, nun."

I had expected it to argue with me. Instead, it sounded listless, defeated. For some reason, I didn't want that. I almost wished I hadn't woken it up.

"I need to talk to you." I shifted back to the window so the revenant would have a view of the nighttime forest rolling past. "I need to know what's happening out there."

"How should I have any idea? I've been imprisoned inside a moldy

old saint's relic for the past century." Finally, I detected a note of annoyance in its weak-sounding voice. *"You're a fool for trying to speak to me."*

That was probably true, but at present, I didn't have any better options. Even if it lied to me, I might learn something useful. "Can't you sense anything?"

My only reply was a prickly silence. Most likely, the shackles were suppressing too much of its power.

Frustrated, I began to turn away—and then something caught my eye beyond the screen. In the darkness of the forest, a wavering light had bloomed. More followed, like ghostly candles lit by an invisible hand. And they kept appearing, unfurling ahead of the harrow, lighting up the forest with their pale silver glow. I felt like we had joined one of the legendary funeral processions of Chant-clere, during which thousands of votives were lit along the streets to lead the mourners onward.

But the lights belonged to wisps, First Order spirits that were waking as we passed, alerted by the life and movement of the carriage. Wisps rose from the souls of dead children and were the only type of spirit known to be completely harmless. Even shades caused headaches and malaise if they accumulated in large enough numbers—but no one had ever been hurt by wisps.

More and more lights bloomed. I had never seen so many in one place. I pictured the thin, frightened faces on the side of the road, the bodies abandoned in the towns. Children were dying. They were dying unblessed, in numbers I couldn't imagine.

"Nun." The revenant's voice sounded insistent. I wasn't sure how long it had been trying to get my attention. *"That metal is consecrated. Nun? Are you listening?"*

I felt a strange tingling in my palm and realized I had pressed it against the screen. When I withdrew my hand and looked at it, the revenant let slip a ripple of shock.

"You've hurt yourself!" it hissed.

"No. That's how it always looks." I showed it my other hand, the scars webbed and shiny in the harrow's dim orange light.

A long silence elapsed. The revenant must not have noticed my hands while they had been covered in blood in the chapel. I expected it to mock me, but it only said, in an odd tone of voice, *"There are a few blisters. Don't do that again."*

"I won't if you help me," I replied.

It paused, startled. Then its fury boiled up like a storm, a snarled black cloud of resentment and spite. But it couldn't do anything while I wore the shackles. I felt its rage break ineffectually against me and subside in a thwarted wave.

"Look out the window," it snapped, giving in. *"If I'm going to sense anything, it needs to be through your pitiful human eyes."*

"We're traveling south through Roischal," I explained as I turned back to the screen. "We've passed hundreds of people fleeing their homes." Briefly, I filled in some of the details I'd noticed, like the blighted injuries and the bodies in the villages. "I heard stories in Naimes, but it's worse than I thought—it's getting worse quickly."

I felt the revenant scanning the countryside. It wasn't trying to control the movements of my eyes, but I was aware of a bizarre doubled alertness as it shared them with me, and I knew somehow that it was observing more than I was capable of seeing on my own. Its attention caught on a distant sword-flash of silver, the moonlight glancing off a broad flat ribbon winding through the hills.

"That must be what you humans call the Sevre," it muttered to itself. *"I've always loathed that river. . . . Such a wide span of running water is difficult even for revenants to cross. . . ."* It lapsed into silence

as it looked around some more. *"Well, I don't see anything useful,"* it informed me at last, with a sort of nasty cheer. *"How tragic."*

Slowly, I raised my hand toward the screen.

"Stop! Fine! Have it your way, nun. There's one thing I know for certain. The attack we fended off—the spirits weren't targeting your convent at random, or even just to kill some nuns, more's the pity. They were sent there to destroy my relic."

I sat up straighter. "What?"

"Do I need to speak more slowly for your pathetic meat brain to keep up? They were sent there to destroy my relic. Almost certainly because I was the closest thing powerful enough to stop them."

A pit opened in my stomach. *Sent there*, the revenant claimed. Something had *sent* them to Naimes, like an officer commanding an army. I remembered the way the thralls had roped their horses to the lichgate, cooperating with one another, just like they were following orders.

I ventured, "The fury—"

"It wasn't the fury. Furies are solitary by nature; it wouldn't have gotten involved unless someone forced it to. And someone did force it—those spirits reeked of Old Magic."

"That's impossible."

"You asked for my help. It isn't my fault if you don't like what I have to say."

"Old Magic hasn't been practiced in hundreds of years. It's heresy."

"So is talking to a revenant, and you seem to be managing admirably." Its voice dripped with sarcasm.

"That isn't what I meant." I swallowed, my throat dry. "No one would dabble in Old Magic after the Sorrow. No one would be that—"

"Stupid? If there's one thing I can always rely upon, it's the reassuring dependability of human idiocy. Give your kind a century or so, and they'll happily repeat the exact same mistakes that nearly wiped them all out a few generations before. The spirits smelled of Old Magic; that's all I know. What you do with the information is up to you."

I gazed out the window in silence, watching the wisps glitter among the trees. The revenant had been wrong about the shackles. Maybe it was wrong about this, too.

But what if it wasn't?

The Clerisy had spent the decades following the War of Martyrs purging all traces of Old Magic from Loraille. Even after the war had been won—the spirits driven back, the seven revenants imprisoned—the cause of the Sorrow remained. Left to fester, it could rise again. An even larger cataclysm could result.

The worst thing about the Sorrow was that it had happened by accident. The Raven King had so badly feared death that he had doubted the promise of the Lady's afterlife. He had been attempting a ritual to grant himself immortality when he had, instead, inadvertently shattered the gates of Death. In doing so, he had granted a worldly existence beyond Death to all. Immortality, of a kind—but a terrible un-life, a cursed half-life. Such was the evil of Old Magic. It twisted back on its users, granting them what they sought in the worst way imaginable. It was a perversion, unfit for human hands.

Maybe the revenant wasn't confused—maybe it was trying to deceive me. But it stood to gain nothing by lying. We were enemies turned fellow prisoners, bound by the same set of chains.

And if it was right . . .

"Suppose you're telling the truth. Why would someone force spirits to attack? How would it benefit them?"

"Why do humans do anything?" it snapped in reply. *"You're far better equipped to answer that question than I am."*

I wasn't certain that I was. Already, I found the revenant easier to have a conversation with than Marguerite or Francine. Deciding not to voice that dismal thought aloud, I looked down at the shackles around my wrists. "After you're exorcised from me, what's going to happen to you?" The answer seemed obvious. "Someone else will wield your relic, won't they? Someone who has training and can come back here and stop this."

It didn't answer for a long time. I began to get a bad feeling. Then it asked, *"How old was the aspirant who died in your crypt?"*

Aspirant—it had used that word to describe Sister Julienne before. "I'm not sure. Old." An image surfaced of Sister Julienne shuffling through the catacombs, her cobwebby hair hanging past her waist. "Eighty, at least."

I felt a strange pinch from the revenant, a pang of some nameless emotion, quickly suppressed. *"She might have been the last. I don't think the Clerisy is training vessels for me any longer. The last two, or three—they were nearly useless. I suspect that over time, the knowledge of how to wield me has been lost."*

I had no idea when a high relic had last been used in Loraille. A hundred years ago, perhaps more. The need for them had faded with time. The Clerisy might have decided that training more aspirants wasn't worth the risk.

If there was no one else . . .

"Those people were traveling north because of me," I heard myself say. "They heard about what happened in Naimes, and they think I can help them. They think I'm a saint."

"They might be right. You're horrid and annoying enough to be one. As far as I can tell, that seems to be the criteria."

I barely heard it speak. *This is the Lady's will.* That was what Sister Julienne had told me in the crypt. What if she hadn't just meant saving the convent? It didn't seem like a coincidence that people needed help, and I was here, traveling right past them, the only person in Loraille who had wielded a high relic within living memory.

But I wasn't a saint. I wasn't even trained. I remembered enough fleeting snatches of the days following the battle to know that the revenant had succeeded in at least partially taking over my body. Without the sisters' efforts, it would have possessed me. And if it had done so, the consequences would have been catastrophic. I had felt its violent intentions as though they had been my own. It would have slain the sisters without a second thought.

And yet another of its emotions dominated my memories, stronger than its rage, its resentment, its hunger—stronger than all of them combined.

Fear.

I watched the light cast shifting patterns on the harrow's wall, turning an idea over in my mind like a dagger's blade, examining it for nicks and scratches. And then I asked, "Revenant, is it true you'll do anything not to go back into your reliquary?"

SIX

Peering through the harrow's screen the next morning, the revenant said, *"That idiot priest has no idea what he's doing, riding with my reliquary out in the open. Do you see, nun? We're being followed."*

Outside, the rising sun glared above the treetops, burning away the fog that blanketed the road. Still sticky-headed with sleep, I took a moment to spot what the revenant was referring to: a ripple in the fog, similar to the eddies stirred by the trotting horses. As I watched, I made out a translucent shape furtively slipping away.

"A gaunt," the revenant supplied. *"It's being used as a scout. They'll attack soon. That will be our best chance to escape."*

Leander rode ahead of us, surrounded by knights wearing suits of consecrated armor. I couldn't tell whether the stab of dislike I felt at the sight of him belonged to me or the revenant.

After what I had learned yesterday, it seemed obvious that the spirits would continue trying to destroy Saint Eugenia's relic. But unlike me, Leander hadn't stayed awake half the night interrogating a revenant.

I leaned toward the screen, trying to catch a glimpse of his onyx ring. "He has a powerful relic—it binds a penitent. Won't he notice that something's wrong? Will the penitent warn him?"

The revenant hissed a laugh. *"Not unless he calls it forth, and I doubt he can afford to use it casually. Look at the way he's sitting. He has to mortify himself to control it."*

"He has to what?"

A flicker of surprise came from the revenant, followed by a wary pause, as though it was wondering whether it had accidentally revealed too much. Finally, it said, *"It's what humans do when the spirits bound to their relics try to resist them. There are a fascinating number of different techniques. Whips, hair shirts, girdles of thorns. Sleeping on beds of nails used to be quite popular. I had one vessel who would kneel on gravel for hours, reciting prayers—I gather the intent was to vanquish me through boredom."* Suspicion crept into its tone. *"You weren't practicing mortification when you used your dagger on yourself in the crypt?"*

"Not on purpose," I said, glancing at the fading marks on my wrist. "I just assumed you wouldn't like it."

"How delightful. Being horrid must come naturally to you."

I shrugged, not disagreeing. I was already thinking about doing worse. Despite the agreement we'd arrived at last night, I knew I couldn't trust the revenant to uphold its end of the bargain. Now that I no longer had my misericorde, I might have to resort to other measures to keep it under control. I was certain I could manage something. Sleeping on a bed of nails couldn't be much worse than sharing a room with Marguerite.

The revenant continued talking, but I had stopped listening, studying Leander. It hadn't occurred to me that there might be a physical explanation for his stiff, straight-backed posture. He had looked that way even back in Naimes.

He seemed young to be wielding such a powerful relic. By that fact alone, I wondered if he was one of only a few people capable of controlling it. If it could have gone to someone older and more experienced, it likely would have. I knew little about penitents, only that they were rare even for Fourth Order spirits—so much so that they hadn't been included in our lessons. Relics binding them had to be even rarer; the Clerisy likely went to great efforts to find suitable candidates to wield them.

I remembered how disdainfully Leander had spoken of lesser relics. Ironically, if he weren't too arrogant to wield a First Order relic like Sister Iris and Mother Katherine, he wouldn't need to limit its use, and he would have been able to sense the gaunt spying on us.

Mother Katherine. Without warning, the memory flashed through my mind: Sister Iris's scream, Mother Katherine limp in her arms. None of my fragmented memories of lying fevered in bed afterward included her, only Sister Iris and the other nuns. Mother Katherine should have been there. If she could have, she would have come.

I couldn't think about that, not now. I wrenched my mind away and stared hard at my hands, turning them palms-up in my lap, summoning the memory of heat and agony and letting it wash over me in a blistering wave, burning everything else to ashes.

"What are you thinking about?" the revenant broke in, its voice low and venomous. I realized I had been silent for several minutes.

"Nothing." I sincerely didn't want to talk about it.

"You're lying," it hissed. *"There's always something going on in*

your detestable nun brain. You're going to betray me, aren't you?
You're already thinking about breaking your promise."

"What?" At first the revenant's accusation merely surprised me.
Then a lump of anger formed in my throat. "No, I'm not."

"If you imagine that you can fool me—"

"You've spent the past week trying to take over my body. Of
the two of us, I should be more worried about you betraying me."

"Ha!" The revenant dragged itself up. I felt it stalking around
the confines of my mind like a caged beast. Then it hissed savagely,
*"You have no idea what you've offered. You promised that if I helped
you, you would do everything in your power to keep me from returning
to my reliquary. Do you truly understand what that means? What
you're sacrificing?"*

Unfortunately, I did. It meant that I was stuck with the revenant indefinitely. My soul would never know a moment's peace.
I would suffer a miserable, profane, defiled existence, constantly
on guard against possession, poisoned by incense and consecrated
steel.

But it was right. Perhaps I hadn't realized the worst part after
all. Back when I'd made the offer, I hadn't known the revenant
would talk so much.

It still hadn't stopped. Now it was saying spitefully, *"Before, you used
the possibility of an eternity trapped in your company to threaten me."*

"I know how you felt when we fought in the chapel," I said
through gritted teeth. "You miss feeling things. You like being in
a human body."

"That doesn't mean I want to be in yours!"

The last of my patience evaporated. "Then we can forget about
last night." My voice sounded like a death knell. "You can go back
into your reliquary. Maybe you'll never get another vessel. How

long do you think it will take Saint Eugenia's relic to disintegrate? Hundreds more years, probably. That's a long time to be imprisoned inside—"

"Stop!" the revenant cried. I felt a painful scrabbling clutch, as though it had sunk its claws into my insides. *"Stop,"* it hissed again, more quietly this time, even though I already had.

I waited, then asked, "Are you finished?"

"The shackles," it muttered after a pause. *"When the spirits attack, we need to rid you of these shackles, or else we'll both be next to useless. And my reliquary—we'll need to retrieve it as well. If the humans believe that I've possessed you, they might decide to destroy it."*

I opened my mouth to argue that the Clerisy would never consider destroying a high relic. Then my eyes fell on the shackles' holy symbols. I swallowed my words.

The revenant might not behave the way I had expected, but it had slaughtered thousands of people. Tens of thousands, the populations of entire cities. It would do all of that over again in a heartbeat if it gained control of my body. The devastation in Roischal was only a shadow of the terror it had wreaked during the War of Martyrs. To prevent that from happening again, the Clerisy would destroy Saint Eugenia's relic if they had no other choice.

With the revenant's power, I could save everyone. But if I lost control, I might burn the world to ashes.

I found it difficult to believe that this was truly what the Lady wanted. In all probability, it wasn't, and She was merely making do with what She had. Which was, unfortunately for everyone, me.

I had come too far to start having second thoughts. We did need to take the reliquary with us, and not just for the reason the revenant had suggested. If it tried to possess me again, I might be able to resist its power for long enough to destroy the relic myself as a last resort. The bone had looked old and brittle enough to crush in my hand.

"All right," I said aloud, before it could grow suspicious. "I'll think of a way to get the priest close to us. He's the one carrying the key." Somehow I knew that to be true. Leander wouldn't entrust it to anyone else.

By the time the sun reached its zenith, I still hadn't come up with a strategy to lure him into the harrow. The revenant was growing increasingly impatient, pacing back and forth in my head as it pointed out every spirit that it noticed in the fog.

"Whatever you plan on doing, hurry. They're close enough that I can sense them even through these accursed shackles."

I was wondering whether I should finally admit that I didn't have a plan when a raven's raucous cawing erupted outside. A horse whinnied, and one of the knights swore. I straightened in my seat. Something about the raven's cries sounded familiar. Looking through the screen, I couldn't see anything useful: a knight had ridden close to the harrow, and his armor filled my field of vision. As I watched, he raised his arm as though to fend off an attack. Another flurry of heckling caws followed.

"It's just a bird," Leander snapped. "Stay in formation."

Wingbeats flapped past. "Pretty bird!" the raven shrieked defiantly.

I tried to stand up, only to get jerked back down by the shackles. "Trouble."

"Oh, do you think so?" the revenant hissed. *"Aside from an impending attack by spirits for which we are completely unprepared?"*

"No, that's the raven's name. Trouble." His timing didn't strike me as a matter of chance. "The Lady must have sent him to help us."

"I would be interested to know how many hours daily you nuns spend inhaling incense. Clearly, it has an effect on your brains."

I ignored it, listening carefully to the knights' disgruntled shouts, the chaotic jingling of tack. It sounded like Trouble was diving from the sky, spooking the horses.

I wasn't worried about his safety. My favorite book in the scriptorium was a collection of parables describing the gruesome fates of wrongdoers who had offended the Lady by harming Her sacred birds. Even the knights wouldn't dare hurt a raven. As the knight blocking the screen rode past, I saw another waving his scabbard in the air, futilely attempting to shoo Trouble away.

Their efforts were in vain. At last, infuriated, Leander called out orders to stop the harrow. As it slowly bumped to a halt, I heard him issue a few more indistinct commands. The loud, grinding vibration of the winch drowned out the rest. I clambered to the floor and crouched there, watching the links rattle into the mechanism.

After the winch stilled, the metal slot in the door slammed open, and a tin cup slid inside. I dragged it over with my foot and gulped down the cold, metallic water. When the knight reopened the slot, the empty cup wasn't waiting for him.

Eyes appeared on the other side, shadowed and unreadable behind the grille of a helmet's visor. I slid the cup partway across the floor, almost close enough for him to reach.

"I need to speak to the priest."

A long silence emanated from the knight. He had probably been instructed not to speak to me. I pushed the cup the rest of the way over.

"There's something I need to confess."

He took the cup. The eyes vanished, and the slot dropped shut.

I waited, hoping Leander wouldn't be able to resist the temptation. I was rewarded a moment later when the bolts began to slide open on the door.

"There's something else," the revenant said quickly. *"You can't let anyone find out that we're talking to each other, or that I'm helping you willingly. If we're ever caught, pretend . . ."* I felt it bristling as it forced out the rest. *"Pretend that you subdued me, and I'm under your control."*

I'd rather not. People truly would believe I was a saint if I made such a claim. But it was right—if anyone found out that we were cooperating, not just the revenant with me, but also the reverse, an exorcism would be the least of my worries. I might even face burning at the stake for heresy. I nodded to show that I'd understood.

The door swung open, flooding the harrow with light. I resisted the instinct to cringe away from the glare and faced the figure standing there with watering eyes. Even through a blur of tears, the tall, spare silhouette unmistakably belonged to Leander. I wondered what he saw in return as his gaze swept over me. My robes stank of sweat, and my unbraided hair hung lank and greasy to the floor. No doubt he found the image satisfying. He had wanted to see me humbled at his feet in Naimes, and he had finally succeeded, though it had taken a chain and shackles to bend me to his will.

The harrow dipped beneath his weight as he stepped inside. His robes blocked out the sun, bringing into focus the key ring hanging from his belt beside his censer. One of the keys looked old and tarnished, a possible match for the shackles.

"That one," the revenant confirmed.

"You may speak," Leander said, as though I had been waiting for his permission. "What is it you wish to tell me?"

He sounded composed, but I noticed that he was standing just outside the distance I could reach him if I suddenly lunged to the end of the chain. My gaze traveled up from the key ring, past the glittering jewels of Saint Eugenia's reliquary, and finally to his face. As I met his eyes, I caught a flicker of emotion in their depths, there and gone again, like the flash of a fish's scales vanishing into a dark pool.

"Stop wasting time," the revenant hissed. *"What is your plan? Don't tell me you're making this up as you go along."*

I racked my brain for something to say, and my thoughts returned inevitably to Sister Iris's scream, the sight of Mother Katherine limp before the altar. "I want to know what happened to the sisters in Naimes. Were any of them injured in the attack?"

"Am I speaking to Artemisia, or the revenant?" Leander returned coolly.

"Can't you tell?"

Our eyes were still locked. He looked away first. "You seem to be in command of yourself, but it can be difficult to tell for certain. Spirits study the human world through their vessels, growing more cunning with each person they inhabit."

A hoarse muttering sound came from above. Trouble had landed on the harrow. His claws pattered across the roof, and Leander tensed, a reaction that might have been a flinch in someone less controlled. Whatever he had seen in the past weeks in Roischal couldn't have been pleasant to have affected even him. The shadows beneath his eyes looked deeper inside the harrow.

But he continued smoothly, "If a spirit as old and experienced as the revenant were to take over your body, it could impersonate you so skillfully that even the sisters who raised you wouldn't be able to tell the difference. Until it ceased the act, and killed them."

"Unlikely. I would rather spend another hundred years in my

reliquary than try to impersonate you. I'd go straight for the killing."

I received the impression that I was going to have to get used to ignoring it in the middle of important conversations. Through clenched teeth, I asked, "Even if I were possessed, how could it be dangerous to tell me?"

"Speaking to you at all is a risk."

"But you came anyway."

Leander's hand twitched—the one wearing the onyx ring. He looked at me again, his expression impossible to read. Then he said in a low, intense voice, "Right now you should be receiving instruction in Bonsaint. You could have had anything you wanted. Instead, you're chained inside a harrow, tormented by a spirit you might have one day learned to control."

"You have no idea what I want," I countered.

"You've seen nothing of the world save a convent and the miserable little town in which you were born. I think it's possible that you don't know what you want."

I gazed back at him expressionlessly. "I want to know what happened to the sisters."

Forgetting himself, he took a step forward. "You should have listened to me," he said. "If you had come with me—"

"*Nun,*" the revenant broke in urgently, at the same time I snarled, "Everyone at my convent would be dead!" I threw myself to the end of the chain, the bite of the shackles drawing me up short.

He jerked back, startled. I had almost reached him—almost touched his keys. His mouth twisted into an involuntary defensive snarl, like a cornered animal baring its teeth, before he drew his composure back into place with a strained effort. "I shouldn't have come." He turned sharply and began to step out of the harrow.

"Nun! They're here!"

My hair had fallen in a curtain around my face. The strands quivered with my breath. "Your Grace," I said. "Don't you want to hear my confession?"

He paused, one hand on the doorway.

"The key! Nun—the key!"

"I'm going to escape," I told him.

Slowly, he turned, his face wiped clean of emotion. Through my hair, I met his eyes. "I'm telling you," I finished, "because there isn't anything you can do to stop me."

Reflexively, he reached for his relic.

Above us, Trouble's mutterings had gone silent. Now he uttered a single clear word. "Dead."

Leander looked up, horror dawning across his face.

"Nun, brace yourself!"

That was my only warning before the harrow exploded.

SEVEN

The next thing I knew, I lay insensible among splinters of wood. My ears rang, and the stink of mud and copper filled my nose. Everything was chaos; hooves flashed perilously close to my face, the sun glancing from their metal shoes. The sounds of horses screaming, men shouting, and Trouble unleashing his harsh cry of "Dead!" sounded distorted and far away, like my head had been shoved underwater.

The sky looked impossibly blue. The light seemed too bright, the shadows too dark. I watched clods of dirt fly through the air.

"Get up, nun!"

My senses came rushing back in a torrent of sound. I rolled over. The chain slithered with me, freed from the harrow's wreckage. One of the carriage horses lay dead on the road, twisted up in its traces. Spirits flitted past, converging on the knights like wisps of fog.

I half fell, half climbed over the harrow's broken frame. And almost collapsed onto Leander, lying stunned amid the wreckage, a trickle of blood running from the corner of his mouth.

"My reliquary. Get my reliquary first. There's a rivener nearby. It's coming—"

That explained the harrow. Riveners were Fourth Order spirits risen from warriors slain in battle, armed with the rare ability to affect the living world with powerful blows that could splinter wood and shatter bone. I had no hope of surviving it without the revenant's power.

I wanted to get the key first, but the revenant sounded panicked. I yanked the chain from Leander's neck and ducked my head through its loop. Thinking quickly, I stuffed the reliquary down the front of my robes, where the thick, bulky wool would conceal its shape.

Leander groaned, then coughed. He was waking now, awareness returning to his staring blank eyes. I fumbled with the key ring at his belt. Sliding the correct key from the ring posed a challenge for my clumsy hands, their stiffness worsened by days of disuse. The revenant's agitation flapped around in my head like a frenzied bat as the tiny key slipped repeatedly from my fingers. Finally, I gave up and yanked the entire ring free, snapping the leather thong that attached it to the belt.

My victory lasted barely a heartbeat before Leander's hand closed around my wrist.

"Behind you!" the revenant shrieked.

I threw myself to the side, dragging Leander with me. The spot where he had lain erupted in flying soil and shards of wood. Debris rained down, pelting my robes and pattering across the carriage's wreckage.

I looked up, and then up some more. The spirit that towered over us was nearly half again the height of a man. It was clad in cracked, battered armor, with broken arrows and spears protruding from its body, like a great bear that many hunters had tried and failed to kill. Two pinholes of light glowed in the cavernous recesses of its helmet.

Recognition smote me—it was the same type of spirit as the one Mother Katherine had called forth in the chapel, bound to her amber ring.

The rivener raised its sword for another sundering blow. I was lodged against one of the carriage's wheels and couldn't move. At my side, Leander gave me a quick startled glance and reached for a spar of wood among the wreckage. He still hadn't let go of my arm.

As the sword descended, he raised the piece of wood between us, which I saw was a slat broken from one of the harrow's iron-studded wheels. The sword struck it and dissolved into a gust of mist that swept over us, as cold and stinging as a winter wind.

Puzzled, the rivener looked down at the empty hilt clutched in its gauntleted hand.

Of course—whoever had built the harrow hadn't taken any chances. Even the wheels were consecrated.

Leander scrambled to his feet, unsteady and panting. First he pointed the spoke at me, wild-eyed, and then at the rivener, whose broadsword had already re-formed and was sailing through the air in his direction.

The keys' jagged shapes bit into my palm, clenched in my fist. As Leander engaged the rivener, I scrambled over the broken wheel and huddled behind it, jabbing the key toward the left-hand shackle's equally tiny keyhole.

"Hurry," the revenant seethed.

"I am."

"Let me do it for you!" I felt a ripple of frustration. *"Never mind, I can't, not with the shackles . . . Just hurry, nun."*

Furiously, I continued jabbing. Out of the corner of my eye, I watched spirits swarm around the knights, who spun this way and that, shaking their heads like boars beset with flies. Some still thundered around on horseback; others had been dismounted, their riderless horses stamping and rearing in the chaos. The knights' consecrated armor helped protect them from blight and possession, but they were being overwhelmed by sheer numbers. Several already lay on the ground unmoving.

At last the lock clicked, and the first shackle fell free. The revenant's power surged eagerly, only to shrink back with a flash of pain that left spots dancing across my eyes. Gritting my teeth, I started in on the second shackle.

Nearby, Leander remained locked in battle with the rivener. He had somehow managed to light his incense and was fighting with his censer in place of the spar. His survival mystified me until he made a sharp gesture with his free hand, and ghostly chains materialized from the air, coiling around the rivener as though alive.

Every Fourth Order relic imparted an ability that could be used in combat. The chains had to be the penitent's power. They tightened cruelly, and cracks split the rivener's armor. It sagged, listing sideways.

Leander might have defeated it easily if it weren't for the other spirits mobbing him, forcing his attention away. He spun to swing his censer through a feverling that had snuck up on him from behind, then a gaunt on his other side. He clenched his relic hand into a fist, and more chains sprang forth, binding several more spirits at once. I had never seen anything like it before, even in the convent's training grounds. He moved as though the battle were a dance, his motions swift and vicious, every strike deadly in its precision. But it wasn't enough. While his focus lay elsewhere, the rivener shook itself free from the slackening chains. Implacably, it advanced, forcing him backward.

"Nun."

The revenant issued its warning in a low voice, as though it were in danger of being overheard. I glanced over in time to see a silvery knobbed spine glide behind the wheel's broken spokes. A second gaunt's bald head rose into view over the shattered remnants of an incense burner, its oversized teeth bared in a morbid grin. The spirits had found me.

The key slid into place. The revenant's power roared up like an igniting pyre, the blistering force of it momentarily blinding me. When my vision cleared, I saw that the second shackle lay in the mud, cracked and smoking. And the two spirits were gone, obliterated: tatters of mist blew from the wreckage in their place.

I got one of my feet under me. My ankle twisted when I put weight on it. The revenant's power rushed downward, bolstering me, and with its support I rose from the wreckage, lifting my bowed head.

At once, the nearest spirits paused. They stared at me. And then they fled, streaming away from the road toward the trees, flickering erratically as they raced over the trampled ground and the bodies of knights scattered across it.

The rest of the spirits hadn't noticed. They were too busy swarming the remaining knights and thronging around Leander. He had been cornered against a weed-choked ditch along the roadside, battling for his life against the rivener's relentless strikes and the half-dozen other spirits surrounding him. No matter his skill, it would take only one of the rivener's blows to finish him if he lost his footing.

"Leave them," the revenant said. It tugged my gaze toward the forest. Leander's dappled stallion stood alertly by the edge of the trees, watching the battle with pricked ears and flared nostrils. Missing his rider, he had bolted.

I took a step in the opposite direction.

"What are you doing?"

"I'm not going to leave someone to die. Even someone I hate."

Leander faltered. Somehow, he had heard me—and my voice had distracted him in a way that the attacking spirits had not.

The rivener's next blow took him off guard. He stumbled as the earth beside him erupted in a fountain of dirt and rocks. The lesser spirits surged toward him.

"Wretched nun," the revenant seethed. Seeing that I wasn't going to change my mind, it said quickly, *"Watch out for the rivener's strikes. I can't protect you from those."*

As I waded from the wreckage, I paused to wrench another spoke from the harrow's broken wheel. Its splintered end dragged on the ground behind me, plowing a groove through the debris. The spirits that saw me coming fled from my path like frightened shades.

The rivener had raised its sword high above Leander, poised for the same executioner's strike that Mother Katherine's spirit had performed in the chapel. Busy fighting for his life against the other spirits, he didn't catch sight of it until it began to descend. His eyes fixed on the blade like a martyr awaiting judgment.

I wasn't going to get there in time. I raised the spoke over my shoulder and threw it. It went spinning through the air and punched through the rivener's form, leaving a hole that swirled with vapor. The rivener's sword froze. Slowly, its helmeted head turned.

"Ah, fantastic. There goes your weapon. And here I thought you nuns were trained for combat."

I braced myself to dodge its next strike. But before the blow came, chains whipped around its body, binding it in place. Then Leander was beside me, a streak of blight darkening one of his cheekbones. That was all I had time to register before he shoved his censer into my hands and turned to use his relic against the spirits behind us.

Unthinkingly, I fell into an offensive stance. My left hand felt empty without a dagger, but now I didn't need it. Streaming incense smoke, the censer's consecrated silver was a weapon in its own right. The revenant's power surged through my limbs as I swung it in a practiced pattern. Censer forms could be used to attack as well as to defend, though the Gray Sisters considered this fighting style reckless and rarely featured it in our lessons.

Bound in Leander's chains, the rivener almost posed too easy a target. By the time they began to unravel, dissolving link by link into mist, my censer had done its work. The spirit went down on one knee, bracing its immaterial weight on its sword. Great gashes rent its form, trailing vapor. It struggled to rise, even just to lift its head, trembling with the effort.

The gesture looked so human that I hesitated. The rivener had been a person once, a soldier who had fought to defend the living. Perhaps it had died in this very pose, refusing to surrender to the last. Even corrupted, even after becoming the very monster it had fought against, an echo of its former self remained.

"Finish it," the revenant snapped. Then it paused and added less harshly, *"Don't make it suffer."*

One final swing, and the rivener collapsed, a cascade of mist spilling over the ground, swirling cool around the hem of my robes. An inexplicable feeling of loss gripped me. No one knew for certain whether spirits returned to the Lady after they were destroyed, or if their souls simply vanished, gone forever.

When I looked up, Leander was watching me, surrounded by the vapor of dispersing spirits. Warring emotions played out across his face. Pausing to catch his breath, he raised a hand to touch the patch of blight on his cheekbone. Then his expression hardened.

"Artemisia," he said coldly. "The revenant is too powerful. You can't control it for long."

I tightened my grip on his censer's chain.

"You don't have a choice. Surrender."

"No," I answered.

In reply, he reached for his relic.

I threw his censer at him. Before he could recover, as he stood there stunned with incense dusting his robes, I tramped into the weeds and shoved him backward into the ditch. There came a splash as he landed in the rank, swampy water at its bottom. Slipping in the mud, I followed him down. When he surfaced, spluttering, I yanked the onyx ring from his finger and hurled it as far as I could. It soared deep into the forest, glinting, and vanished somewhere among the leaves.

Furious, Leander seized a handful of weeds and dragged himself partway out of the water. But it would take only my boot to his chest to push him back under, and judging by his expression, he knew it. "Restrain her," he commanded.

The surviving knights had gathered around the ditch, their swords lowered. They looked at one another, expressionless behind their visors, and then back at me, hesitating.

I scrambled from the ditch and ran.

After the past week, I shouldn't have been able to run, much less quickly. But I whipped through the tall autumn-browned grass faster than I ever had before, almost weightless with the revenant's power. I felt it reveling in the sensations of our flight—the sun blazing on my hair, the way the matted grass tore underfoot, even the rough scratching pulls of the seedheads snagging on my robes. Everything else melted away. We were alive, and free.

Shouts rang out behind me. But the knights weren't fast enough, and a moment later I had caught the dappled stallion's dangling reins and leaped astride. Evidently the horse didn't harbor much loyalty for his former master, because he wheeled around to escape as though he'd been waiting for the opportunity all his life. I bent low over his withers, and together we plunged into the trees in a whirlwind of fallen leaves.

By late in the day, the last signs of pursuit had faded. *"I can't sense them any longer,"* the revenant said. *"They either lost our trail, or they gave up. The priest wasn't with them."*

Good. I imagined Leander crawling across the forest floor on his hands and knees, searching for his relic in the dirt.

I eased his horse out of the creek we had been following to hide our tracks, listening to the wet crunch of the stallion's hooves transition to a solid thump on the soil. Sitting astride a warhorse was exhilarating after learning to ride on the calm old draft horses at my convent. He had carried me at a canter for the better part of an hour before we had finally slowed down, following the winding deer trails over the hills.

I needed something to call him. "Priestbane," I said experimentally, and watched his ears swivel back with interest. He snorted out a breath that I took for approval. Patting his neck, I cast around for a telltale flash of white among the trees ahead. When I caught sight of Trouble flapping through the bare branches, I adjusted our path.

The revenant's scornful voice broke in. *"Don't tell me you're still following that raven."*

"I think he's taking us somewhere. He's flying eastward, which means we're heading deeper into Roischal."

"You do realize that there's nothing mystical about ravens, don't you? They don't gather around convents because they're divine messengers of your goddess. They come because that's where humans bring the corpses."

"That's fine. If he's leading us to corpses, that's where I want to go."

"You must be popular at the nun parties. Do you have any friends? Just out of curiosity."

My hands tightened on the reins. Sophia might count, but she was eight years old, so that seemed embarrassing to admit out loud. "Do you?" I asked without inflection.

"I've been trapped inside a relic for the past century. What's your excuse?"

"I was possessed by an ashgrim as a baby." My voice sounded harsh and ugly. "When I was ten, I stuck my hands in a fire to get it to stop trying to kill my family. The other novices think I murdered them. That's why."

As soon as I finished, I felt blood rush to my face. That was a lot more than I'd intended to say out loud. A profound silence came from the revenant.

"I don't want to talk about it," I added, before it could think of some other way to mock me.

To my relief, it didn't speak again for a very long time.

Eventually, the trees thinned. Priestbane trotted into a clearing, a field hazy with mist flushed gold by the setting sun. I didn't realize we had reached civilization until we startled a flock of grazing sheep, who fled bleating in terror, their rumps sodden with mud.

I reined Priestbane to a halt as their shapes vanished into the mist. The rooftops of a town loomed ahead, eerily silent at a time when children should be shouting, dogs barking, the air fragrant with the smoke of evening cookfires.

"Revenant, can you sense anything?"

The question seemed to draw it out of thought. I wondered if it had been plotting its next attempt to possess me. *"Nothing aside from a few shades infesting those buildings' crypts."*

"Cellars."

"What?"

"When they aren't under chapels, they're called cellars."

"I don't care," it hissed. *"Anyway, there are no humans ahead. At least,"* it added nastily, *"no living ones."*

Trouble had already flown ahead, visible as a shaft of darkness spearing through the haze. I nudged Priestbane back into motion.

As we reached the road, evidence of the town's hasty abandonment came into view. Chicken feathers, scraps of cloth, and clumps of straw littered the rutted ground. An escaped hog rooted in a ditch, grunting industriously as we passed. The first building we reached was an old stone smithy, which had a dark stain above its doorframe where a consecrated horseshoe had been nailed to ward off spirits. Someone had torn it off and taken it with them for protection.

My shoulders tightened as the buildings closed in on either side of the road, their doors and windows gaping. The setting sun painted their west-facing sides a glowering red and plunged the rest into shadow.

I hadn't been to a town since before Mother Katherine brought me to the convent seven years ago. This one was significantly larger than the village where I'd grown up, which barely even qualified as a village. I could still picture the desolate ramshackle huts growing smaller and smaller, receding down the hill as the convent's wagon carried me away.

Even though this place looked nothing like it, I still wanted to get out as quickly as I could. Staring straight ahead, I pressed my heel against Priestbane's side.

"We need to find a place to rest," the revenant objected. When I didn't answer right away, it asked, *"You aren't planning to ride through the night, are you?"*

I didn't answer. I hadn't thought about it.

"You need to stop. Your body hurts." There was an edge to its voice.

I pictured the wisps glittering along the road. "That doesn't matter."

"Well, it matters to me," the revenant snapped. *"Whatever you feel, I have to share it with you. Do you realize you haven't stopped to eat or drink all day? You let the horse stick its nose in a stream a few times, so I know you're at least aware of the concept in theory."*

I was well on my way to ignoring it again, but then it said that, and I found myself looking down at Priestbane. I barely recognized him as the horse Leander had ridden earlier in the day. His dappled coat was dark with sweat, his mane knotted up with burrs. Guilt sliced through me like a knife.

I drew him to a halt near the outskirts of town.

It took longer to work my boots out of the stirrups than I

expected. When I slid from the saddle, the ground's impact jarred through my legs, and my vision whited out with pain. When my senses returned, I was leaning against Priestbane's saddle. He had stretched his head around to investigate, his hot breath gusting over my hair.

"*I told you,*" the revenant said.

"Why aren't you helping me this time?" I gritted out.

"*I can't lend you my power too often. Your body has limits, and not being able to feel them is dangerous. If you push yourself too far . . .*" It hesitated, then said darkly, "*I had one vessel whose heart burst. She barely sent me back into my relic in time. Another who started having fits—she couldn't wield me after that.*"

"How many of your vessels have died, exactly?"

"*I assure you, none of them were my fault,*" the revenant snapped. "*I warned them every time, and they didn't listen.*"

It actually sounded upset about its vessels dying, but then again, it would be, if it had to go back into its reliquary afterward.

"You can't blame us," I pointed out. I tested my balance, then began hobbling toward a nearby stable. If the revenant asked, I would pretend that I had picked it out at random, but the truth was I had chosen it because there hadn't been any stables that looked like it in my village. "All you do is call us names and rant about murdering nuns."

"*Yes, that's all I do, isn't it?*" the revenant hissed. And then it vanished from my mind with a kind of angry flourish, like it had stalked out of a room and slammed the door behind it.

I shrugged. Priestbane followed obediently, his head low and ears relaxed as he clopped up to the stable. The latch came unstuck with a squeak of rain-swollen wood, and the door shuddered open after I kicked the bottom slat a few times. The inside was dim, pungent with the musty odor of mice and horses.

First I took off Priestbane's tack, staggering under the weight of his sweaty saddle, and left him inside. Then I drew water from the well in the yard, filled the stable's trough, and dried him off with handfuls of straw. I found hay in the loft and checked it for mold before I tossed it down to him. While I worked, I felt the revenant slowly creeping back into my consciousness.

"You treat that beast better than you do yourself," it commented sourly, watching Priestbane nose through the pile.

"He's a good horse. He carried me all day. He doesn't deserve to suffer because of the things I ask him to do."

"Have you ever considered that your body carries you?"

I didn't know what to say to that. As I stood watching Priest-bane, the light shining through the gaps in the walls slid upward and disappeared, casting the stable into darkness. The sun must have descended below the rooftops outside.

"Don't sleep here," the revenant said suddenly. *"There's a human building attached to this one, isn't there?"*

"I think so." I had seen something like that out in the yard, possibly living quarters for the inn's ostler. Honestly, though, I didn't see the point. My gaze fixed on the deep drifts of straw piled up along the wall.

It must have noticed me looking. *"Don't you dare. Your pathetic little meat body is on the verge of collapse, and there's a building made specially for humans just a few steps away. Go on, move. And bring the priest's things. You may have forgotten that you need to eat to survive, but I haven't. Nun!"* It gave me a jab that made me sway on my feet. I was still staring at the piles of straw as though I'd fallen into a trance.

My vision seemed to be fading in and out, but perhaps that was only because the stable had gotten darker. Finding that I didn't have the energy to argue, I reached for the straps of Leander's saddlebags and dragged them after me as I stumbled toward the door to the ostler's room. I almost tripped over the threshold on the way inside.

"Build a fire," the revenant ordered, before I could even take in my surroundings. It poked me again, nudging me forward through the dark room until I collided with a stone ledge, fumbled, and heard something clatter to the floor. A mantelpiece, I realized, as my eyes began to adjust, and then I made out what had fallen off: a carved wooden animal, something the ostler had been whittling before he'd left. A child's toy, still unfinished.

I picked it up and carefully put it back on the mantelpiece. For some reason, my hands were shaking.

"What are you doing? Don't bother with that. Light the fire." There was real urgency in the revenant's voice now, not just impatience. I considered telling it that I wasn't going to freeze to death, not this time of year, and especially not down south in Roischal, but speaking didn't seem worth the effort. Numbly, I felt around on the mantelpiece until I found a tinderbox. Crouching, I shoved some wood into the hearth from the bin nearby and went to work with the flint, my clumsy hands striking a few weak sparks.

Power surged forth from the revenant. The next spark flared brightly. Fire licked across the kindling, the dry wood hungrily popping and crackling. A warm glow illuminated my surroundings, which turned out not to contain much: half-repaired bridles hanging from nails on the wall, a straw mattress piled with horse blankets.

The revenant relaxed as soon as the fire blazed to life. My hands also stopped shaking. I stared at them, suspicious.

"Now eat something," the revenant said quickly. *"You haven't*

eaten a legitimate meal the entire time I've been in your body. The nuns occasionally forced some sort of horrid gruel down your throat, but I hardly think that counts."

Once again, arguing seemed pointless. I dragged Leander's bags closer and rummaged through them. Sheafs of parchment, an ivory comb, spare smallclothes. Finally, a bag that contained a loaf of bread, a few wrinkled apples, and a round of cheese wrapped in wax. I hesitated as I shook everything out onto the floor. Something about this seemed like a bad idea.

"The smoke could lead people to us," I concluded finally, my thoughts working at a fraction of their usual speed.

"There aren't any humans close enough. If that changes, which I sincerely doubt, I'll wake you." It was silent a moment. Then it asked, as though it had been mulling over the question for a while, "Fire doesn't bother you?"

"No." Occasionally the smell of burned ham made me vomit, but the revenant didn't need to know that. "It isn't as though someone else shoved me in. I did it to myself."

The revenant was silent again. I started to get the vague sense that there had been something wrong with my answer. Then it said, "Go on, eat."

I felt it monitoring me closely as I took a bite of bread and chewed. Whatever this loaf was, it bore little resemblance to the coarse barley bread we ate at the convent. I had never tasted anything like it before. It melted in my mouth like butter, and its crust looked golden in the firelight. "Another bite," the revenant prompted.

I ate the entire loaf that way. As soon as I swallowed, the revenant would tell me to take another bite, or command me to drink from Leander's water skin. It didn't relent until crumbs dusted my robes and the skin hung empty. Then it let me crawl over to the bed and collapse on top of the blankets. Surrounded by the smell of horses, I could almost imagine that I was back at the convent, sleeping in the barn to avoid Marguerite.

My full stomach felt as heavy as an anchor, dragging me down toward sleep. I had the murky sense that I was forgetting something important. The reliquary. I needed to keep the reliquary within reach, in case . . . in case the revenant . . .

In case the revenant what?

The revenant was saying something, but I couldn't muster up the energy to listen. "Good night, revenant," I mumbled, hoping that for once, it would be quiet.

It stopped. At last, blessed silence. I had almost drifted to sleep before I heard its low reply. *"Good night, nun."*

EIGHT

D ead. Dead! Dead!"

I jerked awake to the sight of Trouble's beak poised above my face, his angry gray eye glaring down at me. As my brain scrambled to catch up, he hopped over me with a flick of his tail and snatched the round of cheese from Leander's half-open bag. He flapped away triumphantly, his cries of "Dead!" muffled by his prize.

By the time the revenant spoke, I had already thrown back the blankets and reached for my nonexistent dagger. *"There isn't anything here—the bird sensed me, that's all. We'll have to be careful about that in the future."* Balefully, it watched Trouble flap away into the stable. *"We could always eat raven for breakfast instead."*

The revenant had to settle for a couple of wrinkled apples. I was back on Priestbane and following Trouble again before the sun appeared on the horizon. I flexed my hands on the reins, testing the gloves I had scavenged on our way out. They were too large for me, so I had tied them around my wrists with twine.

The man on the road had mentioned my scars. In all likelihood, that was the way the Clerisy would try to identify me. I didn't stand out otherwise; my pale skin and black hair could belong to hundreds of other girls in Roischal. I was lucky that this time of year, no one would think twice about a traveler wearing gloves.

My robes, on the other hand, I'd had to leave behind in the village. Their distinctive appearance instantly marked me as a Gray Sister. I still had on my chemise, my boots, and my stockings, but I had found a linen tunic and a tattered, mouse-gnawed woolen cloak in one of the houses to replace the robes. Among all the refugees fleeing their homes, I wouldn't attract attention. Except for the fact that I was riding a Clerisy warhorse.

Priestbane was well rested and energized by the morning chill. His head bobbed in time with his eager strides, and he looked around with his ears pricked forward, seemingly interested in every dripping branch and dew-silvered cobweb. When we flushed a rabbit from the bushes, he snorted at it in challenge.

Saint Eugenia's reliquary bumped against my ribs at the motion. I felt around its edges, ensuring that the shape was still hidden underneath my clothes. As long as I kept the cloak on, I was fairly confident no one would be able to tell it was there.

"Stop doing that. If you keep touching it, someone's going to notice."

The revenant was probably right. I moved my hand away, then felt a flicker of unease. I was beginning to listen to it as though it were a bizarre traveling companion—someone who shared my goals out of more than mere necessity. I couldn't drop my guard.

Last night, I had been lucky that it hadn't tried to betray me. I suspected that my physical weakness had bought me time. It had brought up the consequences of its vessels pushing themselves too far for a reason, and it knew that I wouldn't surrender without a fight—that I would rather die than allow it to possess me. It likely couldn't afford to risk my body failing in a struggle. After what had happened to its previous vessels, it had reason to be cautious.

"Nun, I've sensed something."

I twitched upright in the saddle. "What is it?" I asked roughly, pushing my thoughts aside as though it had walked in on me writing them down on paper.

"I'm not certain," it answered after a hesitation. *"But whatever it is, it's nearby."*

So far that morning, we hadn't passed any signs of life. Right now Priestbane was carrying me through an abandoned field, his hooves crunching over the stubble of harvested grain. I stopped him to listen. Straining my ears, I thought I could hear bells tolling faintly in the distance. And something else—the distant cries of ravens.

Trouble circled above us and cawed once as though in reply. Then he soared like an arrow over the hill ahead, fading to a white speck against the clouds.

Feeling the change in my posture, Priestbane danced forward. I shortened the reins to keep him from breaking into a canter. He took excited, mincing steps all the way up the hill.

When we reached the top, I could only stop and stare.

Below us lay a valley filled with mist. A city's towers speared from the mist into the sky, their points lit reddish gold by the rising sun as their long shadows spilled over a half-obscured jumble of battlements and rooftops below. I struggled to make sense of the bewildering image. I had never seen a city before, or even a building larger than my convent's chapel. This place could swallow the convent whole without noticing.

The clear faraway tolling of a bell carried across the valley.

Pennants streamed from the towers, flashing white and blue.

"That's Bonsaint," I said stupidly. It had to be. Bonsaint was the capital of Roischal, famous for its colossal drawbridge, which had been constructed over the banks of the River Sevre as a defense against the Dead. Crossing it was the only way to enter the city.

"It's nothing compared to the cities that stood before I was bound," the revenant answered scornfully. *"Look, it was even built using the stones of an older one."*

I stood up in the stirrups for a better view. Sure enough, the ancient-looking gray stone of Bonsaint's fortifications matched the look of the numerous ruins scattered across Loraille, one of which stood near my old village. The children had been forbidden from playing there, for good reason. Most of the ruins from the Age of Kings had been abandoned because they attracted too many spirits, their lingering taint of Old Magic irresistible to the Dead. I had heard that in Chantclere, daily rituals of incense and prayer were required to drive away the shades that accumulated in its streets. It seemed likely that similar measures were necessary in Bonsaint.

I could hear the ravens cawing more loudly from my current vantage point, but I still couldn't see them. They had to be down in the valley, hidden by the mist.

As soon as I had that thought, the wind shifted. The sound of the bells grew louder, and with it, men shouting and the distant, tinny clash of steel against steel. The mist was beginning to burn away, peeling back from the green valley like a shroud.

"I can smell powerful Old Magic," the revenant said at once. *"It's coming from the city. That's why I wasn't able to tell what I was sensing earlier. Old Magic, and spirits—nun, there are hundreds of spirits here. No, thousands. Thousands of them, and not just shades . . ."*

It trailed off as the mist blew away from the base of Bonsaint, revealing what I first took to be another layer of mist covering the valley, silvery and low to the ground. Then I realized I was looking at a mass of spirits, so densely packed that their shapes blurred together into a silver mass, an endless sea. An army of the Dead.

They were held at bay by a thin line of soldiers curved in a defensive half-circle in front of the river, fighting for their lives against an almost equal number of their own possessed men. They were hopelessly overwhelmed, about to be overcome at any moment. Behind them, an encampment of civilians stretched along the bank. Even from a distance I recognized the battered tents and wagons of refugees who had fled their homes. People who had come to Bonsaint for refuge but hadn't been let inside.

The giant drawbridge stood upright on the opposite bank, unmoving.

A thought struck me like a single clear toll of the bell echoing across the valley: these people had been condemned to die. The Divine of Bonsaint was prepared to sacrifice them all to protect her city.

I didn't pause to think. I turned Priestbane toward the valley, urging him first into a trot and then a canter.

"Nun, wait. You aren't trained—you need to be careful. You can't ride straight into a battle—nun!"

As far as I could tell, that was exactly what I needed to do. "If you guide me, I'll listen to you." A fierce certainty gripped my heart. "We'll fight the way you used to, before your vessels forgot how to wield you."

The silence stretched on for so long that I started to wonder if the revenant wasn't going to reply. The valley drew nearer and nearer; Priestbane's stride leveled out. Then it said decisively, *"We need a weapon. There."*

The body of a dead soldier lay in our path, his sword jutting from the ground. I seized the hilt as we passed and freed it in a spray of dirt. Trees flashed by, flickerings of sun and shadow. Then we exploded into the battlefield's chaos.

The first line of spirits broke against Priestbane like waves crashing against a stone. I knew the Clerisy's warhorses were shod with consecrated steel, but I wasn't prepared for the bravery with which he charged into the fray, snorting and trampling spirits beneath his hooves. Blight didn't harm animals the way it did humans, and he had been trained to endure the stinging cold of the spirits' touch.

"First we free the thralls," the revenant said rapidly. *"If the soldiers haven't been possessed for long, some of them might still be strong enough to fight."*

A gaunt flitted toward us—more by accident than on purpose, I suspected. With the revenant guiding my arm, I cut it down, and saw its shocked expression as it dispersed. Priestbane charged onward. I had slain several more spirits before I found the breath to ask, "Can you handle that many at the same time?"

"We'll have to do two passes." A swift, calculating pause. *"Ride toward them from the east. Most of the spirits won't have adjusted to their human senses yet, and with the sun behind you, you'll take them by surprise."*

As Priestbane forged us a path, I laid about with the sword. I could feel the revenant drinking everything in: the wind against my face, the flash of sunlight on metal, the shifting of muscles beneath my clothes. Its power soared through my veins like a battle hymn. I had never felt this alive before, as though I were experiencing every sense for the first time, and I understood how one of its vessels had fought until her heart burst. I could fight like this for days without stopping; part of me never wanted the feeling to end.

Through the haze of exhilaration I noted that the spirits around me were all Second and Third Order, their ranks dominated by a type I had never seen before, luminous and indistinct with shifting dark patches, like clumps of slag on white-hot metal. *"Blight wraiths,"* the revenant supplied. As their name suggested, blight wraiths were the Third Order spirits of those who had died of blight—previously rare in Loraille, now a testament to the number of bodies left abandoned in Roischal's villages.

Soon we had gained enough ground to see the soldiers ahead. Their formation had dissolved into a ragged line. Some of the men had lost their helmets, and horror showed beneath the smears of mud and blood on their faces. The thralls they were fighting were their own friends, and would need to be killed to be stopped.

At the revenant's prompting, I released the reins to stretch out my hand. Power funneled through me, and the nearest soldiers crumpled in a wave, the expelled spirits pouring from their bodies. For a heartbeat their former opponents stood stunned; then they set upon the spirits with a roar of victory.

I turned Priestbane away. As we carved an arc toward the other end of the line, a cry went up: "Vespertine!" And again, louder, triumphant. More soldiers joined in. "Vespertine!" It was a rallying cry, a roar of desperate hope.

The battle demanded my full attention. "What does that mean?" I asked, watching a gaunt disperse around my sword.

"It's what you humans call a priestess who wields a Fifth Order relic," the revenant said tersely, preoccupied. I felt it moving from place to place inside my body, driving back the blight from dozens of glancing blows. *"On your left—watch out."*

I cut down spirit after spirit without effort. For a strange moment I felt as though I were watching myself from afar, a lone cloaked figure cleaving through an ocean of the Dead. The chant of "Vespertine!" shook the ground like a drumbeat. I could feel it in my bones.

After the battle ended, I might have to face those men, perhaps even talk to them. The thought filled me with dread. Saving people wasn't a problem—it was the part that came afterward I couldn't handle. If I could figure out some way to slip away unnoticed . . .

"Nun!"

The revenant's warning came too late. Ahead of us, one of the possessed soldiers had turned and sighted his crossbow. I watched the bolt release, watched it spin through the air.

Desperately, the revenant grasped for control. My mind had gone blank. Without thinking, without even truly understanding what I was doing, I granted it permission. My hand snapped up with inhuman speed and caught the bolt a hairsbreadth from my chest, the whine of its flight still buzzing in my ears.

In the drawn-out seconds that followed, my arm didn't belong to me. I could still feel it, but I wasn't the one holding it aloft or gripping the quarrel. A heartbeat passed, another. Conflict roiled inside me. Then the revenant abruptly let go, almost disgustedly, as though throwing down a rag it had used to mop up a spill.

"Pay attention," it snapped. *"Don't forget that you can be injured."*

My pulse thundered in my ears. I cast the bolt aside, its shaft red with blood. It had sliced through my glove. Ignoring the sting, I stretched out my hand. I couldn't think about what had just happened. I concentrated instead on the force of the revenant's power roaring through me as I drove the spirits from the remaining thralls.

The soldiers collapsed as I rode past, one after another, following the sweep of my outstretched hand. Circling around again, I saw that some of the men from my first pass were already being helped upright, marshaled into formation by a knight on horseback.

He was the only one wearing plate armor. The rest were normal soldiers like the ones who had attacked my convent, dressed in mail and leather. The chain mail had to be consecrated, but it wouldn't afford nearly as much protection as full plate. I didn't see any clerics, either. In all the descriptions of battles I had read, there had been clerics on the battlefield, aiding the soldiers with prayer, incense, and the power of their relics. I could only guess that the Divine had held back her forces because she didn't want to risk the city's safety by lowering the bridge.

Grimly, I hacked apart a witherkin, a feverling, a shivering frostfain whose eyes were hidden beneath the curtain of icicles hanging from its brow.

"Nun, there are too many spirits. We can't defeat them this way."

The revenant was right. Even cantering back and forth in front of the line, destroying the spirits one by one, I was barely able to thin their numbers enough for the soldiers to hold their own. And I was beginning to encounter another problem: the spirits had caught on and were starting to avoid me, darting away before I could reach them. A space was opening around Priestbane like the eye of a storm.

"Where's their leader?" I asked through gritted teeth, remembering the fury in Naimes.

"Inside the city. Everything's muddled up with the smell of Old Magic, but whatever's happening in there, we won't be able to reach it from here. Nun, you need to use my full power."

My hands tightened on the reins. Without a word, I wheeled Priestbane around and urged him away from the men, away from the line. Spirits parted around us, shrinking back in fear as Priest-bane's strides lengthened to a pounding gallop. A path opened ahead.

"How far away do we need to be from the soldiers? And Bonsaint?"

The revenant lapsed into silence. I felt it calculating its answer, trying to conceal a sudden spark of hunger. *"Farther,"* it urged at last. *"To the edge of those ruins."*

An outcropping of stone lay ahead. It looked like part of an ancient wall, a leftover remnant of the ruins that had been dismantled long ago to build Bonsaint. I leaned forward in the saddle, focusing on the outcropping's steadily expanding outline as the wind gripped my cloak and tore at my hair. My hood had fallen back, but there wasn't anything I could do about that. When we reached the ruins, I rode past, encouraging Priestbane onward.

The revenant's power surged in outrage. *"We've gone far enough!"* it hissed. *"Release me!"*

The raw hunger in its voice convinced me otherwise. I had been right not to trust it. As Priestbane's hooves devoured the ground, leaving the ruins behind, the revenant's power swelled like an unvoiced scream in my chest. A sharp sting pricked my eye—a blood vessel bursting. The spirits continued to retreat in front of us, more quickly now, leaving a widening gap ahead. We had nearly reached the other side of the valley. The hills grew nearer and nearer.

I couldn't breathe. My vision began to tunnel, darkening and narrowing; the hills seemed to recede, spooling away into the distance. Dimly, I recognized that I was about to pass out.

"Now," I gasped.

The revenant answered. Around me came an unfurling, the

spreading of a great pair of ghostly wings. Silver light hazed my vision as phantom flames danced over my skin. The bright, cold essences of hundreds of spirits blazed across my senses like stars winking to life across a night sky, and then they vanished all at once, engulfed within the flames.

The valley steamed with the fog of dispersing spirits. I could almost smell it, a coppery tang in the air, until I felt wetness on my lips and recognized that what I was smelling was my own blood streaming from my nose.

The observation didn't seem important. Those spirits hadn't been enough. If anything, they had only made the hunger worse. We were still galloping toward the hills, so I turned Priestbane around in a wide arc, back toward the remaining bulk of the forces.

The stallion shivered beneath me. His ears were laid flat against his skull, and the whites showed around his eyes. Part of me wanted to lay a reassuring hand on his neck, but that same part didn't dare. I knew I would burn his life away the instant I touched him. It took all my willpower to drive back the flames licking at his heels, greedily tasting his strength.

There were fewer spirits left than I expected, at least a quarter of the army already burned away, half or so of the rest retreating toward the trees in ghostly streams. I bore down on a knot of them before they could reach the forest and felt their sparks flare and extinguish like moths igniting in a pyre. I swept through the spirits beyond, incinerating them as I passed. The silver fire streamed from me like a cloak, leaving a broad swath of steaming ground in my wake.

Nothing could stop me. A third of the army was decimated— then half—the rest scattering, fleeing in every direction. It was time for me to curb the revenant's power. But that thought seemed far away, feeble in comparison with the terrible hunger that gripped my body, growing ever stronger. It twisted like a knife in my gut, like a hand around my throat leaving me choked and breathless.

The spirits weren't enough. I needed more than the cold, meager remains of the Dead. I could feel the bright living souls of the soldiers and refugees growing nearer and nearer, and I couldn't look away.

Soon I had drawn close enough to see the soldiers' faces. Silver light reflected in their eyes as they gazed at me in wonder. They had lowered their swords. They thought they no longer needed them.

Closer . . . closer . . .

At the last second, I wrenched on Priestbane's reins and pressed my knee to his side. The pinion-edge of the flames sheared past the soldiers, the grass browning and shriveling at their feet. Priestbane's hooves pounded onward, carrying me past.

Anguished, the revenant shrieked—or maybe I was the one screaming. I couldn't tell. The reliquary grew hot against my skin, first itching, then burning. I gripped its edges through my robes.

"That's enough," I gasped. "Revenant, enough."

At first I thought it was going to fight me for control. And it could. If it tried, I might not have enough strength left to fight it. A terrible moment passed—and then its power rushed from my body, leaving me gasping and hollow, as though something essential inside me had been torn away.

Priestbane slowed to a walk, his head drooping. I dropped the sword and bent over his saddle, pressing my face to his hot, sweat-dampened mane. His sides heaved like a bellows. Grass stretched dead around us for as far as I could see.

I didn't know how long I sat there. The sun beat down on my cloak. My mouth tasted like blood. I heard shouts from the soldiers as they chased the last few spirits across the valley, sometimes close, sometimes far away, and remembered to pull the hood back over my head to hide my face. I focused on the smells of horse and hot leather, the green stink of the battlefield's churned-up turf, so I didn't have to think about anything else. The revenant said nothing. It had retreated somewhere deep inside me, far enough away that I could no longer sense its presence.

A shadow fell over me. Too late, I heard the jingle of another horse's reins.

"Lady vespertine," said a man's gruff voice.

My shoulders tensed. Maybe if I ignored him, he would go away.

"Lady? Are you injured?"

It had been worth a try. Reluctantly, I lifted my head. Peering sidelong from the shadows of my hood, I saw that it was the knight who had led the soldiers in battle. As I watched, he pushed up his mud-spattered visor with the back of his gauntlet, revealing a brown, careworn face. There were exhausted-looking pouches beneath his eyes, but his gaze was kind—too kind.

I wished he would stop looking at me that way. It made me feel flayed open and pinned, like one of Sister Iris's anatomical specimens.

"No," I said hoarsely, sounding uncertain.

A murmur went around. "You see," a child's voice declared with authority. "That's Artemisia of Naimes. I told you. She's a saint."

I flinched. After an awkwardly long pause, I lifted my head higher, expanding my field of vision beneath the hood's ragged fringe.

Immediately, I wished I hadn't. A crowd encircled me, soldiers on the inside, refugees on the outside—hundreds of people, dusty and bedraggled in the midday sun, all staring in wide-eyed silence.

Seeing me looking, several quickly signed themselves. The rest joined in, and a flutter of motion passed through the crowd, hands touching foreheads in the sign of the oculus, accompanied by hushed and reverent whispers. One old woman started weeping.

I didn't know what to do. Granted, I was used to making people cry, but it usually happened for different reasons. These people—I had nearly killed them all. None of them had any idea how close I'd come to slaughtering them instead of saving them. If they did, they would be fleeing in the opposite direction.

Why did they all have to stare like that? Even the baby hoisted up in its mother's arms was staring at me. I doubted anyone could see my face beneath the hood, but the knowledge didn't help. I just wanted to get away.

I was wondering if I could drag the revenant out of wherever it was hiding and use its power to immolate myself like the saints of old when the knight said "lady" again, and I realized he was holding out his water skin. I had my own, courtesy of Leander, but I had forgotten to use it. My throat suddenly felt so parched that I didn't hesitate. I took the skin from his hand and swallowed the warm water in thirsty gulps, briefly forgetting about the crowd.

"I'm Captain Enguerrand," the man said gently. "Lady, this isn't the first time you've saved my men. I heard what you did for the soldiers in Naimes."

I wiped my mouth on my sleeve. "They survived?"

"All but four. And today, before you appeared, we had nearly lost hope—"

He ceased talking abruptly, his gaze fixed on my sleeve. My mouth had left a smear of blood on the fabric.

"It's nothing," I croaked, handing back the skin. "I had a nose-bleed."

The movement shifted my cloak. The light slanted beneath my hood, and Captain Enguerrand's eyes widened in surprise. "You're young," he said, sitting back. "You can't be any older than my daughters."

Just then, a commotion came from the direction of the river. The giant drawbridge was being lowered over the Sevre. Riders had gathered on the other side to cross it: knights, their armor blinding in the sun, and a handful of robed clerics. They were so far away that they looked like toys.

As the bridge touched the bank and the procession stepped onto it, a single figure separated from the rest to ride forward, cantering toward us across the valley. I didn't recognize him until he drew the horse up short a distance away, the sun bright on his golden hair.

"That girl has stolen the relic of Saint Eugenia," he called in a clear, carrying voice. "She is in danger of being possessed. Seize her, by the order of Her Holiness the Divine."

NINE

The silence that fell was so profound I could hear the distant flapping of the pennants over Bonsaint. Everyone seemed to be holding their breath.

"Revenant," I muttered, too quietly for Captain Enguerrand to hear. It didn't reply.

The soldiers traded glances. They looked battered and filthy compared to the polished splendor of the knights on the bridge. Behind them, a discontented murmur ran through the crowd. I stole a wary look at Enguerrand under my hood, only to find him watching me with a complicated expression—resignation, unhappiness, determination. He looked like he was steeling himself to make a decision that he knew he was going to regret.

"Sir," pleaded one of the soldiers.

Enguerrand sighed. He turned to his men and nodded.

Everything seemed to happen at once. The soldiers moved. I tensed. At the same time, the old woman collapsed, wailing. One soldier immediately swerved to help her, tripping a second, who was making a halfhearted grab for my stirrup that already seemed calculated to miss. The cry spooked Enguerrand's horse, which jostled sideways into its neighbor. Except I was close enough to see that it hadn't really spooked; Enguerrand had jabbed his heel into its side.

The results were dramatic. Suddenly there were horses rearing and whinnying. The baby turned red as a beet and started howling. The little girl who had identified me as Artemisia of Naimes took one delighted look at the mayhem, clenched her fists at her sides, and exuberantly began to scream.

A young soldier approached me in the chaos, ducking to avoid a rotten turnip flying through the air. Fervently, he signed himself. "Lady, run," he said, and slapped Priestbane across the flank.

Priestbane lunged into motion. Dazed, I caught his reins and laid a hand on his shoulder in silent apology. Cantering heavily, each stride accompanied by a labored, snorting breath, he carried me away. Civilians and soldiers alike moved out of my path, pausing to sign themselves as I passed. Some reached out to brush their fingers across my shoes or Priestbane's side, like pilgrims touching a saint's effigy for its blessing.

I didn't see the point in trying to escape. Priestbane was spent; he wouldn't be able to outrun our pursuers this time. But then I heard a raucous cry of "Crumbs!" and glanced over my shoulder. Trouble had returned, diving at the crowd with a vengeance. I saw in disbelief that the riot had spread across the entire encampment, engulfing the procession as it tried to exit the bridge. The caparisoned horses balked, too hemmed in to give chase. People had even closed in around Leander, miring him in a sea of bodies.

I turned back around, leaning over Priestbane's withers. More faces flashed past. Outstretched hands surrounded me; shouts battered my ears. And then suddenly I burst free from the claustrophobic noise and stink and press of the crowd, open ground stretching away around me like a flung-out tapestry.

On one side the battlefield unfolded, the once-green valley reduced to a brown wasteland by the revenant's power. On the other, the river glared like a sheet of hammered steel, winding its path toward the forest. Ahead lay the shadows of the trees.

As the crowd's noise receded and the hills drew nearer, juddering up and down with each stride, it was difficult not to feel as though I were running in the wrong direction. What I'd done today wouldn't last—those people still needed my help. I needed to get inside Bonsaint. I had to find a way, even with all the Clerisy's forces in Roischal bent on my capture.

"Revenant, I need you."

Silence.

Unexpectedly, its rejection stung. Even though I didn't trust it, I had gotten used to relying on its advice. For a brief, horrible instant I had no idea what to do.

I shook off my uncertainty. I would get to the woods. Then I would figure out what to do next, with or without its help. I didn't have a choice; I couldn't ride Priestbane like this for much longer without hurting him.

The hills loomed above me. The shadows of the branches stretched over my cloak, breathing forth the forest's damp, cool air. Priestbane's hoofbeats muffled to a soft drumming on the leaves.

And then a shout rang out behind me.

I risked a look, already knowing what I would see. Leander. He'd escaped the crowd, galloping after me. My glance left me with a fleeting impression of green eyes blazing against a pale face.

Captain Enguerrand thundered a few paces behind, his own stallion flagging, its black coat flecked with foamy saliva.

Leander's mount was fresh, rapidly closing the distance between us. As I scrambled for an idea, I heard a *thunk*, and with a sickening weightless lurch found myself flung from the saddle. Priestbane's hoof must have struck a root, I thought, even as the world turned upside down. I saw a flash of sky, and then I hit the ground.

The impact slammed the breath from my lungs. Unable to halt my momentum, I tumbled end over end down a hill, lashed by undergrowth, dead leaves choking me, tangling in my hair, stuffing their prickling edges into my sleeves and collar and stockings.

At last I slid to a partial stop at the bottom of an incline, still gradually slipping down in a stupor. Distantly, I heard shouting. Blood roared in my ears. I flung out an arm to steady myself, and my hand met empty air.

I blinked away dirt and realized the roaring wasn't my blood after all. I'd slid to a halt at the edge of an embankment that abruptly cut off in a steep vertical plunge, the roots of the trees anchored along its edge dangling in midair over the roaring span of the Sevre. The river's current raged, throwing up spray against sharp rocks that studded the frothing water like teeth.

For a moment everything else stopped existing. The white spray and jagged, glistening rocks seemed to expand, filling my vision like an animal's gaping mouth. Even this high up, fine droplets of water misted my face. Slowly, I felt myself sliding over the edge.

In a rush, I came back to myself. I wrenched myself away, scrabbling, grabbing fistfuls of leaves. Loose dirt sifted into my gloves as I clawed for the roots beneath, tearing handfuls of them from the ground in my desperate scramble up the slope. When I reached a leaf-filled hollow behind a tree, I threw myself onto my side, panting.

And then, a voice. "I've found her horse, Your Grace."

Enguerrand.

"That's my horse," Leander said coldly, his voice raised to make himself heard over the noise of the rapids. "She stole it from me."

Every muscle in my body went rigid. Moving in stiff increments, I burrowed deeper into the leaves, hoping the Sevre would drown out the quiet rustling of my movements.

"Your Grace?"

"Never mind. Where did she go? She must be nearby. She couldn't have run far."

A pause followed. I shifted my head so I could peer through the leaves, bringing the two of them into focus on the trail above the slope. Captain Enguerrand held Priestbane's reins. I guessed that he and Leander had continued their pursuit of the stallion before discovering that he was riderless and doubling back to find me. Enguerrand was gazing down the steep incline to the Sevre below, where my uncontrolled tumble had scuffed an obvious path to the edge of the precipice.

Leander followed his gaze, and the blood drained from his face. For a heartbeat he looked stricken. I thought this had to be a performance for Enguerrand's sake, but Enguerrand wasn't look-ing at him—and when the captain turned back around, Leander struggled to bring his expression back under control, appearing briefly horrified before his face smoothed into its usual pious mask.

"We've lost her," Enguerrand said grimly. "I would wager she hit her head when she fell from the horse, and went over stunned. It wouldn't be the first time. We lost a soldier last year the same way. It isn't easy to judge how close the river is from the trails."

As Enguerrand spoke, Leander's hand spasmed. Reflexively, he reached for his onyx ring. Then his fingers stopped a hairsbreadth from the relic.

I held my breath, waiting to see what he would do. I noticed for the first time that he looked even worse than he had yesterday, the skin under his eyes bruised instead of merely shadowed, a match for the dark streak of blight on his cheekbone. He had likely forced his way out of the crowd by using his relic. He would have had to use it on dozens of people to manage that.

The moment stretched on. At last Leander laid his hand back down. He had little cause to suspect that Enguerrand was lying to him. The tracks spoke for themselves. The path I had clawed on my way back up overlapped too closely with the original for me to tell them apart, so I doubted Leander could, either.

Admirably, Enguerrand hadn't looked at the relic. He didn't seem to have even noticed Leander's struggle. "She went over the edge," he repeated, steadfast.

"Then have your men search the river," Leander snapped.

Enguerrand hesitated. "Your Grace, does she know how to dismiss the revenant?"

"Of course not. She's untrained."

"Even Fifth Order spirits are said to be weakened by the Sevre. I don't know as much about this as you do, Your Grace. But if she fell in with the revenant still summoned . . ."

He didn't need to finish. The frothing water and jagged rocks would claim even a strong swimmer. Someone sharing a spirit's weakness to running water wouldn't stand a chance.

Leander's eyes were drawn back to its current. For a long moment he stared into the rapids. After a few seconds, he started to look sick.

"Your Grace?"

"Search the banks," he said, returning to himself. "As far south as necessary. Don't stop until you find . . ." His face was white, his eyes stark. "Until you find her," he finished, and wheeled his mount away.

Captain Enguerrand lingered a moment longer, studying the tracks I had left in the leaves. New lines already seemed to be etched into his weathered features. I wondered what he was risking by helping me—his family, the daughters he'd mentioned on the battlefield.

He raised his head, and his gaze brushed over my hiding place. Then he turned his horse to follow, drawing Priestbane after him, calling orders to his men.

I didn't move until dark. At least what passed for dark in the woods, which barely counted for someone with the Sight. Wisps had emerged as dusk painted the landscape in shades of blue and purple, and now hundreds of them sparkled among the trees, casting a ghostly silver glow over the hills, illuminating my path.

I didn't allow my gaze to linger as I trudged past. I knew from experience that I wouldn't be able to see any sign of the children their souls had once belonged to. Even up close, wisps merely resembled hazy spheres of light hovering a handspan or so above the ground.

No one had ever bound a wisp to a relic. According to convent legend, Saint Beatrice had needed to starve herself for weeks to make her body weak enough for a shade to try possessing it, and even then it had barely been a shiver in her mind, effortless to subdue. The only stories about wisps were those describing how Sighted travelers had survived getting lost in the wilderness by following wisp-lights, which had floated ahead of them, guiding them to safety. I had never seen anything like that, but I hoped it was true.

There was a plot outside my old village where children were buried in unmarked graves. In a village like mine, far outside the route of the convent's corpse-wagons, only those who could afford it sent their dead children to convents to get the bodies blessed. Wisps couldn't hurt anyone, the reasoning went, and it cost money to borrow a horse, which most families needed to get the body to the convent in time. Spending that coin could mean a second child starving for lack of bread.

At night, peeking through the knotholes in the shed's walls, I had been able to see the plot and the lights of the wisps hovering above its graves. My family had been keeping me in the shed for months by that point. I'd had no idea what the wisps were or what their presence meant, but their lights had comforted me all the same. Somehow, they'd always felt like kindred souls signaling to me across the dark.

At last, I reached the edge of the forest. I must have been lost in my thoughts, because I nearly stumbled into a group of people, hearing the loud crash of their footsteps through the undergrowth too late. I withdrew in time to avoid being spotted, cowering behind a bush like a startled animal.

"As if she would really fall into the river and drown! I'm telling you, the captain might as well have winked."

"I doubt the old man knows how to wink," another voice replied, with obvious pride.

"Did you see the silver fire?" a third was saying, also male. "I've never seen anything like it. No one has. A real vespertine—did you think you'd ever see a vespertine?"

"Not a vespertine," corrected a quiet voice. "A saint."

Following this pronouncement, everyone lapsed into reverential silence. Fabric rustled. A pattering sound followed.

I took a closer look through the leaves, and instantly wished I hadn't. It was a group of young soldiers relieving themselves at the edge of the trees. Firelight glinted off their chain mail.

I could ask them for help. By the sound of it, I could probably trust them. But as they finished and turned to leave, and I tried to rise from behind the bush, I discovered that I couldn't move. I tried again, to no avail. The mere idea of approaching them had immobilized me. Speaking to a group of strangers would have posed a challenge for me at the best of times. The idea of doing it now, after everything they had just said, made me want to turn back around and hurl myself into the river.

I watched them go, their figures silhouetted against a sea of flickering cookfires. Not too far away, the sides of tents and wagons danced with leaping shadows, painted red in the shifting light. Laughter and the smell of woodsmoke carried on the breeze. I had emerged from the forest in a different place than I had entered it, following the Sevre to make sure I didn't get lost. In doing so, it appeared that I had stumbled across the far side of the refugee encampment.

It looked significantly larger up close than it had from far away. There had to be thousands of people camped out along the river. Suddenly I was grateful I'd remained hidden. No one in Roischal aside from Leander and Captain Enguerrand had seen my face closely enough to recognize me. My hood had fallen back during the battle, but I'd been enveloped in the revenant's ghost-fire afterward, so I doubted the soldiers had gotten a good look.

Better if I remained dead, a body floating down the Sevre. The Clerisy might not be fully convinced of my demise, but at the very least, they would waste some time searching for me in the wrong direction. Meanwhile, I could vanish among the refugees without a trace.

I stumbled toward the fires, drawing my cloak closer around my body. As I picked my way across the dark field, alone in front of the vast, glittering sprawl of humanity, I was more conscious than ever of the continued silence inside my head. If I had consecrated steel, I would try using it to draw the revenant out. I had muttered a few prayers earlier while waiting for the sun to set, but disappointingly, the words hadn't produced any interesting effects—no smoking welts or festering boils.

As I entered the encampment, the dazzle of the fires confused my sense of direction. Sounds and smells washed over me in waves, overwhelming my senses. The reek of sewage merged nauseatingly with the savory aroma of roasting meat; disorienting bursts of laughter erupted around me without warning. I averted my eyes from the groups gathered around the cookfires, searching for a dark, abandoned spot where I could huddle down and sleep. My steps weaved like a drunkard's. Distantly, I wondered whether I should try to find something to eat. Sometimes I forgot.

Have you ever considered that your body carries you?

Someone had said that to me recently. Mother Katherine? No— the revenant.

A loud cheer went up, and I instinctively shrank away, crouching against the side of a cart. The cheer went up again as I pressed my face against the rough wood, retreating from the barrage of sound. It was my name, I realized. They were cheering my name.

I didn't want to move. But eventually the cheering died down, and I had the unsettling sense that I was being watched. Reluctantly, I raised my head. Two grimy-faced children were regarding me solemnly over the edge of the straw-filled cart bed. After a moment of consideration, one of them broke off a piece of bread and held it down, as though I were a shy creature to be coaxed from the shadows.

"Are you alone?" someone else asked.

I hadn't noticed the woman standing beside the cart, her face drawn with worry. She looked as though she had been watching me for a while. She reached for my shoulder, and I flinched. Slowly, she lowered her hand.

"Don't worry—it's all right. Are you looking for somewhere to sleep?" She was using the same gentle voice as Captain Enguerrand. It was how the sisters had spoken to me when I'd first arrived at the convent, a starved, voiceless child with burned hands and staring eyes.

When I didn't answer, she went on, "You can sleep behind our cart if you want. We won't bother you. Look, here's a spare blanket. . . ."

She moved away to lift a bundle from the cart. A man lay propped up against the leaned-over end, his face and neck mottled with blight. He was lucky to have survived. Since spirits could only possess people with the Sight, whatever attacked him wouldn't have been interested in keeping him alive. Its goal would have been to drain the life from him as quickly as possible. Whenever the convent received corpses who had died of blight, Sister Iris would ride out the next morning to investigate, tracking down the stray witherkin or frostfain responsible.

My thoughts had wandered. Motion drew my attention back to the woman. She had spread the blanket across the ground in the shadows some distance from her family's fire. "Here," she said, patting the blanket as though I might not understand words.

I was used to that. Too exhausted to care, I dragged myself over to the blanket as the children watched my every move in fascination. I didn't want to spend the night getting stared at, but I also didn't have the energy to go anywhere else. It was either sleep on the blanket, or pass out on the ground. At least I had some comfortingly non-human company. There was a mule tied up behind the cart, which laid back its ears and flashed me the white of its eye before resuming its quest for a weed trapped under one of the wheels.

The woman returned to the fire and gathered her family around her, speaking quietly. I couldn't make out what she was saying.

"The poor girl," the man said. "She's so thin. I wonder what happened to her family."

I caught a snatch of her reply. "Better not to ask, I think. That look on her face . . ."

As far as I knew, I hadn't been making any particular expression. She was likely referring to my normal one, which I supposed, in certain lighting, could look somewhat disturbed. I burrowed deeper into the blanket.

I didn't emerge when she stealthily returned to set something down nearby: close enough to reach, not close enough to frighten me. I looked after she had gone and discovered that she had left a crust of bread. I wondered if it was the same one that the children had been eating previously. They were still in the cart, watching.

Her charity made me uncomfortable. I should eat, but the children needed it more. I rolled the bread over to the cart and waited for one of them to pick it up before I turned away.

The revenant would be angry when it came back and discovered that I hadn't eaten, but it had chosen to abandon me, so it didn't have the right to complain.

As I drifted off, I listened to the man and woman speak in

hushed voices. I learned that they had originally left their town to visit Bonsaint for the festival of Saint Agnes. They'd gotten caught up in the attacks during their journey, and by the time they had arrived at Bonsaint, the drawbridge—which they called the Ghostmarch—had already been lifted for everyone except those bringing supplies into the city.

At home we celebrated Saint Agnes with only a single holy day, but she was the patron saint of Bonsaint. She had died attempting to bind a revenant, and in the process had destroyed it instead, burning her entire body to ashes. That qualified her as a high saint, even though she hadn't left a relic behind. Bonsaint devoted several days of festivities to her memory. People traveled far for the celebration, even from outside Roischal.

That might be useful to keep in mind, if the Old Magic practitioner in Bonsaint was using the festival to cover their actions. Materials could be smuggled into the city as supplies for the festival; strange actions might go unnoticed amid the preparations. I was busy mulling this over when I heard the man mention the Ghostmarch again and realized they were talking about the drawbridge finally being lowered to let the refugees inside.

"Why wait until tomorrow?" he was saying angrily. "They saw what happened—they know the danger we're in."

"It's all right," she said, reaching out to clasp his hand. "Artemisia of Naimes is watching over us tonight."

Faith shone in her eyes. I thought that was a ridiculous thing to say, but in all fairness, I couldn't argue. I was lying on her blanket.

Unfortunately, I was more or less useless without the revenant. It occurred to me how disastrous it would be if I had to try to save someone while it was absent throwing a tantrum. Whenever it came back, we were going to need to discuss that. It couldn't vanish whenever it pleased, at least not without warning me first.

Unless—

The thought struck like a torrent of cold water. I rolled over and drew out the reliquary with unsteady hands, fumbling with the latches. My chest still felt tender from how hot the metal had grown at the end of the battle. I imagined the air inside simmering, the delicate bone splintering, the revenant destroyed just like the one fatally bound to Saint Agnes.

I had been a fool not to think of that earlier. The relic was old; there might be a limit to how much power it could channel at once. It took me an agonizingly long time to get the latches open, cursing myself every second of the way.

Even after I had opened the reliquary, I couldn't see well enough to tell whether the relic looked damaged. I pried the bone from its velvet notch and turned it over onto my hand.

With shocking speed, the revenant came boiling up from the depths of my mind and slammed into full power with a force that left me reeling. *"Stop that,"* it hissed, spitting with fury. *"Put it away!"*

"Revenant," I whispered hoarsely. "You're still here."

It paused, its emotions a confused, sharp-edged jumble. Relief clearly hadn't been the reaction it had expected. *"You aren't going to destroy my relic?"* it asked finally, in a tone of lingering disbelief.

"I was checking to see if it had been damaged. I thought that was why you disappeared. Where were you?"

It hesitated. Then it snapped, *"I'm entitled to some privacy, aren't I? It isn't as though there's much to go around. Being trapped inside your body isn't the panoply of delights you might imagine. Oh, pardon me, you're a nun. Silly of me to suggest that you've ever imagined a single delightful experience in the entire span of your dull, miserable, hateful nun existence."*

I had almost missed talking to the revenant. At least I wasn't worried about making it cry. I glanced over my shoulder at the couple, but they didn't seem to have noticed anything amiss. Even if they did overhear me muttering to myself, they would likely mark it down as a sign of my ordeal. The children appeared as though they had fallen asleep.

"The priest almost caught me," I whispered. "I could have used your help."

"Please. If you had truly needed me, I would have intervened."

I nearly dropped the relic in shock. "You were watching that entire time?"

"It isn't as though I have much else to do," the revenant snapped. *"In any case, if the priest had caught you again, what do you suppose I could have done about it? Since you're so determined not to hurt any humans, even the ones who deserve it."*

"Did those people you tried to kill on the battlefield deserve it?" My voice had gone as cold and dull as lead.

The revenant didn't answer. It seemed to have realized it had gone too far. I still held the relic on my palm, and it looked suddenly pathetic, a fragile nub of ancient, brittle bone.

For a moment I had been worried about the revenant—actually worried that I might have lost it, and not merely because I couldn't help the people of Roischal without its power. Even after it had nearly slaughtered hundreds of people using my body as a vessel, including the woman who was helping me and her family. I didn't understand how I could still spare a single scrap of concern for it after that.

"What I hate about you is that you aren't some mindless creature," I said tonelessly. "That's what I thought you would be, when I first opened the reliquary—a more powerful version of the ashgrim. But you can talk. You can think. Which means that when you do something, you're making a choice to do it, like a person. I had started to think of you as a person," I realized aloud, disgusted. "I suppose that was stupid of me."

"Yes, I suppose it was," the revenant retorted, but there was a note in its voice I couldn't interpret. It had listened to that entire speech in silence. It was probably waiting to see whether I was about to crush its relic in my hand.

Using slow, deliberate movements, I placed the relic into its velvet slot, shut and latched the reliquary, and tucked it back underneath my clothes. Then I drew the blanket over my head and stared into the dark.

TEN

Today I would have to cross the Ghostmarch. Its shape loomed above the encampment in the pre-dawn gloom, leashed to the city walls with a complex array of ropes and pulleys as though it were a beast in danger of breaking free.

I vanished from the family's camp before dawn, leaving them asleep in the murky half-light. Before I left, I pried one of the smaller, less recognizable gems from the reliquary and placed it carefully in front of the woman's face as she slept on unawares, ignoring the revenant's hissed objections. I was certain the Lady would want her family to have it.

People were already stirring, but the smoke of last night's banked cookfires hung low above the ground, shrouding everyone's movements. No one bothered me as I passed.

As I neared the edge of the encampment, the roaring of the Sevre grew louder, and louder still as I picked my way up the rocky escarpment that overlooked the river, its weathered boulders pock-marked with pools of standing water. No one had camped here, likely because the wind kept blowing the river's spray in drenching sheets over the bank. I found an outcropping of rock to crouch behind that shielded me from the spray but still afforded me a view of the drawbridge and the city.

Up close, Bonsaint lost some of its grandeur. My view was mostly of the walls. The banners hung sodden with dew, the high gray battlements that thrust from the tumbled rock of the bank mottled with lichen from the endless moisture of the Sevre crashing below. The soldiers patrolling the battlements were so high up they looked like toy figures, their positions betrayed by the occasional glint of steel. From this vantage, I would be able to study the Clerisy's defenses before I crossed the bridge.

Eerie groaning and creaking sounds shuddered across the bank, like the whale song we sometimes heard on the coast of Naimes, echoing up from the depths of the sea. They were coming from the Ghostmarch, the revenant explained, as the colossal wooden beams expanded and contracted in the damp, straining against the drawbridge's metal components.

"The metal is consecrated, of course, but that won't be the unpleasant part. I haven't crossed the Sevre since before I was bound, and I'm not looking forward to doing it again."

"Won't walking on a bridge make a difference? We'll be high above the water."

"Certainly, it will make a difference. You can't drown from on top of a bridge. You can, however, ardently long for death as you vomit over the rail. I'll be able to suppress my power to reduce the effects on your body, but you'll still feel sick as we cross, and you'll need to hide it from the other humans. Your Clerisy will be watching for signs of possession."

Neither of us mentioned that the problem could be avoided entirely if I were able to dismiss the revenant back into its relic, even just for a few minutes.

"*Lean over and look into that puddle,*" it said suddenly.

"What?"

"*Your reflection,*" it said impatiently. "*I want to see what you look like.*"

Soon it was going to regret saying that. "Just don't scream."

"*Why would I scream?*"

I shrugged. That was how Marguerite had reacted when she'd first arrived at the convent and discovered me watching her from beneath the bed of our shared room. But possibly, hiding under the bed had been a factor.

I bent over the puddle, watching my reflection materialize in the shallow water. Gray eyes, stark against a filthy face smeared with dirt and dried blood. The skin underneath ghastly in its pallor, surrounded by a tangled curtain of long black hair, snarled like a bird's nest with burrs and leaves. Overall, not the worst I had ever looked first thing in the morning.

I felt the revenant recoil.

"If we come across the priest, he won't recognize me," I pointed out.

"*If the Clerisy sees you like this, they'll think you're a thrall!*"

"My eyes aren't glowing."

"*That isn't always a reliable sign,*" the revenant snapped. "*Experienced spirits know how to prevent it. In any case,*" it hurried on, possibly realizing it had revealed too much, "*we don't want to give them any reason to pay special attention to you, and you look precisely like a thrall that's spent a fortnight blundering through the wilderness, trying to eat twigs and moss because it has no idea how to care*" *for its human vessel. And you smell like one, too, for that matter.*"

A fair observation. I soaked a corner of my cloak in the puddle and scrubbed my face, which the revenant endured in prickly silence. I got the feeling it wanted to complain about the cold but couldn't, since I was acting on its advice. *"Clean that cut on your hand while you're at it. I would consider it a personal affront if you got this far only to die of wound fever.*"

I had forgotten about my hand. The thin, shallow gash looked like it had been sliced by the bolt's fletching, right through my glove. I more regretted the damage to the glove. My scars made it impossible to handle a needle and thread.

After I had cleaned the wound to the revenant's satisfaction, I shoved the wet handful of cloak beneath my tunic and scrubbed away at my armpits and the other parts of my body that I could reach. The revenant seemed utterly uninterested in the proceedings, just as it had on the occasions when I'd relieved myself in the woods or the harrow's chamber pot.

"Is it true that spirits can't remember anything about their human lives?"

"Yes," it answered tartly.

I had never considered before now that someone would have needed to speak to a spirit to learn that information. I had always merely accepted it as one of the Clerisy's teachings. "So you don't know whether you were a man or a woman in life."

"No, and I don't see why it matters. Humans are so tedious. Oh, you have dangly bits. Congratulations, you're going to put on armor and swing a sword about. Oh, you've ended up with the other kind. Too bad—time to either have babies or become a nun."

It wasn't exactly that simple, but I decided that I didn't want to argue about the Clerisy's hierarchy with a Fifth Order spirit. Also, it had a point. "It would be useful if you did remember something. We still don't know why your soul turned into a revenant."

"No doubt because I was horrifically nasty and evil," it spat.

Probably, but I received the impression that I would upset it if I agreed. Instead, I said nothing, giving my dirty fingernails a final halfhearted scrub before I tugged my gloves back on. "How is this?" I asked, leaning over the now-murky puddle again.

It gave me a grudging inspection. *"Better,"* it admitted, then added darkly, *"But you're going to have to do something about that hair."*

We spent the rest of the morning going over the various obstacles that we might encounter on the bridge and what I might have to say if I was stopped for questioning. By the time the sun rose above the city's battlements, I had nearly succeeded in picking most of the burrs from my hair. We were debating whether I should claim I was from Roischal or Montprestre when a ratcheting sound echoed across the bank, and I looked up to see the towering span of the Ghostmarch move. In slow, ponderous jerks, the bridge slanted away from the city walls and began to descend over the river, producing a tortured, drawn-out groan like a living creature in agony.

I tensed behind the outcropping, the back of my neck prickling. I had never seen anything like this before. It seemed impossible that something so large could move, much less at the whim of humankind. Up along the wall, I glimpsed the furious spinning of winches and pulleys as workers let out the ropes. In the river below, massive pilings stood anchored in the rapids, waiting to receive the bridge's weight. The Ghostmarch plunged them into deep shadow before at last, with a crunch and scrape of rock, it settled in place against the opposite bank.

A crowd had already gathered, but no one approached the end of the bridge. I thought it likely that some were remembering the effects of Leander's relic from the day before. Thankfully, though I was too far away to make out details, I didn't see any sign of his black robes among the knights and clerics gathered on the other side.

"Those clerics will be using their relics," the revenant warned.

"Will they be able to sense you?"

"Not while I'm suppressing myself. But, nun, I won't be able to stay hidden and lend you my power at the same time. While we're over the river, I won't be able to use my power at all. You'll be on your own."

I bit back a number of possible replies about its performance yesterday, which it seemed to be doing its best to pretend hadn't happened. In silence, I clambered down, slipped out from behind a boulder, and merged with the crowd.

I had chosen a spot away from the front, not wanting to be one of the first to cross. I regretted it as a sea of humanity closed in around me, shoulders jostling mine, bodies pressing close, dozens of voices vying for supremacy in my ears. Babies were crying, couples arguing. Nearby someone was consoling an elderly man on a cart, begging him to drink a little water. My head swam. I wished that I could pull my hood up, but the revenant and I had agreed earlier that hiding my face would seem too suspicious.

"What's wrong with you?" Its voice sounded muted. Suppressing itself, I guessed. *"You already feel like you're going to vomit."*

"It's the people," I muttered under my breath.

"What about the people?"

"There are a lot of them."

"You could have mentioned that this would be a problem earlier," the revenant hissed.

I hadn't known it would be. I took measured breaths through

my nose, focusing on the ground in front of my feet. The crowd inched forward in fits and starts, clogged with carts and wagons, periodically halted by balking mules that refused to set foot over the river.

And then I reached the bridge. The moment I stepped onto the planks, I felt as though all the blood had drained out of my body through my feet. I could feel the power of the current raging beneath me, snatching my strength and carrying it away, hurling it onward down the river, pummeling it to nothing. I didn't feel my next shuffling step. My legs had gone numb.

For the revenant, the effects seemed to be worse. It had curled itself into a tight knot to hide, and now I felt it struggling not to unravel, radiating feeble pulses of misery. I doubted it would be able to speak even if it tried.

Through the waves of dizziness and nausea, I slowly became aware that the knights stationed along the bridge were paying special attention to dark-haired girls. Some they drew aside to be scrutinized by a funereal-looking old man in crimson and silver vestments, which I recognized from the convent's books as the robes of a sacristan. As we drew nearer, I caught the red glint of a ruby on his finger. One of a sacristan's duties included lighting the cathedral's candles and incense, like Sister Lucinde had done for our chapel in Naimes.

But the ashgrim wasn't his only relic. An oval-shaped moonstone pendant gleamed at his breast, too large to wear as a ring. I noticed that he was waiting on the far side of the bridge, where he would be able to use his shade to examine the girls as they stood over the Sevre. Even worse, there was a raven perched on his shoulder, which seemed to fix me with a beady stare as I hunched inward, hoping to pass unnoticed.

It was no use. A knight loomed from the crowd to block my path, his visored face impassive as he gestured me over to wait. Unable to think of any way to escape, I joined the group of girls clustered by the rail. Some of them were looking over it at the frothing chaos of the Sevre, the mere idea of which made bile creep up my throat.

The nearest girl turned and gave me a tentative smile, which quickly changed into a look of alarm when she took in my expression.

"I have the flux," I croaked, and she sidled away with gratifying haste.

One by one, the knights motioned us forward. The reliquary hung as a leaden weight beneath my tunic, and the raven's attention seemed focused on me as the other girls filed past. Finally, my turn arrived. A gauntleted hand halted me mere steps from dry land.

My vision blurred. I had an impression of rheumy eyes peering at me from beneath dark, silver-shot brows, and a deep, sonorous voice asking me a question.

"Anne," I replied, hoping the sacristan had asked for my name. "I'm from Montprestre. I came to visit my aunt, for the feast, but then—on the road . . ."

I couldn't remember the rest. The story that I had rehearsed with the revenant slipped from my mind as the sacristan stooped closer, his spidery fingers brushing over the moonstone pendant.

A tickling, crawling sensation washed over me, as though tiny insects had been released to skitter over my skin, searching for a way inside. I struggled not to react. Only a Sighted person would be able to feel the effects of the relic. But the revenant had reached its limits—I felt its knot beginning to fray. Any moment now the sacristan would sense something. And out of the corner of my eye I saw the raven ruffle its feathers, preparing to deliver a pronouncement.

A loud, harsh caw broke the spell. It hadn't come from the raven on the sacristan's shoulder, but rather from somewhere behind me. Mirrored in his giant moonstone, I glimpsed a flash of white pinions.

He looked up, frowning. At the same time, a decisive voice said, "That isn't her."

A horse's hoof thudded against the bridge. My gaze wavered up to Captain Enguerrand, who was looking down at me in turn with no trace of recognition.

"Move along," he said, already glancing past, as though I were of no more interest to him than the dozens of other pedestrians crammed onto the bridge.

I ducked my head and obeyed, shouldering past the people in my path, barely registering their protests in my urgency to reach solid ground. A jumble of ropes dangled threateningly above as I passed into the dripping, echoing shadows of the gatehouse.

My first impression of Bonsaint wasn't a favorable one. As soon as I emerged from the gatehouse's darkness, color and sound whirled around me like a spinning top. My stomach heaved, and I blindly stumbled to a gutter and threw up. I crouched there for a long moment with my eyes squeezed shut.

I smelled urine, the sour stink of spilled ale, and pastry frying in grease. Around me, dogs barked. Children laughed, shrieking as they ran past. Vendors shouted about hot pies and fresh cold mussels straight from the Sevre.

The other half of the clamoring voices sounded completely nonsensical to my ears. I briefly panicked before I realized that I was hearing different languages. Sarantian, and perhaps Gotland-ish. Gotland had fallen in the Sorrow's aftermath and was now an uninhabited wasteland to our northeast, overrun with spirits. The Gotlanders who had survived the cataclysm now thrived in Loraille's cities, with entire districts given over to their language and trade.

Sarantia had escaped the worst of the Sorrow by collapsing the mountain pass that connected it to Loraille. Once our closest ally, it now traded with us only by sea, wary of risking overland contact. Nevertheless, the shared history between our two nations was such that many people in Loraille had varying degrees of Sarantian heri-tage, evident in their brown complexions and dark, wavy hair.

Now that I was listening properly, I could identify the lilting cadence of Sarantian without doubt. I could read it passably, since some of our convent's texts were written in it, but here it was being spoken too quickly for me to follow.

Cautiously, I shaded my face against the sun and opened my eyes.

I was in a square larger than the grounds of my convent. The shops that crowded its sides were each as tall as the chapel—high, narrow buildings of stone and white plaster, whose tiled roofs and chimneys stretched so far toward the sky that following them upward made me list sideways and almost fall before I caught myself against the gutter. I averted my eyes from the spires beyond, which soared even higher, the flocks of ravens flapping around them as tiny as gnats.

The bustling view below wasn't any safer to behold. I focused on the statue of Saint Agnes that stood at the center of the square, her feet strewn with offerings of wilted flowers. Beggars crouched around its base, holding out bowls for alms. A smaller statue of

Saint Agnes stood in the cemetery in Naimes, erected over the grave of a pilgrim. Her familiar marble countenance was the closest thing to a friend that I was likely to see in Bonsaint.

My heartbeat gradually calmed. I was trying to work up the balance to stand, feeling like a sailor recently deposited onshore, when a voice above me said, "Are you all right?"

Unmistakably, the question was addressed to me. I longed for my life in Naimes, where the only new people I'd had to meet had been corpses. I spat to clear my mouth and looked up into a pair of curious brown eyes.

Eyes that I recognized. They belonged to the young soldier who had slapped Priestbane's flank and told me to run. Now he had his helmet tucked beneath his arm, revealing a handsome, brown-skinned face and a tousled head of black hair.

My stomach plummeted. I braced myself for recognition to dawn, but his expression didn't change. He didn't know who I was. He must not have seen my face beneath the hood.

"The captain sent me," he went on, speaking a little more slowly, as though I might have difficulty following. I gathered that the way I was looking up at him didn't inspire confidence. "Captain Enguerrand, that is, the captain of the city guard. We're supposed to bring everyone who's sick or injured to the convent so Mother Dolours can have a look at them." He glanced around, then knelt beside me in a confiding pose, his bent arm resting casually on his knee. "The captain said to mention there's a sanctuary law at the convent, which means that for as long as you stay there, you're under the abbess's protection. He thought it might make you feel better."

I knew about the sanctuary law; it applied to every convent in Loraille. Famously, it had once been used to shelter the scholar-turned-heretic Josephine of Bissalart from burning at the stake. I stared at the soldier, trying to figure out what a normal person would say. In the end I bent over and vomited again, which seemed like a better alternative to speaking.

"Oh, sorry," he said, and leaned over me to look. "At least nothing's coming up. You must not have eaten in ages."

"Stop looking," I ground out.

He grinned unrepentantly. "Well, you're definitely sick," he said, sounding very cheerful about it. He jammed his helmet onto his head and stood at attention. In an authoritative voice, he declared, seemingly for the benefit of passersby, "Madam, I have no choice but to escort you to the convent."

Going with him didn't necessarily seem like a good idea. Some of the sisters would be carrying relics. I wished I could consult the revenant, but at the moment it was queasily sloshing around in my head like a stunned fish in a bucket, occasionally rolling belly-upward. I didn't think it was going to have anything useful to say for a while.

Captain Enguerrand had saved me twice now. Both times, he had been aided by Trouble. Maybe it was foolish to believe that the Lady had sent Trouble to help me, but that was all I had to go on. If this was what Captain Enguerrand thought I should do, then I would do it.

I tottered to my feet, shaking my head in refusal of the soldier's offered arm. Then I ended up grabbing it anyway when I made the mistake of looking up. The riot of motion and color in the square hadn't grown any less overwhelming since I had last seen it. I thought I might be sick again.

He gave me a knowing look. "Your first time in a city, isn't it? I've seen that expression before. Where are you from?"

"Montprestre," I muttered, releasing his arm. I would stand out less if I claimed I was from Roischal, but my story would quickly unravel if anyone began asking questions. Meanwhile, I could probably get away with lying even if I was unlucky enough to meet another person from Montprestre. Mostly, the province was known for having a lot of goats.

"That explains it," he said sympathetically. "Well, you'll get used to Bonsaint eventually. In the meantime, keeping your eyes on the ground might help. My name is Charles, by the way."

"Anne," I returned, doggedly trailing after him as he set off across the square. If he said anything else, I didn't hear it. I hadn't been prepared for how painful it would be to use my old name again. The sound of it echoed cruelly in my head, conjuring up memories of ropes around my wrists, the musty stink of the shed. I should have chosen something else. Francine, or even Marguerite.

To my relief, Charles didn't seem to notice that I was behaving oddly. The helmet had already gone back beneath his arm. Several times, I caught him glancing at his reflection as we passed a stall and artfully rearranging his tousled hair. This resulted in no difference that I could perceive, but nevertheless a girl carrying a basket of flowers blushed and smiled at him as he passed.

He led us onto a narrow, winding avenue where stalls crowded the cobblestone lane. Steam hissed from a nearby booth, followed by the rhythmic clanging of a hammer. Heat billowed across the street as a man drew a red-hot lump of metal from a forge.

"Consecrated steel amulets!" the vendor shouted. "Protect yourself from the unseen! Effective against wights and ghasts of every order!"

I frowned, giving his stall a closer look. Dozens of pendants hung glinting from the awning. Melted down from Clerisy horseshoes, I guessed, and almost wished the revenant were fit to comment, just so I could hear its scornful reaction. Pieces of consecrated steel that small would barely deter a shade.

Another vendor's voice drew my attention. "The crossbow bolt that struck Artemisia of Naimes, miraculously recovered from the battlefield! Just a single copper pawn to touch it and receive her blessing! Guaranteed to heal wounds, guard against blight, restore imbalanced humors!"

For a moment I barely believed what I had heard. But then a different voice declared, "Splinters of wood from the holy arrow, stained with Saint Artemisia's own blood! The genuine article! Buy a piece for only five pawns!" He glared across the street at his competitor.

I stared in disbelief at the long lines crowding each of these stalls. Then anger boiled up in my chest, stopping me dead in the middle of the street. Charles walked a few paces ahead before he noticed I had lagged behind, and hurried back.

"What's wrong?" He took in the direction of my gaze and scoffed. "Unbelievable, isn't it? I hear they're dipping so many splinters of wood in pigs' blood that the butchers are starting to run dry. That's just the way things are, I suppose. Do you know they're already calling it the Battle of Bonsaint? Like something from the War of Martyrs. Oh," he added suddenly, standing on his toes to see farther down the street. "Come on, we need to get out of the way."

There was some sort of procession coming down the narrow lane. That was all I managed to grasp before Charles drew me aside into an empty stone doorway. The rest of the foot traffic did the same, squeezing between stalls or into alleys. Charles briefly glanced upward as he shuffled to make room, and I nearly joined him before I caught myself. Shades clotted the top of the archway like old cobwebs, their grasping hands and contorted faces swirling in and out of view. Shades that Anne of Montprestre shouldn't be able to see.

"I saw it happen, you know," Charles said. I felt a jolt of alarm, but when I glanced at him sidelong, he wasn't looking at me. He was gazing in the direction of the stalls, his expression far away. "I was there on the battlefield, fighting. I saw her—Artemisia of Naimes. I even touched her horse."

"What did she look like?" I asked warily.

"Beautiful," he said, his eyes shining. "Like the Lady Herself, surrounded by silver fire. The fairest maiden I've ever seen."

He definitely hadn't seen me, then.

I was starting to wonder how long we were going to be stuck in this doorway together when I felt the revenant stir, feebly clawing at me for attention.

"Nun," it hissed. *"Watch out. Relics . . ."*

A hush had fallen over the street. In the newfound quiet came the chiming of bells and the haunting rise and fall of voices harmonizing in a sacred chant. Gooseflesh pricked my arms. I pressed my back against the stones as a slow-moving procession of white-robed priestesses came into view, their veiled faces downcast, gently swinging silver censers. Pearl rings gleamed on their fingers. As incense fogged the street behind them, the shades lurking in the shadows mingled with the smoke and dispersed.

They had to be orphreys, priestesses who devoted their lives to purification. Their undine relics allowed them to submerge themselves in sacred pools for hours on end to prepare for cleansing rituals like the one they were currently performing.

And they weren't alone. At the end of the procession, six knights carried a litter. The parted curtains showed glimpses of a woman within, resplendently robed in silk and brocade. A miter rested atop her head, heavily embroidered with gold. Onlookers touched their foreheads in reverence as she approached.

It was the Divine. To my eyes she appeared no older than she had in Naimes four years ago, though her age was difficult to tell for certain. With her hair pinned up beneath her miter and her delicate features caked with white maquillage, she looked more like a painted wooden doll than a person. Her many relics completed the effect—rings on every finger, an amber pendant at her breast, and a jeweled scepter across her lap, encrusted with diamonds.

My gut clenched as the litter drew level with the archway. The smoke that curled from the censers burned my throat and stung my eyes. If the Divine happened to be using any of her relics, I doubted that the revenant would be able to hide itself in its current condition. But as I waited, holding my breath, her white face didn't turn. She was speaking to someone on the other side of the litter, their identity concealed by its frame. Whoever it was, it was clearly someone she admired. Gone was the air of loneliness that had haunted her in Naimes. Her wide eyes looked eager, even devoted. Tension bled from my body as the litter moved past, until its changing angle revealed the figure walking alongside.

Leander.

His gaze was fixed on the Divine. If he moved his eyes even a fraction, he would see me standing in the doorway beside Charles. I knew I shouldn't stare, in case doing so alerted him to my presence, but I couldn't look away.

He looked unwell. One of his hands was resting on the side of the litter as though conscientiously helping guide it forward, but there was a subtle strain in his pale hand and rigid posture that suggested he was instead using it for support as he walked.

Now that he was no longer traveling, he wore his full confessor's vestments. I could see why he hadn't donned them on the road. The elaborate silver stole draped over his robes would have gotten dirty in the countryside, the matching cincture likewise. The robes themselves were identical save for a silver oculus embroidered at his throat just below his collar, bright against the black fabric, framed by the stole on either side—whose pattern, I realized, depicted interlocking chains.

I wondered how many people he had hurt yesterday to have strained himself so badly. How many more he would hurt pursuing me, if he found out I was still alive. Though he had to be in pain, his expression was as calm and remote as a carved saint gazing piously down from a vault, untouched by the suffering below. His holy-seeming composure made him appear more the Divine's equal than her subordinate.

The litter passed around a bend, vanishing out of sight behind a group of stalls. I loosed a breath as the eerie chanting faded, replaced by the voices of the vendors hawking their wares.

But I felt the revenant's attention following the procession long after the traffic resumed and Charles led me back out onto the street. It remained strangely alert as we wound through the noise and stink of the city beyond, my eyes fixed on the cobbles.

"I need to tell you something," it said finally, *"but you have to promise not to react."*

I glanced at Charles, then dipped my chin in a nod.

"I've figured out where the smell of Old Magic is coming from in this city. Nun, it's been right in front of us all along. It's coming from the priest."

ELEVEN

I haven't smelled Old Magic this powerful since the Sorrow," the revenant continued, sounding almost excited by the development. "He positively reeks of it. He must have resumed practicing it upon his return to the city. He didn't smell of it on the road."

So much for not reacting. I almost tripped over a cobblestone. I waited until a cart rattled past to speak, watching Charles out of the corner of my eye. "Why didn't you notice yesterday after the battle? I thought you said you were paying attention."

"Through your senses. I wasn't using my own. But I assume he smelled of it then, too. It's the same scent that I detected from beyond the walls, and on every spirit we've fought since Naimes."

I forced myself not to glance over my shoulder, a useless reaction; Leander had long ago passed from sight. "How is he doing it?" I managed. "Why?"

"Don't ask me. If I could read humans' minds, I wouldn't have *ended up trapped inside a little girl's finger bone. You're the one with the meat brain. Why don't you take a guess?"*

"But—"

"We'll have to speak later, nun. We've nearly reached the convent."

I opened my mouth to ask how it knew, but frustratingly, it had already gone. I looked up to discover that we had entered an older, quieter section of the city, the buildings constructed uniformly of the same plain gray stone and the cobblestones worn nearly smooth underfoot. The daylight hadn't dimmed, but I felt as though a shadow had fallen over the street. A chill hung in the air that hadn't been there before.

I wondered if this was how Loraille had felt before the Sorrow. There must have been rumors, whispers. A sourceless darkness. A nameless fear.

Charles led me around a corner, and the convent's moss-speckled walls came into view. They looked like they had once stood outside the city, only to be later absorbed by Bonsaint's sprawl. The lichgate stood open, its gateway wide enough for two corpse-wagons to pass abreast, and refugees were being helped inside: some walking unaided, others limping with an arm draped over a companion's shoulders. One lay swathed in blankets, carried on a makeshift litter—their single exposed arm appeared dead, purple from shoulder to fingertip with blight. Sobs and moans of pain filled the air.

As we approached the gate, a sound drew me from my thoughts. A hostile whispering was emanating from inside the convent, like a group of sisters feverishly reciting litanies under their breath. Though it grew louder and louder the nearer we drew, no one else seemed aware of it. I glanced at Charles, but he only gave me an encouraging smile, oblivious.

Beyond the entrance, I saw nothing out of the ordinary—

nothing that might explain the mysterious whispering. The hair stood up on my arms. I wondered if I was losing my mind.

The lichgate's tarnished iron throbbed strangely in my vision. The air thickened, growing difficult to breathe. As its shadow fell over me, individual voices resolved from the confusion of sound, some calm, others angry, leaping out as though hissed directly into my ears.

"Lady, we beg mercy for Your servants. . . ."

"Begone, foul spirit!"

"We ask protection for those within. . . ."

"We cast you out! We banish you into the dark!"

"May our prayers stand fast against evil. . . ."

"The Dead are not welcome here!"

"May our faith stand as iron though our bodies are dust. . . ."

A shudder tore through me. The whispering was coming from the lichgate. These were the voices of the long-dead sisters who had forged the gate, their prayers driven into the molten iron with every stroke of the hammer. The living couldn't hear them, but spirits could. This was what a lichgate felt like to the Dead.

Each voice stabbed at me like the beak of an attacking raven. I hunched inward to protect myself from their invisible assault, stubbornly pressing forward. An elderly woman being helped past gave me a worried look, but if she spoke, I didn't hear her.

I sagged with relief as we finished crossing the threshold. A few whispers followed me, their condemnations pelting my back like sleet, then fell away. We were inside the convent. I had an impression of somber stone buildings, their slate rooftops spattered white with raven droppings, and the chapel's bell tower rising above them in the distance.

It was only after Charles paused, taking me in, that I realized he had been talking to me as we passed through the gate. His eyes widened. "Are you all right? Your nose is bleeding."

Unsurprised, I pressed my cloak against my face to stanch the flow. "It happens sometimes," I said colorlessly. "I have a condition."

"Nice try, but I've been called worse," the revenant sniped, roused from its silent lurking.

Charles seemed unconvinced. "I think I'd better take you to one of the—"

A resounding bellow interrupted him. "I see you there! Out! OUT, if you know what's good for you!"

The voice belonged to a hugely stout nun who was charging toward us with alarming speed, her face purple with anger and her gray robes billowing behind her. My heart almost stopped. She had arms as big around as vinegar barrels, the fabric straining to contain their girth. Like Mother Katherine, she didn't wear any adornments of rank, but the numerous relics glinting on her fingers suggested she was the abbess.

I stood frozen as she approached, but it wasn't me she was after. She bustled past, stirring my cloak in the wind whipped up by her momentum. I had been so distracted by the lichgate, I hadn't noticed the pair of clerics lurking just within, wearing identical expressions of disapproval as they watched the refugees trickle inside. Their blue robes and moonstone relics identified them as low-ranking Clerisy officials called lectors, who were responsible for the somewhat frivolous task of reciting holy texts during ceremonies. They jumped as the abbess bore down upon them like a furious eagle descending on jays, already roaring at the top of her lungs.

"Look at the pair of you, standing idle while the sisters break their backs in the Lady's service. And you call yourselves clerics.

Useless!" Her voice boomed from the walls like thunder. "Do you have anything to say for yourselves? No? Not a word? Well, I know who sent you. If Her Holiness wishes to stick her prying nose into the care of the sick, the injured, the elderly in this convent, tell her she's welcome to come get an earful in person!"

She punctuated each sentence by stabbing her finger at their chests. With each jab, the lectors took a step backward, growing increasingly pale until they lifted their robes and fled. The abbess planted her large fists on her hips and watched them go. Then she grunted in curt dismissal and turned toward the nearest refugee.

"Infirmary," she declared, already bustling over to the next. This time I saw her brush her hand over one of her relics. "Guest dormitory, be quick about it—and get some pottage in her; she's about to drop."

Charles leaned toward me. "That's Mother Dolours. Do you see those rings she's wearing? They're healing relics. She's saved the lives of more soldiers in the guard than any of us can count."

"All of them?" I asked in surprise. I counted at least five rings, likely more.

He grinned. "Every last one."

I had never heard of someone wielding so many Third Order relics. Healing relics were difficult to master, and greatly sought after. Each conveyed a different healing power based on the type of spirit bound to it—a feverling to treat fevers, a witherkin to treat wasting illnesses, and so on. Our healers in Naimes hadn't used relics at all, treating us instead with herbs and tinctures.

A tremor ran through the revenant when the abbess's attention swung in our direction. Its presence shrank inward, but not before an icy prickle of fear escaped.

"We can't let the fat nun use her relics on you," it said, its voice

muffled. *"I won't be able to hide myself from her."*

I looked more closely at Mother Dolours. I couldn't tell whether it was my imagination, or whether I truly perceived a slight distortion in the air surrounding her, the holiness radiating from her body like consecrated steel. The revenant had felt fear in the presence of nuns before, but that was different—it had feared what they represented, imprisonment in its reliquary. This time it feared Mother Dolours herself.

"Where are you going?" Charles asked.

"The stable." My feet had begun to carry me there before I had consciously decided on a direction. This convent was laid out differently than mine, but the manure-coated wagon tracks and telltale odor of pigs were as good as any sign pointing the way.

"Wait! You haven't been assigned a place to sleep. I think they've started setting people up with pallets in the refectory. Anne, you really look like you should sit down."

Ignoring him, I glanced around. The more mobile refugees had been given small tasks helping the sicker ones—carrying blankets, distributing bowls of pottage. There were too many outsiders in the convent for the sisters to keep track of everyone. Their attention would be divided between accommodating the refugees and caring for the city's dead. If I looked like I knew what I was doing, which wouldn't be difficult to feign, the sisters would probably leave me alone.

Besides, I couldn't sleep in the refectory. I remembered how crowded it had been in Naimes when we'd hosted the novices for the evaluation. I wouldn't be able to speak to the revenant if I was surrounded by people, and someone would eventually notice that I never took off my gloves. Also, there was the part about being surrounded by people.

Charles trotted up beside me. "Anne—"

"How is Mother Dolours able to speak against the Divine like that?" I asked to distract him. An abbess ranked far above a pair of lectors, but challenging a Divine bordered on treason.

He gave me a speculative look. "I probably shouldn't tell you this, but everyone in the city knows by now, so it isn't much of a secret. Mother Dolours was almost elected Divine four years ago. Her Holiness only got the position because Mother Dolours turned it down."

I paused in surprise, considering what I knew about the Holy Assembly in Chantclere, who were responsible for electing new Divines when the old ones died. "Isn't the Assembly's vote binding?"

"It's supposed to be." He grinned. "The story's legendary. Mother Dolours got around it by handing in her curist's robes to join the Gray Sisters—that was the only way she could defy the vote and continue to practice healing. . . ."

Charles trailed off. He halted in the middle of the lane and began rapidly unbelting his sword. As I watched in bewilderment, he shoved the whole mess into my hands—belt, scabbard, and all. "Hide that," he instructed, and nodded in hasty approval as I dubiously placed the sword behind my back.

Ravens took off from a nearby roof, cawing harshly. They had been disturbed by an enormous shape rising from the building's shadows. Someone cried out in fear as the figure took a lumbering step into the light, revealing a huge, muscular frame swathed in bandages. He was the largest man I had ever seen, nearly the size of a rivener. His strangely blank eyes were trained unblinkingly on me and Charles.

"Don't worry, he won't hurt you," Charles assured me, and

then went to the huge man and put a steadying hand on his arm. "Jean, it's all right. The sword's gone now. Jean? It's me, Charles. Your friend."

His pleas seemed lost on the giant, who continued to lumber forward, dragging Charles with him. Swollen patches of blight, dark against his pale skin, distorted his already ugly features—small eyes, a heavy jaw, a nose flattened by a poorly healed break. He was so tall that as he approached, I had to lean my head back to keep looking at him.

"I promise, he won't hurt you." Charles sounded desperate now. He frantically cast around, and understanding dawned as his eyes alit on my face. "I think it's the blood. Jean? You can calm down. She isn't hurt."

The man—Jean—didn't give any sign of registering what Charles had said. His stark, wild eyes were still fixed on me unblinkingly. Seeing him up close, I realized he was near Charles and me in age; his imposing size only made him appear older. And it was also obvious, at least to me, that his gaze wasn't angry or threatening. It was haunted.

I wiped my nose on my sleeve. "Look," I told him. "It's just a nosebleed. It's already stopped. See?"

Jean's expression didn't change, but some of the tension left his broad shoulders. Judging by the gratitude in Charles's eyes, I guessed that this wasn't normally the way people reacted. Based on personal experience, the normal way probably involved screaming.

"He's a soldier?" I asked.

Charles hesitated, then said in an undertone, "He got possessed in the battle yesterday. He . . . he hurt a lot of people. Our friend Roland . . ." He didn't need to finish. One look at Jean's size and obvious strength made it clear Roland hadn't survived.

"*Fascinating,*" the revenant put in. I felt it inspecting Jean. "*He still smells faintly of Old Magic. That might prove useful to us later.*"

"He hasn't spoken since," Charles went on, thankfully unaware of the revenant's remarks. "Things keep setting him off. Mother Dolours thought it would be best to keep him here, since there are so many weapons in the garrison. Not that he'd use them to hurt anyone," he added quickly. "They just—"

"Upset him. I understand."

He let out a breath, relieved. "The way some people react to him, after hearing what happened—you'd think he was still possessed." He lowered his voice further, looking pained. "Whatever's wrong with him, Mother Dolours can't heal it. She says it's an injury of the mind."

"I used to know someone like him," I said. "He just needs time."

Charles's face brightened. "They got better?"

I remembered hiding under the bed from Marguerite. Jerking away whenever the sisters tried to touch me. Sitting alone in the refectory while the other novices whispered. "Mostly," I said at last.

"What did you mean when you said that Jean might prove useful?" I asked once I had shut the stable's door and found myself alone with the horses. Most were the large, well-muscled draft type bred to pull the convent's corpse-wagons. Their heads hung inquisitively from their stalls, greeting me with soft snorts and nickers.

"*Not now. The brute might overhear you. He's standing right outside.*"

"Don't call him that," I replied, but I moved deeper into the stable until I found the ladder leading up into the hayloft. The revenant winced as a rat fled squeaking across the rafters.

"You aren't planning to sleep in here, are you?" it asked in disgust.

I shrugged, peering into the loft's murky darkness, trying to make out whether I would bang my head against the slanted ceiling if I straightened to my full height.

"I suppose it is filthy and depressing, just the way you like it. Open that window," it demanded, a trace of urgency entering its tone. *"You might thrive in this vile miasma, but I don't have to suffocate to death while you're at it."*

I decided not to point out that the revenant was already dead. I went to the loft door and cracked it open. The revenant relaxed as clear sunlight and a flood of cold, fresh air swept inside. Looking out, I saw that Jean was still standing in the yard below. He had followed Charles and me all the way to the stable.

Charles was still there too, wandering aimlessly around the muddy yard, kicking bits of straw and pointlessly examining the chickens. Stalling for time.

"I'm leaving now, Jean," he said at last.

Jean didn't move. I could only see the top of his shorn, blight-mottled head, but it was enough to tell that he wasn't paying attention, staring instead into nothingness.

Charles looked down and took a deep, reinforcing breath. Then he squared his shoulders and raised his head. "That's all right, Jean. Maybe tomorrow." He came over to give Jean a pat on the arm before he went to retrieve his sword from where I had stowed it behind a water trough. I watched him walk away, defeated.

Jean might not have been possessed if I had woken earlier and reached Bonsaint sooner. Their friend Roland might not have died.

If I hadn't paused to eat those apples, if I hadn't sat gaping at the sight of the city on the horizon . . .

I could drive myself mad thinking that way. With the power I had now, I could measure every choice I made in human lives.

Exhaustion crashed over me. I slid down the wall, feeling splinters catch in my cloak, and thumped into the hay. My eyes felt gritty, as though they were full of sand. I squeezed them shut before I said, "We can talk now. Jean won't be able to hear anything from down there."

"What if I don't want to?"

"You always want to talk." I knew that much about the revenant by now.

"Perhaps I could use a little peace and quiet during the rare moments in which you aren't trying to get yourself killed."

Ignoring it, I said, "I don't think you're right about Leander being the one in control of the spirits. They attacked him when they ambushed the harrow. And back in Naimes, he was surprised to learn about the possessed soldiers."

"I didn't say he was controlling them," the revenant snapped. *"Not all the time, at least. I said he's been practicing Old Magic. Do you know the least thing about Old Magic? It's a notoriously fickle art. If it has one rule, it's that it always—"*

"Twists back on its users," I interrupted, surprised to find the answer on the tip of my tongue. "Like it did to the Raven King."

Now that I thought back to the memory—Leander standing opposite the page, holding the folded missive—surprised didn't seem like quite the right word. He hadn't been surprised. He'd been angry. As though . . .

"Just because he's been influencing them doesn't mean his command over them is complete. Suppose, for example, he orders a group

of spirits to destroy Saint Eugenia's relic. They fail in the attempt. Then he gains custody of the relic and no longer feels that it needs to be destroyed. But he hasn't commanded the remaining spirits to stop trying; he hasn't realized he needs to. And then he's in for a nasty surprise when they proceed to attack him, because he's the one bearing the relic. It doesn't matter that he's the ritual's practitioner—their orders are clear. Destroy the relic. They'll keep trying until they succeed, or until they're destroyed themselves."

"And the possessed soldiers . . . he might have ordered the spirits to do something, but he didn't order them to do it by possessing people. Except he didn't expressly forbid it, either."

"Yes, precisely. Rituals need to be highly specific about their boundaries to go according to plan. Even adepts make terrible mistakes from time to time, and no matter how clever he is, the priest is no adept. Anyone who tries practicing Old Magic now will be working with incomplete resources—scavenged pages, half-burned manuscripts."

I was still thinking about those first possessed soldiers. What if they had fallen victim to nothing more than an early test of Leander's command over Old Magic? I wondered how many people had died. If any of the soldiers had lived. "How do you know?"

"I was there," the revenant answered. *"I saw them burn."*

A shiver ran through me. But its answer shouldn't have come as a surprise. The revenant was ancient; no doubt its power had been used to battle Old Magic before.

"That still doesn't explain what he wants."

"What do you know about him? Think, nun."

I cast back through my memories. The first to leap out was the look of disgust on his face when I'd told him I wanted to be a nun. *Why would you ever want such a thing?* And then, in the harrow, when I had continued to defy him—*I think it's possible that you don't know what you want.*

"He wants power," I said slowly. "It's so important to him that he can't understand other people not wanting it."

"Go on."

I thought of the way the Divine had gazed at him. Fondly, adoringly. But he was still her inferior and always would be. Despite his young age, he had already risen as high as he could in the Clerisy's ranks. He had obtained the most powerful relic he could control.

"He can't get any more of it through the Clerisy," I finished. "If he wants more power, he has to find it elsewhere."

"I've seen a thousand humans like him. If it helps, they always end up dying in ghastly ways. I would happily volunteer, but unfortunately, we can't just kill him and be done with it. We need to find out more about the rituals he's been practicing first. Old Magic persists beyond its practitioner's death, and we need to know exactly what he's set in motion."

I glanced out the loft door. Jean had abandoned his vigil beside the stable to sit down on the ground among the chickens, looking huge and forlorn as they pecked the straw around him.

"Is that what you want to use Jean for?"

"Right now, if I tried extending my power far enough to locate the ritual site, any human using a relic inside Bonsaint would sense my presence immediately. We need a trace to follow more discreetly. He should do nicely as a starting point."

This was the second time I had detected a suspicious undertone of excitement in its voice while talking about Old Magic. It didn't just know a great deal about the subject; it was also interested. "Will that hurt him?" I asked, trying not to let my suspicion show.

"That's what you care about?" I felt a jab of annoyance. *"No, he shouldn't feel a thing. I'm not an amateur."*

"Then let's do it now," I decided.

"What? Absolutely not."

"Why?"

"You're too weak. You need to rest first. No, listen to me. You've barely eaten since you became my vessel. You've barely slept—don't argue!" it hissed, when I opened my mouth to object. *"Passing out from exhaustion doesn't count. You need to recover your strength before you tax yourself again."*

"We don't have time. Now that we're in the city, we've left everyone outside Bonsaint defenseless. The spirits could attack other provinces next. We have no idea what Leander is planning."

"It will take time for the spirits to rebuild their numbers after yesterday. Old Magic can't call forth an army that no longer exists."

"Hundreds of spirits got away."

"And thousands didn't. The rest will be in hiding now, too afraid of my power to emerge until they're compelled again."

"But more will rise," I argued. "Even if most of Roischal's dead become shades—"

"I know what I'm talking about," it interrupted. It sounded angry now. *"I've devoured more souls, living and dead, than your pitiful mind can even begin to fathom. Most spirits would rather leap into the Sevre than cross me. Don't ever forget what I am, nun."* It gripped me and gave me a fierce internal shake, hard enough to rattle my teeth.

It had been a while since the revenant had done something like that. I wished I had my dagger on hand. Then again, even if I did, I wasn't certain I had the energy to use it.

"I won't," I said simply. I was surprised by how tired I sounded, my tongue thick in my mouth. My head felt heavy against the stable's wall.

The revenant was silent a moment. Then it said, *"The Old Magic will take time to fade. Meanwhile, in your current condition—if I attempted to trace it, you might not survive. And I assure you, you won't be able to help anyone if you're dead."* Its voice seemed to be getting quieter, farther away. *"Sometimes, if you want to save other people, you need to remember to save yourself first."*

I slept. And slept. Once, I partially awoke to hear the tolling of the fifth bell. The late light slanting through the loft door was the color of melted butter, motes of dusting swirling lazily in its beams.

The next time I awoke it was to the revenant shaking me again, urging sharply, *"Nun, you need to wake up. You aren't well."*

I groaned. My body sweltered in the sun's merciless heat, but that couldn't be right, because when I cracked open my eyes, the sunlight had gone. A square of night sky hung beyond the loft door. My chemise clung to my body with sweat.

"You're feverish. You need to drink water."

I pushed myself upright, then sagged back down to my side. My eyelids felt heavy, drooping shut of their own volition.

The revenant paused. Then its voice came rushing back, vicious with malice. *"It would be child's play to possess you in this state. I could claim every soul in this convent. Every loathsome nun, every stinking peasant, and you would have to watch."*

The loft wobbled around me. I had bolted upright, standing knee-deep in the hay, my legs trembling like a newborn foal's.

"Now go down the ladder," the revenant instructed, still using

the same cruel tone. Muddle-headed, I hastened to obey. I felt it steadying my shaking hands on the rungs. I blundered through the door, stumbled out into the darkened yard, fell to my knees in the mud beside the well and drank thirstily from the bucket's ladle.

"You're in worse shape than I thought, nun," the revenant mused to itself. It sounded angry, but not at me; I was barely conscious, an afterthought. It paced back and forth in my head as I leaned against the well's cool stones, soothed by their chill against my brow. *"Of all the problems I expected to have managing an untrained human, this wasn't one of them. My previous vessels at least understood how to take care of their bodies. Here's what we'll do,"* it said to me, but I was already fading away. The last thing I heard was *"Nun? Are you listening to me? Nun!"*

TWELVE

Consciousness returned in a flood of white. This alone assured me that I was still alive. Holy texts described the Lady's afterlife as a place of restful dusk, lit eternally by stars. Here, wherever I was, the air smelled astringently of healing herbs. Murmuring voices surrounded me, echoing faintly as though carried down a corridor; distant footsteps rapped briskly to and fro. Shifting experimentally, I discovered that I was surrounded by linens. I felt weak and oddly light, like the dried-up husk of an insect.

"Are you awake this time, nun? Ah, you are."

I dragged in a breath, my heartbeat quickening.

"No, don't try to get up again—you've done that before. They might resort to restraining you instead of merely drugging you. As it turns out, you're a nightmare to deal with even when you're half-conscious and insensible with fever."

I recognized the taste of the syrup that coated my mouth; it was the same kind I had been given in Naimes. I cracked open my eyes, only to squeeze them shut again, finding my surroundings painfully bright. I parted my dry, cracked lips.

"Don't bother trying to speak. I'm sure I can guess what your questions are. Let's see. No, they haven't figured out who you are. No, I haven't been trying to possess you. Tempting though the prospect was, I wouldn't have been able to do anything with your useless body aside from stumbling it around and smacking it deliriously into walls. Anything else?"

A scratchy, questioning sound escaped my throat.

"Yes, you were very ill. You still are, but you're through the worst of it now. There's another human helping you," it added, an inexplicable darkness creeping into its tone. *"She seems to know you. She's claiming to be your friend."*

That was unsettling. My lack of contacts in Bonsaint aside, I couldn't think of anyone who would claim me as a friend even under threat of torture. Straining to listen, I made out that two people were conversing in soft voices nearby. They didn't seem to have noticed that I had awoken.

One of the voices was too quiet for me to hear. The other replied, "Thank you for watching over her so closely. You've been such a help to us these past days."

"That one's the healer who's been using a feverling relic on you," the revenant explained.

No wonder it seemed tense. All this time it had been trapped helplessly in my weakened body, waiting to see if a healer would sense it and alert Mother Dolours.

"Let us know if anything changes," the healer went on. "Otherwise a few days of strict bed rest should put your friend to rights."

Strict bed rest. A few days. I didn't have the time. I waited for the rustle of fabric as the healer moved away, then tried opening my eyes again.

A whitewashed ceiling swam into view. I lay on a pallet with the linens drawn up to my chin. The pallet was on the floor at the end of a hall, below a small window with the shutters cracked open for fresh air. Other patients rested on pallets nearby, the closest appearing deeply asleep. The only other person in the room was a girl standing at the foot of my pallet. She was facing away from me, but her plump figure and chestnut hair were unmistakable. I had slept in a bed opposite them for seven years.

"Marguerite?" I asked in disbelief, my voice a terrible rasp.

She started and whirled around, her blue eyes bright above her flushed cheeks. Frantically, she scrabbled for something beneath the neck of her tunic and thrust it between us. A protective amulet, like the ones the vendors had been selling on the street.

We stared at each other. The last time I had seen Marguerite, she had been collapsed in the chapel, half-dead from blight. Now she wasn't wearing her novice's robes; she was dressed like a refugee in a drab, patched tunic. The blight on her hands and face had faded to dull splotches of green and yellow, like week-old bruises.

"What are you doing here?" I asked hollowly.

"What are *you* doing here?" she whispered back fiercely. Her hand was shaking. "A soldier found you collapsed in the barnyard this morning. He said your name is Anne of Montprestre. Now I've had to pretend I'm from Montprestre, too. Do you have any idea how many stories I've had to make up about goats?" Her voice trembled. "I don't even know anything about goats!"

"So you do know this human?" the revenant asked in distaste.

My thoughts moved slowly, thickened by the syrup's lingering fog. "Why?"

She glanced down the corridor, checking the sleeping patients and the sisters walking back and forth through the intersecting hall farther down. "I had to," she whispered, "to keep the sisters from seeing your hands."

An ugly jolt of terror shot straight down my guts into my bowels. I pulled my hands from beneath the covers. My gloves were gone, replaced with ridiculous-looking bandages that encased my hands like mittens.

"I told them I knew you. They still think you're some Unsighted girl from Montprestre. I said your hands were blighted and wrapped them up before anyone could see them. If you hadn't tied those gloves on, the sisters would have gotten them off before I could say anything. . . ."

My heart was hammering. Gradually, it occurred to me that my uncharacteristic panic didn't belong to me alone. It was coming from the revenant.

"She took my reliquary," it said, while Marguerite kept on babbling.

I shoved back the covers and fumbled with my clothes, clumsily lifting the neck of my chemise, which was all I was wearing; my tunic and cloak had been taken away. And so had the reliquary. I gazed at the naked patch on my chest and then raised my eyes back to Marguerite.

She had fallen silent, watching me. She must have seen something in my eyes, because she said quickly, in a low voice taut with fear, "If you attack me, I'll scream."

I wasn't sure what was worse—losing Saint Eugenia's relic or having to reason with Marguerite. "You can put down the amulet," I said in resignation. "I'm not possessed."

She slowly shook her head. "Everyone saw you after the battle in the chapel. The sisters dragged you away screaming. You bit Sister Lucinde."

"Ah, sweet memories," the revenant hissed.

I didn't remember that at all. "Then why haven't you reported me to Mother Dolours?"

She bit her lip. She glanced down the corridor again, but not before I saw a flash of uncertainty cross her face. "I—everyone's talking about you. About the battle. All the people you saved . . . and you saved me, too, in the chapel. But I haven't made up my mind yet," she added in a rush. "Even if you aren't possessed, you're still dangerous."

She was right about that, at least. "Give the reliquary back."

"No."

Taking her eyes off me had been a mistake. I lunged from the pallet and clapped a bandaged hand over her mouth before she could scream. I hooked the other beneath the leather thong that hung around her neck and yanked it until it snapped—*"Be careful,"* the revenant said, alarmed—but nothing else came free with the amulet, which chimed delicately as it bounced away across the flagstones. Marguerite wasn't wearing the reliquary.

She trembled in my grip, taking short, rapid breaths like a frightened rabbit. I waited until she made eye contact, then moved my hand away enough for her to speak.

"I don't have it with me." Defiance shone through her fear. "I hid it. Somewhere no one will find it."

I shouldn't have gotten up. The infirmary tilted sickeningly around me. I backed away, reaching the pallet just as my legs gave out and deposited me in a pathetic heap. I had the humbling realization that even if I'd found the reliquary concealed somewhere else on Marguerite, I wouldn't have had the strength to take it from her.

She was looking at me strangely. After a moment I realized she had never seen me in a state like this before. Whenever I hadn't felt well in the convent, I had always crept off and hidden in the stable until the malady passed. Probably, from her perspective, that had made it seem as though I never fell ill. Perhaps she hadn't even imagined it was possible.

She hesitated and then said, "You were really sick, you know. If that soldier hadn't found you, you could have died."

I didn't want to talk about it. "What are you doing in Bonsaint?" Terrible possibilities filled my mind: more thralls attacking Naimes, the chapel burning, the sisters fleeing.

She frowned. "I ran away, obviously."

I stared at her, speechless.

She turned slightly red. "I told you I would rather die than stay in Naimes!"

"I didn't think you were serious."

Her face hardened. "That's right. No one ever thinks I'm serious. Everyone thinks I'm just a stupid, silly little girl without a single useful thought in her head. Well, I've been planning it for weeks. None of the nuns noticed. *You* didn't notice, and you lived with me. They probably haven't even noticed I'm gone."

"Of course they've noticed. You can't believe that." But seeing her expression, I wasn't so sure. I wondered if she had even told Francine. I'd thought she told Francine everything; I never imagined she was capable of keeping secrets. "You could have gotten possessed."

"As if you're one to talk. Anyway, I thought of that. Obviously." She hugged herself and evasively glanced away, rubbing her arms as though to scrub away my touch. She was still keeping an eye on the corridor.

Of course. The sisters here didn't know she was a novice. "You're afraid I might tell someone you're a runaway," I realized.

She rounded on me. Her furious blue gaze reminded me of the day I had returned to our room to find her aunt's letters strewn across the floor. "They can't send me back to Naimes," she declared, angry tears welling in her eyes. "They *can't*."

I wasn't certain I could handle watching Marguerite cry. "I'm not going to tell on you." She didn't look reassured, so I added, hopefully more convincingly, "I couldn't do that without explaining how I know you, and then I would get caught, too."

That seemed to get through to her. I watched her scowl and wipe her eyes on her sleeve. If she was so afraid of being sent home, why had she risked her own cover to help me when she could have simply faded into the background and watched me get taken away by the Clerisy? I didn't understand.

She's claiming to be your friend.

Something twisted in my chest. I wondered if the fever had caused organ damage. "The same is true of you," I went on. "All we need to do is keep each other's secrets."

The revenant had been listening to our exchange with something approaching horror. *"Oh, I don't see how this could possibly go wrong."*

"But I can't stay in the infirmary," I finished, ignoring it.

Marguerite rocked back. "You have to. Didn't you hear what I said? You almost died." She was giving me that look again.

"I'm better now."

"No, you aren't," Marguerite and the revenant said in unison. The revenant cringed. "You can't even stand up," she continued. "Anyway, healers take an oath not to talk about their patients. If one of them sees your hands, they won't let word of it spread outside the infirmary."

That was what I should have been worried about. In actuality, I had merely been thinking I might go mad surrounded by this many people, especially if any of them tried to talk to me. Pretending otherwise, I asked, "How do you know that?"

She stiffened as though I'd reached up and slapped her. "You never noticed where I spent all my free time in the convent, did you? Ever since Mathilde had the sweating sickness." Her expression turned bitter when I didn't answer. "I need to go now. You aren't the most important person in the entire world. I have other patients I need to look after." She returned a moment later, her cheeks pink, snatched up the fallen amulet, and hurried away again.

The revenant thoughtfully watched her go. *"Well, it appears we have no choice. We're going to have to torture the location of my reliquary out of her, and then kill her."*

I slumped back, exhausted. "We aren't killing Marguerite."

"Just think how satisfying it would be to dispose of the body."

"Revenant."

"I know a great deal about thumbscrews," it said. *"One of my previous vessels—not my favorite one, mind you—liked to use them as a self-mortification technique."*

I pulled the covers over my head, as if in doing so I could block out the revenant's voice. At the very least, it would prevent anyone from noticing that I was talking to myself.

"We need to get my reliquary back," it hissed angrily. *"She could hand it over to the nuns at any moment."*

"I doubt she will," I answered, imagining how that conversation would go. "She could have died trying to come here. She wouldn't throw all that away unless she felt she had no other choice."

"Providing prior examples of her poor life choices fails to reassure me, nun."

I wasn't so sure. Marguerite had hatched a plan to run away—a successful one—and I hadn't had the slightest inkling of it. She had survived the journey, then managed to conceal her identity in Bonsaint for days. If she'd been helping out in the infirmary for a while now, as the sister had suggested, she might have managed to sneak inside the city with one of the supply caravans. All that took planning.

Disturbed, I wondered if I even knew her at all.

"I think it's better to let her keep your reliquary for now. We would draw too much attention by fighting with her." Not least of all because, in my current condition, she might win. "And if the Clerisy discovers that I'm still alive, the absolute last place they'll expect to find Saint Eugenia's relic is with Marguerite."

The revenant didn't agree. We argued until our heated back-and-forth made me dizzy, and I had to curl up and close my eyes as the world tipped around me. It fell silent then. I would have thought it was sulking if not for its cold, careful touches glancing around my body, as though it was examining me for injuries. My last thought before I drifted away was that I must have been worse off than I had realized for it to be so concerned.

I dozed on and off for the rest of the afternoon. Eventually, the revenant alerted me to someone approaching.

"Whoever it is, they smell like incense, porridge, soul-numbing misery . . . Ah, yes. A nun."

I poked my head out to discover that it was a sister carrying a tray, which she carefully set down at my bedside, revealing a hunk of dark-brown barley bread and a steaming bowl of pottage. Then she looked up and exclaimed, "Shoo!"

A raven's indignant muttering answered. I followed the nun's gaze, already knowing what I would see. Trouble had landed on the window's ledge, his eye fixed greedily on the tray. The sister flapped her hand at him until he squawked and flew away.

"That bird—Lady, have mercy," she said as she helped me sit up. "Someone's even taught him to speak—a naughty little girl, by the sound of it. Don't let him steal your food, now, dear. The healers say you need to eat. I expect to find this bowl as clean as a confessor's kerchief when I come back. I don't need to watch you, do I?"

She looked at me sternly until I awkwardly maneuvered the wooden spoon into my bandaged hands. She had barely nodded in approval and set off when I heard a flutter of wings. Trouble had reappeared, tilting his beak inquisitively at my bread. I bit off a piece and spat it onto my hand.

"Don't," the revenant warned. *"You heard the nun."*

"It's just a crumb."

"Crumbs!" Trouble agreed, hopefully fluffing up his feathers. "Good bird!"

"It's more than you've eaten since the day of the battle. That raven can take care of itself, unlike you." Its vehemence startled me. I paused, looking Trouble over. His bright eyes and glossy feathers suggested that he had been eating well despite his outcast status among the other ravens. I reluctantly returned the bread to my mouth and considered the pottage, letting the revenant examine the lumpy green mash that filled the bowl.

At last it said, *"I might have argued differently if I'd known you would be fed this appalling gruel."*

"It's peas pottage."

"You say that like it's an improvement. Well, go on. Eat it while I suffer."

Fortunately, that seemed to be the end of its complaints. It spent the rest of the meal in uncharacteristic silence, until it said,

"Nun, I need to ask you something," and the food instantly turned to lead in my stomach. Something about its tone suggested that I wasn't going to enjoy this conversation.

"What?" I asked.

"Can you not tell when you're hungry?"

I sat back without speaking. I didn't know what to say.

"Or tired," it added, *"or in pain, for that matter."*

"I don't know."

"How can you not know?"

I pushed aside the empty bowl. Somehow, "I don't know how I don't know" didn't seem like an answer that would satisfy the revenant.

"It isn't just that you're sick. Every time you move, it hurts. You have a cracked rib; you almost broke it yesterday when you fell from the horse. And I wrenched your shoulder, catching that thing the thrall shot at you—"

"It was a crossbow bolt."

"Never mind what it was. You feel wretched. You're in nearly the worst physical condition of any vessel I've ever inhabited, but it's as though you haven't even noticed."

"It's better to not think about it. I've gotten used to ignoring things. I had to, in the shed."

"In the what?"

"It's a—"

"I know what a shed is," it snapped. *"Why were you in a shed?"*

I had forgotten that the revenant didn't know. "When I was possessed by the ashgrim—" I couldn't decide how to finish that sentence. A flash of memory lit the inside of my head like lightning, an oddly still image of me suddenly lunging for my little brother. I saw myself from the perspective of an observer standing outside my body, a hollow-eyed, snarling child, fingers bloody, nails torn: I had clawed through the rope. That time, I had managed to yank out some of my brother's hair before my father had wrestled me to the ground.

I felt a stir of impatience from the revenant and realized that I still hadn't answered its question. "My parents kept me tied up at first. Then, when that stopped working, they locked me in the shed behind our house."

Silence. Then, *"They didn't try giving you to the nuns?"*

"They didn't know I was possessed. They thought I was mad. Mother Katherine believes the ashgrim found me when I was a baby, so to them, it seemed as though there had always been something wrong with me."

I hoped I didn't need to explain further. Most people manifested the Sight later in childhood, when they were old enough to tell someone. Developing it in infancy wasn't unheard of, but on the rare occasion it happened, the babies seldom survived. Few were aware that it was possible to be possessed so young—my family certainly hadn't been. All they had known was that I'd gone from a screaming, difficult infant to a toddler who bit and scratched like an animal, driven by strange and violent whims they didn't understand. No one in my village had had the Sight, so if my eyes had ever glowed silver, they wouldn't have been able to see it.

"I didn't know that I was possessed, either," I added, before the revenant could ask the obvious question—why didn't you ask for help? "No one told me about spirits. People don't talk about them in villages like the one I came from. It's considered bad luck."

Not that anyone had ever tried speaking to me, anyway. They had only come by to stare. Often I had woken up to eyes pressed to the shed's knotholes, the village children peering in at me, whispering. There hadn't been anywhere I could go to hide.

"*Idiots. Humans simply love inventing superstitions and then get-*
ting killed because of them. Or better yet, using them as an excuse to
kill other humans." It paused. "*What did you think was happening*
to you?"

I almost answered that I didn't want to talk about it. Then it
occurred to me that perhaps for once, I did. The revenant wasn't
human; I doubted there was anything I could say to it that it would
find truly shocking. Whatever had happened to me, it had seen and
done worse. I didn't want to find that idea reassuring, but somehow it helped.

"That the ashgrim was a part of me. An evil part that wanted
to do bad things. Hurt people. Or, if there weren't any people
around . . ." I stared at a crack in the ceiling, remembering.

"*It would make you hurt yourself.*"

"I'm not sure. It might have been the ashgrim. It might have
been me doing it to stop the ashgrim. I couldn't tell the difference."

"*And the humans left you there to your own devices.*"

I felt the revenant drawing conclusions as I did myself. Surprisingly, sharing those memories aloud for the first time allowed me
to see them in a new light. How I had learned, in the shed, that
no one would come if I needed help. There would be no comfort
when I was in pain. No guarantee of food when I was hungry. That
there was nothing I could do to change that; I could only endure
it. Now, deprived of my routine in Naimes, I had fallen back into
old habits.

I found the revenant almost comforting in its lack of judgment. To it, a creature that had had to learn how human bodies
worked through trial and error, my problems weren't even out of
the ordinary.

"I'll remind you," it said finally. *"Rather than expecting you to remember on your own. When you need to eat, when you're sick or hurt, and whether it's serious enough to seek help. But you have to promise that you'll listen to me. Nun?"*

I had been quiet, wondering whether having an evil spirit inhabiting my body might turn me into a halfway normal person. I turned my face toward the window, letting the sunlight sting my eyes. "Yes," I answered. "I promise."

I slept deeply again. Sometime after dark, I awoke to hear the sisters singing evening prayers. Their voices floated across the grounds from the chapel and into the infirmary as though carried by the moonlight spilling through the shutters. As I listened to them, an ache of homesickness swelled inside my chest.

I remembered hearing the choir in Naimes for the first time. In my village, I had sometimes listened to my neighbor humming out of tune while she did her washing near my shed—that was the only music I had known before I heard the sisters raise their voices in song.

It was difficult to describe what I had felt then. I had spent my life believing that everything about me was as small and dim and dirty as the inside of that shed. But the high, clear notes had seemed to echo in the unlit chambers of my soul, revealing its shape, vaster than I had ever known. And the sound had filled me with longing for something I didn't understand—like a desperate thirst, except it wasn't for water, or anything else that existed in the life I had led before.

Mother Katherine had found me afterward, gripping the pew's back in front of me like I'd been swept out to sea. She had shown me how, across the chapel, the flames of the candles were standing still.

I understood now, away from my convent for the first time since I had arrived there, that the longing I had felt that day and many days since was homesickness. Homesickness for a place I had never been, for the answers to questions I carried in my heart but for which I had no words. I hadn't recognized it then, because I hadn't understood what it felt like to have a home.

I had nearly drifted back to sleep when voices carried softly through the wing, accompanied by the quiet scuff of footsteps. A pair of sisters patrolling the hall, making sure that nothing was amiss with the patients. They walked past the sleeping bodies, some of whom were snoring, others motionless in slumber. Though I was fully awake now, I lay still and pretended to be among them.

"Two days since the battle, and there hasn't been a sighting of a dangerous spirit anywhere in Roischal," one sister whispered. "Do you think it's possible? That Artemisia of Naimes is truly a saint?"

The other nun sighed. I felt the revenant tense and knew before she spoke that it was Mother Dolours. "I fear that an age of saints and miracles isn't something to celebrate, Sister Marie. The Lady sends us such gifts only in times of darkness. Do you recall the writings of Saint Liliane?"

The sister was silent a moment. Then she murmured, "And so the silent bell wakens to herald the Dead; and the last candle is lit against the coming night. . . ."

I strained to hear more, but their voices had dwindled as they passed outside the hall, leaving a cold lump in my stomach and the lingering image of a single, steady candle flame slowly burning itself down, the only remaining light to hold off the dark.

THIRTEEN

The next morning, I woke to a different world. Everywhere, people lay moaning on pallets, sisters hastening back and forth between them. Marguerite came by, her cheeks flushed with exertion, and explained that a sickness had reached the convent. So far it was only affecting the refugees who had slept in the camp, but there was fear that it would spread.

Soon, barely any room remained for the sisters to pick their way through the halls. Hastily assembled pallets encroached on mine until I could have stretched out an arm and touched three other patients, not that I tried. I braced myself against both the unwanted company and the rising stench. Going back to sleep wasn't an option. Sisters were constantly hurrying past to help ailing patients to the privy, sometimes failing to reach it in time, with explosive results.

The revenant watched the tableau unfold in such horror that I felt my hair trying to stand on end.

"Disgusting," it hissed, as one man bent retching against the wall. *"How many different fluids can they possibly have in their bodies? If there's one thing I haven't missed about having a vessel, it's being forced to endure the appalling quantities of effluence you humans spew out of every orifice at the slightest opportunity."*

"They aren't doing it on purpose," I said, not worried about being overheard. My neighbors were too preoccupied with their own misery to notice. "It's involuntary."

"And that's supposed to make me feel better?" it retorted shrilly.

The revenant had been carrying on like that all morning, which meant it was nervous. I had noticed by now that its talkativeness increased when it was working itself up into a panic. I decided that the best strategy was to ignore it. Instead, I focused on watching Marguerite.

To my surprise, she hadn't scurried off somewhere to hide. She was working alongside the healers, bundling away soiled linens and coaxing patients to take sips of broth. Some of it she did with her face screwed up in dismay, but she did it anyway, her shoulders squared in determination. Yesterday, I had found her claim that she'd helped in the infirmary in Naimes difficult to believe; I had envisioned her loitering in the hall, occasionally fetching unguents for the sisters, using the assignment as an excuse to avoid more unpleasant chores. Now I wasn't so certain.

The revenant had prodded me several times about its reliquary, but I couldn't begin to guess where she had hidden it. I was starting to realize that I knew much less about her than I had thought. Perhaps that shouldn't have come as a surprise. Over the past few years, I had made it my primary goal to avoid her as much as possible. In some ways I still thought of her as the little girl who had screamed at her first sight of me hiding beneath the bed.

Everywhere patients moaned, vomited, prayed to the Lady for mercy. And that turned out to be the relaxing part of the day. It wasn't long before the whispers of plague began.

I first grew aware of the change in the air when I noticed two lay sisters comforting a sobbing novice. I couldn't hear what they were saying, but the rumors quickly spread. Somewhere in the infirmary, a patient had died. The lay sisters delivering fresh linens and broth began to look tense, their grips tight on their trays. At the second death, panic struck. Someone screamed at the sight of the limp, shrouded figure being carried out the doors to the fumatorium.

With so many ill and injured patients being cared for in the infirmary, it was inevitable that some of them would die. But the threat of plague still haunted Loraille even a hundred years after its last appearance. Cities ravaged by pestilence gave birth to plague specters, Third Order spirits whose trailing miasma seeped beneath doors and through the cracks in windows, infecting anyone it touched. Only a single relic capable of curing plague existed, and it was located far away in Chantclere.

The scream shattered the hall's fragile calm. Some of the patients tried to bolt, while sisters rushed to restrain them. The healers shouted for order—in the mayhem, the patients who were unable to stand were at risk of being trampled. A lay sister dropped her tray with a crash of broken crockery, then sank to the floor in tears.

"What in the Lady's name is going on in here?" boomed Mother Dolours.

She swept into the room like an advancing storm, the skirts of her robes bunched in her hands to keep them off the floor. She paused to take in the scene, then looked directly at a patient lying on a pallet nearby. He paled, shrinking against the wall.

"Goddess grant me patience," she said. She waded toward him

through the sea of pallets, bent, and took his arm. "It isn't plague!" she roared.

The hall went still. As everyone stared in shocked silence, she slapped a hand to the man's chest. Color flooded back into his pallid face, and he shot up from his pallet, gasping. Mother Dolours roughly patted his cheek, much as one would pat an obedient horse, then grunted in satisfaction at whatever she saw and moved on to the next patient.

The revenant had gone quiet along with everyone else, huddling down to watch. I had never seen someone healed by a relic before. I had been taught that the process was slow and taxing; the bound spirit needed to be carefully controlled, or else it would worsen the illness instead of curing it. But Mother Dolours moved to another patient, and another, without so much as pausing for breath between them. Silence reigned as it became clear that she intended to heal the entire hall.

"The relic she's using binds a wretchling," the revenant said. *"That explains it—these humans must have been drawing their water downriver from the city, where it's tainted with refuse. I've seen it happen before, but naturally no one ever listens when I warn them about it."*

It fell silent again as Mother Dolours started down my side of the hall. I felt it squashing itself out of sight, an uncomfortable sensation, as though it were wedging itself beneath my rib cage to hide. I tensed with the certainty that Mother Dolours would be able to sense it anyway, but when she reached me, she merely gave my bandaged hands a perfunctory once-over. "You don't have it, child?"

I shook my head, resisting the instinct to flatten myself against the wall like the first man had. Dozens of people healed, and she wasn't even out of breath. "Blight," I lied. "I'm feeling better."

"Good girl." And she moved on to the patient beside me.

By the time Mother Dolours left, the wing was full of dazed-looking patients sitting up and wolfing down bowls of porridge. The first man she had healed fearfully signed himself every time her voice thundered in from an adjoining hall. All seemed to be well until a young novice skidded around the corner, panting.

"Curists are being sent from the cathedral," she announced. "Her Holiness is investigating the reports of plague!"

The sisters, who had all sat down in exhausted relief, leaped up and rapidly began tidying. Marguerite joined them in bundling away armfuls of linens. She kept giving me pointed looks that I eventually realized were intended to communicate something to me, but I had no idea what, and the stare I sent back attempting to convey this made her blanch and flee to the other end of the hall.

"Next time, you need to do that into a mirror so I can see what it looks like," the revenant remarked, sounding slightly impressed.

I wondered if she had been trying to warn me that the convent's sanctuary law might not hold up against the threat of plague. The Divine might be able to use the fear of an outbreak, even a rumored one, as an excuse to search the refugees. The remainder of the evening became a race for Mother Dolours to finish healing the other halls before the curists arrived.

"There are too many," one sister whispered. "She'll do it," another insisted. Even the revenant was invested. *"Once I saw a curist try to heal a third this many humans, only to get partway through and keel over dead into a chamber pot."*

The chapel's bells rang the fifth hour; lamps were lit to stave off the dark. Meanwhile the novice ran in and out, thrilled to be the bearer of important news. "She's in the north wing!" she reported. "The east wing! There's only half the wing left!"

Sighs of relief filled the hall.

Moments later, the curists arrived. I received my first glimpse of them when they paused in the adjoining corridor, resplendent in their cream-colored robes and half-capes trimmed in gold. I guessed which one was the head curist by the number of rings on her fingers: a diminutive woman with elegant Sarantian features, a hawklike nose, and black hair streaked dramatically with gray.

"Where is the abbess?" she asked, casting a keen glance around our hall.

"Dead, most likely. And good riddance—"

It choked on its words as Mother Dolours came striding into view. "As you can see, Curist Sibylle," she said in her resonating voice, "there is no sickness here."

"I do see that, Mother," the head curist said dryly, still surveying our hall. "How curious, that out of hundreds of patients, not one of them appears to be ill."

A lay sister squeezed out a shrill, nervous giggle before the others managed to hush her. The head curist raised her eyebrows but didn't comment. She turned back to Mother Dolours. In a softer voice, she said, "We will cause the least disruption that we can, Dolours, but Her Holiness demands a thorough report."

I didn't think I imagined the note of disapproval in her voice as she spoke of the Divine, and was certain of it when Mother Dolours laid a grateful hand on her arm.

Once she had gone, the sisters rushed over to guide Mother Dolours toward a stool, hastily shoving it beneath her when she tottered dangerously on her feet. She collapsed onto it with a great whoosh of air and over the next few minutes, to the awed astonishment of everyone in the hall, proceeded to drink her way through several mugs of ale, passed along to her by a chain of sisters with practiced efficiency. Then, ruddy-faced and restored to full vigor, she charged off to resume her duties. I felt the revenant wince as she went by.

"She could exorcise you, couldn't she?" I asked, and knew I was right when it sourly refused to answer.

Full dark had fallen by the time the curists left. They passed my pallet on their way to the door at the end of the hall, speaking to each other in low voices. I was doing my best not to look suspicious in any way—and failing miserably, according to the revenant—when amid their low-voiced conversation I caught a familiar name. *Leander.*

As soon as I lurched out of bed, Marguerite appeared as though my disobedience had summoned her. "What are you doing?" she demanded. "You need to get back in bed."

"I can't believe I agree with this human," the revenant said. *"Though I still think we should kill her. We could always stuff her body down a latrine."*

"I need to follow them," I said.

"Why?"

"I need to hear what they're saying about Confessor Leander."

Her mouth fell open. "That horrible priest who gave us our evaluations?"

I hesitated. My legs were already wobbling. I couldn't follow the curists without her help, and I doubted she would cooperate unless I gave her a good reason.

"He's involved in the spirit attacks." I hesitated again, then added, "I found out he's been practicing Old Magic."

Her eyes went round. As I had hoped, there was only one force stronger than Marguerite's terror of me: her insatiable hunger for gossip. "I knew it," she said with conviction. "I *knew* there was something evil about him. Come on."

Our differences momentarily forgotten, she shrugged out of her cloak and tossed it over my chemise. Then she glanced left and right and bundled me out the door.

"You're lucky she didn't ask how you knew about the Old Magic." The revenant clearly didn't approve. *"If you tell that to anyone with half a brain, it won't take them long to figure out we're working together."*

I already knew that; otherwise I would have gone to Mother Dolours for help. I wished I could. But I strongly doubted she would let me go free if she found out that I was conspiring with a revenant.

We followed the curists to a small courtyard behind the kitchens. Lay sisters were working strenuously inside, scraping loaves of bread out of the ovens on long-handled wooden peels, sweating in the heat. Billows of steam poured from the windows, rich with the smell of herbs. As the curists collected their suppers, Marguerite drew us into a shadowed entryway. Judging by the gritty kernels of grain on the cobbles beneath my feet, it led to the granary. A few shades swirled around the stone ceiling, goggling down at us as though we had barged into their house without knocking.

"Confessor Leander saw them," the youngest curist was insisting, anxiously twisting her stole in her hands. "He told me so last week. Dead rats, without any marks on their bodies, as though they simply dropped where they stood."

"It isn't plague, Camille," said the head curist, Sibylle. "There are no swellings, no rashes. It is merely a flux."

"Perhaps you shouldn't take Confessor Leander's claims as fact." This was the only man in the group, white-haired and stooped, with bushy eyebrows that gave him the look of a kindly sheepdog. "He's a favorite of the Divine, this is true, but he is far too young for the burden placed upon his shoulders. There are only two penitent relics in all of Loraille, and most clerics are near my age when they take up the mantle of confessor. He has the ability, yes . . . but the strain upon him is great. Have you not noticed how changed he has been since his return to Bonsaint? The death he has seen in the countryside these past weeks, the suffering—he has hardly been sleeping since. He has been spotted wandering at odd hours. I fear the ordeal was too much for him after the loss of his elder brother."

"Gabriel of Chantclere," murmured one of the other curists to her neighbor, who had looked up inquiringly.

Marguerite let out a tiny gasp. "I know that name," she whispered. "If it's the same Gabriel, Aunt Gisele mentioned him in some of her letters. He was expected to serve on the Assembly one day."

This surprised me. The gift of Sight was rare enough that it was unusual to hear of two Sighted people from the same family, let alone both achieving high ranks within the Clerisy.

"How did it happen, Curist Abelard?" asked the youngest, Camille. "How Gabriel died. No one will tell me."

"He drowned in the sea. It seems that he"—here the old curist, Abelard, hesitated minutely—"fell from the battlements of Chantclere."

"Or someone pushed him," the revenant remarked, but I only half heard it speak; I was remembering the look on Leander's face as he stared into the Sevre, believing I had drowned.

Curist Abelard went on, "Some might say it is necessary for a confessor to be submitted to adversity. To experience failure and pain. Only those who bear a great burden of guilt are able to control a penitent. But there is a reason why most confessors do not retain the post for long. The responsibility breaks them; it is not uncommon for them to lose their wits before they retire."

"Enough of this. We do not encourage idle talk among our ranks," said the head curist, to which Abelard raised his open palm in rueful agreement.

"But you see, Camille, why it may not be wise to listen to him about the rats," he finished gently.

She nodded, looking meekly at her lap. Their conversation turned to other topics, the winter's stores and how long they might last the city's increased population. A moment later they were drowned out by a noisy group of children who ran shouting into the courtyard, playing a game that seemed to involve one chasing the others around with a large stick.

The revenant mused, *"Not sleeping well, keeping odd hours . . . It sounds as though he's been sneaking out at night."*

I turned the old curist's words over in my head. *A great burden of guilt.* "Maybe he did murder his brother." A twisted thought occurred to me. "I wonder if he did it so he would be able to wield the penitent relic. He might not have shown an aptitude for any other kind. That could have been his only opportunity to advance within the Clerisy."

"Oh!" Marguerite gasped. I had been addressing the revenant, but she couldn't tell. "He must have been awfully jealous of Gabriel, don't you think? Aunt Gisele made it sound like everyone in Chantclere adored him. She never even mentioned that he had a younger brother. Living in someone else's shadow like that, never being noticed, always second best . . ." She trailed off, looking at me.

"Yes?" I ventured, hoping that was the right thing to say.

It wasn't. She pressed herself against the wall, as far away from me as she could get. "You weren't talking to me, were you?" she accused. Her frightened eyes glittered in the dark, reflecting the silver light of the shades.

An icy finger drew down my spine. The revenant had gone very quiet, and very tense. "What do you mean?"

"You keep pausing like you're listening to someone speak. In Naimes, in the chapel—you were arguing with it." Her voice thinned to a whisper. "With the revenant."

I thought back to the aftermath of the battle, when the revenant had been trying to possess me, and winced. I had been too distracted at the time to consider what that must have looked like to everyone watching. Marguerite, on the other hand . . . "You were unconscious."

In the same tiny whisper, she said, "I heard the sisters talking about it."

Of course they would have talked about it. Everyone had seen it, not just the sisters. Sophia had seen it—she'd seen me holding a dagger to my chest, threatening to plunge it between my ribs. The thought made me feel sick. I stared at Marguerite. I had no idea what to say.

"Fine. Don't answer me. You don't need to, anyway." She backed up a step toward the granary, then seemed to realize she couldn't escape in that direction. She flattened herself against the opposite wall and edged past me instead, which would have been comical if I weren't so tired of her being scared of me. I watched her start to leave, then waver, taking in the way I was slumped against the stone, remembering I couldn't get back to the infirmary on my own.

Her mouth twisted unhappily. She gripped the pocket tied to her belt as though for reassurance. I guessed that it had her amulet inside—it was too small to be the place she was hiding Saint Eugenia's reliquary.

I noticed in the shade-light that there were a few minor burns on her fingers. They looked new. Which was odd; I didn't think she had time to help in the kitchens.

She saw me looking. "I'll send a healer to come get you," she blurted out, and fled.

As soon as she left, the revenant roused itself. "We aren't killing Marguerite," I said. "She isn't going to tell anyone."

"Are you certain about that, nun?"

There was a silkiness to its tone that made the hair stand up on my arms. I realized I had no idea what it would do if it thought we were at imminent risk of being discovered. Anything, I suspected, to avoid going back to its reliquary, even if that meant breaking our agreement.

The group of children ran past, laughing and screaming. None of them noticed me lurking in the shadows. I remembered the way the revenant's ghost-fire had poured across the convent's grounds, eager to devour even the grass and the worms in the soil. If my control slipped, if it unleashed itself here, nothing would survive.

The tension strained to a breaking point, and then it eased. A sister had entered the courtyard, glancing around with a slight frown of impatience. By the looks of it, Marguerite had told her that I'd gotten lost on my way to the privy. Our secret was safe. I felt the revenant relax as it reached the same conclusion.

As I stepped into the light, using the wall for support, the stick the children were playing with went flying across the courtyard and clattered to the ground at my feet. Instantly I found myself enveloped in a waist-high squabble. "No, it's *my* turn!" they shouted. "It's mine!" Standing in the middle, I might as well have turned invisible.

Finally a girl snatched up the stick, brandishing it at her competitors. "Now *I* get to be Artemisia of Naimes!" she declared boldly, and ran.

I stared dumbfounded as the children raced away, fighting over their makeshift sword. Their running back and forth was a reenactment of the Battle of Bonsaint: one of them playing me, others the soldiers, the rest the army of the Dead.

The revenant was observing me, assessing my reaction. *"Is that so difficult for you to believe?"* it asked at last.

I didn't know how to answer as I watched the children go.

FOURTEEN

The next day, I felt well enough to make a trip to the privy on my own, though I ended up regretting it. The privy took the form of a small stone garderobe that jutted from the convent's exterior wall over the Sevre. Inside it smelled of damp and echoed with the river's muted roaring. A wooden bench with a hole in it emptied into the water below. The revenant's weakness overtook me the moment I entered, and by the time I staggered out, pale and sweating, everyone waiting in line for their turn looked like they were having second thoughts.

The revenant was in a foul mood, which turned fouler as we entered the infirmary. *"Oh, just what we need,"* it snapped.

Charles was standing over my pallet, glancing around. The healed flux patients had been discharged earlier that morning and their bedding removed, leaving my abandoned place on the floor one of only about a dozen left in the hall, and it seemed that his bafflement was starting to give way to alarm. I watched as he knelt and gingerly lifted one of my pallet's corners as though I might be hiding underneath it. When he saw me, he sprang upright, looking embarrassed.

"Anne!" he exclaimed, relieved.

"Charles." I wasn't used to people looking glad to see me, and I had no idea what to say. I settled on, "Thank you for bringing me to the sisters." I knew he had to be the soldier who'd found me in the barnyard; none of the others knew my name.

"I should have done it earlier. Your hands . . ." I felt an unpleasant squirm in my stomach before he went on, "Why didn't you tell me about the blight?"

"It wasn't important."

Apparently, that was the wrong thing to say. Looking concerned, Charles stepped toward me. Instinctively, I stepped back. I was grateful that the sisters had laundered my clothes and returned them to me, so I wasn't standing in front of him wearing only my chemise.

He opened his mouth, but he never got the chance to speak. Outside, someone screamed.

I recognized the scream. Not long ago, I had been the cause of it on a nearly daily basis. "Marguerite."

Charles gripped his sword's hilt and hurried outside at my heels. Marguerite had been avoiding me since yesterday; I hadn't seen her since we had eavesdropped on the curists last evening. We found her in the courtyard in front of the infirmary. A crate lay broken at her feet, its load of glass jars and the straw they had been packed in spilled across the cobbles. She was clutching one arm to her chest in pain. Jean's massive silhouette loomed over her, backlit by the low winter sun. A crowd had already gathered around them, muttering restlessly.

"He tried to hurt her!" someone called.

"No," she protested weakly. "He just surprised me, that's all—he was trying to help—"

Her objections were lost in the rising din of angry voices. "I saw it—he grabbed her! He nearly broke her arm!"

It wasn't difficult to piece together what had happened. Marguerite had been struggling to carry the heavy crate, and Jean, likely waiting outside for Charles, had noticed and tried to lift it from her arms. But that wasn't the picture everyone else saw. Ugly, swathed in bandages, a full head taller than a normal man, Jean looked like a monster threatening pretty, blue-eyed Marguerite. He didn't show any sign of being aware of what was going on, except for the way he had backed up, his huge fists balled and a muscle clenching rhythmically in his jaw.

"That strength of his, it isn't natural," the woman in front of me whispered. Another was saying, "Not right in the head, I heard . . . possessed . . ."

I didn't think the situation could get much worse. Then Charles shouldered his way forward, and Jean's eyes fell on the sword. He let out a bellow like a wounded animal and flung out an arm, knocking someone over. They went down with a cry of pain.

Charles swore and began unbelting his sword, but the damage had been done. "Calm down," he urged. "He isn't going to hurt you," but no one was listening. I could see that he was trying to help, but it was only making Jean more upset. At least one friend had already died because of him, and the agitated mob too closely resembled another battle.

"Stop," I grated out. No one heard me, either. I shoved my way through the crowd until I reached the space in the middle and planted myself in front of Jean. "Stop!"

I couldn't remember the last time I had shouted. It hurt, as though my voice had been torn raw from my chest. Everyone quieted and looked at me in confusion.

Thankfully, no one was staring at Jean any longer. Unfortunately, now they were all staring at me instead.

After what they had lived through, I couldn't blame them for being afraid. Some of them had seen groups of possessed soldiers ransacking their towns, killing people they loved. I knew what it felt like when something reminded you of terrible things that had happened to you. But more than that, I knew what it felt like to be Jean.

The mutterings were starting up again. My harsh question cut through them like a knife. "Do you know how he got like this?"

No one answered, but at least they went quiet again.

"He was a soldier," I said. "He was fighting to save your lives."

That seemed to penetrate. Shame colored many of their faces; a few people looked away. Then a defiant voice piped up, "Artemisia of Naimes saved us."

I searched the crowd until I found the man who had spoken. "Maybe. But if he hadn't fought for you first, you would have been dead by the time she got there."

I hadn't meant for that to sound like a threat, but apparently it did. He took a step back, bumping into the person behind him. Then he muttered something that sounded like an apology and slunk off with his head down.

"Oh, I really need to see what you look like when you do that," the revenant said.

As quickly as it had formed, the crowd's remaining energy evaporated. They weren't bad people, just people who had been through too much. They left quietly, helping up the bystander who had been knocked to the ground, some shooting guilty looks at Jean, who was hunched over with his arms in front of his face as though to fend off a blow, unresponsive to Charles's careful efforts to lower them. I was watching everyone disperse when my back prickled—the telltale warning of a stare boring into me.

It was Marguerite. She was looking at me with wide eyes and a slightly parted mouth, as though she wanted to say something.

Whatever it was, I didn't want to hear it. I had the uncomfortable feeling that I wouldn't be able to bear it. I turned away and vanished with the crowd.

"Artemisia."

It was dark, and Marguerite had woken me by shaking me. At first I had the mortifying thought that she wanted to talk about what had happened with Jean. I considered pretending to still be asleep, but that wasn't possible because I had flinched violently when she'd touched me, and she definitely knew I was awake.

I felt her silent, hesitant presence hovering over me. I braced myself and rolled over. The lanterns burned low behind her, turning her hair into a frizzy glow around her darkened face. It was the dead of night, and everyone else was asleep.

"You need to hide," she whispered. "Leander is here. He's searching for something."

Searching for you, her expression said, though she wasn't meeting my eyes. She pushed a bundle into my bandaged hands and withdrew, waiting. Relief flooded me when I saw what it was: my gloves, the one item the sisters hadn't yet returned to me. I made short work of tearing off the bandages and tugging the gloves on in their place. But I shook my head when Marguerite glanced questioningly at my boots. It would take my scarred hands too long to lace them, and I didn't want her to watch.

"The graveyard," I said.

Marguerite had always hated going into the graveyard in Naimes. She shivered as she walked with me across the darkened grounds, even though I was the one walking barefoot, the pebbled earth icy beneath my feet. Once she almost shrieked when a windblown leaf skittered across her path, and I realized she'd thought it was a spider. Marguerite was terrified of spiders; this had proven one of our earliest points of contention, just days after we started sharing a room. I had only wanted to show her that they were harmless, but when I had tried to demonstrate that by picking one up and offering it to her, she hadn't spoken to me for a week.

She paled when I tugged her toward a mausoleum, a dark, ominous shape with its gate standing slightly ajar. Shade-light shone through the rusty bars, outlining the withered flowers that littered its steps in silver.

"I'm fine here by myself," I told her. "You can leave."

She shifted from foot to foot, her cloak drawn tightly around herself. She seemed like she wanted to argue. I hoped she wasn't going to offer to stay with me. As surprisingly generous as that would be coming from Marguerite, I imagined it would increase my chances of getting caught substantially.

I peered more closely at the mausoleum and said, trying to sound enthusiastic, "I bet it's full of spiders. I can't wait."

That was all it took to send her scurrying back across the grounds.

I slipped through the open gate into the mausoleum. The floor was damp and gritty, with slippery mats of decaying leaves piled in the corners. Small mortar-sealed drawers lined the walls to the ceiling, filled with cremated remains. The shades swirling around them reached for me, then shrank away, making horrified faces. I guessed that they had sensed the revenant. Despite myself, I felt bad for them. They had only wanted a little of my warmth.

"Merely out of curiosity, when choosing a hiding place, do you always select the most unpleasant option available to you?"

I took in our surroundings. "Revenant, you're dead."

"That doesn't mean I like being around other things that are dead," it snapped, which I supposed was fair enough; I usually didn't like being around other humans, either. We waited in uncomfortable silence for a time before it said without warning, *"I can sense the priest. He's walking in this direction, speaking to a nun."*

My breath stopped. I had expected Leander to check the dormitory, the refectory, the infirmary. Not to be here.

Voices carried faintly in the cold air. I climbed onto the molding and hoisted myself up, finding fingerholds in the crumbling mortar, to peer through the tiny barred window set into the mausoleum's wall. Darkness blanketed the graveyard, but I picked out the dim movement of two figures walking along a path. The sister's gray robes were easier to make out. If it weren't for Leander's pale skin and golden hair, he would have blended completely into the night. He seemed to be heading somewhere with purpose. I relaxed slightly as it became apparent that he wasn't searching for me; he was in the convent on some other business.

Hardly sleeping. Wandering at odd hours. If he wasn't here for me, his visit had to be related to the Old Magic.

"I can't hear what they're saying," I said in frustration.

"I can."

The revenant paused, and then the world around me changed. The walls of the mausoleum grew smoky and translucent, like stained glass. I no longer needed to peer out the tiny window;

I could see straight through the stone around me to the grave-yard and the tombstones beyond, their outlines shifting like vapor trapped in overturned jars. I could see the shades swirling inside the other mausoleums, unimpeded by stone, their forms a bright mercurial silver. And in the distant buildings of the convent—the dormitory, the infirmary—golden lights shone like candles, except they weren't candles; I watched one glide slowly past a neat row of other lights, and realized it was a person, a sister patrolling between the pallets of slumbering refugees. They were souls—living souls.

Warmth radiated from them even from a distance. I felt a shivering cramp in my stomach. A straining urge to get closer, as though I were lost in the cold on a winter's night, lured by the distant heat of a fire.

I gripped the bars, my hands no longer flesh, but shadows veined with gold. "What did you do to me?"

"This is how I perceive the world, at least partly. Oh, calm down, nun. If you were trained, you would have learned how to do this. It's a basic skill. Even clerics with shade relics can do it, though naturally a shade's senses pale in comparison to mine." I opened my mouth, and it chided, *"Be quiet and listen."*

I steeled myself, searching the phantasmal graveyard until I regained sight of Leander and the sister, now a pair of shadowy figures whose souls lit them from within like lanterns. A poisonous-looking red haze clung to the censers hanging from their belts—incense, I guessed. Their voices rang as though echoing down a long tunnel, slightly distorted but much louder than before.

"It must be tonight," Leander was saying, sounding annoyed.

"Can you not consult the cathedral's records?"

"I tried that first. The documents I seek are unavailable." Or, I inferred, someone had noticed he was poking his nose into subjects he shouldn't and had locked the texts away.

"Then go to the scriptorium, Your Grace. That is where we keep our writings." Though I couldn't see the sister's expression, her steady voice held an undercurrent of fear.

"Not all of them," he said.

"I'm not certain . . . This isn't allowed. Only sisters are permitted . . ."

Leander's figure stopped, and turned.

"Yes, Your Grace," she said in a cowed murmur. I couldn't tell what had transpired between them, but watched as she passed him something—possibly a key. Head bowed, she departed.

Now that Leander walked on alone, I noticed something different about his appearance. Darkness billowed around him like a cape fashioned from living smoke. As it moved, it left a smoldering trace on whatever it touched—the path behind him, the overhanging branches—as though they had been licked by flame. My skin crawled at its wrongness.

"Is that Old Magic?" I asked.

"Yes. A residue."

I watched Leander disappear behind a mausoleum, his soul's light obscured by a tangle of shades. "Wherever he's going, we need to follow him."

"The trail he's leaving will show you the way."

I had expected it to protest, but beneath its wariness I detected a shiver of interest, even excitement. It wanted to know what Leander was up to as badly as I did—but perhaps not for the same reasons. I'd had an inkling of its fascination with Old Magic before, but now I knew for certain. I would need to be careful of more than just Leander on this errand.

I stole out of the mausoleum, following the trail of shadow. To the revenant's senses, the graveyard lay colorless beneath a chalky moon. The living smells of damp earth and moss had bled away, replaced by a stale odor of nothingness. I was aware of the grass pricking my bare feet, but numbly, as though my feet were frozen almost past the point of sensation. The wavering outlines of the graves disoriented me; I had to focus to keep my steps from weaving. If this was how spirits experienced the world, I wasn't sure I could blame them for seeking human vessels.

A prickle traced my spine as I grew aware that I wasn't alone. Someone nearby was disjointedly mumbling a prayer in a frail and broken whisper—*"Lady . . . watch over . . . Have mercy . . ."*—and I cast around for the light of another person's soul until the revenant instead drew my attention to an amulet lying at the foot of a tombstone. I realized that the voice belonged to a long-ago nun, just like the lichgate, its prayer fractured upon the amulet's reforging.

Leander's trail ended at the high, overgrown wall that bordered the cemetery. The traces of Old Magic seemed to vanish straight into the ivy. That was all I could observe before a wave of dizziness left me sagging against the nearest gravestone. "Revenant," I managed.

Warmth returned; sound and sensation came rushing back. I pressed my forehead against the gravestone out of a sudden need to prove to myself that it was real. The lichen plastering it was wet and green-smelling, the rough stone reassuringly solid. I sucked in desperate gulps of air, disturbed by how badly the experience had affected me.

"Most humans aren't able to withstand a spirit's senses for more than a few seconds at a time. That wasn't bad for a first attempt. You'll get better at tolerating it if you practice."

"I'm not sure I want to," I answered honestly.

"Probably for the best. Some of my vessels wouldn't have noticed incoming danger if it had cartwheeled naked in front of their noses."

I could guess where this was going. "And they all ended up dying in gruesome ways?"

It didn't answer. A sarcastic remark didn't seem to be forthcoming. For some reason I remembered asking it, before Bonsaint, how many of its vessels had died. Finally it said, *"They were trained not to listen to me. They didn't hear."*

"You can't have let that stop you." Not the revenant. The idea was laughable.

"Oh, but I did." Its voice held a note I couldn't interpret, almost dangerous, like the silky way it had spoken last night outside the kitchens. *"There's a technique to block out a spirit's voice entirely. Would you like me to share that with you, too?"*

My skin crawled. I imagined it raging at its vessels. Then pleading. Shouting warnings that fell on indifferent ears. No wonder it had been surprised when I had answered it in the crypt. How long had it gone without speaking to someone before me?

"No," I said.

Silence. I couldn't guess what the revenant's purpose had been in asking that question. I only had a sense of danger narrowly averted and an inexplicable knot in my chest at the idea of its vessels treating it that way. Before I could pursue the feeling too closely, it offered in conciliation, *"Look over there. The priest went through a door."*

Approaching the wall, I saw that it was right. Stairs led down beneath an ivy-choked archway, with a door hidden at the bottom, swallowed up by leaves. What I could see of it was ancient and rust-clad, forged from consecrated metal. I knew, somehow, that it was an entrance to the convent's sacred chambers, even though I had never seen such a door in Naimes.

But then a memory surfaced—flashes of an unfamiliar passageway, of statues watching me with unseeing marble eyes as someone carried me past. Of a table covered in chains, the air hot and foul with incense and thickened by the coppery stink of drying blood.

I had been inside the sacred chambers before. Mother Katherine had taken me there on the night of my exorcism.

I stepped back from the wall, sickened.

A flutter of wings sounded nearby, accompanied by a flash of white in the darkness. Trouble circled once overhead and then landed in the ivy above the door. He regarded me in rare silence, his gaze expectant. The message was clear.

A surge of bitterness overcame me. If the Lady willed it, I would go. Moving quickly so I wouldn't lose my nerve, I descended the steps and reached for the door. Leander hadn't locked it behind himself. It swung open heavily, revealing a curved, poorly lit stair beyond.

"Be careful," the revenant warned as I stepped over the threshold. *"This place isn't welcoming toward the Dead."*

FIFTEEN

My senses aren't going to work well down here," the revenant went on. "Too much consecrated stone. Move slowly, and I'll warn you if I notice anything unusual."

The stair reminded me of the one that led down to the crypt in Naimes, winding deep beneath the earth in a tight spiral. Except this one was clearly even older, the stone pitted like an old bone where it wasn't worn smooth with the passage of feet. The cobwebby shades that haunted it were slow-moving and almost featureless, barely reacting as I ducked between them.

I descended carefully. A corridor awaited me at the bottom, the low ceiling ribbed in an unfamiliar style. Here and there a statue of a saint stood in a niche, hands clasped in prayer. Age hung in the air as thickly as dust. More shades floated overhead in misty, motionless tangles, as though time itself had congealed them.

"They're old," the revenant explained. "Shades have little in the *way of conscious minds to begin with, and even that fades in time without human company."*

The thought of the shades' minds slowly eroding chilled me in a way my surroundings hadn't. I wondered if it would be a mercy to destroy them. But I couldn't—I needed their light to see.

I pitched my voice low, gripped by the eerie feeling that speaking too loudly might wake something that was sleeping. "Which way did the priest go?" To my left, there was a shadowed archway; to my right, another stair.

"There." It drew my gaze to a spatter of fresh blood on the flagstones straight ahead.

It could only belong to one person. I paused to look more closely at our surroundings, but I didn't see anything that might have injured Leander. I felt the revenant doing the same. Its attention lingered on the statues.

"Take a look at the third statue on the left. Be careful."

I started forward, grateful I wasn't wearing boots. My bare feet made it easier to move without a sound. As I neared the statue, the marble saint's lips seemed to curve in a secretive smile. Its eyelids seemed to lower demurely. Only a trick of the light, I told myself, like Saint Eugenia's effigy in the crypt of Naimes.

"Stop!" the revenant hissed suddenly, sinking in its claws. *"Don't step on that flagstone."*

I pulled my foot back. It didn't take me long to work out what the revenant had seen. The center of the corridor had weathered centuries of traffic, but the flagstone I had nearly stepped on looked noticeably less worn than the others.

"A trap. There will be more. The Clerisy built a number of places like this during the War of Martyrs."

My mouth was dry. The statue continued to regard me with its subtle half smile, as though waiting patiently for me to take another step. "Why?"

"One of my vessels seemed to think they were designed to slow down invading thralls, but I suspect that the Clerisy was just going through an especially sadistic phase in the twelfth century. Keep going, nun. That statue is giving me hives."

We moved onward. Sometimes I caught glimpses of the hidden traps that the revenant was guiding me around—a gleam of metal tucked between a saint's clasped hands. The teeth of a spiked portcullis slotted into the ceiling, poised to fall. As we wound our way deeper, it made me pause more often, scrutinizing each crack and irregularity before allowing me forward.

The droplets of blood led us down another spiraling stair, at the foot of which I almost tripped over the body of a nun sprawled across the flagstones. Her eyes were open; her staring, upturned face was contorted into a tortured expression of guilt. Heart hammering, I knelt to check her pulse.

"Still alive, unfortunately. But the priest didn't hold back with his relic. She won't wake for another hour or two, at a guess." Casting its attention down the corridor, it suddenly went alert. *"Quickly— hide."*

I squeezed behind a statue the revenant identified as harmless, flattening myself into the shadows. A door stood nearby, huge and grimy with age, heavily banded in iron, with a pair of hooks bracketing it on either side. One held a lantern, and the other was bare. I watched as the door swung open, revealing Leander on the other side.

He paused for a long moment, listening. Then he stepped out, slipping a piece of parchment into his robes. In his other hand, he held the missing lantern. When he turned to hang it back on the hook, it nearly slipped from his grasp.

It took him three tries to hang it. Afterward he slumped against the wall, his face blank with pain. He pressed an unsteady hand to his side. When he drew it away, blood shone red on his fingers. His harsh breathing was the only sound in the corridor.

His hand tightened into a fist. Slowly, he straightened to his full height. He stood for a moment with his eyes closed, almost as though praying. Then he lifted the skirts of his robes and wiped the blood from his fingers. When he set off, only a slight limp betrayed his injury. He stepped over the unconscious sister without looking down.

It struck me as his footsteps receded up the stair that if I had only seen him then, I wouldn't have been able to guess that he was injured, such was the skill of his acting.

"He's growing reckless," the revenant observed.

Attacking a sister was a risky move. The curists had already noticed the change in his behavior. Either his actions were growing desperate, or he was so close to executing his plans that he cared less about discovery. Neither possibility boded well.

I waited a moment longer before I snuck out and took down the other lantern—the one Leander hadn't touched. Before I entered, I glanced over my shoulder. The corridor lay empty behind me, the half-smiling statues gazing silently into the dark.

All other thoughts fled after I closed the door and raised the lantern. Its light trickled over a dusty confusion of jewels, gold, carved chests, books bound in leather. Some were arranged on shelves, others piled unceremoniously in the corners. An iron chandelier the size of a cartwheel hung overhead, frozen waterfalls of wax cascading from its unlit candles.

"Stop gaping like a peasant," the revenant said. *"This is nothing. You should see the vault in Chantclere; you can get lost in it."*

I lifted the lantern higher. "There's an entire suit of armor down here."

"That isn't just armor. That's a dreadnought."

I picked my way over, interested. The armor had been fashioned for a true giant, a man Jean's size. Though crusted black with tarnish, the intricate engravings on the metal still showed through. The ball of a mace sat on the ground beside it, attached to the chain and hilt of a flail. The ball's spikes almost reached my knees. Even for someone of near-inhuman strength, I wasn't sure its weight would be possible to wield in battle. "Was that a type of knight?"

"No one wore it. It's a construct animated by Old Magic. It walked around on its own with no one inside. Don't worry, nun," it said at my reaction. I hadn't moved a muscle, but my heart had almost stopped. *"It's an antique. It's been inert for centuries. Do you see that small hole in the center of its breastplate? The key that belongs there is carried by the human who controls it. Doubtless it got lost hundreds of years ago."*

I swallowed, sweeping the lantern's light around, seeing the room's contents anew. The light fell on a silver reliquary shaped like a hand, the base decorated with seed pearls to resemble the edge of a lace sleeve. I had heard of a reliquary like that—the one containing the hand of Saint Victoria. Rarely for a saint, she had left a whole hand behind intact, its withered skin and fingernails still attached. According to legend, it bound a fury so violent and maddened that no one could control it after her death.

This wasn't a treasury. It was a room where dangerous things, forbidden things, were locked away.

I tore my gaze from the glittering objects before I could recognize anything else. Leander had left with a piece of parchment. I went over to inspect the books, setting my lantern down nearby.

They were piled together in a heap, a tangle of chains securing them to the shelves.

The wealth they represented was staggering. The scriptorium in Naimes had only a handful of books like these, with leather covers and gilt flashing on their spines. Most had been scrolls or sheafs of sewn-together parchment. I had learned my letters by copying them, stooped over a desk trying to force crabbed shapes from my scarred hands under Sister Lucinde's patient instruction. To have been exiled down here, left in a haphazard pile despite their worth, these books had to be brimming with heresy.

Shiny fingerprints marked the dust on the covers. It wasn't hard to identify the volume Leander had handled. When I lifted it, its chain rattled unexpectedly loudly in the silence, and I froze; but after a moment's waiting, I heard no answering sound from the corridor outside.

I could tell even in the dim light that the book was old. Its cracked, flaking cover showed patches of fabric beneath the leather, and when I opened it, it smelled as musty as the inside of Saint Eugenia's reliquary. But to my surprise, it wasn't filled with unsettling diagrams or dark incantations. It seemed to be a list of items.

Year of Our Lady 1154, I read. *A gold-plated candelabra, fashioned in the shape of lilies, set with three rubies and eight sapphires, gifted to the Cathedral of Bonsaint by the Archdivine.* I turned the pages, frowning. More descriptions of precious objects awaited me, relics and paintings and altar cloths embroidered with thread of gold.

"This is a record of treasures bequeathed to the cathedral." What was it doing down here? I flipped onward until I came to the empty space where the missing page had been, the vellum cut near the binding.

"Interesting," the revenant said. *"I think the priest might be*

looking for an artifact." It hesitated. *"Nun, do you remember what I told you about the shackles in the harrow?"*

"You said they were Old Magic," I said cautiously.

"I wasn't lying to you. Those were Old Magic runes. You know them as holy symbols, but there's a simple explanation."

My stomach dropped. Even though I had anticipated this, some small part of me had still hoped the revenant wouldn't try to mislead me. I kept my voice calm, betraying nothing. "Go on."

"In the immediate aftermath of the Sorrow, your Clerisy hadn't banned Old Magic yet." I felt it choosing its words with care, as though picking its way around unseen traps it might trigger if it wasn't careful. *"At that point, you understand, it wasn't officially ruling over Loraille. When the humans weren't busy dying, they were all arguing with each other about what should replace the monarchy. Then, of course, there were saints popping up everywhere, and the Clerisy was practically drooling over how quickly it was rising to power—"*

"Get to the point," I interrupted. "What does this have to do with Old Magic?"

"Fine, since you're asking so nicely. The truth is, a number of Old Magic artifacts were used in the war to battle spirits. I faced them from time to time."

I tried to envision that—Old Magic being unleashed side by side with the saints on battlefields. Instinctively, I shook my head in denial. Nothing I had read about the War of Martyrs mentioned anything like that. But people had been dying by the thousands to the swarms of newly risen spirits, facing impossible odds. If they had been sufficiently desperate . . .

When the possessed soldiers had attacked Naimes, if there had been an Old Magic artifact capable of holding them off—saving everyone . . .

"That's how I know about dreadnoughts," the revenant contin-ued. *"They couldn't do much against unbound revenants, granted, aside from tickle us a little—but I can't emphasize enough how dis-tracting it is to have someone tickling you in the middle of a battle. It completely spoils the mood."*

I studied the dreadnought. If that mace were consecrated, it could tear through spirits like cobwebs. But it wasn't consecrated. It couldn't be. Old Magic was anathema to the Lady; it had destroyed the order of Her creation. It couldn't coexist alongside Her blessing. Could it?

There was an easy way to find out—I could touch the armor. Then I would know.

I looked at the dreadnought. I didn't move.

"You're rambling again," I said hollowly.

"Some might call it rambling. Others might call it a valuable firsthand account of one of the most important events in—fine, stop!" I had started to reach for Saint Victoria's reliquary, which was defi-nitely consecrated. The revenant continued sourly. *"After the War of Martyrs, amid all the confusion and death, it seems likely to me that the origins of many Old Magic artifacts were forgotten and their power instead attributed to the Clerisy. Those shackles, for example, were probably stored in a crypt somewhere as the sacred manacles of Saint Mildred the Hideous or similar."*

I saw an obvious flaw in its logic. "Not everyone could have died. Someone must have known what they really were."

"Certainly, but were they going to say to the other humans, 'These shackles are capable of subduing a revenant, but oh well, the Cler-isy has decided that they're evil, so let's destroy them'? Of course not. Humans are stupid, but not that stupid. So the humans who knew the truth kept the knowledge to themselves. And over time . . ."

"Everyone forgot," I finished slowly. "Old Magic runes gradually became seen as holy symbols." That was where the revenant was headed with this, and to my unease, I found myself lacking a convincing counter-argument. We were taught that holy symbols were the Lady's divine language, their secret meanings revealed to the minds of the saints as shapes etched in sacred fire. This explanation had satisfied me as a novice; now it seemed somewhat weak. But I wasn't ready to trust the revenant's explanation, either. I ventured doubtfully, "So you believe an Old Magic artifact like the shackles might have ended up among the cathedral's treasures, and Leander's searching for it."

"Yes." It sounded relieved. Perhaps it had been worried I would have a crisis. *"Without the missing page, we can't know for certain. But it seems very likely."*

Regardless of whether the revenant was spinning clever half-truths or lying outright, the fact remained that Leander was looking for something. It didn't have to be an artifact. He could be searching for a powerful Fourth Order relic, like Saint Victoria's hand. His penitent was useful, but it couldn't do everything.

I was still holding the book. I glanced back at the entries before and after the missing page. The final entry read, *Year of Our Lady 1155, A tapestry depicting the Battle of the Lakes.* And the next, after where the page had been sliced out: *Year of Our Lady 1155, A marble statue of Saint Agnes.*

I thought aloud, "Whatever it was, we know it was given to the cathedral in 1155, around fifty years after the War of Martyrs ended." That didn't help narrow things down much. I slid the book back onto the shelf and turned to go, picking up the lantern.

A flash of gold caught my eye. The light had reflected from another book, its pages shining brilliantly even through a layer of dust. I paused.

"You don't need to look at that," the revenant said hastily, which made up my mind. I turned back, raising the lantern.

It was an illuminated manuscript. I had seen illuminated manuscripts in Naimes, but never one like this. Unable to help myself, I leaned closer.

The open pages depicted a swirling mass of gaunts, painted in vivid color and shining with gilt. The scene seemed to move dizzily before my eyes. At any moment one of the gaunts' heads might turn, its grasping hands might close, the withered stalks of grain woven around the border might rustle in the wind. I felt like if I leaned too close, I might tumble into the image as though through a window.

"The Great Famine of 1214," I said under my breath. The picture didn't need words. I simply knew, such was the skill of its creator.

With careful reverence, I removed one of my gloves and set my fingertips to the edge of the thick vellum page. Another illustration awaited me on the next, this one of a plague specter trailing its miasma as intricate designs through a mazelike array of city streets. The closer I looked, the more details I picked out. A cat peeking from a window. A child's doll abandoned on the cobblestones. Three rats investigating a spilled tankard.

Now that I had started looking, I couldn't stop. I turned more pages, each seeming to breathe with life, even as they depicted images of Death. An ashgrim, its fire-blackened skull half-concealed within a whirl of smoke and silver embers. A diagram highlighting the differences between a witherkin and a wretchling, enclosed in interlocking circles whose scrollwork seemed to spin like wheels before my dazzled eyes. I paged past shades and feverlings, undines and furies. The whole time, at the back of my mind, I wondered what was here that the revenant hadn't wanted me to see.

Then I reached the manuscript's final section. The introductory page was ornately lettered, shimmering with gilt. It read THE SEVEN REVENANTS, HERALDS OF DEATH.

SIXTEEN

S ilence came from the revenant.

I thought of the faded tapestry in Naimes, the one of Saint Eugenia confronting the revenant, and knew I had to look, even if I ended up regretting it. Slowly, I turned the page.

The spirit that confronted me was unlike anything I had seen before. It was a skeletal, six-winged figure radiating a starburst of lines that I took to signify light, like the rays of the sun. A halo shone behind its head. It wore a half-melted crown, the gold dripping in shining rivulets down its skull. At the bottom, letters read CIMELIARCH THE BRIGHT.

I turned the page. The next revenant lurked in a pall of shadow, only the bones of its arm and hand clearly visible, holding a set of scales. This one was labeled ARCHITRAVE THE DIM.

A chill crawled down my spine as I turned more pages, met each time with unearthly skeletal figures, veiled or crowned or holding objects—the scale, a sword, a chalice—and all of them winged, some with a single pair, others more. And beneath them, spelled out in gilt: CAHETHAL THE MAD. OREMUS THE LOST. MALTHAS THE HOLLOW. SARATHIEL THE OBSCURED.

"You have names," I realized aloud.

"Names given to us by humans," it said in distaste.

I gazed at Sarathiel the Obscured, taking in its remote, beautiful countenance, the eyes serenely half-closed. A fine crack ran diagonally across its features, dividing them in two, as though its face were a porcelain mask. Mist poured from the tipped chalice held in its skeletal hand, pooling beneath its silver pinions. Three sets of wings framed its body, one pair spread and the others folded. It shouldn't have come as a surprise to me that revenants had wings—I had felt them. But the images almost defied comprehension.

No one knew how the revenants had been created. Perhaps they weren't human souls. Maybe there was nothing human about them at all.

The silence lengthened. At last the revenant said, *"Sarathiel is the one who was destroyed by Saint Agnes. I hear that Oremus's relic was destroyed as well when it stopped cooperating with humans, and Cahethal went insane and buried its last vessel beneath a rockslide. Cahethal's reliquary might still exist intact, but if it does, it's trapped beneath a mountain where the humans can't reach it. There are only four of us left."*

I hadn't heard any of that before. I'd known about what happened with Saint Agnes, but not the others. Only four high relics remained. That knowledge wouldn't have troubled me a few months ago, when the idea of needing high relics to protect Loraille had seemed like something out of an old tale, but now it seemed woefully inadequate.

If Sarathiel, Oremus, and Cahethal were gone, that left Cimeliarch, Architrave, Malthas, and one other. I felt inexplicably certain that I hadn't yet seen the revenant—my revenant.

I turned the final page.

RATHANAEL THE SCORNED, read the lettering.

Above it hung a skeleton twined in a ragged shroud, with two pairs of tattered, crowlike wings. Its fleshless skull grinned out at me, the eye sockets bound behind dark wrappings. It held an iron torch clasped in front of its rib cage, the top spiked like a crown, the flames roaring up, enveloping its body and wings in fire. The silver of its form had a dark, tarnished look like an old mirror, but I couldn't tell if that was intentional or a result of the gilt flaking with age.

Some powerful spirits held objects, like riveners did swords. It represented something important about their nature, but I had no idea what the torch might signify and doubted the revenant did either—only how ironic it was that I'd ended up with the revenant associated with fire.

I absorbed its deathly visage, trying and failing to match it with the voice in my head. The revenant had devoured the populations of entire cities; it was also the entity who ordered me to eat my pottage.

"I'll have you know that I'm very good-looking by undead standards," the revenant remarked, after I had stared for a long time without speaking.

I frowned in annoyance. Just like that, the spell was broken. "Why are you called 'the Scorned'?" I asked.

"Let's just say the other revenants don't like me very much. Or didn't, as is ever so tragically the case for some of them."

"I can't imagine why."

"You haven't met them, nun. I consider it a compliment."

Curious, I closed the manuscript to see what it was called. The gold lettering spelled out a familiar title. *On the Hierarchy of Spirits.*

"This is the work of Josephine of Bissalart," I said in surprise. That explained why it was locked away. Josephine's work was brilliant but tainted. She had gone from the celebrated scholar who had sorted the spirits into their five orders to a heretic pursued by the Clerisy for her increasingly deviant beliefs. She had narrowly avoided execution by first sheltering in a convent, then escaping on a ship to Sarantia.

Running my fingers over the title, I wondered for the first time what those beliefs had been. Whether, if I heard them, I might find something to agree with.

A sound drew me from my thoughts—a long, slow scraping, like two pieces of metal grinding against each other. Startled, I jerked my glove back on and glanced around. At first the room appeared unchanged. Then I saw it.

The dreadnought's helmet had turned. It was looking directly at me.

"Run," the revenant shouted. *"Run!"*

I slammed my shoulder against the door and dove from the room. Perhaps I should have grabbed something to use as a weapon, but just as quickly I realized it wouldn't have mattered; even a sword wouldn't be strong enough to withstand a blow from that flail.

Heavy footfalls shook the ground behind me as I dragged the unconscious sister out of the way—*"Leave her!"* spat the revenant, but I couldn't let her die—and pelted up the stairs, taking the steps two at a time, my lungs already on fire.

I was faster than the dreadnought. But unlike me, it wouldn't tire. The tortured groaning and squealing of rusted plate chased me up the stair's spiraling turns. At the top, I burst out into another corridor and tore down its length, statues flashing past. *"Don't step on that flagstone,"* the revenant hissed, wrenching me aside.

Abruptly, without warning, the din of crashing armor ceased. I risked a quick glance over my shoulder. My feet pattered to a stop.

The dreadnought had halted at the top of the stairwell. It stood with a slumped-over posture, one shoulder lower than the other, dragged down by the weight of the flail. Even then, its helmet almost scraped the ceiling. Its monstrous bulk filled the corridor, swallowing up the shade-light. If I looked closely, I could see through the bars of the helmet's grille into the hollow space behind them.

Somehow it was worse seeing the dreadnought like this, knowing that any second its armor could twitch, move, explode violently into action. "Is there a trap ahead?" I asked under my breath. "What is it doing?"

"It didn't animate of its own accord. Someone's controlling it— they commanded it to stop."

Slowly, I backed away. I turned sideways, shuffling along so I could watch my path and the motionless dreadnought at the same time. Soon I reached the next intersecting corridor. It was the one with the portcullis trap, I remembered, and a sense of foreboding gripped me even before I approached the corner and saw that the portcullis had dropped, its bars blocking off the exit route. A black-robed figure waited on the other side.

I barely swerved back in time to hide myself. Peering out from behind the corner more cautiously, I saw Leander's lips curve into a thin, rueful smile that quickly fell away, replaced by a meditative expression. Only his eyes looked alive in a face turned as still as marble. When he spoke, his voice was unexpectedly soft.

"I knew I was being followed. Show yourself, and I'll call off the dreadnought. I truly would prefer not to harm you."

He opened one of his hands. On his palm lay a key. It was large and blocky, with one square tooth at the end. I gathered it wasn't the key he had taken from the sister to gain entrance to the chambers. After revealing it, he tucked it away behind his back.

The revenant winced. If its senses hadn't been muffled, it would have been able to tell that Leander had tampered with the dreadnought.

"Are you certain?" Leander asked. A few heartbeats had passed. He waited a moment longer, then turned. He said over his shoulder, "Very well. If you insist." Resting against the small of his back, his hand closed around the key.

Metal shrieked as motion erupted behind me.

"There has to be another way out," the revenant spat as I ran. *"Try those stairs,"* it ordered. *"Turn left. Left! Watch out!"*

Something flashed past my face and thunked against the opposite wall—a crossbow bolt, I thought. I couldn't look. My feet had lost sensation; every breath burned. Even if the revenant unleashed its full power, its fire's soul-devouring ability would be useless against an empty suit of armor. It could temporarily increase my strength, but I was still made of flesh and blood. And my endurance was flagging; the dreadnought was catching up. The deafening clamor of its stride filled my ears. I could taste its hot stink of rusted metal.

I veered into another hallway and found it looked familiar—I had traveled down it before. The stair leading up to the graveyard lay at the end. My heart leaped with hope.

Then the mace slammed to the ground behind me, cracks racing through the flagstones beneath my feet. The dreadnought swung again; shards of stone went flying. I threw myself away, and didn't recognize my error until too late. A statue's patient half smile filled my vision. Metal glinted in the dark.

"Careful!" the revenant shrieked as I dodged the blade: a misericorde clasped between the saint's folded hands, sharpened to a deadly point.

I skidded, rebounded off the wall, and lunged for the stair as the dreadnought's next impact narrowly missed my head. Pieces of what had once been a statue hailed down, throwing powder and fragments of rock across the steps. I scrambled over them, ignoring the bruising gouge of the stone pieces, dizzily chasing the spiral upward.

There, at last, stood the door. But we weren't safe yet. My survival hinged upon whether Leander had left it unlocked behind him. He might not have bothered, trusting the dreadnought to finish me off. Or he might have left it unlocked deliberately, granting me one last chance to escape, like a cat toying with a mouse.

I flung myself against the door, and it sprang open, tumbling me out into the graveyard's damp. I didn't have time to feel relieved. I threw my weight back against it, trying to force it shut.

Metal clashed against the other side. The dreadnought's helmet appeared in the gap. It pushed relentlessly as the revenant fed an answering burst of power into my body—the best it could do, I guessed, without alerting the entire city to its presence. The armor's joints squeaked, then groaned, but the extra strength wasn't going to be enough. I was weakening. The nearness of the door's consecrated iron blazed against my face like heat radiating from an oven.

Suddenly there were hands braced on the door beside me, muscles straining as they pushed. Another pair, much smaller, joined them on my other side. Inch by torturous inch, the door creaked shut. It thudded into place.

I looked up, meeting Jean's and Marguerite's wide eyes.

"What *was* that?" Marguerite bleated. I clapped a gloved hand over her mouth.

"Dreadnoughts are too stupid to tell a door apart from a wall," the revenant hissed into the ensuing tense silence. *"If it loses sight of you for more than a few seconds, it will think you've escaped."*

I stood there waiting, barely breathing, until I heard metal scrape against stone, ponderous steps moving away—the dreadnought retreating.

I dragged Marguerite down with me as my legs wobbled and gave out. Jean reached to catch us before we hit the ground, then suddenly balked. He backed up skittishly, his big hands held uselessly aloft as though he feared they might betray him.

A pang of sympathy shot straight to my core. I knew what that felt like—the horror of your own body turning on someone without your permission. In Jean's case, he hadn't merely hurt people. He had killed them. It would take him a long time to regain trust in himself, if he ever did.

Marguerite was glaring at me. I took my hand away. She wiped her mouth on her sleeve before saying, "I saw the priest on my way back to the infirmary, and I knew you were going to get into trouble." She looked uncertainly at Jean, who had curled into a huddle against the wall. "I didn't know who else to ask for help."

"It's good you chose him. I don't think anyone else in Bonsaint would have been strong enough."

"Strong enough for *what?*" she demanded. "What was that? What was the confessor doing?"

Reflexively, I glanced up at the graveyard, wondering if he was about to come swooping down on us.

"The priest is gone," the revenant said. I got the impression that

if it had its own body, it would be collapsed beside us against the door in an attitude of stunned exhaustion. *"Next time, nun—not that I expect there to be a next time—remind me not to call a dread-nought an antique."*

My spine prickled. In the ivy-draped darkness of the stairwell, Marguerite was watching me.

"You're doing it again," she said. "You're listening to it."

My stomach turned over. "If you tell anyone—"

"I wasn't going to." She frowned, avoiding my eyes. "You obviously aren't possessed."

"How do you know?"

I could tell she was frightened; she was gripping her pocket again, the one she kept her amulet inside. But she said defiantly, "I shared a room with you for almost seven years. You're just as weird and creepy as you were before. Being possessed by a Fifth Order spirit would probably make you less weird."

"Astonishingly," the revenant said, *"I find myself agreeing with this pink human a second time."*

"And anyway," she muttered, "you know things that only you would know. Like how much I hate spiders."

She was taking this much better than I had expected. "Thanks," I said after an awkward pause, also avoiding her eyes.

In a sudden decisive movement, she clambered to her feet, standing over me. She took a deep breath, then extended her hand. I stared at it. In all the years I'd known her, I couldn't remember her ever willingly offering to touch me.

"Will you tell me what you're doing? I want to know. I promise I can keep it a secret." She stubbornly lifted her chin. "And I might—I might be able to help."

I continued to stare at her, nonplussed.

"Believe it or not, I do actually have a brain," she said, turning a little redder. "And you need help. Whatever you're up to, you can't do it alone."

"I have the revenant."

I felt it stifle its surprise—for some reason, it hadn't expected me to say that—as Marguerite retorted, "That's not enough."

"It's gotten me this far," I said.

"Can a spirit cover for you if you go missing from the infirmary?" she challenged. "Or if you pass out and someone sees your hands? Does it know all the latest news in the city? It isn't just gossip, you know," she said with unexpected heat. "Sometimes it's useful information. There's nothing wrong with paying attention to what's going on around you."

I leaned back, wishing the ground would swallow me whole. I recognized the signs that Marguerite was getting emotional about something, but as usual, I couldn't tell what.

When I didn't answer, she made a frustrated sound. Clearly releasing a long-pent-up grievance, she declared, "Just because you can survive by being scary and intense all the time doesn't mean you should judge everyone who can't."

So that was what she was angry about. I looked from her face to her extended hand and back again. The truth was, she had come to my rescue twice now. She had helped hide me, and tonight she had probably saved my life. All that time in Naimes, I had underestimated her.

Reluctantly, I took her hand.

SEVENTEEN

Marguerite and I sat opposite each other on the stable's floor with a lantern flickering between us. I had just finished relaying everything I knew to her, ending with the revenant's explanation of the dreadnought. She had watched me in horrified fascination the entire time, her expression exaggerated by the flame lighting her face from beneath.

"It really said all that?" she squeaked.

If only she knew. "It said a lot more. I'm only sharing the important parts."

She looked away, chewing her lip. She still had a death grip on her pocket. I considered telling her that her amulet wouldn't protect her from the revenant, but I didn't want her to take it as a threat, so I didn't say anything. I waited.

"It's—you know, it's smart?" she asked finally. "Like a person?"

It is a person, were the first words that jumped to mind. Instead,

I said, with the revenant's indignation needling me to speak, "It thinks humans are all idiots."

"That's an understatement," it hissed.

I wasn't fooled by its nasty tone. Now that Marguerite knew about it, I could tell it was secretly enjoying having a conversation with someone new, even with me acting as the intermediary. For a being who liked to talk so much, going for hundreds of years without anyone listening to it must have been torture.

"I thought it would be more like . . ." Marguerite shook her head. She took a deep breath, collecting herself. "Never mind. So you think you can use Jean to help find out where Confessor Leander has been practicing Old Magic. And it really won't hurt him?"

I followed her gaze to Jean. He was sitting outside the candle-light, gazing forlornly at the horse in the nearest stall with his hands knotted in his lap. Despite his size, he looked like a little boy who wanted to pet the horse but had been denied permission. "The revenant says it won't."

"And you believe it?"

That was a good question. I still didn't know why the revenant was so interested in Old Magic. However, I could say with complete certainty, "If the revenant wanted to possess me and kill everyone, it would have already tried. That isn't what it wants."

I felt a startled hitch from the revenant, and then it went very still. Apparently it hadn't realized that I was onto it. That was what it got for assuming all humans were idiots.

Fortunately, Marguerite seemed reassured. She rose and went to Jean, moving carefully, as though approaching an injured animal. "Jean," she said softly, reaching for his shoulder. She flinched when he turned to face her. Then she set her jaw in determination and completed the gesture, her hand tiny against his bandaged shoulder. "Will you come sit down with us?"

He rose, startlingly big in the stable's gloom, shedding pieces of straw. He stared down at her hand as though he barely recognized what it was, but he still allowed it to guide him. Marguerite settled him onto the floor opposite me and then looked up with a question in her eyes. Her mouth was pressed small, her brows furrowed.

"How does it work?" she asked.

The revenant said, *"All you need to do is touch him, and I'll get an impression of the place where the ritual was cast. I doubt either of us will recognize it—some hideous dungeon filled with whips and chains, I expect; you would never believe what priests get up to in their spare time—but I'll be able to trace its direction, and we can follow it to the source."*

I wasn't sure how much of our earlier conversation Jean had overheard, if any. I shook my head at Marguerite, requesting her silence.

"Just touch him," the revenant prompted. *"I'll do the rest."*

I tried to move, and found that I couldn't. Jean was sitting there looking at the ground, showing no indication of being aware of what was happening. He might not feel anything I was about to do to him, but it felt wrong to use him without his knowledge.

"I'm like you," I told him impulsively. "I got possessed, too. By an ashgrim."

That broke through the fog. He looked up, his dark eyes meeting mine. It was the first time he had truly looked at me. I could see the pain deep within his gaze, the tortured hope, like an open wound. My chest tightened.

He needed to know. If I was going to use him for this, he deserved to know everything. *"What are you doing?"* the revenant hissed as I stripped off my gloves.

I held my hands out for Jean to see. I was so used to their appearance I rarely looked at them closely, but now I saw them as a stranger might, red and oddly wrinkled in the candlelight, the left permanently curled, missing the fingernails on the last two fingers. Those fingers were the most badly burned, left with only shiny knobs of flesh at the shortened tips.

Out of the periphery of my vision, I saw that Marguerite was holding her breath. Jean's own hands reached out very slowly to cradle mine, holding them as though they were something precious that might break. No, not that. As though they were unbreakable—the one thing in the world that he knew he couldn't hurt.

"My name is Artemisia of Naimes," I said.

He didn't react. Wet tracks shone on his cheeks beneath the craggy line of his brow. He already knew. An echo of a voice came back to me, the man on the road to Bonsaint. *She has scars. We will know her by her scars.*

"I'm sorry," I told him. "I should have gotten there faster." He was shaking his head, but I went on, my voice harsh. "I should have stopped what happened to you. I'm trying to make sure it doesn't happen to anyone else. But I need to do something to you to figure out how. Will you let me?"

A tear dripped to the ground between us, a dark blot in the dirt. He nodded.

I gripped his hands in mine.

The stable shifted. The walls turned to smoke-colored glass; the horses in their stalls became dark shapes threaded with gold. That was all I was able to observe before the floor opened up and the stable dropped away.

I plunged silently into darkness. In the void, a vision materialized before me. Shards of color reared upward from the emptiness, assembling themselves into seven tall, narrow shapes. A plinth of some kind lay below them, blazing white. A bent figure straightened neatly from behind it, tall, slender, dressed in black. His hands were filled with shadow.

He looked directly at me, his face cold and his eyes as green as moonlit glass. His lips formed a word. *Artemisia.*

My heart stopped.

The vision drained from me along with my strength. The world tipped sideways, but I didn't hit the ground. Disoriented, I struggled to identify the warmth surrounding me until I realized that Jean had caught me in his arms. Marguerite hovered over us, anxious.

"Did he see us?" I demanded of the revenant, too panicked to care what they would think.

"No. It was just an imprint—a memory. It happened the night after you escaped from the harrow."

The night after I escaped from him. I wondered if my flight had driven him to desperate measures, if the ritual he had carried out that night had been because of me. The army of spirits had gathered outside Bonsaint the next morning. The timing couldn't be a coincidence.

I squeezed my eyes shut. The revenant had said it would be able to find the place we had seen in the vision. Concentrating hard, I thought I felt something—a subtle yet insistent pull, like the tug of a ghostly string.

"We need to go," I said.

"You need to rest."

"I've rested enough."

"You said you would listen—"

"Artemisia." Marguerite's tentative voice broke in. I opened my eyes.

She looked unsettled. Jean was staring at me, but he hadn't

let go. I wondered what all that had looked like from the outside. Probably not as threatening as it could have, since the revenant had obviously been scolding me like an overprotective nanny.

Marguerite opened her mouth, closed it again. Then hesitantly spoke. "It's almost sunrise."

"Good," I said. "The streets will be empty."

"Nun," the revenant snapped.

"No—what I mean is, today's the first day of the festival. There's going to be an effigy of the Raven King in the main square. Practically everyone in the city will be there." She was twisting one of her chestnut curls around her finger, winding it up hard enough to look painful. "Maybe. . . ."

I had forgotten about the festival of Saint Agnes. Something Leander had said to the sister in the graveyard came back to me. *It must be tonight.*

"I need to go," I said in alarm. "Leander might be planning to do something during the ceremony. Whatever he was looking for tonight could be part of it."

"That's exactly what I thought," she agreed in a rush, then flushed with embarrassment. She hurried on, "It's just, it's the biggest event Bonsaint has all year. If he's planning on doing something really awful to a lot of people, that would be the best time to do it. And the square is right in the middle of the city, so you'll probably need to go through there anyway, right?"

She was watching me anxiously, waiting for my reaction. "I would imagine so," I offered, trying not to sound too surprised that she had thought of all that on her own.

She took a fortifying breath, as though she were preparing to plunge into cold water. Then she said, "If you're going, I'll go with you."

I looked at her in disbelief. "It could be dangerous."

"I know," she said. "That's why I should go."

My first instinct was to say no. But she had traveled all the way from Naimes to Bonsaint on her own. Everything I had witnessed through the harrow's screen, she had seen too, except closer up and without the protection of armed guards. She might not have known what true danger meant before, but she did now.

"All right," I said, ignoring the revenant's hiss of protest.

Her eyes shone as Jean helped me upright, setting me on my feet as though I weighed nothing. The moment he let go, I stumbled. Marguerite gave a little cry of surprise and tried to catch me. When we collided, something fell from her pocket to tumble glittering into the straw.

She gasped and snatched it back up. But not before I saw it, and recognized it. An ancient silver ring set with a tiny moonstone, like countless others in Loraille, except I knew this one—I could see it anywhere and not mistake it. The relic of Saint Beatrice, worn on Mother Katherine's hand.

Before she could return it to her pocket, I caught her wrist. She tried to yank herself free, but I didn't budge.

"It was just sitting on the altar," she said hotly. "No one was using it. Let go of me."

Instead, I gripped her tighter. "So you stole it?"

"I only thought of the idea because of you," she countered. "Before, I couldn't figure out how to protect myself from possession when I ran away. But then I realized a spirit can't possess you if you already have another one taking up room inside your body, even if it's just a shade."

"That's actually quite clever," the revenant said in surprise.

"So I've kept it summoned ever since I left Naimes," she continued. Her vehemence faltered. "And it's—it's been helping me."

I was so startled I let go of her. "It speaks to you?"

"No. It doesn't know words. It reminds me of . . . of a child. When it wants to warn me about something, it's like a little tug on my cloak." She looked down, frowning, rubbing her wrist defensively. I remembered the burns on her fingers—they must have been caused by her amulet. "I don't think the nuns can sense it, or at least they aren't looking for it, since there are so many shades in the convent already. And it isn't like they can possess people or anything. Another one doesn't make a difference."

"She's right." The revenant briefly shifted my vision, showing me Marguerite's soul. Caught up in the network of golden veins was the tiniest silver glint, far too subtle to notice if the revenant hadn't drawn my attention to it. *"Even I wasn't watching for a shade."*

Swiftly, she went on, "I thought I would hate it, having it inside my head all the time, not knowing how to put it back into its relic. But I don't. It's so happy. It just likes having company. And while I was traveling . . . I nearly ran into a group of thralls. It saved my life by warning me off the road."

"The human who wielded the relic before her must have been kind to it." The revenant sounded distant, its emotions shuttered. *"It's rare for spirits to willingly help their vessels, even ones as simpleminded as shades."*

"Mother Katherine," I told it reflexively, and then Marguerite's earlier words sank in.

No one was using it.

Marguerite looked at me with something terrible in her eyes. Grief, pity. I didn't know which was worse. "Artemisia, I'm sorry."

I stumbled away as though she had struck me. Barely thinking, only wanting to get away, I grabbed for the ladder leading to the hayloft and started to climb.

"I loved her too," she said, her voice thick.

I couldn't turn around. I didn't want her to see my face.

I didn't know why I was so upset. I had known for a long time now that Mother Katherine had died in the attack. I just hadn't been willing to admit it to myself. But my throat still ached as though I'd swallowed a stone. Heat prickled painfully behind my eyes.

I wondered if I was going to cry. I hadn't cried since I was a child, before I had come to the convent, and I didn't want the first time I did it again to be in front of the revenant. I felt its presence hovering: too close, seeing everything.

"Go away," I said, even though there was nowhere else for it to go.

"*Nun.*"

Whatever it wanted to say, I didn't want to hear it. It would have killed Mother Katherine itself that day if it had gotten the chance. I had no way to articulate the misery of the shed, the light that had come pouring in when she opened the door. I hadn't been able to see her face, but I had known she was there to save me. Later I had found out how it had happened: that the story of a girl who had thrust her own hands into a fire had reached the convent, and Mother Katherine had left at once, in the middle of morning prayers, to travel to my nameless town and find me. Like I was worth something—like I was wanted.

Leave me alone, I thought to the revenant. To Marguerite, to the thousands of people who needed my help, to the Gray Lady Herself. *Leave me alone.*

The revenant seemed as though it wanted to say something else, but I turned my face into the hay, and it was silent.

* * *

When I woke, I knew I wasn't alone. The weight of someone else's company filled the loft. I cracked open my eyes, sore and swollen from crying, and found Marguerite sitting near the edge with her knees drawn up to her chest, her arms wrapped tightly around them. She looked like she hadn't slept much. I remembered with a twist of dread that I had agreed to go with her to the ceremony today.

Seeing me stir, she bent to do something out of my line of sight. I heard water dripping as she wrung out a cloth. "Here," she said, passing over the wet rag. "Put this over your eyes. I promise it helps."

You would know, I thought, then felt bad for thinking it. She was right—it did help. Also, it gave me an excuse to cover my face.

Into my private darkness, she said as though she had heard me, "Crying doesn't make you weak, you know. It's just a reaction your body has, and there isn't anything you can do about it." She sounded sullen. "I know what you're probably thinking, and it isn't like I do it on purpose. I don't want to go around crying all the time. But usually, I'm not even feeling that emotional when it happens. I just leak more than most people."

I wasn't certain how to answer. If I tried, I knew I would accidentally say something horrific and ruin the moment.

But Marguerite obviously wanted me to say something. "I told the sisters you had left the infirmary and I would be checking on you to make sure you're all right." The silence drew out. "Artemisia," she said, "I couldn't stay in Naimes."

"Why?" I asked. My voice sounded awful, like a croak throttled from a half-dead raven.

Fortunately, she was used to that. "I hated it there. I didn't want to be a nun, and no one gave me a choice. Wearing gray for the rest of my life, being surrounded by dead people, never leaving the grounds . . . It was a nightmare."

I wasn't sure what to say to that, either.

"I'm not like you," she answered anyway. "I didn't belong in a place like that." She took a deep breath. The next time she spoke, her voice shook with something almost like anger. "When I ran away, I knew I might die, or worse. But it would have been worth it. Worth it to live for a week, a day, even a minute outside those miserable gray walls. Being stuck there was like dying already, except so slowly that I barely noticed."

I risked a glance at her from underneath the rag. She wasn't looking at me; she was staring out into the stable, seeing someplace else, her jaw set and the color high in her cheeks.

"I want to go places," she declared. "To see the world for myself, not just read about it in letters. I want to travel all the way to Chantclere. I'm going to see it. I'm going to see the ocean. Aunt Gisele said it's blue down there, not gray like it is in Naimes. And I'm going to see it."

Those words had the quality of being repeated over and over to herself like a prayer. I wondered again why her aunt had stopped sending her letters. I didn't know a great deal about her family, only that they had visited her often in the early years of her novitiate, but over time their visits had dwindled. I supposed it would be easy to forget about a daughter locked far away amid the rocky cliffs of Naimes—easy to justify not making the long, dull, treacherous journey to see her.

"I'm glad you took the relic," I said.

I heard a sharp intake of breath. I couldn't bring myself to look at her again, but I imagined her hesitating, wondering if I was playing some sort of trick. "You're glad that I stole it, you mean?"

"The revenant told me that the shade's been helping you because Mother Katherine was friends with it, and it's learned to like people."

"I didn't put it that way," the revenant snapped. *"I didn't say they were friends."* So it was listening after all.

"Oh," Marguerite said quietly.

"If you hadn't taken it, it would be trapped alone inside its relic right now. Someone else would have gotten it eventually, but they might not have treated it well, and they wouldn't have kept it summoned for long. It's better off with you. I think Mother Katherine would like that—knowing it's gone to someone who cares about it." Incredibly, crying all night seemed to have left me clearer-headed, which wasn't a result I had anticipated. "She would want you to have it."

A morose sniff came from Marguerite's direction. "I still stole it."

"I'm not sure it counts as stealing," I said, grim with the certainty that I was inching toward the same kind of heresy that had nearly gotten Josephine of Bissalart burned at the stake. "You can steal a thing. You can't steal a person."

The revenant didn't say anything. I had the sense that it was crammed into a corner of my mind, nursing some complicated emotions. I risked a look at Marguerite and saw her swipe roughly at her eyes with her sleeve.

She mumbled, "Saint Eugenia's reliquary—if you want it back . . ."

"Finally!" the revenant exclaimed, at the same time I said, "Keep it."

"No!" it hissed.

"Really?" Marguerite sounded dubious.

"Nun!"

"It's the only way the revenant can be destroyed," I explained.

"Don't tell her that," it snapped. *"Why are you telling her that?"*

"Which means it's dangerous for me to carry," I continued doggedly. "There's no sense in me wearing it, especially in battle. Having someone else keep it safe for me is the best way to protect it."

The revenant shuddered, its presence sinking away to sulk. But if it would only stop and think rationally for a moment, it would realize I was right. Also, it still didn't know the reason why I had wanted to keep Saint Eugenia's reliquary on hand. Hopefully it would never find out.

Marguerite gave a damp-sounding laugh. "I was always jealous of you, you know," she admitted.

The rag nearly fell off my face. "What?"

"You were always so sure of yourself. You knew exactly what you wanted to do, and everyone could tell you were going to be good at it. All the sisters liked you. They hated me."

"No, they didn't."

"Fine." Her voice deadened. "They didn't notice me. That's worse."

I remembered what she had said in the infirmary, *They probably haven't even noticed I'm gone*, and how much she had sounded as though she'd believed it.

"I'm sorry I talked about you behind your back," she went on. "It was mean, and I shouldn't have done it. I never meant it. I just wanted the other girls to like me. I wanted to be friends with *someone*, and you obviously didn't want—"

"I wanted to be friends with you," I interrupted, the terrible words erupting forth without my permission, as though they had been lurking somewhere inside me for years, waiting for the worst possible moment to be spoken.

Marguerite swiveled around and stared at me in shock while I fervently wished I could obliterate myself on the spot. "You tried to put a *spider* on me," she said finally.

"Just to show you it wouldn't hurt you."

"Oh. I didn't . . ." She trailed off, looking away. She gnawed on her lip, then glanced at me sidelong, as though to make sure I was still myself and not an Artemisia-shaped imposter. "I wish you had told me that," she said.

Instead of silently trying to make a spider crawl up her arm. In hindsight, I saw where that had gone wrong.

I had begun to feel cautiously optimistic that we might be finished talking when she confessed in a sudden rush, "I never knew what to say to you! I always felt like I was saying the wrong thing. The way you looked at me sometimes, it was like you wished I would just jump out the window and *die*."

"I wasn't thinking that," I protested, surprised. "I was probably trying to figure out how to answer you. I never knew what to say to you, either."

"Really?"

She looked skeptical. This was why I hated trying to have conversations with people. I said in frustration, "You wouldn't have died if you had jumped out the window. We were only one story above the ground. At worst, you would have broken an arm. And if I had really wanted you to go out the window, I would have pushed you myself."

A smile touched her mouth before she forced it away. "You would have," she admitted.

"This is nauseating," the revenant put in. I felt it loitering at the margins of my consciousness, revolted. *"Hurry up and get it over with."*

"Marguerite, I never hated you," I insisted.

She looked down. Then the smile crept back onto her face. "You might hate me soon."

I tensed. "Why?"

She climbed down the ladder and came back up with a basket of white flowers. I recognized them. They were called Lady's tears, the only flowers that bloomed this time of year, sprinkling the barren hillsides with their starry blossoms. It was a tradition to weave them into your hair on Saint Agnes's holy day.

I had never participated. My hands couldn't manage a task as delicate as braiding, and also no one had wanted to touch me, to my profound relief—I hadn't wanted to touch them, either.

She said with the same shy smile on her face, "I was thinking, Confessor Leander is probably going to be there, and he knows what you look like."

I leaned away slightly. "He knows what you look like, too."

"I doubt he remembers me. I was in there for less than a minute, and he barely looked up from the desk. Anyway, this would be a perfect disguise. No one would expect to see you with flowers braided into your hair."

With any luck, Leander wouldn't expect to see me at all. As far as I knew, he still thought I had drowned in the Sevre. But I had the bleak suspicion that this was Marguerite's equivalent of trying to hand me a spider. I needed to participate in this activity to secure our friendship, which for some reason was something I wanted.

"Fine," I intoned, as though staring into my own grave.

EIGHTEEN

I sn't it marvelous?" Marguerite asked, her wondering face tipped upward at the colorful banners flapping overhead, while I stared hard at the cobbles and tried not to lose my breakfast.

I had thought Bonsaint's sights and smells were too much on a normal day. As it turned out, Bonsaint during a festival was a hundredfold worse. I shuffled along behind Marguerite like an invalid, my stomach clenched against the odors of sweat and greasy street pies. The jeering voices of puppet shows vied with the clamor of vendors loudly hawking their trinkets; my head itched from the flower stems poking my scalp. The revenant kept making me pause to look at my reflection—first in a polished tin plate, then a lady's mirror on display in a stall. It would never admit it, but I strongly suspected that it had enjoyed the hair braiding.

"Don't worry," it assured me. *"We're traveling in the right direction. The pull is growing stronger by the moment. In the meantime, at least we've escaped from that miserable convent for a few hours."* It

was taking in our surroundings with enthusiasm, sounding unnatu-rally cheerful. *"I'm relieved to see that human fashions have improved over the last century. The nuns had me fooled; you're still wearing the same wretched gray sacks as ever. Look over there,"* it added with interest. *"Are those hats?"*

Marguerite noticed them at the same time. "Hats!" she squealed, rushing over.

"Maybe Marguerite should be your vessel instead," I muttered into the revenant's appalled silence.

She was dangling over the sill of a shop, staring wide-eyed into its interior. Funereally, I shuffled over to join her. Inside, a variety of ridiculous-looking floppy objects drooped limply from stands, made from different colors of silk and velvet and decorated with feather plumes. Left to my own devices, I wouldn't have been able to figure out that they were supposed to go on people's heads.

Something else caught Marguerite's eye, and she rushed to the other side of the street as I straggled pallidly behind. Lace hand-kerchiefs, it turned out. Then buttons carved into the shapes of flowers. I wished Leander would hurry up with his evil plans.

A familiar voice caught my attention, raised in laughter. It was Charles, coming down the street. He looked like he was parting ways with a group of other off-duty soldiers; none of them were wearing swords. To my surprise, they had Jean with them, and looked like they were congratulating him about something, cheer-ing and thumping him on the back.

I grabbed Marguerite's arm to drag her out of sight, but Charles's face lit up; he had seen us. "Marguerite!" he called out, hurrying over. "Anne," he added in surprise. "You look different."

"I'm having fun," I said sepulchrally.

He coughed. "I meant your hair. It looks nice."

"I braided it for her," Marguerite volunteered, then blushed furiously for no discernible reason. Across the street, Charles's friends were elbowing one another.

Charles snatched an onion from the stall behind us and lobbed it at them. Once they'd dispersed and Charles had sheepishly paid for the onion, I asked, "What's Jean doing here?"

He had followed Charles over, blocking out the sun. Incongruously, there was a yellow ribbon pinned to his shirt.

Charles proudly punched him on the arm. "Yearly tradition. He's won the barrel-throwing contest for the last three years running. We weren't about to let him break his victory streak. Our whole unit got the day off—the captain authorized it."

Jean kept gazing in slight wonderment at the ribbon, as though he half expected it to disappear as soon as he looked away. Being treated normally by his friends was good for him, I realized, as long as nothing happened to upset him. It seemed like none of them blamed him for the fate of their friend Roland. They weren't afraid of him. I wondered what that would be like.

"Are you two going to see the effigy?" Charles went on hopefully. "I can help find you a good place to sit—it's harder than you'd think—and stop for something to eat on the way. Bonsaint's festival pastries are famous; you need to try one."

Marguerite bit her lip. "Anne, what do you think?"

I couldn't warn Charles not to attend the ceremony. Not without inviting questions that were impossible to answer in the middle of a crowded street. Also, if I claimed to be Artemisia of Naimes, he would probably think I had gone insane. The mere idea of having that conversation made me want to crawl into a hole and die.

The revenant noticed me sizing up an escape route. *You had better not, nun. Ideally the priest won't be looking for you at all, but he certainly won't be looking for a version of you that's voluntarily socializing with a group of humans. Also, I want to try a pastry."* I felt obscurely betrayed.

"All right," I agreed reluctantly.

Charles wasn't discouraged by my lack of enthusiasm. He chattered happily the entire walk to the food stall. I found out that he came from a family with five sisters, in a province several days' journey to the south, and had manifested the Sight at the relatively late age of nine. Knowing no one at the monastery in Roischal, he had become an honorary member of Jean's family. Jean's parents had died when he was young, so he'd been raised by an aunt, a tiny, ferocious woman whom Jean lifted over puddles when it rained. She was like a mother to many of the young men in the city guard who didn't have family nearby.

I found myself listening with a lump in my throat. Some of the girls at my convent had family close by in Naimes, but I had avoided them whenever they'd visited. I hadn't wanted them to see me and think the sisters abused the girls in their care.

After he bought the pastries, we sat down on a building's steps to watch a minstrel show set up in the middle of the street. I retreated into my cloak, barely tasting the pastry's mushroom filling as bare feet thumped across the stage in front of us. The Raven King, traditionally played by a beggar, gamboled over the boards wearing an old cloak of raven feathers and a crown of twisted metal scraps. Every time coins pattered onto the stage, he doffed his crown and grinned with blackened teeth. Jean flinched whenever one of the copper pawns struck him, but seemed to calm down when he saw that the man wasn't hurt.

I had heard about this festival custom, but seeing it firsthand made me uneasy. I supposed that for most people, mocking their fear made it seem weaker. The more they laughed at it, the less power it held over them. But that had never been my experience with the Dead.

The revenant was watching too, its attention focused on the stage. *"Nun, that human has the Sight."*

"The beggar?" I asked in surprise.

Charles leaned over to see if there was someone sitting on my other side. "Who are you talking to?" he asked, puzzled, when he found the space empty. The group of girls sitting next to us— oddly, they had been lurking nearby ever since we had joined up with Charles—all erupted nonsensically into giggles.

"I'm praying," I lied.

"Oh." He raised his eyebrows. "That's, ah—very pious of you."

"You don't know the half of it," Marguerite assured him, her eyes sparkling. "Back in Montprestre she used to pray over the goats every morning, wearing a hair shirt, kneeling in the cold."

Charles nearly choked on his pastry. Gravely, I signed myself.

"Yes, the beggar," the revenant said, waiting impatiently for us to finish. *"In places where the risk of possession is low, it isn't as uncommon as you might think. Your Clerisy can't round up everyone with the Sight. The humans who escape their notice typically live like this one, pretending to be mad. That way no one will think twice if they seem to see and hear things that aren't there."*

I stole a glance at Marguerite. I had never seen her so happy. She reminded me of the healed patients in the infirmary, revived from the brink of death. She was right—she wasn't suited for the life of a nun. That had been obvious from the moment I'd met her. But then why had the Lady given her the Sight? Why give it to the man on the stage? And what kind of future awaited her now? These questions troubled me long after we left the stage behind.

I recognized one of the streets we took on our way to the square; it was the narrow, winding avenue where the procession had passed my first day in Bonsaint. Now it was lined with stalls selling festival food. A puppet show occupied the archway that Charles and I had crammed into, the Raven's King puppet wailing in cowardly despair as the puppeteer pelted him with cloth ravens. Children's laughter rang in my ears.

Suddenly, the festival's bright colors seemed garish. The good cheer felt artificial, as though everyone had to keep celebrating, or else the horrors of the countryside would darken their doors. Sister Lucinde had once claimed that nothing bad ever happened on a high holy day. Soon I would find out whether she'd been telling the truth.

"Nun, we're getting closer to the ritual site. I think the pull is coming from that building in the distance. The one with the spires."

I followed the tug on my gaze to a collection of spires rising above the rooftops, their shapes nearly lost in the glare of the late-afternoon sun. They were the same spires I had been dizzied by upon my entrance to Bonsaint. Standing still for a moment, I felt it too—the insistent tug of the invisible string urging me in that direction.

Charles noticed me looking. Squinting, he shaded his eyes with his hand. "Have you seen the cathedral yet?"

"The what?" I asked stupidly.

"The Cathedral of Saint Agnes. It's the second biggest in Loraille, after Saint Theodosia's in Chantclere. There are seven spires, one for each high saint. Anne?"

The realization had hit me like a bucket of cold water. The cathedral's sanctuary. The seven tall shapes in the vision had been stained-glass windows; the white plinth below them. . . .

Leander was conducting his rituals at the altar.

I should have realized it earlier, but the idea was so profane I could barely wrap my head around it even now.

"Anne?" Charles repeated, concerned.

"I forgot!" Marguerite exclaimed loudly. "How could I forget? Anne *always* gets sick when she eats mushrooms." She grabbed my sleeve and turned me around, mouthing, *What's wrong?*

"I'll tell you later," I muttered. There wasn't anything we could do about it now, and Charles was hovering, looking concerned. At least I didn't have to fake my unhealthy pallor.

I saw the effigy first as we neared the square, a straw figure towering high above the crowd, its face shaped into a rough approximation of human features and the top of its head worked into a crown. The low sun lit it gold against a windy sky torn with clouds. As a representation of the Raven King, it was intended to look sinister, but something about this one's appearance made my skin crawl. In Naimes, the effigy we used was only about the size of a novice. It had always struck me as looking a little forlorn, as though it knew the fate that awaited it. This one looked like it was waiting to be worshipped.

Charles whistled at the sight of it. "That's the biggest one yet."

The ravens had already gathered, numbering in so many hundreds that they looked like a living black cloth draped over the rooftops. They flapped and croaked above the crowd, animated by the excitement in the air.

The buildings' chilly shadows fell over us as we entered the crowd. Without everyone catching sight of Jean and hastily moving out of our way, I wasn't sure how we could have gotten through. People were packed into every inch of space, even perched on the statue of Saint Agnes in the center of the square, laughing and eating festival food, pointing at the ravens.

Eventually we found a storefront awning that no one had claimed yet, most likely because they couldn't reach it. This presented little challenge to Jean, who boosted us up one by one onto the warm slate tiles. From there I could see that the effigy had been raised on a wooden platform, similar to the minstrel show's stage, but larger and elevated higher above the crowd.

"Look," Charles said to Jean. "There's Brother Simon."

Marguerite and I craned our necks to see the gray-robed figure swinging his censer over the platform. I had never seen a Gray Brother up close. There weren't as many of them as there were Gray Sisters, since so many Sighted boys went on to become soldiers.

I tried to imagine Leander being raised by monks. Sleeping in a crowded dormitory, laboring away at menial chores. It was almost impossible to picture, even though he couldn't be far past his boyhood in a monastery—he was only a few years my elder. Where had he gotten his first taste of Old Magic? A locked-away artifact, a forbidden scroll?

"Do you know," the revenant inserted into my dark ruminations, *"it took me nearly a hundred years to figure out that monks existed? All that time, I just assumed they were unusually hairy nuns."*

Any further observations were mercifully cut short by a commotion in the crowd: hooves clattering, cries of excitement. The Divine's litter had arrived in the square, escorted by a group of clerics, including the hateful black-robed figure riding in a position of honor alongside. He wasn't on Priestbane, I noticed; he was seated atop the same white horse he had been riding when he had chased me into the forest.

I remembered the rock and worried Priestbane had been lamed, until Charles leaned over to say, grinning, "Did you hear that Artemisia of Naimes rode the confessor's old horse into battle? Turns out, it was actually his all along—she took it from him on the way to Bonsaint. Apparently he can't ride it anymore, because people recognize it. He gets mobbed by crowds wanting to touch it for her blessing."

My mouth twitched with the rare urge to smile.

The revenant said, *"I don't sense anything unusual yet, but I can't extend my power far with so many clerics nearby. Keep an eye on the priest for any behavior that looks suspicious. Perhaps your pathetic human senses might actually prove useful for once."*

It took some time for the Divine to make her way to the platform. The impressively armored cathedral guard had created a path for her through the crowd, but she stopped frequently as she walked along it, pausing to speak to the festival-goers clamoring for her blessing, stretching out their arms and hoisting up their babies. She spent so long greeting them that the clerics began to look impatient. I watched her bend her head over an old woman's crippled arm, and it struck me that this wasn't the behavior of a ruler who would callously bar refugees from the city.

Perhaps the decision hadn't been hers. Leander was still at her side. To an ignorant observer he probably just looked annoyed by all the babies, but I guessed that his subtle air of discomfort had more to do with his concealed injury. Did he ever leave the Divine alone? I remembered comparing her to a painted doll, but perhaps she was more of a puppet, with Leander tugging her strings.

The group finally reached the platform, dwarfed by the giant straw effigy stretching overhead. I could guess why they'd made it so large this year—the spectacle would come as a much-needed reassurance of the Lady's goodwill after the devastation that had befallen Roischal.

Based on the crowd's anticipatory hush, the Divine was going to speak. In Naimes, Mother Katherine had never bothered. She had simply gestured at the dejected-looking effigy, smiling a little sadly, and the Lady had answered in a thunder of wings.

The Divine paused to give Leander a swift, searching look, as though seeking his approval. Then she took a deep breath and wrung her hands before stepping forward. Her sweet, youthful voice spilled across the square.

"People of Bonsaint." She sounded breathless in her earnestness. "The Lady has delivered us from danger. By Her grace, the Dead have been driven from our fields." Had Leander convinced her of that? He wasn't watching her, instead gazing coldly across the crowd. "On this day, we honor her by denouncing the Raven King, bringer of the Sorrow, ruin of the Age of Kings. May his face remain forgotten. May history scorn his name."

"May history scorn his name," echoed the crowd.

"Lady, we give thanks." The Divine made the sign of the oculus and bowed her head.

The crowd held its breath. Everyone knew what would happen next: the ravens would descend on the effigy in a great black cloud and tear it apart, straw by straw, just as they had the king's real body three hundred years ago, when they had been sent by the Lady to destroy him. He had been known only as the Raven King ever since, his true name struck from Loraille's records in disgrace.

The held breath stretched on. And on, and on, until confused murmurings started to fill the square. Not a single raven had budged. No longer flapping or croaking, they roosted in watchful silence, hundreds of dark eyes gleaming. As the sun sank below the rooftops, the slice of red light illuminating the effigy slipped upward, casting more of it into shadow. Soon only the crown blazed against the darkening sky, like it had been set on fire.

The Divine stood frozen, a pale blot in the shadows. Her hands tightly gripped the platform's rail. Beside her, Leander spoke. Whatever he said seemed to jar her from her horrified trance, and she quickly bent her head in prayer. Leander joined her, but I could tell he wasn't truly praying; instead, he was watching the crowd beneath his lashes.

I had never heard of this happening before. The Lady always answered. Beside me Marguerite was gripping her pocket, consulting her shade. "Does the revenant sense anything?" she whispered, her eyes wide and frightened.

"Not yet," it snapped, preoccupied. I got the impression that it was extending its senses as far as it dared. I shook my head, and almost jumped when Marguerite's other hand reached out to seize mine, holding it as tightly as Sophia had in the crypt.

The murmurs were growing agitated. "Artemisia!" wailed a voice suddenly. "Artemisia of Naimes!" At once, a confusing outcry filled the square. I couldn't tell what had prompted it until another voice shouted, "The white raven!"

Leander's head jerked up, his gaze fixing on the statue of Saint Agnes. I followed it to see that Trouble had landed on the statue's head, his white feathers striking in the gloom. My stomach plunged. Some of the people here had to be refugees; they must have seen Trouble in the aftermath of the battle, diving at the clerics to aid my escape. And if they had made the connection between me and Trouble, Leander certainly had too. Looking back, I found that he had gone very still, his fingers poised over his onyx ring. Beside him, the Divine looked overwhelmed, glancing around as though searching for someone to tell her what to do.

The shouting continued, growing bolder. "It's a sign! Saint Artemisia is with us!"

"There's something here," the revenant said suddenly. *"An unbound spirit. It reeks of Old Magic. It's possessing someone."*

I cast a horrified eye over the hundreds of people gathered in the square. There were too many possibilities. Dozens of soldiers, visibly uncertain whether to contain the crowd or help disperse it; the monks who had helped set up the effigy; even the clerics and knights standing on the platform with the Divine. Each of them Sighted, vulnerable to possession.

Nearby, alarmed cries rang out, more of disgust than fear. I learned forward, trying to see the cause of the disturbance. People were jumping away from something on the ground. It was rats—rats scattering beneath their feet, fleeing across the cobblestones.

"There it is," the revenant hissed triumphantly.

Marguerite's shade must have sensed it too. She was staring at a shape in the crowd, a dark figure limping along behind the rats, shoving people aside. My breath caught as the dwindling light glanced from a piece of metal on the figure's brow. It was the beggar from earlier, the one playing the part of the Raven King. He was still wearing his crown and cloak of feathers. Now his face was contorted, his teeth bared in a grimace. His head wagged from side to side like a maddened bear. I felt the revenant recoil at whatever it sensed within him.

"That human wasn't possessed when we saw him earlier. Nun, the spirit inhabiting him knows we're here. It's looking for us."

As though it had heard the revenant speak, the thrall jerked to a halt. The beggar's eyes met mine across the crowd, flashing silver in the dusk.

"It's been sent to find us."

NINETEEN

The beggar bared his blackened teeth in a rictus grin. Then he ducked his head and continued shoving through the crowd, his limbs moving in labored fits and jerks.

"It's powerful," the revenant was saying, speaking more to itself than to me. *"Fourth Order, certainly, but the stink of Old Magic is obscuring it. . . . Nun?"* It sounded alarmed. *"Whatever you're thinking of doing, don't."*

All I cared about was that the thrall had come for me, which meant that anyone nearby was in danger. Charles wasn't carrying his sword; even if Jean had had one, he was in no condition to fight. And I couldn't let anything happen to Marguerite.

Roughly, I shoved her hand away. "I need to go," I grated out, and jumped off the awning, hardening myself against her cry of protest.

"Nun!"

I didn't answer. As soon as my boots hit the cobbles, I was weaving through the crowd, shoved from side to side by the unpredictable lurch of bodies. I paused to let the beggar catch sight of me, willing him to follow. Then I yanked my hood over my face. If I managed to lead him out of the square, I might be able to fight the spirit inhabiting him without anyone getting hurt.

"You are the worst vessel I've ever had," the revenant hissed.

At first my strategy seemed to work. I caught a few glimpses of the beggar over my shoulder, twitching and grimacing as he prowled along my trail. Then I heard a scream.

"Blight!" someone shouted. "The Dead are among us!"

As though this were a signal, the ravens took flight at last, erupting over the crowd in a storm of beating wings. Their voices echoed the cry of "Dead, dead, dead!"

I jerked to a halt as panic raged around me. The thrall had stopped in the middle of the square near the statue of Saint Agnes. His bloodshot gaze locked on mine as his hand snapped out and grabbed a passing woman's wrist. He let go as soon as she screamed, and she was carried away by the crowd, terror boiling in her wake. No one else could see the silver sheen that glazed his eyes. As far as these people knew, anyone around them could be possessed; the square could be full of spirits, and none of them would be the wiser.

The message was clear: it wasn't going to let me lure it away. It would hurt people until I stopped and faced it here. Whatever it was, it was intelligent, or it was following Leander's orders.

The ravens blotting out the sky made it difficult to see what was happening on the platform, but it appeared as though the clerics were trapped with the crowd blocking the stairs. Through the gale of flickering black wings, I saw someone drop a censer, which rolled across the boards until it struck the base of the effigy, showering the robes of nearby clerics with embers. The Divine frantically pat-ted at her smoking vestments—and just like that, Leander was no longer at her side.

My hands curled into fists. Ducking my head, I shouldered toward the beggar, who stood waiting for me, eerily still in the midst of the chaos.

"Wait," the revenant said hurriedly. *"It wants you to fight it. This is a trap. The aim isn't to destroy my relic; it's to force you to reveal your presence to the Clerisy."*

"Then what am I supposed to do?"

The harsh cries of the ravens drowned out my voice, but I knew the revenant had heard me. The answer hung in the silence between us. *Run. Leave these humans to their fate.* At least it didn't bother saying those words out loud. It knew me too well for that.

The thrall briefly vanished from view as someone staggered past clutching a bloodied face. I needed to move quickly. Soldiers had begun pushing their way forward, halting people to look into their eyes. Organizing them was an armored knight who I hoped was Captain Enguerrand, not a member of the cathedral guard.

I pushed forward, straining in the opposite direction as the people fleeing past. I had barely managed a few steps when a body slammed into me, bowling me to the ground. What followed was a disorienting muddle of churning legs and stamping boots. A burst of heat flooded my ear, and then the revenant yanked me back up so forcefully that I thought for an instant it had taken over my body. I gasped for air as though surfacing from underwater.

My ear stung. Someone had kicked me.

"You could have been killed," the revenant snapped. *"Right now the humans pose a greater threat to you than the thrall."*

"Help me fight it," I panted, undeterred.

"Have it your way, nun. Get as close to the thrall as you can." It sounded bitterly angry. *"This is a foolish thing to even attempt, but while the clerics are distracted, they might not be able to tell my power apart from the spirit possessing him."*

No matter how dangerous it was, I had to try. If I could just flush the spirit from hiding, the Clerisy's forces should be able to fight it. The Divine carried at least one Fourth Order relic, and she wouldn't have been ordained if she were incapable of using it.

A few more steps, and I broke into a small clearing created by the crowd surging around Saint Agnes's statue. The beggar stood waiting. As soon as I stepped back into sight, his eyes rolled up, locking on to me through the flitting shapes of ravens, the whites so bloodshot they burned red in the twilight. Then he charged.

His weight bowled me to the cobblestones, his frame thin but wiry, clawing at me in a frenzy of motion empowered by the spirit's unnatural strength. His scrabbling hands closed around my throat and squeezed. I wrenched myself to the side and sent us tumbling over each other across the ground, into the path of people fleeing past. A boot clipped my shoulder; another struck the beggar's head. His grip loosened enough for me to drag in a painful, fiery breath. Only then did the revenant's power push forth, a trickle compared to its usual violent flood. The beggar collapsed, convulsing.

Veins bulged in his face, and his mouth opened in a silent scream. His lips were tinged blue, his tongue purple and swollen. I grabbed his head in both hands so he wouldn't crack his skull on the cobbles. His eyes fixed on me with a terror that I couldn't identify as his own or that of the spirit possessing him.

"You're killing him," I said.

"I'm doing my best," the revenant retorted, its voice strained with effort.

I bit back a terse reply, remembering the limitations of my own hands. I could hold a sword, but not a sewing needle. The revenant's destructive power likewise wasn't designed for subtlety—but for my sake, it was trying.

The beggar went limp. At first I thought he had died. Then silver light hazed his eyes. The terror in them vanished, replaced with an expression of cold condemnation.

"Traitor," he declared.

I almost released him in shock. That deep, rasping voice wasn't the thrall speaking. It was the spirit possessing him.

"Betrayer of your own kind," it went on, the beggar's mouth contorting strangely around the words. With another, greater shock, I realized that it was speaking to the revenant.

"Do you not see," it rasped, "that the humans will destroy you if we fail? There is no path for you, Scorned One. No mercy, no escape. Wherever you go, you will be—"

I didn't get to hear the rest. The revenant interrupted with a final, vicious shove of power, like the twisting of a knife. The beggar's eyes fell shut and his lungs rattled in a long exhale. A gout of silver vapor poured from his body, twisting away in a gyre above the crowd.

Whatever form it took, the Clerisy could handle it now. It might be powerful, but it was only one spirit against the combined might of Bonsaint's forces. I had seen Leander alone take on a rivener.

As far as I could tell, my struggle with the beggar had gone unnoticed amid the chaos. I dragged his unconscious body toward the statue and hauled him up on the plinth, where he wouldn't get trampled. Every breath burned my bruised throat like fire. I imagined that I tasted smoke. Not incense, but the stench of something burning. The pain must have brought back a memory of my family's hearth, the heat of the fire as I plunged my hands inside.

When I looked up, one last person fled past, leaving behind an expanse of empty cobbles, littered with debris—scraps of food, crushed blossoms. I looked up farther, bringing a circle of boots into view. Drawn swords. Soldiers.

I hadn't been fast enough. They had finished combing through the crowd. Converging at the square's center, they had all stopped dead around me. Ravens still swarmed overhead, panic still churned behind them, but it was as though the space surrounding Saint Agnes's statue had turned into the eye of a storm, briefly quiet and still.

A loud, metallic clatter shattered the illusion. One of the soldiers had dropped his sword. He didn't seem to notice he'd done it; he was too busy staring at me.

"Oh, fantastic," spat the revenant.

These soldiers had the Sight. They had seen everything. Not just two people fighting on the ground, but the spirit I had driven from a thrall's body—even if they had seen nothing else, they couldn't have missed its silver light twisting overhead.

I was still holding the beggar's arms. Slowly, I lowered him to rest against Saint Agnes's feet.

They didn't know my face. Perhaps they wouldn't recognize me. Who would look at me and think I could possibly be Artemisia of Naimes? The real Artemisia could have slipped away, and I was just some bystander she'd left behind. That was how I felt, like an imposter at risk of being mistaken for myself.

"I told you she couldn't have drowned," said one of the men. They were gazing at me in wonder.

"Anne!" came a ragged shout.

I flinched. I was still imagining that I smelled smoke, and the sound of my old name belonged to that same pain-filled darkness, an echo of reproval, of fear. I wasn't ready for Charles to break into the circle of soldiers, elbowing them aside. He looked frantic. He must have jumped down from the awning to look for me. I remembered, dazed, that he had five sisters.

First he looked at me; then his eyes slid to the unconscious beggar at my side. He glanced around at the soldiers, confused. "Anne?" he repeated, lost.

"That isn't my name," I said.

He looked at the other soldiers again and then back at me, his gaze dropping to my gloves. Understanding began to dawn. He was realizing that he had never seen my hands.

I didn't know what I had expected him to do once he figured out who I was—laugh, maybe. Look disappointed or betrayed. He did none of those things. Instead, he dropped to his knees on the dirty cobbles.

"Lady vespertine," he said, gazing up at me. His eyes were dark and sincere beneath the lock of sweaty hair plastered to his forehead.

The smell of smoke was growing stronger. The air was too hot. I couldn't breathe. I wanted Charles to stop kneeling—to get up. I tried to stand, but my legs folded. Charles lunged forward and caught me before I fell from the statue's plinth.

"Nun, what's wrong?"

I couldn't think. The revenant's alarm swirling around in my head was only making me dizzier. "Is something burning?" I asked.

A new soldier answered, using the gentle tone that meant I had asked a strange question, one with an answer so obvious that a normal person shouldn't have needed to ask. "Lady, the effigy caught on fire."

Of course. The sparks from the dropped censer would have

easily ignited the dry straw. That seemed clear enough. But my thoughts were dizzy, muddled. For a confusing moment I felt the grit of my family's hearth beneath my knees, saw the red, living pulse of the coals before I thrust my hands inside. But that had happened years ago. Hadn't it?

My skin was clammy with sweat. I had the sickening awareness that something was wrong with me, but I didn't know what it was.

"You told me fire doesn't bother you," the revenant said suddenly, as though solving a mystery that had troubled it for days.

"It doesn't." I sounded uncertain.

"Lady?" asked one of the soldiers. I felt Charles touching my scalp.

"You idiot," the revenant said with feeling. Yet for once the insult wasn't aimed at me. I thought it might be calling itself an idiot, even though that didn't make any sense. *"This isn't an ordinary cookfire—of course it's affecting you."*

"I don't think she took a blow to the head," Charles was saying. And then, in a different voice, "Captain!"

Over his shoulder, I had a woozy impression of armor, its polished surface reflecting the dancing glow of flames. Enguerrand.

"Get her out of here," he ordered. His voice was rough, as though he had been shouting. "She needs to be brought to safety. The spirit is Fourth Order—we don't know what kind yet. Talbot, Martin—"

He was giving orders, but I didn't hear the rest. A terrible scream split the noise of the crowd. Silver light flashed across Captain Enguerrand's armor.

"What's happening?" I rasped. This was wrong—the Divine and her clerics should have destroyed the spirit by now. A red glow lapped against the buildings, alive with the shadows of people running. Heat rolled mercilessly across the square. I fought against the arms restraining me, then recognized who they belonged to and tried to stop. It was Charles. I didn't want to hurt Charles.

"They're taking you away. It's over now. You don't need to see."

"Show me!"

"Nun—"

Worriedly, Charles called out to someone, "I think she's delirious!"

Perhaps the revenant feared that if I didn't shut up, someone would figure out I was talking to it. It relented, and my vision shifted. This time I was prepared to see the world through its senses—or thought I would be. But there was more than just the translucent, smoked-glass tint to the world, the muffling of scents and sounds. Something impossible was happening in the square. Silver forms were darting through the crowd, hunting, swooping toward the soldiers and the clerics on the platform. Spirits.

"Blight wraiths," the revenant supplied.

But where had they come from?

Anticipating the question, it tugged my eyes toward the spirit we had exorcised. It hovered above the crowd, invisible to the Unsighted multitude below. Pointed slippers encased its skeletal feet; lavish robes hung from its emaciated frame. A miter crowned its head, the trailing ribbons framing a withered face, the desiccated skin stretched tightly over bone, giving its hollow-cheeked visage an expression of sour disdain.

Below it lay a scattering of large black lumps on the cobbles, like doused coals—bodies.

As I watched, it bent to lay its thin hand on the head of a passing woman as though in benediction. The moment it touched her, she collapsed to the street, dead of blight. It assumed a stance of prayer above her, and the golden light swirling within her chilled to cold, lifeless silver.

A white vicar.

These were the worst of the Fourth Order spirits, risen from clerics who had met violent ends. They were so feared that even clerics who died of natural causes were given elaborate rites to protect their souls from any risk of corruption. Supposedly, their kind had been eradicated from Loraille centuries ago.

The white vicar pointed, and the silver funneled out of the dead woman's body, taking shape as it went. The newly formed wraith joined the others streaming through the crowd.

The revenant must have decided I'd had enough, because my senses flooded back in a roar of fire. The effigy had transformed into a tower of flame, lapping out folds of greasy black smoke, the heat of it blistering my face even from across the square. Everything was lit red with deep blue shadows in between, and embers swirled in the air overhead.

My eyes caught on a soldier engaging a blight wraith nearby, its silver glow illuminating the openmouthed terror on his face. I wasn't conscious of reacting, but I must have tried to throw off Charles's grip. Another soldier came into view, steadying me, blocking the wraith from sight.

"Nun," the revenant snapped. "Nun! You've done enough. Let them help you."

I shook my head, both in denial and in a hopeless attempt to think. As though jostled loose, a terrible thought sprang into clarity. "Charles." My fingers tightened on his back. "Where are Marguerite and Jean?"

"They're together," he said into my ear. "They're safe. I left them behind on the—" He broke off, perhaps realizing that that had been before the white vicar, before the wraiths. They might have been safe on the awning before, but they weren't now. He stopped and scanned the people streaming past.

"Charles," shouted the other soldier, barely audible through the din. "We need to go! We have our orders."

Charles didn't seem to hear. He had gone rigid. I followed his line of sight.

A possessed soldier had backed a group of people against a building. I couldn't tell whether they were city folk or refugees, or a mixture of both; soot streaked their faces and clothes from the flying embers. The light made everything strange, like a scene from a nightmare. I wouldn't have recognized Marguerite and Jean if it weren't for Jean's distinctive size—even hunched over, he was the largest person in the square.

Startlingly small in comparison, Marguerite had placed herself in front of him and the others, her arms spread as though trying to protect them from the thrall. I wondered what she thought she was going to accomplish. Even if she were armed, she wasn't any good at fighting. The thrall would kill her more easily than a kitten.

I was already moving, throwing off Charles's slack arms. If the other soldier tried to intervene, I didn't feel his touch. I didn't feel the people who ran into me or shoved me or trod on my boots. I only grew aware of the revenant speaking at the very end.

"Keep going," it was urging sharply. *"Don't fall over, you horrid nun. You're almost there."* And then it said, *"Grab him."*

When the thrall saw me coming, he started to bring up his sword, but his angle was poor. I seized his arm and wrenched it, and the sword went clanging to the ground. Before he could think of rushing me, I planted a hand on his face and drove him down. With the revenant's strength, he went easily, and the spirit came boiling out from his mouth and nose and eyes, streaming between my fingers. I wasn't sure if the revenant had exorcised it, or if it was so desperate to escape that it had abandoned its vessel on purpose.

The revenant said viciously, *"Don't let go,"* and I felt the spirit being drawn inward, *into me*, siphoned up like breath, until all that remained of it was a cold half-sated hunger numbing the pit of my stomach like frost. The revenant had devoured it.

There was a pause in the square—a brief cessation of noise, in which I heard a strange gasping, sighing exhalation. Marguerite's hands were on me, helping me to my feet, her astonished face lit silver, and then I saw it: across the square, the blight wraiths were abandoning their vessels en masse, pouring upward as pillars of light. I stared in confusion, wondering if the Lady had intervened with a miracle. Awe swept coldly over my body.

Then I remembered what the revenant had said in the hayloft. *Most spirits would rather leap into the Sevre than cross me.*

The spirits knew it was here. They were fleeing in terror—all of them at once.

The white vicar still remained, its radiant form suspended above the square. But as soon as I looked, a thin, earsplitting scream rippled through the air: the debilitating wail of a fury. The sound grated in my ears like fingernails scratching down a pane of glass, but it didn't freeze me the way it had in Naimes. This time, it hadn't been aimed at me. Across the square, silhouetted by the conflagration, the Divine had finally raised her scepter. The vicar wore a look of deathly scorn, but the relic's power had caught it fast, and already the soldiers were closing in.

A face leaped out from the crowd nearby: Leander, illuminated by the ghost-light. He was gazing upward at the fleeing spirits. He looked young and almost vulnerable as he watched his plan collapse. Then his mouth twisted. He shoved forward, his hand wrapped around his ring. The first person to get in his way fell writhing to the cobbles. Then Captain Enguerrand's armored figure stepped from the crowd to block his path.

I didn't see any more. The heat was smothering me; the smoke was filling my lungs. Distantly, I registered that the people Marguerite had been trying to protect were watching.

"It's her," one of them said. "It's Saint Artemisia."

I often wanted the ground to open up and swallow me whole. Just this once, I received my wish. The world turned sideways, and everything went dark.

TWENTY

I awoke on a bed in an unfamiliar room, full of unfamiliar people staring at me. They drew back when I yanked myself against the headboard, exchanging glances and whispering. Most of them signed themselves; an old woman even got down and prostrated herself on the floor.

My heart slammed dizzily against my ribs. The first thing I noticed was that I could still faintly smell smoke. Perhaps it was coming in from outside, or it was clinging to everyone's hair and clothes. The second thing I noticed was that I wasn't wearing my gloves.

"Where are my gloves?" I asked.

"Calm down, nun," said the revenant, as Charles hurried into the room.

"You're awake," he said, his expression relieved until he saw my face. He dropped to his knees beside the bed. "Artemisia, it's all right."

Artemisia. He was calling me Artemisia in front of these people.

But it didn't matter; they already knew. "Where are my gloves?" I repeated. For some reason, it hurt my throat to speak.

He reached for my shoulder, then seemed to think better of it. "Elaine's washing them, along with the rest of your clothes. You don't remember? The smoke—you told us about the smoke. How the smell bothers you."

I didn't remember saying that, but I wasn't about to admit that in front of a roomful of people who were likely well on their way to being convinced that I was mad. Strangely, a small prick of guilt came from the revenant.

"Where are we?" I asked instead, trying to make my voice sound less harsh. There was a little boy clinging to the skirts of a woman who I thought might be Elaine, and I didn't want to frighten him.

The woman stepped forward; the little boy shyly hid behind her legs. "This is my house," she said softly, her gaze lowered. "We brought you here after you saved us."

"They're helping hide you," Charles added, turning back to me, his gaze earnest. "The Clerisy doesn't know you're here."

"Yet," the revenant put in darkly. *"If there's one thing I've learned about humans, it's that your kind loves to gossip. Nuns are no exception, by the way. The ancient and terrible knowledge I harbor about Sister Prunelle's bunions would make even you beg for mercy."*

A thousand questions crowded my mind. I wanted to ask everyone to leave, but I was their guest. I assumed that this room, with its multiple cots and cushion-covered chests, functioned as the sleeping chambers for the entire household. It looked like everyone I had rescued from the thrall had returned here, not just Elaine's family. There were perhaps a dozen people in the room, about half of them seated, the others standing as though they had forgotten how to sit. I didn't recognize any of them except for Jean, crouched in the corner with his big hands wedged between his knees. The old woman was still prostrated on the floor, mumbling prayers.

"Please," I said. "Don't do that."

Elaine bent and murmured something to her, gently drawing her up, leading her over to a seat on one of the chests. Then she hesitated, wringing her hands. "Is there anything you can tell us?" she asked in her soft voice, still keeping her gaze averted, as though I might blind her. "About what happened? About why the Lady—"

Suddenly, a jumble of voices filled the room, all asking questions simultaneously. "How did the spirits get into the city?" "Why didn't the Lady send Her ravens?" "Has She forsaken us?" "Are we—" "My father was in—" "Can you—"

My pulse began hammering. Some of the people who had been sitting were starting to stand up. The little boy hid his face, frightened by the adults yelling.

If it weren't for him, I wouldn't have been able to speak. But I focused on him and forced out the words. "I think it was a warning." I wasn't certain whether anyone would be able to hear me through the noise, but silence fell as soon as I began to talk. "She was trying to warn us of the danger. She didn't forsake us. She never does."

Not even when you wanted Her to.

"You speak to Her," Elaine said, her eyes filling with tears. From across the bedspread, Charles was looking at me with something approaching awe.

"No," I said quickly, roughly. "About the effigy, that was only a guess. I've never . . ." There were some who heard the Lady's voice—Sister Julienne had, certainly. Mother Katherine, I suspected. And probably Mother Dolours as well. "I'm not a saint. It isn't like that."

Everyone just stared. I was speaking the words, but they weren't hearing me. I had lost them. I remembered the shed, where there had been nowhere to hide, and I started to feel as though the air were vanishing from the room, that there were too many bodies inside breathing it in, that I was going to suffocate.

Charles glanced at me in dismay. An idea crossed his face. "Artemisia needs to pray," he blurted out.

"Of course," Elaine said quickly, looking relieved. This, she understood. "Of course. Come along, everyone."

"Put your head between your knees," the revenant ordered, in such a curt, unsympathetic tone that I obeyed without thinking. *"Good,"* it said. *"Now breathe. There's plenty of air in here for your disgusting flesh lungs. Whoever made this building had the architectural skill of a village drunkard. There are drafts coming in through every nook and cranny."*

Bizarrely, that helped. My pulse began to slow. I couldn't begin to guess what Charles thought; he was staying perfectly silent and still. Eventually, after my breathing returned to normal, I heard him stand, his boots scuffing against the rug.

"Marguerite's at the market finding out what she can," he said as though nothing had happened. "What the Clerisy's doing about last night, and things like that. She should be back soon." I glanced up at him and saw that his brow was knit with worry. To gather this information, she was putting herself in danger.

I felt a pang, remembering what she had said to me in the graveyard. *It isn't just gossip, you know.*

He moved to leave, then hesitated. He took in my face, seeing something there—I had no idea what. Then he came back and knelt again.

"Lady vespertine," he said.

"Stand up." My voice sounded awful.

He didn't listen, just squared his shoulders in determination and bowed his head more deeply against the coverlet. A lump formed in my throat. I wanted him to understand that I wasn't Saint Artemisia; I wasn't who he thought I was. He should have realized that by now.

"You said I was the fairest maiden you'd ever seen," I reminded him.

He lifted his head. "You were," he said. "You are. You saved us—me, Jean, the captain, everyone. I saw it happen. I'll never forget it. You can't live through something like that and not remember it every day for the rest of your life." In his eyes, I could almost see a reflection of the revenant's silver fire. The light that had saved him, and nearly killed him.

I swallowed. Of the two of us, Charles was braver. He had fought on the same battlefield, and he had done it even though he had believed he was going to die. He had faced his own possessed friends to keep others safe. Charging into battle with the power of a Fifth Order relic wasn't nearly as difficult. If power were a measure of worth, Charles wouldn't have needed me at all.

I wished I were better at speaking. All those thoughts were in my head, but I didn't know how to get them out.

Seemingly unperturbed by my silence, he stood. "Thank you, lady vespertine," he said kindly. "That's all I wanted to say."

The wait for Marguerite's return tensely dragged on. A little while after Charles had left the room, Elaine's family hauled in a wooden tub so I could scrub the last of the smoke's lingering stink from my body before I put my clean clothes back on. Elaine handled them reverently, as though they were spun from gold, even though the cloak had holes in it and still smelled of damp wool. They weren't finished drying, but I was grateful to be dressed; I could hear hushed voices in other parts of the house that the revenant identified as belonging to new arrivals. They were entering in a steady stream through a back door that opened out into an alley. It wasn't difficult to guess what they had come to see.

Before long there were faces peeking in at me from around the door, despite Elaine's audible efforts to herd them away. I had the sense that she had shared the news of my presence with a few close friends, only for word to spread through the neighborhood. The revenant was annoyed to be proven right about this particular aspect of human nature.

"They say it's her hands," someone whispered. "That's where the scars are."

"How old is she?" whispered someone else. "What happened?"

"I could devour their souls for you," the revenant proposed. *"It would be fun. Don't pretend you aren't tempted."*

I braced myself when a cloaked figure barged inside, thinking this was the dreaded moment at which someone was going to throw themselves at my feet and beg for a miracle—only to relax when the intruder shook a hood back from her hair, her cheeks flushed from the morning chill. Marguerite had returned.

"Artemisia!" she exclaimed in surprise. "You're clean." She wrinkled her nose at everyone's horrified stares. "Don't worry, we grew up together. Is there anything to eat? I'm starving."

I never could have predicted how grateful I would be to see Marguerite. She cheerfully took charge of the household in a whirlwind of activity, somehow managing to transport me to the kitchen in a shuffle that placed me between her, Charles, and Jean, to the disappointment of everyone craning their necks for a look. At the table, she ushered me to the least visible corner in the back. Meanwhile

Jean sat nearest the door, blocking everyone's view from the hallway. He was drawing his own share of looks, but not for the reason
I thought. I learned from Marguerite that he had carried me in his
arms all the way here. People had seen, and were treating him as
though he were part saint himself.

The little boy, whose name was Thomas, helped set the table. It
was too early for the midday meal, but Elaine brought out a haddock
and fig pie she appeared to have baked specially for the occasion, pre-
senting a slice to me nervously, as though the Lady might smite her
for offering me such lowly fare. When I tried to thank her, she fled.

We ate in a huddle, speaking in low voices. I couldn't block out the
awareness of being watched—the feeling that everyone in the house
was committing every detail of this scene to memory, and a dozen
different versions of it would be spread across the city by nightfall.

"There are all kinds of rumors," Marguerite was saying. "Everyone thinks you were in the square, but as far as I can tell, there isn't
any proof. I heard too many different stories about what happened
for any of them to be useful to the Clerisy. Some of them were
really ridiculous—they got your hair color wrong in most of them,
and in one you even brought somebody back from the dead. It's
obvious the soldiers who saw you kept their mouths shut."

"Of course they did," Charles said, offended.

She flashed him a quick smile, a dimple appearing on her cheek,
before she turned back to me. "So the Clerisy isn't officially searching for you yet, but there's too much confusion to know for sure.
They could be looking in secret."

"They won't want to arrest her during a holy festival. People
would riot. I mean, they would anyway," he added, shooting me a
meaningful glance, "but having it happen around Saint Agnes's day
would make it worse."

VESPERTINE

"You're right—I hadn't thought of that."

"What about Captain Enguerrand? Did you hear anything?"

"Oh!" She gave him a sympathetic look, her heart in her eyes. "He's been detained. They put him in the garrison's dungeon. Someone else is leading the guard."

Jean hadn't given any indication of listening before. Now his hand clenched around his knife. Charles asked quickly, "Did you hear the name of the acting captain?"

"I think it was something like Henry. Hubert?"

"Halbert." Charles swore. "He's a bootlicker," he explained. "He'll do anything he's told to do. What are the charges against the captain?"

Marguerite didn't know. "Defying the will of the Clerisy," I guessed. It was the first time I had spoken. The sound of my voice inspired a renewed flurry of whispers from the hallway outside, though I doubted they could hear what I was saying. "After Leander's plan failed, I saw him trying to find me in the crowd. Captain Enguerrand stopped him. Leander probably claimed he was there to fight the white vicar, but Enguerrand knew the truth."

Quiet fell around the table. Then Charles said, "Wait. Leander's plan? The confessor?" and we had to explain about Leander and the Old Magic, watching him grow progressively more shocked.

"The *altar?*" he asked loudly once I'd finished, and Marguerite quickly hushed him. He lowered his voice, leaning over the table. "Then you think Confessor Leander was the one who summoned the white vicar?"

Marguerite glanced at me. "It follows the pattern," I said carefully. So far, we'd managed to skirt around the revenant's role in uncovering the Old Magic.

"We think he might have been planning to do something during the ceremony," Marguerite added, "but when he realized Arte-misia was there, he had to change tactics."

"Or the vicar was his plan all along," I said. "We don't know."

"But where did it come from?"

"It might have come into the city possessing a thrall," I said, listening to the revenant's suggestion. "The priest—Confessor Leander has enough influence to arrange passage for someone. Maybe he was keeping it in reserve for an emergency."

"Or it could have been inside Bonsaint already, minding its own business," the revenant added. *"It was old, and very intelligent."*

Intelligent enough to speak. I'd forgotten about that until now. Traitor, it had called the revenant. Scorned One, just like in Jose-phine's manuscript. I supposed the vicar had known the revenant was helping me of its own free will. Except—to have earned that title in the first place, had the revenant cooperated with a human before? It hadn't spoken to its previous vessels, the ones who had been trained. But Saint Eugenia . . .

Charles placed a hand on the table, interrupting my thoughts. "We should go to the cathedral right now," he said, starting to stand. "The service starts at fourth bell."

The hallway outside the kitchen looked more crowded than when we had sat down. There were more people in the house, watching us with eyes as wide as saucers. My presence wasn't going to remain a secret for long.

I said, "I'll go, but I need to do it alone."

"We already talked about this!" Marguerite cried.

"Both of you have been seen with me since then. Marguerite, you're the only person who knows where Saint Eugenia's reliquary is hidden. You need to keep it safe in case something happens. And, Charles, you need to stay with Jean."

They both opened their mouths to object. They were forestalled by a shuffling sound beneath the table, which stilled upon being noticed. Then a small voice demanded from beneath the table, "Do they hurt?"

"Thomas!" someone exclaimed—Elaine.

I knew what he was asking about. I had taken my gloves off to eat. I shook my head to let her know it was fine.

"No," I answered, watching Thomas emerge from hiding and clamber onto an empty stool beside me. Guessing what he wanted, I held out my bad hand. "You can touch it if you want to."

He diligently felt my scars, then grew bolder and tried to straighten my curled fingers. A collective indrawn breath filled the hallway, followed by a pause as everyone waited, I assumed, to see if the Lady was going to send a lightning bolt through the window to punish him. When nothing happened, everyone relaxed—except for Thomas, who was too busy inspecting my hand to notice.

Marguerite was watching with an oddly soft expression. "Artemisia," she said, "you know you don't need to do everything alone."

I glanced around at her, Charles, Jean. The people in the hall. I felt the revenant, bristling with impatience. And I realized she was mistaken—I hadn't been alone, not for some time.

TWENTY-ONE

In the mostly deserted streets, I saw the aftermath of the fire. I had to walk through the main square, and I passed the building that had stood behind the effigy, its shutters charred, a huge black scorch mark cast against its stone edifice like a shadow. Below, the Clerisy's platform had been reduced to a jumble of brittle burned sticks. The stink of damp charcoal hung in the air, its last resentful smoldering extinguished by the morning dew.

The square was deserted now, clearly being avoided after last night's events. The few people I came across looked fearful and ducked quickly back inside. Litter had accumulated around the base of Saint Agnes's statue. I wondered what had become of the beggar—whether he had survived. Whether he had people to care for him, or if he was out there on his own.

I discovered where everyone in the city had gone when I reached the cathedral's square. It was packed full of people, their numbers barely contained by the shops and counting houses that hemmed the area in. And everywhere, I heard my name.

"A scrap of cloth from Saint Artemisia's cloak!" shouted a vendor ahead. "As powerful as any relic!"

"Its smell is, at any rate," the revenant said. *"This way."*

I pushed through the vendor's line, ignoring the protests of the customers who stood waiting. Farther in, other vendors were trying to sell various items that I had supposedly touched, like pieces of Priestbane's tack, and even in one case, "a lock of hair from the maiden's own head." *"Blond,"* the revenant supplied. *"Also, they got it from a horse."*

The crossbow bolt was still the most common ware being hawked, but no one was calling it that any longer. It had become the holy arrow instead. I supposed that sounded nicer. The buyers most likely didn't know any better, or they were simply eager to believe that the more romantic-sounding version was the truth. Some might remember that the story had begun differently, but perhaps once they heard other people call it the holy arrow enough times, they started to doubt their memory, then started to forget.

And it appeared the strategy was working. The vendors were selling out nearly faster than they could make them. With my head down, I watched a boy working in a stall surreptitiously dip a splinter of wood into a jar of pig's blood and then stick it in a bowl of sand to let it dry. I wouldn't have seen it if I hadn't been looking down and happened to glimpse him working through a tear in the stall's fabric.

Perhaps this was how history treated saints. It didn't matter what was real, what had truly happened. Even as they lived, their lives passed into legend.

"Nun?"

I had halted in the middle of the square, the traffic flowing around me as though I'd turned to stone. A sudden impulse had seized me to tear off my glove and look at the cut on my hand. It hadn't even finished healing yet. I felt as though I needed to prove it still existed as around me a dozen voices shouted my name, desperate to own pieces of me, uncaring of the truth: even if they butchered me like an animal, there wouldn't be enough blood in my body to anoint their holy arrows. They would martyr me themselves to satisfy their hunger for a saint.

"Nun?" the revenant repeated.

"Nothing," I said, and put down my hand.

A moment later, a shadow fell over me. I was distracted, so for the first time since entering the square, I made the mistake of looking up. Panic descended on me like the stroke of a gavel. When my wits returned, I found myself crouched in an alley with my heart hammering, feeling like an idiot as the revenant flitted through my body searching for injuries, finding nothing.

"What happened?" it demanded for the fourth or fifth time. *"What's wrong with you?"*

A lot, no doubt. I wasn't certain I should tell the truth, since "the cathedral is big" didn't seem like something that should send a person careening into an alley in mindless terror. But the cathedral was big, and I couldn't have come up with a lie even if I'd wanted to.

"The cathedral," I mumbled finally.

The revenant went quiet. Possibly it was remembering that I had spent a considerable portion of my life locked inside a shed. Then it said, *"Keep your eyes on the ground, like you were doing before. Close them, if you want to. I'll tell you when we're close."*

The rush of gratitude I felt in response was so potent that I was certain the revenant could sense it. Thankfully, it didn't say anything as it guided me back into the square.

Now that I had seen it, the cathedral's presence loomed. I felt
the weight of its age-blackened stone towering above, encrusted
with carved figures of saints and spirits, its spiny, intricate spires
piercing the sky like the points of misericordes. It seemed that it
might come crashing down at any moment, too huge and terrible
to support its own weight.

It was no less crowded in the cool, dank shadows surrounding
the cathedral, but here the voices were hushed, people huddled
together as though for safety, waiting to be let inside. I picked
through them until I found an empty space on the ground. Many
of my neighbors looked like refugees; I wondered what it must feel
like to have come to Bonsaint seeking shelter, only to discover that
even the city wasn't safe. To them, the cathedral represented the
last bastion of refuge in Roischal, its holiness impenetrable.

After what I'd seen in Naimes, I knew better.

The first change I noticed in the square was a nervous ripple
among the vendors. They started flipping cloths over their wares,
hastily laying out different items. A figure was approaching through
the crowd.

"The priest," warned the revenant, right before Leander strode
into view.

People stumbled to get out of his way. They would have done
so even if he were a stranger, his reputation unknown. He looked
immaculate in his full black and silver regalia, his beautiful face as
cold as a drawn blade. From the looks he sent the vendors, it was
clear he knew what they had been selling. They flinched, their eyes
darting to his onyx ring.

I sat still, watching. From this distance, in the shadows, it would
be impossible for him to pick me out from the crowd.

He strode the rest of the way across the square and up the

cathedral's steps. As though cowed into obedience by his approach, the great doors hastily swung open to admit him. I caught a flash of the sacristan's crimson vestments amid a flurry of movement, suggesting Leander had startled a group of clerics inside. It took a moment for the incident to get sorted out and for the sacristan to begin admitting the waiting congregation.

"Pauper's balcony!" a strident voice cried, directing those of us sitting on the ground toward a different door. I hadn't noticed it before: it was a grimy side entrance set almost invisibly into the cathedral's wall. As I joined the others in shuffling toward it, I watched the sacristan methodically turn aside those he deemed too slovenly for the main entrance, gesturing them toward our line instead.

We filed up a dim, sour-smelling stair, our shoes thumping on wood worn black and shiny with the passage of generations of dirty feet. We emerged onto a plain standing-room balcony. A wrought-metal screen separated the balcony from the rest of the cathedral, so the congregation seated in the pews below wouldn't see us—or smell us, I assumed.

Looking out, I had to lean against the rail for balance. The vaulted ceiling soared upward until its details vanished in a haze of incense smoke. Seven towering stained-glass windows captured the sun and filled the nave with light. I recognized them from my vision in the stable, though I hadn't been able to make out the details then.

Now I saw that each one depicted an image of a high saint. Saint Agnes occupied the central place of honor: pale and sorrowful, her hands crossed over her breast as though she lay on a funeral bier, surrounded by white lilies. Beside her stood dark-haired Saint Eugenia, wearing a shining suit of armor and clasping a sword. She smiled serenely down at the congregation from her lofty height, engulfed in silver flames.

A chill gripped me. I had never seen an image of Saint Eugenia wielding the revenant's fire. I was conscious as I hadn't been for some time that it was her fragile bone I had carried across Roischal's countryside, that I had held in the palm of my hand.

As though sensing my thoughts, the revenant said in a tone I couldn't read, *"That doesn't look anything like her."*

It nudged my gaze down to the altar. Beneath the white altar cloth, it was surprisingly crude in appearance, roughly hewn from dark stone. I guessed that it bore some spiritual significance—perhaps it was a saint's sarcophagus, or it had been chiseled from a sacred place, like the site of a martyrdom. Since this was the Cathedral of Saint Agnes, I could hazard a guess as to whose. I felt the revenant inspecting it too, drawing its own conclusions.

Murmuring voices surrounded me as worshippers continued to pack onto the balcony. Through them, the revenant said, *"This is unexpected."*

It didn't say it in a good way. My mouth went dry. "What?"

"This spell . . . it's strange, nun. It's the same Old Magic I've been sensing all along, but it isn't a new working. It's hundreds of years old, at a guess."

"Then Leander didn't create it." My voice merged with the balcony's steady stream of chatter.

"No, but he's certainly interacted with it in a way that no one else has. Perhaps he found out how to awaken the ritual and harness its power." It paused, then said, *"I can't tell any more from here. We need to get closer. You're going to have to touch it."*

Of course I was. At least that wouldn't be difficult. After the service, it was customary to line up along the nave to touch the altar. Considering yesterday's events, I predicted that a lot of people were going to want its blessing.

Just then the Divine appeared, heading toward the chancel, the long train of her robes gliding behind her. And as my luck would have it, Leander followed after her like a wolf trailing a lamb. I was so busy wondering how I was going to avoid him that I almost didn't notice the way some of the clerics were giving him sidelong looks and gossiping behind their hands. I suspected he was aware of it; his back was very straight going up the steps to the sanctuary.

The balcony was packed full now. A hush descended. Everyone watched the Divine the same way they had looked at me in the house, desperate for guidance. Despite myself, I pitied her. I remembered how sorrowful she had looked in Naimes. The knowledge that she had been the second choice for Divine surely weighed on her. She couldn't afford to fail her people again.

She folded her hands. Her sweet, clear voice filled the nave: "Goddess, Lady of Death, Mother of Mercy, bless us with the stillness of Your regard."

The Lady rarely sent a sign in response to the traditional invocation. In my seven years at the convent, I had seen it happen only a handful of times. But today the Divine was clearly hoping for one. Everyone could see it. After her voice fell silent, there came a long, waiting pause, the congregation holding perfectly still, suspending its breath, trying not to exhale and disturb the candles.

At first it seemed it might work. The flames were tranquil, betrayed by only a few slight flickers here and there. Then the candles on the altarpiece ruffled in an unmistakable draft. The Divine bent her head. Only then, when it was obvious no sign was forthcoming, did the cathedral rumble with hundreds of voices repeating the refrain.

Beside me, people fearfully gripped each other's hands.

The Divine had no choice but to continue. She spoke of the soul's tribulations, of the Lady's mercy in troubling times. I let her voice wash over me as meaningless noise, using my hidden vantage behind the screen to observe Leander.

He was pretending to listen, but I caught him giving the Divine narrow-eyed looks, as though making calculations. I wondered if she had begun to suspect him, if the clerics had said something to her. Perhaps she was beginning to doubt his advice.

It struck me as darkly ironic that they interacted with Leander daily, spent hours standing around the altar, and had no inkling of the Old Magic's presence. If any of them had bothered making friends with the spirits bound to their relics, they could have saved themselves a great deal of trouble. Perhaps none of this would have happened in the first place; Leander never would have gotten away with it.

That was when understanding dawned.

They were trained not to listen to me, the revenant had said. *They didn't hear.*

Mother Katherine liked to say that our Lady was a merciful goddess, but She wasn't a nice one. I remembered the sorrow on her face when she passed me the candle in the chapel, and it struck me that she could have sent anyone: one of the sisters, someone who had been trained to wield a relic, someone older and more prepared. But the Lady had spoken to her. She had sent me.

Someone with training wouldn't have asked the revenant for its help. They wouldn't have listened to it. They wouldn't have learned about the Old Magic, and wouldn't have followed it here.

If you wish to stay in Naimes so badly, perhaps that is the Lady's will.

Wandering the convent at night, I had sometimes caught

glimpses of Sister Iris and Sister Lucinde playing a game of knights and kings through the refectory window, their faces still with concentration as they moved the carved figures across the board. One piece selected over another, its neighbor sacrificed so that it could advance. I thought of Sister Julienne dead on the crypt's floor. And I felt the Lady's shadowed hand behind me, hovering.

I understood what She wanted me to know. She had chosen me for this role, but She wouldn't hesitate to sacrifice me, too, if doing so allowed Her to win the game.

Except it wasn't a game; the stakes were the lives of everyone in Roischal. I thought of the carved toy abandoned on the mantelpiece, the child in the camp holding out a piece of bread, Thomas touching my scars. If I had to die for them, then so be it. If I had to suffer, then I would. The Lady already knew that. She didn't need to hear me say it. But still I felt Her presence, waiting in silence, and knew there was nothing She had done to me that I had not accepted first.

I prayed bitterly, *Do what You will.*

The Divine was still speaking when the Lady answered—when the flames of the candles on the chandeliers, in the sconces around the pillars, in the candelabra on the altarpiece all stopped flickering, filling the cathedral with shining, still light. Gasps and sobs rose from the congregation. The Divine slowly raised her head, tears luminous in her eyes, her face transformed with joy.

A strange sensation filled my chest as everyone around me laughed and cried, embracing one another in celebration. I thought it might be the humorless urge to laugh.

"Was that your doing?" the revenant asked. *"On second thought, don't tell me. I suspect I'm better off not knowing."*

A mood of almost delirious relief suffused the cathedral as

the service ended and the congregation began to stand. As I had hoped, people were already queueing up along the aisle, bending one by one to touch or kiss the altar. From the shuffling movements on the balcony around me, it seemed we would join the end of the line.

I silently willed Leander to leave, but he remained in the nave, conversing with a lector. Eventually I had no choice but to merge with the descending crowd. If I waited until I was one of the last to reach the altar as the cathedral emptied, I would risk drawing his attention even more.

I kept an eye on him as the line inched forward. His back was turned to the aisle. Worshippers still sat scattered in the pews, their heads bent in solitary prayer. I watched them gradually depart as I made my halting progress up the aisle.

Halfway there. Two-thirds. Finally I reached the steps of the chancel.

I waited as the woman in front of me lingered over the altar, ostentatiously signing herself as her lips trembled in prayer. A tear dripped from her chin onto the altar cloth. "The blood of Saint Agnes," she whispered, touching the altar with shaking fingers.

The stone did have dark marks on it, but they weren't blood, not even old blood. After spending the past seven years around corpses, I would know. They looked more like scorch marks from a fire—as though at some point in its past, the altar had been engulfed in flames.

Someone behind me coughed impatiently; another shuffled from foot to foot. Oblivious, the woman continued praying, tears streaming down her face in earnest. Occasionally we had gotten pilgrims like that in Naimes, ones who liked to put on a show. The sisters had always been able to tell they were faking it.

At last she turned to leave, glowing as though the Lady had answered her prayers. I hoped not, because based on personal experience, I was fairly certain she wouldn't like the results. I moved forward for my turn, tugging off my glove. I'd gone only one step before noisy tears erupted behind me. I glanced over my shoulder to see the woman sinking to the carpet, her face raised as though beholding a vision in the air.

"Saint Agnes!" she cried in rapture. "I see you—I hear you! Reveal your message to me!"

Everywhere, conversation halted. Across the pews, Leander began to turn.

My stomach dropped. I ducked my head and reached for the altar, hoping the revenant could make do with a glancing touch before I vanished behind the line. I moved too quickly to react to its startled warning of, *"Nun, wait—"*

My fingers brushed the stone, and pain exploded in my skull, worse than anything I had ever felt: a shrieking, red-streaked abyss, devouring thought and memory. For a moment I didn't remember who I was or where, or why any of that mattered. All I wanted was to escape from the pain, even if it meant someone bludgeoning me over the head to make it stop. Something inside me was being torn apart, and the feeling was terrible beyond comprehension.

I thought nonsensically of the whirlwind of bats descending on the chapel's bell tower, only in reverse: siphoning out in unnatural backward flight, the solid, dark mass disintegrating into scraps of wind-whipped black, scattering away across the night until nothing was left.

I realized someone was screaming, thinly and from what seemed like far away. I blinked until images swam into focus, their blurry edges haloed in light.

I wasn't the one who was screaming—it was the woman collapsed on the carpet while bystanders collected around her. She was still crying out to Saint Agnes, and like an awkward participant in her act, I had fallen to my knees in front of the altar with my red, scarred hand extended, plain for everyone to see.

But no one was looking. Everyone was riveted by the drama unfolding at the center of the aisle, except for one. Across the aisle, behind the pews, Leander was staring at me. The lector he had been speaking to was saying something—asking him a question—but he didn't seem to hear her as he took a step forward, slowly reaching for his onyx ring.

I had to get out. Something had happened to the revenant, something terrible; I couldn't feel its presence inside me at all. I scrambled up, away, pain driving through my skull with every step, and didn't notice when my glove dropped from the folds of my cloak to lie forgotten on the flagstones.

TWENTY-TWO

illars reeled past; a saint's face gazed down at me, pieced together in stained glass. A banded door, the darkness of a stair—and then came the choking clouds of incense, rushing into my lungs like fire. Statues reared from the gloom, staring tranquilly from their dark niches. Fleeing in half-blind desperation, I had stumbled into the cathedral's crypt. I felt my way along the niches for a door. There would be a way out, a way into the catacombs.

Staggering along, I almost collided with a pale candlelit shape in the smoke: a young woman in white, frozen in surprise. An orphrey.

"Leave us," said a voice from the stair, and she obediently turned and vanished, slipping past the tall, forbidding figure on the steps.

"Artemisia," Leander said. His face looked composed, but his eyes were rimmed in red. "Did you fall?"

The revenant's fate obliterated all other thought; everything else seemed trivial in comparison. I looked at him uncomprehendingly, and he repeated, "Into the river—did you fall?" I didn't say anything, but my face must have given him the answer. He laughed, a breathless, disbelieving sound. "You didn't. You played me for a fool."

"I thought you were used to that," I said, and went back to feeling for the door.

I hadn't meant it as an insult, only the truth, but he seemed to take it as one. Steps rang against stone, and a hand closed on my shoulder and yanked me around. Spots floated in front of my vision as he bent to put our faces level. Now that he was closer, I saw that he wasn't as calm as I had thought. His lips were bloodless, his expression strained, his eyes a wild, vivid emerald even in the murky gloom of the crypt. I remembered what Curist Abelard had said about confessors—that they eventually lost their minds.

"You know about the altar," he said, his hands gripping my shoulders, twisting up the fabric of my cloak. "Why were you touching it? What are you trying to do?"

I was surprised he had to ask. "To stop you," I rasped.

He squeezed his eyes shut, looking pained. "Then I was right all along. You aren't in control of the revenant, not completely. Whatever you are, you aren't a saint. We're alike in that, you see." Something about that seemed to strike him as horribly funny. I thought he might laugh again, or even let out a sob, but instead he gave me a little shake and said, "Artemisia, whatever it's telling you—whatever it has convinced you is true—you can't trust it. You need to stop listening to it. It's a monster."

Didn't he understand? The revenant was no longer here. There was a raw, bloody place inside of me where it had been torn away. Through the pain, I focused on Leander's face, so he would know that when I answered him, I meant it. "I know."

His eyes widened the instant before my head slammed against his nose with a sickening crunch. I barely felt it—which probably wasn't a good sign—but he staggered and fell, half-catching himself against a saint's statue. He touched his lips and looked at his fingers, then back at me.

"You won't escape from me again," he said, and brought his bloody hand to his ring.

This time, something happened that I hadn't seen before. Silvery vapor came pouring out of the relic, boiling upward into a shape. And then I realized I had seen something like it once. This was what Mother Katherine had done in the chapel, when she had summoned her rivener outside of its relic to drive the other spirits back.

I knew I was in trouble even before the spirit finished taking form: a robed figure draped in chains, its broad shoulders bowed beneath their weight. Nothing showed within its hood, not even pinpricks of light for eyes—only darkness. In one gloved hand, it held a bell.

The shadowed hood regarded me, its attention weighted with a sense of somber despair, a silent crushing judgment. I redoubled my efforts to find the door. Without the revenant, I couldn't fight it; I could only escape.

But it didn't attack. Instead, it turned, slowly, to look down at Leander.

He had pulled himself up a little, his pallor sickly in the candlelight, sweat shining on his brow. When the hood turned to him, he gazed at it a moment frozen, as though seeing something terrible in its emptiness. Then he seemed to come back to himself. With trembling hands, he fed his censer a fresh cone of incense and held it aloft, shielding himself behind the smoke. And he bared his teeth, which were stained with blood.

"You *will* obey me," he said. *"Subdue her."*

The penitent turned back to me slowly, as though disappointed by the command. With every sign of great reluctance, it raised its bell.

A surface gave beneath my hand: a latch. I pushed through the door and slammed it shut behind myself just as the bell rang. The sound that reverberated through the wood was not the chime of a small hand-bell, but the deep, melancholy toll of a funeral bell—giant, cast in iron, held aloft with chains. The sound struck me like a physical blow, driving me to my knees. My vision grayed.

An agony of guilt consumed me. I had failed the Lady. I had destroyed the revenant. Without its power, everyone in Roischal would die, and it was my fault. The revenant wasn't coming back.

"Revenant," I begged, but still I felt nothing. I knew, somehow, that it wouldn't have abandoned me like it had after the battle—not now, not like this. Not by choice. It wouldn't leave me alone again.

As the bell's echoes faded, a fragment of my wits returned. Knowing the door would earn me only a few seconds, I forced myself to stand. I was in the catacombs now, surrounded by bone-filled niches. I staggered to the nearest one and fumbled through the dry bones, hoping one of the clerics had been interred with their dagger. Nothing. I moved on to the next, feeling the ancient, cobwebby shroud crumble to dust at my touch. Shades flitted away, taking their silvery light with them, making fearful, gape-mouthed faces at me from the ceiling.

The door opened just as my ungloved hand closed on something harder and smoother than bone. The bell tolled again, merciless, fogging my thoughts with misery. I tore the dagger from its niche, barely keeping my grip on it as I sagged against the wall.

When I managed to look up, the penitent was advancing, with Leander behind it, censer in one hand, the other clenched in his robes over his heart.

He met my eyes in determined anguish. A tear fell shivering from one eye, and more glistened on his lashes. As much as I hated him, I didn't envy whatever the penitent was making him feel.

I backed up a scuffling step, bringing the dagger in front of me in defense. Only then did I notice that I had grabbed it by the blade. I clumsily adjusted my grip, feeling as though I had never been trained to wield it.

The penitent towered over me. It made no effort to avoid the dagger as I struck it again and again, the silver-edged wounds sealing almost as soon as I dealt them. Within the empty darkness of its hood, a shape began to resolve: a pale, blurry, indistinct smudge, like a face pressed against the outside of a window at night. As the blots of light and dark sharpened into focus, I saw that it was a face—my little brother's, eyes wide with fear, mouth stretching wide in a scream. Before I could be certain of what I had seen, the face morphed instead into Mother Katherine's, ghostly white and unsmiling. Dead. The misery was like a stone in my chest; I couldn't breathe.

The bell tolled on and on. The penitent's face changed again. It became a skull, the eye sockets bound with frayed wrappings: the revenant, whom I had destroyed. My knees bent, and my vision swarmed black.

"Yield," said Leander from somewhere far away, speaking through his teeth, as though enduring incredible pain.

The dagger slipped from my hand. I didn't remember falling, but I found myself on the ground, my cheek against the dirt, my arm flung out before me.

My vision dimmed and narrowed until I saw nothing beyond my own hand. Strangely, a welt marked my palm that hadn't been there before. Struggling to think, I realized that it was where I had held the dagger by the blade. My scarred skin hadn't felt the pain, but the consecrated steel had burned me.

Impossible—but the welt was there. And its existence could mean only one thing.

"Revenant," I said. "Attend me."

Without hesitation, the presence lying wrecked and shattered inside of me gathered the last of its broken strength to obey. Power rushed into my veins, my limbs, my heart. My vision blazed white as I stood. I saw the penitent awash in a light a hundred times brighter than its own, its hood empty after all, and then I stepped through it.

Vapor fell away around me. Silver flames danced over my cloak, bathing the catacombs in their radiance, chasing away the shadows.

Leander was on the ground, braced against the tunnel's wall. Tears streaked his uplifted face. In his eyes and slightly parted lips I saw fury and shame and horror mixed with tormented, fearful longing. That he might have been wrong; that he might be look- ing not at Artemisia of Naimes, but Saint Artemisia. He gasped a breath and tried to rise, only to slip back down. His eyes were fluttering shut; he was on the verge of passing out.

"*Kill him,*" whispered a voice.

I froze. The order sounded like it had been breathed directly into my ear: less a voice than a draft from an opened tomb, a hiss of cloth slithering over a grave.

"*If you let him live . . . ,*" the voice went on awfully, as though whispered from a deathbed, but this time I recognized it.

"Revenant," I said.

It didn't respond; it had used the last of its strength. The light faded as the silver flames burned lower and guttered and then died, throwing the tunnel back into shadow. Leander had lost consciousness, a fresh rivulet of blood trickling from his nose.

A clanging sound came from the crypt, the upper door being opened, its latch released. Someone was coming. Even if by some miracle no one had sensed the revenant, the orphrey might have gone for help. I had to make a decision, and quickly.

I bent to pick up the dagger. I could kill Leander. It wouldn't be difficult. I knew exactly where to put the blade and how hard to push it in. In certain scenarios, I wouldn't have hesitated. But he wasn't crouching over the altar, about to awaken a sinister ritual. He wasn't hurting anyone; he wasn't even conscious to defend himself. I would have to kill him as he lay helpless and bleeding, stripped of his defenses, collapsed against the wall of the catacombs like a martyred saint.

I didn't know what the Lady wanted me to do. There were no candles here, no signs. I was alone.

In the crypt, a voice called out. I turned and ran.

I stumbled through the tunnels, my path illuminated by shades. They tangled themselves up in the corners as I passed, the holes of their mouths and eyes frozen open in silent screams. I went through doors and branching passageways until the niches grew older and then vanished altogether, replaced by bare earth shored up with portions of stone walls. Remnants of the old city, its ruins buried beneath the streets.

Once, a grate in the ceiling opened into the world above. Bright light and noise poured down into the tunnel, voices shouting, the rattling of carts. I cringed away from it and continued stumbling along like a wounded animal looking for a place to die.

The revenant didn't speak again. Every once in a while I touched the dagger to my arm, just to make sure it was still there.

Eventually I found a grate that opened to a quieter part of the city, one I might be able to use without being spotted, but I had no idea how to move its thick iron bars without the revenant's help. I made scratches on the walls with my dagger so I could find my way back, and kept going.

I heard the trickling of water and thought I had better drink, or the revenant would be angry with me when it recovered. I didn't allow myself to consider the alternative—that it wasn't coming back, not the way it had been before.

Following the sound, I limped through a doorway that was half tumbled-out rock. Shade-light cast an ethereal glow over shapes that might have once been arches and pillars, and glittered brightly from a pool on the ground. Drawing closer, I saw that the water bubbled up from a spring with pieces of masonry scattered around it, the remains of an ancient fountain. I crouched and took cold, metallic-tasting gulps from the cracked stone basin, the water glimmering with the reflections of the shades, its ripples dashing my reflection to pieces. In some of them I saw Artemisia. In others, only Anne.

I didn't want to stay, but I didn't think anyone would find me in this place—not after the twists and turns I had taken in the catacombs. And I had nowhere else to go that I knew would be safe. I dragged myself to a corner and huddled there, gripping the dagger tightly. Silence pressed in. Without thinking, I moved the blade toward my arm, already patterned with welts.

This time, I felt a stir. *"Stop,"* the feeble voice whispered.

My hand paused. I felt my pulse beating in my throat. "Revenant. What happened to you?"

"The altar—made to destroy a revenant. That's what killed . . . the other one. Sarathiel."

"Is there anything I can do?"

"Talk about this . . . later."

It thought I wanted to talk about the Old Magic. To resume planning again, to figure out our next step. I said, "I meant if there was anything I could do to help you."

There came a long, uncertain pause. *"Sleep,"* it whispered at last.

I slept and woke and slept again, occasionally creeping back to the pool to drink. Whatever the altar had done to the revenant had hurt me, too, though I suspected what I was feeling was the revenant's pain, just as it felt mine.

Time passed. Eventually I jolted to wakefulness in the near dark, in a cold sweat with my stomach in knots. I had a dreamlike impression of watching some rats go scurrying past—not a dream, I realized, as I heard telltale squeaking and scuffling, and felt the revenant's senses chasing after their tails as they fled into some dark crevice.

"That's impossible," it hissed, as though it were arguing with someone nearby.

Under other circumstances, I would have been relieved to hear the revenant sounding better. But I couldn't shake the eerie feeling that I had walked in on it speaking to an invisible third presence, an impression heightened by the darkness and a prickling sensation of being watched. It was harder to see now—most of the shades had gone, possibly frightened away. I reached for the dagger and found it already in my hand.

"What did you sense?" I asked.

I almost regretted speaking. An unsettled silence came from the revenant, as though it hadn't noticed I'd woken up and was disturbed by the failure of its own perception. Then it said, *"Nothing. I was mistaken. I'm not entirely—myself."*

I didn't need it to tell me that. Its presence felt tremulous and strange, like it had risen from a sickbed too early. If it were a person, I would make it lie down.

It went on feverishly, *"There's precedent, you see. Occasionally, in the relic, I used to sense things—things that weren't there. . . . Nun, we need to get out,"* it said suddenly. *"Back to the surface."*

I hesitated, wary. "The Clerisy's going to be looking for us. Is there anything dangerous down here?"

It seemed to consider the question. Then it said, *"Me,"* in a low tone that made the hair stand up all over my body.

I rolled to my feet and made for the doorway at once, casting around for my marks on the tunnel wall. There. The scratches were illuminated by the wispy light of a lone shade, which fled as we approached, flitting ahead. In its fragile, quivering glow, I made out another scratch farther along the tunnel, then a third, marking a fork in the passageway.

"There's a grate not too far from here."

"Hurry," the revenant said, and then a moment later, *"Hurry, you wretched nun,"* with more force behind the command.

"I almost thought you were done calling me that," I said, gripped by the sick certainty that something bad would happen if it stopped speaking. Now it felt less as though the revenant needed to lie down, and more like I needed to keep it awake.

When it didn't respond, I went a little faster, stumbling over the uneven ground. I could see the shade ahead of us, but my immediate surroundings were pitch-black. As its light receded, the tunnel grew darker and darker. Soon I would no longer be able to make out the marks. I searched for something to say, anything to break the silence.

"At least neither of us is afraid of the dark," I gasped, out of breath.

Silence emanated from the revenant, and suddenly I remembered the way my hands had begun shaking in the ostler's room when it had made me light a fire for no reason; how it had made me sleep with the loft's door open, letting in the light.

My hands were starting to shake again now, and there was a terrible pressure in my chest like a fist closing around my lungs, slowly squeezing.

"You are," I realized aloud.

"I suppose you find that amusing," it said in a sinuous, deadly voice, with a suggestion of hysteria bubbling underneath.

"No," I said, feeling extremely out of my depth.

"You're a nun, after all. You'll be glad to stuff me back into the reliquary as soon as you're finished with me—"

"Revenant."

"I know you will. It's what all of you do, you loathsome nuns. It's what Eugenia did—even after she promised—"

"Revenant!"

"—after she promised she wouldn't sacrifice herself, and you're just like her—you would throw your life away in an instant if you thought it would serve your accursed Lady—"

Its voice had increased in pitch. Dizziness churned through me; my heart was pounding shallowly and too fast. I thought I might pass out. "Revenant, calm down."

"Calm down?" it hissed. *"Calm down? Do you imagine that you can even begin to comprehend what the reliquary feels like, after a few years in a pathetic little human shed? I was trapped there for centuries*

in the silence and the dark. I'll kill all of you before I let you put me back. I'll kill all of you," it snarled, and seized me like a dog with a carcass, driving me to my knees.

In an absurd twist of fate, the grate lay just ahead. I could see it now from my angle on the ground, a square of watery gray light in the tunnel's ceiling. But I couldn't get there, because the revenant was trying to possess me.

Its presence swarmed through me, foul and oily with malice, blotting out my senses. Blood thundered in my ears; the patch of sky showing through the grate pulsed from light to dark. I brought the dagger to my arm and heard my skin sizzle, but the revenant only thrashed harder. I tasted copper.

Before, in Naimes, I had thought that I'd fought it off at its full strength. Now I wondered if it had been holding back.

I was at its mercy. I didn't even have the reliquary. When I had let Marguerite keep it, I had been placing my trust in the revenant as much as in her, because I had known that threatening to destroy the relic was no longer an option. I wouldn't have been able to go through with it—not after coming to see the revenant as a person. I couldn't have threatened it that way any more than I could have kicked that scared goat in Naimes to make it obey, or locked my own silent, shivering ten-year-old self back in the shed.

As it fought me, it kept repeating things like, *"I'll kill you all,"* and *"I'll rend your miserable soul to shreds,"* except it struck me suddenly that it might not even know what it was saying. I shouldn't have told it to calm down, because it couldn't, any more than I had been able to overcome the stink and heat of the effigy's fire or ignore the people staring at me in Elaine's house.

That was when I realized it wasn't trying to possess me on purpose.

Not that the revelation helped; I still didn't know what to do. Grasping, I thought of the goat again, the one that had been kicked and hit and yelled at until all it had known to do was bite. Talking to it had seemed to make a difference, even though it hadn't understood the words.

"It's all right," I gasped. "You'll be all right."

"I'll murder you," it snarled.

"It's all right. No one's going to hurt you."

I wasn't sure where I'd learned those phrases as a child. Someone must have said them to me for me to have repeated them to the goat, though I didn't have a memory of it. Not my parents, I knew. Possibly it had been Mother Katherine, carting my possessed and burned body all the way back to the convent, stroking my hair because she couldn't hold my hand.

I couldn't tell if the revenant was listening, but I was able to regain enough control to reach out an arm and drag myself across the tunnel's floor, toward the weak light spilling in from the grate. I wasn't certain I could get there, but I had to try, one agonizing inch at a time.

I said, "I'm not going to let anyone hurt you again."

It was an absurd thing to say to a creature like the revenant, but it also wasn't, because I was certain that no one had ever said anything like that to it before in all the long centuries of its existence. And it worked. The revenant stopped speaking in words. It started shrieking instead, howling wordlessly and tearing at me with its claws. It hurt, but it was a familiar pain, the same pain I had inflicted on myself so many times in the shed. I knew then that we really were going to be all right, because I had survived it before, and I would survive it again.

"We're almost there," I told it, and used the final breath of my failing strength to heave myself into the gray pool of light on the tunnel floor.

The revenant let out a horrible cry and renewed its thrashing, but it felt weaker now, a different kind of struggle—the despair of knowing that after the fight ended, it would have to face what it had done. I recognized that feeling too.

Me, the goat, the revenant, we weren't very different from each other in the end. Perhaps deep down inside everyone was just a scared animal afraid of getting hurt, and that explained every confusing and mean and terrible thing we did.

Leander had been right, earlier. I was the one he had misjudged. The revenant might be a monster, but it was my monster. I wrapped my arms around myself and held on as it screamed and fought and clawed. I held on until, finally, it went limp.

TWENTY-THREE

Neither of us wanted to talk about it afterward, to my profound relief. I was sore all over, and I had plenty else to occupy my thoughts. Some of them were ideas I didn't want to examine too closely, circling beneath the surface of my mind like sharks. Now that we were back aboveground, I knew it wouldn't be long before I had to face them. The scorch marks on the altar. Saint Eugenia's fire-blackened finger bone, her body burned to ash.

But for now I focused on my current problems. The first thing I had discovered after hoisting myself aboveground was that night had fallen; the gray light trickling through the grate had belonged to the moon, glaring over the city's rooftops like a bright silver coin. The street outside the alley where I had emerged looked empty, but I still checked to make sure no one was watching before I shoved the grate back into place.

The revenant's presence felt like a bruise, a dull and miserable ache. It had barely spoken to me as I'd climbed through; it had only said, *"the dagger,"* in a listless voice, leaving me to mostly figure out on my own that I was supposed to use the blade as a lever to pry up the grate. And now it said nothing as I tucked the misericorde through my belt, where it would be hidden beneath my cloak, and ventured out onto the street.

Moonlight starkly etched the cobbles and rooflines in silver. The windows were dark behind their shutters, and silence hardened the air like frost. All seemed unnaturally still—I saw no one, even though I judged the hour too early for everyone in the neighborhood to be asleep. My skin prickled with the same feeling of being watched that I had had in the tunnels. I scanned the sky until I located the points of the cathedral's spires poking above the rooftops.

Newly oriented, I drew my cloak tightly around myself and hurried down the street, weighing my options. I couldn't go back to the convent—that would be the first place Leander looked. Elaine's house was out of the question.

Candlelight flickered on a wall ahead, accompanied by low voices. I waited for the light to recede before I cautiously looked around the corner. More light glittered ahead, silhouetting a group of young women carrying candles, their breath white clouds, their faces smeared with ash. Their excited whispers scattered from the alley's walls like birds taking flight. "This way, hurry . . ."

Reaching the intersecting street, I felt as though I had stumbled into a dream. People stood everywhere, holding candles that lit the street with a dancing glow. It took me a moment to recover, disoriented and blinking. When I did, gliding into view was a solemn procession, silk gleaming in the candlelight, banners rearing from the darkness, drawing nearer to the rhythmic chiming of bells.

I crept forward and peered through the bodies. Impressions

came to me in snatches: the liquid glinting of gold candelabra, candles guttering; a painted icon of Saint Agnes sailing past, carried on a swaying platform, her gaze raised beatifically toward the canopy's fringe. Clerics walked in orderly, hooded ranks, chanting and swinging their censers, their robes sprinkled with ashes to honor the sacrifices of the saints. Once I even caught a glimpse of the sunken face of an ascetic, downcast beneath his cowl. I guessed that the glint of gray agate on his finger belonged to a gaunt relic, whose power allowed him to go for weeks without eating.

It was clear now that the Divine had ordered a procession, likely in response to the sign in the cathedral. For an event of this magnitude, every able-bodied cleric who didn't have other essential duties would be expected to attend. I stood very still, waiting. And then, as though I had summoned him, Leander appeared.

An immediate stir ran through the onlookers. One person said to another, "I heard they found him collapsed beneath the cathedral. . . . Some trouble with his relic, it sounds like . . . overpowered him . . ." Only for a third to join in, "It was worse than that—it nearly possessed him! Clerics sensed it from all over the square. . . ."

Slowly, it grew apparent that Leander hadn't told anyone about me. He had lied about what had happened—even covered for my use of the revenant's power. That was what the clerics had sensed, I was sure, not his penitent. Perhaps he didn't want anyone else to capture me; he wanted to save me for himself. Or perhaps he had another reason, one I couldn't begin to guess.

Feeling suddenly uncertain, I studied him. He hadn't changed out of his ceremonial vestments, the dust from the catacombs disguised by a sprinkling of holy ashes. Bruises discolored his austere face. His eyes were downcast beneath golden lashes, his expression impossible to read. A silver censer hung at his side—the same one, I realized, that he had given me in the battle with the rivener, before he had spun around to fight at my back. A lost memory resurfaced—the fleeting brush of his hand against mine.

I shivered, watching the procession swallow him up again.

What was his plan? What did he want?

"You didn't kill him," the revenant observed, startling me.

I quickly stepped back into an alley where I wouldn't be heard, my heart thumping against my ribs. "Are you all right? You said the altar was made to destroy revenants."

"Yes, which doesn't make any sense." Its voice sounded dull. *"As far as I can tell, it wasn't designed for any other purpose—certainly not for controlling spirits. It could be that the priest is using it as a source of power for a different ritual, but I don't think . . ."* It trailed off, thought for a moment, and then surprised me by saying, *"It's just as well you didn't kill him. We may need him. That page he took from the convent—I need to know exactly what he found."*

"You suspect something," I realized aloud.

"A misgiving, not a suspicion. I expect to find evidence that will disprove it."

"Can you tell me what it is?"

"For now, knowing wouldn't help." It hesitated. *"If it becomes relevant, I'll let you know."*

That's impossible, it had said underground. It might not have a logical explanation, but it had thought of something else, something that didn't quite make sense. Something it didn't want to tell me. I swallowed. Whatever it was thinking, it didn't want to be right.

"Unless Leander is carrying the page with him, it's probably in his quarters. The cathedral should be nearly empty right now. If the doors are locked, can you get us inside?"

"If I'm not using my full power, and I don't need to hide myself from many clerics . . . yes, that shouldn't be difficult, assuming you don't mind heights. You don't, do you?"

Mystified, I shook my head.

"Good. Once we're inside, I expect I'll be able to locate the priest's chambers by smell. Even if he hasn't left traces of Old Magic, the stink of priestly repression is impossible to miss. Let's go."

"Not until you answer my question."

"What question?" It sounded a little testy. I waited for it to think back over our conversation, and felt its tremor of surprise before it cut itself off, as though slamming the lid on a chest filled with keepsakes it didn't want me to see. *"Of course I'm all right,"* it snapped. *"Stop dawdling."*

I didn't take it personally. I knew why it had reacted that way: it wasn't used to anyone caring.

The route to the cathedral twisted confusingly through a maze of shops and houses. I could tell I was growing close when I heard a lonely voice calling out, "Only five pawns! Five pawns for a splinter of the holy arrow!" and then I looked up to see the cathedral's mullioned windows glowering above me in the night, each pane of glass cut into a diamond, winking dimly as I passed. I gave a wide berth to the cathedral guards stationed around the entrances and squeezed through a filthy alley in the back, relieved not to have faced the full scope of the cathedral. It was easier to look at up close, under the cover of darkness.

Meanwhile, the revenant searched for a place where we could climb without being spotted. *"There,"* it said at last, drawing my attention to a panel of false archways carved with a frothing mass of spirits. I guessed the scene was meant to evoke a battle in the War of Martyrs, though it was hard to tell, since most of it was caged behind scaffolding for repairs. No one was standing guard, likely because there weren't any possible entries: only a windowless wall above and a stinking gutter below.

I clambered up the scaffolding, and at the revenant's direction set my boot against one of the lowest outcroppings of masonry at the top. A rush of power propelled me upward, tingling through my limbs and outward into my fingers and toes. I flowed up the wall as though I weighed nothing, the revenant effortlessly finding handholds in the dark.

More statues awaited me above, standing in endless carved rows. There were hundreds of minor saints in Loraille, one for every spirit bound; I didn't know all their names even after seven years as a novice. I sent silent apologies their way as I hoisted my way past, boots scraping on their heads and arms.

Spirit-shaped grotesques crouched along the nearest roofline, which connected a series of flying buttresses to a higher wall above. I grabbed a downspout shaped like an undine, whose grimacing mouth would spew water from the gutter when it rained, and squirmed over the edge.

Warmth still radiated from the lead roof, baked into it by the sun. I drew in a deep breath of night air. Even from up here, I could faintly smell the procession's incense. Stars spread coldly overhead, and far below, the procession looked like a long ribbon of light twisting through the streets, its many candles sparkling.

"*This way,*" the revenant said. I clambered along on all fours until I reached a walkway that stretched behind the buttresses. Here I could no longer see the procession, my view obscured by a jumble of rooftop angles. The wind moaned in the dark, passing through the multitude of carved saints and spirits. I felt the revenant shiver, and moved a little faster.

The door it prodded me toward wasn't locked. It opened easily, admitting me into a narrow, dusty stair that I guessed was used to access the roof for repairs. My pulse started quickening as soon as I closed the door behind me, shutting out the wind and what little light remained. I was panting by the time I burst out the door at the bottom, into a musty wood-paneled hall illuminated by a single round window. The walls were hung with old paintings of dour-looking clerics, whose shadowed eyes seemed to judge me as I bent over my knees, catching my breath.

I wanted to ask the revenant how it could be afraid of the dark if its senses allowed it to see straight through walls, but I doubted it would welcome the question. I could tell it felt touchy about me merely knowing its secret in the first place.

"I only sense one human with a relic here," it said once I'd straightened, heading off any possible conversation on the subject.

"That's probably the sacristan," I said. It was his duty to look after the cathedral's valuables in everyone else's absence.

Another door lay at the end of the hall. This time I emerged onto a high marble gallery that looked out over the darkened nave. There were no lamps here, but the huge windows cast fragmented pools of moonlight over the collection of holy objects lined up on display.

I didn't approach the balustrade, knowing that if I did I would bring the altar into view below, and I didn't want to look at it again if I didn't have to. I walked along the wall instead, watching my dim, distorted reflection ripple over the dented bronze of a church bell, probably recovered from an important chapel that had fallen during the Sorrow. Next I passed a saint's yellowed linen smallclothes, reverently preserved beneath glass. Halfway down the gallery I encountered a giant wagon wheel, each of its spokes longer than I was tall. I paused to read the engraving on its plaque: A WHEEL OF THE SIEGE-ORGAN OF MARSONNE.

I had read about the siege-organ before: a colossal pipe organ mounted on a wagon drawn by two dozen draft horses, its consecrated pipes unleashing a thunder of holy sound that disintegrated any spirit within range. Though powerful, it had proven impractical to use in battle, its delicate valves and bellows constantly breaking as it bumped over the roads of Loraille. It now stood in Chantclere's cathedral, stationary forevermore, probably used to blast shades out of the vault every evening.

As I stood gazing at the wheel, a chill crept over me. I had an eerie premonition of spirits swarming the countryside unchecked with only antiques left to battle them. Of the pipe organ's ancient, groaning bulk dragged beneath the sky for the first time since the War of Martyrs, dusted off like the harrow, turned to as a last resort. That could be Loraille's fate if I failed.

We made it the remainder of the way to the living quarters without incident, except once when I had to hide to avoid the sacristan. I watched him go past through the crack behind a door, muttering endearments to the raven on his shoulder, its loud croaks and warbles a counterpoint to the quiet scuff of his velvet slippers. The candles flared to life at his approach and snuffed out one by one after he had gone.

The clerics dwelled in private chambers in a wing of the cathedral that reminded me of a dormitory, though vastly better appointed. I found a lantern and used its light to peer inside the doors I found ajar, discovering that some were full apartments with their own sitting rooms and garderobes. The revenant directed me past them and down a few more halls, where the surroundings grew noticeably plainer. When it guided me to Leander's room, at first I thought it had made a mistake.

Like most of the other chambers, the door wasn't locked. I found myself in a plain cell with a single bed and a tiny latticed window, bare of decoration except for a small painted icon hanging on the wall above the writing desk—Saint Theodosia, the patron saint of Chantclere. The room looked unused, the wardrobe shut, the bed neatly made.

I looked around, frowning. "Are you sure?"

"It might not belong to him, but he's certainly sleeping here. The stench is unmistakable."

Skeptically, I set down the lantern and opened the wardrobe. Leander's clothes hung within: two sets of severe black travel robes and an empty space for his full regalia. There weren't any signs to suggest that he shared the room with another priest or priestess, a friend or lover he visited from his own more lavish quarters. The room belonged to him and him alone.

As a confessor, he should have had his pick of any apartment he wanted. He wouldn't have been forced to take this room. For whatever reason, he lived here by choice.

Thrown off-balance by that idea, I searched his robes, which looked oddly lonely hanging amid the unused space inside the wardrobe. I found nothing, but once accidentally stuck my finger through a rent in the cloth whose placement matched the wound he had received from one of the traps in the sacred chambers. Judging by its size, he had been injured more badly than I had thought. Afterward, I fruitlessly checked the drawer at the bottom of the wardrobe, which contained his smallclothes, undershirts, stockings, and a pair of black leather gloves. On the revenant's advice, I felt across the drawer's underside. Still nothing.

We searched beneath the mattress, under the desk, behind the icon of Saint Theodosia. We paced the room for loose floorboards.

I was starting to wonder if he hadn't kept the page—if he had tossed it down a well or burned it—when the toe of my boot struck something that went sliding under the bed.

Bending to retrieve it, I discovered that it was a slim, ordinary prayer book. I turned it upside down and shook it, but nothing fell out. Rifling through its pages likewise yielded nothing. It contained columns of common prayers, its margins crammed with notes written in a precise, angular hand that I guessed belonged to Leander. The only other writing belonged to a dedication inside the cover: *Study hard. I'll see you soon. —G.* Frustrated, I sat down on the bed.

But the revenant seemed interested. It urged, *"Take another look at those notes. The ones near the end."*

Of course. Back home, novices had passed notes to each other during lessons by writing inside prayer books and swapping them around when the sisters weren't looking. Scanning the pages, my eyes caught on a particular phrase.

Leander had written, *A. of N.—not possessed? Deceived by R.? What does it want? Biding its time? No mass murder thus far.*

"Not for lack of enthusiasm," said the revenant, at the same time I realized the "R" stood for either "revenant" or "Rathanael." Given Leander's status, not to mention the research he had been doing, it wasn't surprising that he knew the revenants' names and which one was bound to Saint Eugenia's relic. Still, the idea made me uneasy.

The next several lines of notes were crossed out too thoroughly to be legible; the revenant emitted a flicker of irritation. Then they continued in an unsteady hand, the ink blotted: *A. not deceived— willing ally?* Underlined, *In control?*

That was where the writing ending. A bloody thumbprint marked the bottom of the page. He must have scribbled those final notes today after our encounter in the catacombs. I sat looking at the thumbprint for a moment, imagining Leander stumbling into the room, scrawling those words, the book falling from his fingers to the floor. Unsure what compelled me, I drew back the bed's neatly made coverlet.

Blood spotted the linens. When I had fought Leander earlier, he had already been wounded, perhaps seriously. He couldn't have gone to a healer without drawing attention, so he must have treated the injury himself, alone. Concealed the evidence beneath his spotless robes, his carefully made-up bed. Hidden it from everyone but me.

His voice echoed in my mind: *You know about the altar.* The dark thoughts circled. I couldn't put them off any longer.

"There's something I want to know," I said. "How did Saint Agnes die trying to bind Sarathiel if the altar destroyed it instead?"

"The altar was part of the binding ritual," the revenant replied, distracted. Its attention was still roaming back and forth over the crossed-out portion of Leander's notes. *"Or at least, it was intended to be. Whoever created it failed to draw the runes properly, with catastrophic results."*

I thought again of the scorch marks on the altar, the fire-blackened appearance of Saint Eugenia's relic. The ashes sprinkled on the robes of the clerics. I remembered the way the revenant had spoken in the convent's underground vault, choosing its words so carefully, leaving too many things unsaid.

And I thought of holy symbols, revealed to the saints as shapes written in divine fire.

My voice sounded hollow as I asked, "Why was she trying to bind a spirit with Old Magic?"

Silence fell, the revenant realizing what it had revealed too late. After a moment it ventured, *"Nun, what you need to understand* about Old Magic is that it isn't inherently evil. It's merely a source of power. A forge can be used to create a sword, or one of those things you humans use to dig around in the dirt—"

"A plow," I said.

"Yes, whatever that is. My point is—"

"The saints used Old Magic. They did, didn't they?"

I felt the revenant considering and discarding a number of complicated replies. Then it said, simply, "Yes. If it's any consolation, your kind would have been obliterated otherwise. And Old Magic hadn't been declared a heresy yet, though it was swiftly falling out of favor."

I sat staring at the bloodstains. "It was wrong."

"What?"

"Putting spirits into relics. It was wrong. Whoever came up with the idea—they were wrong."

"The Old Magic—"

"I don't care about the magic. That isn't what made it wrong. Destroying spirits—that has to be done. But trapping them in a relic is different. It's cruel. I didn't know that before, but I do now."

The revenant was very quiet. "You would have died," it said at last. "All of you."

Where my emotions should have been, there was a hard black lump inside my chest, burning like a coal. "Maybe we should have."

I felt it digesting my reply. Then it said, "Check the book's binding."

I suspected it merely wanted to distract me, but I checked anyway. As I ran my fingers over the binding, I reflected that I wasn't surprised—only bleakly disappointed. If someone could bind a spirit through sheer force of will and the Lady's grace alone, then I would have done it to the ashgrim. I would have burned all of myself, not just my hands, to be rid of it. I thought of Eugenia's smiling face—*that doesn't look anything like her*—and thought of the vendors hawking my blood and hair and clothes and wondered who she had truly been, if she had thought of herself as a saint or just a girl, if she had been glad to immolate herself so that the only thing people could take from her was the one she could control. I could ask the revenant. Perhaps after this was over, I would.

But for now I'd found where the stitching had been cut, creating a hidden pocket between the two sheets of parchment that made up the prayer book's back cover. Pressed within, revealed by an uneven edge of sliced vellum, was the missing page.

I tugged it free and moved to Leander's desk stool, bringing it to the lantern's light. The revenant read faster than I did, but it could only read the writing that my eyes were focused on. It jerked my gaze down the page until it reached the entry: *Year of Our Lady 1155, A small casket crafted of gold and ivory, set with twelve rubies and eight sapphires, heretofore stored in Chantclere, containing the Holy Ashes of Saint Agnes.*

"*Those fools,*" it hissed. "*Those festering imbeciles! They should have scattered her ashes in the Sevre, the ocean—they shouldn't have kept them!*"

I was getting a bad feeling. "Revenant, what did you sense in the tunnels?"

"*I thought that I had imagined it. The darkness, the silence—after a time, I start seeing things that aren't there. . . .*" A tremor ran through it. "*I sensed another revenant. Here, in the city.*"

For a moment, the words didn't make sense. I stared at the page, its text suddenly incomprehensible. "You don't mean a revenant bound to a relic."

"*No. I felt Sarathiel's presence. Impossible, of course, unless it wasn't truly destroyed; unless it was merely weakened to the point that*" *it seemed to be and has been hiding in the ashes for the past three hun-dred years, slowly rebuilding its strength."*

"Spare relics that aren't used very much are often stored inside the altar, beneath the altar stone." My thoughts had begun careen-ing like a wagon down a hill, gaining speed. "The casket might be there too. But wouldn't someone have sensed it? They use the altar every day."

"Weakened, its presence may not have been noticeable. As it recov-ered, it would have regained the ability to hide itself. Out of all of us, Sarathiel was always the best at concealing its presence." I remem-bered its page in the manuscript—Sarathiel the Obscured, its tipped chalice pouring mist. *"The better question is how it's managed to recover in the first place. It wouldn't have been able to heal without consuming life of some kind. . . ."*

"The rats," we both said at the same time. I found that I was standing, the stool toppled over. I hadn't heard it fall.

Leander had found dead rats, the curist had said, their bodies unmarked. I wondered how many rats had been discovered dead inside the cathedral over the centuries, a few here, a few there, and no one had paid them any mind.

"We need to destroy it now," the revenant said urgently. *"Before it takes a human soul. That's when it will have enough strength to leave the casket, and it will act soon. It almost certainly knows I'm here—"*

It stopped at a faint sound. Somewhere in the cathedral, echo-ing, came the panicked cries of a raven.

TWENTY-FOUR

I was halfway to the chapel before I realized I had left the lantern behind in Leander's room, but there was enough moonlight to see by, to take the stairs down from the gallery two at a time. A raven was flapping in circles above the pews. "Dead!" it screamed. "Dead!" Its shrill voice rang from the high, shadowed vault.

The stairs let me out into the transept. When I reached the nave, I drew up short. The sacristan lay collapsed at the center of the aisle, just shy of the sanctuary's steps, in a heap of crimson velvet. His eyes were still open, his waxen face frozen in an expression of surprise. And behind the altar, an almost perfect match for my vision in the stable, stood Leander: his robes swallowed up by the dark, the casket in his hands. The altar's slab had been pushed a few inches to the side, revealing a hint of the cavity where it had rested.

I drew my dagger. "Put it down."

"I'm afraid I can't do that," he replied. He didn't seem surprised to see me; there was no emotion in his voice at all. "I went to some effort to leave the procession unseen, and this might be my only chance. Do you understand how rarely the cathedral is empty? It's a pity about the sacristan, though I never did like him."

"Put it down," I repeated, stepping over the body and onto the stairs.

"Are you going to fight me?" he asked, remote.

"Don't," the revenant interjected tightly. *"Sarathiel is still confined to the ashes, but it's nearly strong enough to escape. If there's a struggle—if the casket falls . . ."*

"If you do, you'll win," Leander admitted. Drawing closer, I realized I had been wrong about his lack of emotion. His hands were steady around the casket, but now I saw the strain in his eyes, vivid against his bruised face. He was trying his best to hide it, but he was afraid.

I mounted the last step and faced him across the altar. He took an immediate pace back, putting himself against the altarpiece. I stared at him, trying to figure out how to take the casket.

"Talk to him," the revenant urged.

I raised my eyes to Leander's face, at which he was unable to hide a flinch. I asked, "Why did you lie about what happened in the crypt?"

He swallowed, noticeable only by the slight movement of his collar. "The answer to that is complicated." He hesitated. "The most practical reason, perhaps, was that I didn't wish the death of any cleric who tried to apprehend you."

"I'm not the one who's been killing people."

"What?" For an instant, he looked thrown. Then his face shuttered. "Believe what you like of me, but I've never used my relic to take a life."

"I was talking about the Old Magic," I said. "Or does murder only count if you commit it with your own hands?"

"You thought—" He broke off as though unable to finish. He glanced at the sacristan, then back at me. He began again, slowly, with a very strange expression on his face, "You thought I've been practicing Old Magic?"

I already knew he was a skilled liar, or at least he was talented at concealing the truth. I didn't believe his act for a moment. But the revenant gave a forceful hiss, as though letting out a swear. *"Nun, ask him if this is the first time he's touched the casket."*

I repeated the question aloud, and Leander gave me the same narrow, piecing-things-together look he'd given the Divine earlier. "No," he said carefully. "I examined it the night I returned to Bonsaint after you escaped from the harrow. I had been meaning to take a closer look at it for some time." That was the night of the vision—the point at which he had started smelling of Old Magic. "I thought it was strange," he went on, seeming to take my silence for permission to continue, "that all records pertaining to it seemed to have mysteriously vanished from the cathedral's archives."

Was that what I had seen in the vision? He hadn't been practicing Old Magic. He had been straightening after touching the casket. Looking at it now, I noticed for the first time how firmly he was holding it shut.

"Do you know what's inside?" I asked, not meaning the ashes.

He met my gaze. Beneath his forced calm, I saw a bottomless well of horror. "As of two nights ago, yes."

"I was wrong," the revenant said. *"The smell of Old Magic has been coming from Sarathiel—from the ritual that nearly destroyed it. It's been leaving a trace on everything it touches. It's been in command of the spirits all along. The attack on Bonsaint may have*

been a response to the priest discovering its reliquary."

Leander asked, "Is Rathanael saying something to you, or are you just thinking? I can't tell. Your face is very hard to read."

The question's directness sent a ripple of shock through me. But if he meant to throw me off-balance, that wasn't going to work. "It doesn't like being called that," I said.

He let out a soft, disbelieving laugh. He was looking at me in a way I didn't understand—an intense, burning look, as though I were the only thing that existed in the world. Around us, time seemed to have stopped. Shafts of moonlight streamed through the stained-glass windows, and motes of dust winked within them like particles of frost. "In the crypt, you said you wanted to stop me. When you said that, you meant—"

"I thought you were responsible for the attacks on Roischal. Practicing Old Magic."

"I see." He hesitated. His lips parted, but nothing came out. I had never seen him appear so uncertain. "I've been investigating the situation for some time," he said finally, swiftly, with an air of disbelief that he was revealing this out loud. "Before the first soldiers were possessed, there were a few suspicious incidents here and there. But the more I looked into them, the more I found myself being assigned . . . errands. I was sent to Naimes, to conduct evaluations. Sent to the countryside, to battle spirits. And then—"

"Sent to retrieve me in the harrow," I finished.

He gave me a humorless smile. I wondered if he was thinking the same thing I was. All along, even then, we had been on the same side. The anger I had seen on his face in the evaluation room, learning about the possessed soldiers—that was because it had happened while he was leagues away from Roischal, forced to put his life-and-death investigation on hold to administer tests to dozens of giggling novices. No wonder he had wanted to get it over with.

I thought of the notes filling the margins of his prayer book. The impersonal emptiness of his chamber. This had consumed his life for months, I wagered, and until now, he had confided in no one. With an uncomfortable twist in my stomach, I realized that the dedication must have been written by his dead brother, Gabriel.

"So the revenants aren't in league with each other," he said slowly, almost to himself. "Rath—your revenant wants to stop Sarathiel, not free it? When it sent the thralls to Naimes, that was to *destroy* Saint Eugenia's relic, not find your revenant a vessel."

"They don't like each other very much," I explained.

"This is mad," Leander said. "I shouldn't . . ." He glanced away; a muscle shifted in his jaw. Then he looked back at me and said as though it cost him, "Help me. I understand that you hate me, but this must be done. I need to see it through."

I had forgotten I was still holding the dagger. When I stuck it back through my belt, he relaxed minutely.

"Ask him what he was planning to do with the casket," the revenant said.

"What were you planning to do with the casket?"

"I was going to throw it into the Sevre." He paused, looking at me warily, and I realized he was addressing the revenant when he asked, "Will that work?"

"Most likely." I waited for the rest of the revenant's answer, then relayed, "It would be easier to dump the ashes over the altar and let the Old Magic finish the job, but there would be a risk of Sarathiel escaping."

"And tell him to keep holding the lid shut," the revenant added. *"Right now I'm fairly certain that's the only thing keeping Sarathiel inside. The lid must have been left a little ajar for it to have snuck out*

enough of its power to kill the sacristan. I'll bet the priest picked up the casket just in time."

Hearing this, Leander turned a shade paler beneath the bruises. "Ah," he said calmly. He stepped out from behind the altar and went down the chancel's steps, avoiding looking at the sacristan's body. It struck me that he hadn't even known whether his plan would work. Any mistake could have killed him. This was a burden he had been prepared to shoulder alone.

"Why have you decided to trust me?" I asked, catching up with his long strides and his dramatically billowing vestments.

He shot me a sideways glance. "In the crypt, you didn't kill me. I was unconscious and at your mercy, and you let me live. If Rath—if the revenant were in control . . ."

"I'm not a saint," I said, because I could see where this was going.

Looking down the empty transept ahead, he smiled. It wasn't his condescending smile from before, but instead a rather pallid real one.

"What?" I demanded.

"Nothing," he said. "The procession is due to return soon, but we have enough time to slip out the back. From there the walk to the parapets overlooking the river will take us only a few minutes. Anyone who sees us will keep their distance. I've made certain enough of that."

Anger throbbed to life dully in my chest. "Is that why you torture people with your relic?" I asked. "To ensure they don't get in your way?"

"We've already established how much you dislike me. If it's any consolation, I don't like myself, either. One can't, in order to be a confessor." He stated it plainly, as though he hardly cared, but opening the door to the vestry, he paused. "When I used Saint Liliane's relic on you in Naimes, I will admit—I was not entirely . . ."

He trailed off. The Divine was standing in the vestry, her many layers of ornamentation being removed by an attendant. The smell of cold winter air and incense clung to her robes. With her miter set aside, I saw that her hair was brown and curly, cut short for tidiness, which made her look even more girlishly young.

"Leander?" she asked in confusion.

Both of us stood frozen: Leander in the open, me halfway behind a garment rack, still conspicuous to anyone who bothered glancing in my direction.

She said in her gentle voice, concerned, "I noticed you had gone missing—I grew worried. I called an early end to the procession. You've been so unlike yourself these past days." She noticed me first, followed by the casket in Leander's hands. Her eyes widened. "What are you doing?" She dismissed the attendant with a gesture.

Her beseeching gaze lingered on me; I saw the moment she figured out who I was. She looked back at Leander in shock. "Leander, you must put that down," she said softly.

"I know everything," he replied, unmoved.

"You don't understand. Please."

It came to me in a flood. Someone had tampered with the cathedral's records. Someone had repeatedly sent Leander away from the city to hinder his investigation. Only one person in Bonsaint had the authority to issue such commands.

Perhaps someone had even purposefully moved the casket's lid and left it ajar.

The Divine lunged for the casket with a cry of despair. At the same time, Leander dove back out the door. Together, we slammed it in her face.

A pause followed. Leander wore a look of disbelief at what he had just done. I imagined the Divine standing on the other side, stunned, having probably never been treated with that much disrespect at any point in her entire life. Then she let out a shout and started banging on the door.

"The bench," the revenant said. I left Leander with his back against the door to grab the wooden bench standing against the wall nearby. It had to be at least twice a man's weight, a huge old antique bulging with carvings, but the revenant wasn't trying to hide itself now. When I finished dragging it into place, Leander was staring at me.

"This way," he said, emerging from his trance. He wheeled back toward the nave, his robes flying behind him as his pace broke from a jog into a sprint. Behind us, the door shuddered ineffectually with blows from the Divine's fists. Then all fell silent.

"I doubt that's a positive development," the revenant remarked, right before wood exploded across the transept.

I paused to look over my shoulder. The Divine stumbled from the wrecked doorway wearing an expression of piteous shock, clutching a bloody-knuckled hand to her chest. From her robes, she had drawn forth an amulet set with an amber stone—a rivener relic. She drew up short when she saw the sacristan's body. "No," she whispered, in what seemed like genuine grief, then looked back at us with red-rimmed eyes. She began to raise her scepter.

The revenant blazed to its full power so quickly that I staggered and had to steady myself against a pillar. Silver flames rolled over my cloak, dripping ghostly embers onto the carpet.

"Run," I told Leander.

The fury's shriek rippled across the cathedral, summoning a wind that lifted the draperies and sent dust streaming from the chandeliers. The noise ground harmlessly in my ears, held back by the revenant's power. Out of the corner of my eye, I saw Leander vanish into one of the doors in the opposite transept.

With a cry of frustration, the Divine flung out her other hand. The pews beside me burst into kindling. As I leaped behind a pillar to avoid the flying shards, the candelabra fixed to the pillar's side violently erupted into flame, roaring toward the vault in a twisting column of fire. When I stumbled back, another pew exploded in my path. The Divine was panting, her white and gold vestments smeared with blood.

No one could wield more than one relic at a time, not even a Divine, but she was switching from one to the other so rapidly she might as well be. And she was incredibly strong—I had never heard of an ashgrim relic being wielded like that before. My cheeks still stung from the heat.

But her relics also gave her weaknesses, as I knew intimately from my time with the revenant. I scrambled toward the sacristan's body and yanked at the censer attached to his belt. As I had hoped, the incense was lit; he must have noticed something amiss before he died.

"What are you doing?" The Divine sounded upset. She had paused, the rivener amulet clenched in her hand. "Please, leave him alone."

She couldn't attack me with the rivener's power without potentially mangling the sacristan's body, and she wasn't willing to risk that, I noted with surprise. I finished tugging the censer free, then charged her.

"Stop!" she cried, throwing out her hand.

A fissure split the floor in front of me, fracturing the flagstones. It wasn't a calculated attack; I barely stumbled as the cracks raced beneath my feet toward the sanctuary, zig-zagged up the steps, and struck the altar with a great clap of sundered stone, breaking it in two. The Divine froze with her hand still outstretched, staring in horror at what she had done. Then I tackled her, and she went down in a tangle of robes.

We clawed at each other like a pair of brawling novices. Holding my breath, I shoved the censer close to her face; she coughed and choked on the smoke. When she turned her head aside, I drew my dagger. Her grip on me slackened as she felt the misericorde's point press against her throat.

"Please," she whispered, hoarse from the incense. Tears glittered in her eyes. "I've waited for so long. This isn't—this isn't fair, this isn't how it was supposed to happen. . . ."

She trailed off, distracted by a flicker of motion. Leander had reappeared in the transept, glancing repeatedly over his shoulder. Looking hunted, he swiftly crossed to the other side and tried a different door. I guessed that the clerics returning from the procession had blocked his escape route. By now they had to be sensing some of the chaos transpiring in the chapel.

We were nearly out of time. I knew the clerics wouldn't pause to listen to our mad-sounding story, not after they discovered us attacking the Divine.

Thinking furiously, I didn't react quickly enough when she wrenched an arm from my grasp. Too late, I noticed that she was still holding the scepter. The fury's shriek rippled past, distorting the air with its power. Across the nave, Leander fell to his knees. The casket tumbled from his hands.

As though time had slowed, I watched it bounce once and then split open, flinging Saint Agnes's ashes in a powdery spray across the carpet.

We all sucked in a breath, staring. A heartbeat passed. The ashes looked utterly harmless. Then something vast and silver erupted from them like a great flower opening, a bloom of wings unfurling. The force of it flung me aside as though I weighed nothing. My head cracked against a pew, and my vision exploded white.

Through the ringing in my ears, a thread of sound emerged, whining like a mosquito.

"Nun, get up," the revenant urged, shrill with panic. *"Get up!"*

I couldn't move. I couldn't even blink. The scarlet threads of the carpet swam into focus in front of my nose, each individual filament lined in silver.

"Nun!" The revenant shook me frantically.

A cool breeze stirred my hair. I had the impression of something colossal bending over me as I lay stunned on the floor, studying me as though I were an insect. I recalled how Sarathiel had looked in the illuminated manuscript, its serenely masked face and half-closed eyes, its multitude of wings. Monstrous but somehow also holy—a figure that could be cast in bronze above an altarpiece, worshipped as much as feared.

The revenant was still trying to rouse me. *"Artemisia!"* it shrieked, and then its presence flooded my veins like fire.

Suddenly, I could move. My arm stretched out. My hand gripped the pew. I pulled my feet under myself and stood. Except it wasn't me controlling my body; it wasn't me who lifted my head to the nightmare hanging suspended overhead, the ravaged face of Sarathiel.

"This is *my* human," the revenant snarled through my mouth, and blazed into a torrent of silver flame.

As the ghost-fire roared up around me, obscuring my vision, I felt strangely calm. I tried to make sense of what I had seen. The six wings, some half-furled and others spread, their ghostly immensity stretching from balcony to balcony. The singed edges of the pinions, blackened and curled. And the terrible face, where the diagonal crack in the mask had split and one half had fallen away, leaving it preternaturally beautiful on one side, a bare and grinning skull on the other.

When the flames cleared, Sarathiel was no longer there. Silver embers danced in the air above the nave, winking out one by one. The disturbed draperies settled back into place with whispers of silk against stone. Except for the epicenter of destruction around us, the cathedral looked eerily untouched, peaceful in its darkened majesty. From the stained-glass windows stretching above, Saint Eugenia gazed down with a hint of a smile.

Then, voices. Shouts of alarm. The thump and groan of the cathedral's doors shuddering open, bringing into view the shimmering glow of hundreds of candles gathered outside. At the periphery of my vision I had vague impressions of shocked faces lining up along the gallery, but I couldn't see them properly. My eyes weren't looking in that direction. When I tried to make them do it, nothing happened.

Leander stirred. My head jerked around sharply at the first sign of movement. I watched as he attempted to climb to his feet, slumped down as though he were exhausted or had forgotten how to stand, then tried again.

The Divine gave a little cry and hurried over, her bloodstained skirts bunched in her hands. She helped him upright, clutching at him.

"That has to be the most idiotic human I've ever seen," the revenant marveled in disgust, in my voice, out loud.

If the Divine heard it, she gave no sign. She was too busy tenderly lifting Leander's face, looking into his eyes. "Sarathiel," she breathed.

TWENTY-FIVE

N o one else was close enough to hear her say it. The clerics were arrayed along the galleries and balconies, standing in the shadowed arches around the nave, emerging from cover like timid creatures after a storm. The cathedral guards reacted first, starting forward with a coordinated clanking of armor. The Divine looked up and noticed her audience for the first time. She was cradling Leander's head protectively, lost in her own world.

"Stay back!" she called out breathlessly. I didn't think she was faking her distress.

Shocked murmurs filled the vault. At once, I saw how this scene appeared. The clerics had sensed a revenant, but they thought it was my revenant, its power too entangled with Sarathiel's to be told apart. The sacristan lay dead nearby, with his censer at my feet; the Divine was bloody and distraught, Leander seemingly injured. Behind us, the altar had been sundered in two. And I was the only person who could be responsible.

I took a step forward, nearly lost my balance, and caught myself against the back of a pew. At least it felt as though I did; but it was the revenant making me move, each action accompanied by a clutch of uncertainty as I discovered what my body was about to do.

My head was pounding, my stomach a sour knot of terror and fury. An image assaulted me of the city going up in a pillar of silver flame, the soul of every soldier and cleric and civilian in Bonsaint extinguished like candles, blazing so brightly that even the holy sisters in Chantclere would turn their eyes northward in fear. No one would be able to touch us then—not the Clerisy, not Sarathiel. My fingers tightened on the pew's back until the wood splintered.

Once, I had believed that this was what the revenant wanted. Now I felt the trembling in my arms and knew that it was afraid. I wasn't sure what to do, but I reached out anyway—a silent offer to take over again, like an extended hand. The revenant hesitated. Then, in a grateful rush, it withdrew.

The next breath that I drew in was a breath at my command. Experimentally, I tried turning my head to look at the clerics on the balcony, and my body obeyed.

Their expressions of dread turned to confusion. A ripple of relief passed through the cathedral. They could no longer sense the revenant.

"They can't sense Sarathiel, either," the revenant said, its presence inside me a roiling tangle of emotions. *"It's hiding itself. It will try to impersonate the priest."*

Nearby, the Divine had succeeded in drawing Leander to his feet, though he was still leaning heavily against her. "Confessor Leander is unharmed!" she called out. "He will—he will recover from the attack. Bring the shackles of Saint Augustin, quickly. Artemisia of

Naimes—" She broke off, listening as Leander murmured something against her breast. Then she finished, "Artemisia cannot control Saint Eugenia's relic."

I wondered what he had said to her—or rather, what Sarathiel had said to her. Clerics scattered at once to do her bidding.

In the following hush I grew aware of a dull, muted rumble, like the crashing of surf against a distant shore. It was coming from the candlelit crowd gathered outside the cathedral's doors. Their movements were restless, threatening to press inside. They were beginning to chant a word. At first I couldn't make out what it was, but a familiar cadence emerged as more voices joined in and the rhythm strengthened, thrumming through the chapel like a pulse.

"Artemisia. Artemisia. Artemisia."

The wind shifted direction, blowing in a gust of night air that smelled of smoke and sweat and the wild places beyond the city, untouched by humankind. And with it came a dangerous energy, the unleashed violence of a building storm. I felt it prickling across my skin; I could almost taste it. The hair stood up on my arms.

"Artemisia. Artemisia! Artemisia!"

"Close the doors!" ordered the Divine, wide-eyed.

Guards scrambled to obey, dimming the noise to a muffled thunder. The bar fell into place with a reverberating thud that reminded me of the day the thralls had attacked in Naimes. Then, the doors hadn't succeeded in holding back the Dead. I wondered if they would hold back the living now.

I didn't dare try speaking to the revenant. There were too many people watching me; they might see my lips move. All of them ignorant of how close they were to death, trapped inside the cathedral with an unbound Fifth Order spirit. I felt as though I were an open flame held aloft beside dry kindling. One wrong move could ignite everything.

The Divine worriedly touched Leander's cheek, smoothed back his hair. He tolerated this for a moment, then looked at me. No—*it* looked at me. Leander's face appeared the same, but something dead and ruined and ancient gazed out from within his eyes. He stepped toward me, the Divine clutching at his arm.

"We must not kill her," the Divine whispered. "You promised there would be no more killing. What did you do to my sacristan? When I moved the casket's lid for you—"

Leander's expression was implacable, serene. "One life. That was all I required. And he was old, Gabrielle. I could sense his strength ebbing—he wouldn't have lived out the winter. He would have made the sacrifice himself if he had known the truth."

"That I am your destined vessel," she said, her face lighting.

"It is the Lady's will," it agreed tranquilly.

"Very well. But we won't harm Artemisia."

"Of course not," Sarathiel soothed. "We only need Saint Eugenia's relic, and then she will no longer be a danger to you." It turned to me. "Give me the reliquary."

"I don't have it."

Sarathiel regarded me with mild surprise, as though it hadn't expected me to prove capable of speech. "Where is it?"

"I don't know."

With the Divine anxiously looking on, he began to search me— *it* did, I reminded myself, as Leander's elegant hands smoothed down my tunic, lifted my hair as though it were an animal's tail to check beneath. This was just Leander's body, a vessel, his mind locked away as a prisoner inside. I wondered if his consciousness was buried too deeply to be aware of what was happening, or if he was watching, feeling every touch.

Sarathiel finished and stepped back. It didn't appear angry or disappointed to have not found the reliquary. A trembling lector returned with the shackles, made his obeisance to the Divine, and then stared at me uncertainly. I obviously wasn't what he had expected of Artemisia of Naimes. I wondered what he had envisioned—someone older, or more beautiful.

The chain had been removed, but they were unmistakably the shackles I had worn in the harrow. While the cuffs had been left warped and scorched by my escape, they still appeared functional. I instinctively stiffened, prepared to resist.

Sarathiel leaned in close, closer, until Leander's warm lips brushed my ear. "We could quarrel with each other here, little vessel," it murmured, breath soft against my cheek. "But how many humans would survive a battle between revenants? Rathanael knows. Why don't you tell her, Rathanael?"

The revenant tugged my gaze upward, and my heart stopped. A translucent, barely visible silver mist was pouring silently down the cathedral's walls, creeping over the stained-glass windows, collecting in ghostly pools in the corners. It rolled across the carpet and seeped between the pews, reaching its fingers toward the preoccupied clerics standing in the aisle.

"Its mist is like my fire," the revenant said. *"It will kill anything it touches."*

I imagined the mist reaching the first clerics, their bodies dropping limply to the carpet. The brief panic before the others fell, one by one, like puppets with cut strings. And then I would be standing alone with Sarathiel in a cathedral full of corpses. Chilled to the bone, I extended my hands.

The lector closed the cold, heavy weight of the first shackle around my wrist. A flash of blistering pain stole my breath. I barely felt the second, my thoughts dazed and swimming.

"Forgive me, lady," said the lector, distraught. He began to bow to me the same way he had to the Divine, caught himself, and scurried off instead. Sarathiel watched him go like a cat drawn to the movement of a fleeing mouse.

I seized the chance to speak to the Divine. Roughly, I said, "Whatever it's promised you, it's lying."

She smiled at me, and I felt a wash of despair, realizing that that was the same thing Leander had told me in the catacombs, nearly word for word. I hadn't listened. And now neither would she.

"Have patience, Artemisia." A light and certainty illuminated her features in a way I had only seen once before, after the appearance of the sign in the cathedral. "I can't explain everything to you now, but the Lady has answered my prayers. I know it's difficult to believe, but you *will* understand—I'm certain of it. You need only a little time."

They placed me in a room in one of the cathedral's spires. It was shaped like a halved birdcage with curved walls and a half-moon floor, its limestone bare save a straw pallet tucked in one corner. Wind moaned through a small barred window; ancient water stains wept down the sill. The main source of light was a torch in the hallway outside, its glow spilling beneath the door.

I went to the window. With the revenant's power, I might have been able to bend its bars. Standing on my toes and peering through it at an angle, I could see a section of the courtyard far below, still sparkling with the protestors' candles. From this high up, their chanting blurred into a meaningless ebb and flow of sound.

I willed them to disperse, to go home. To pack their things

and leave the city. Otherwise they would die, and it would be my fault. The hopeless weight crushing my chest felt like the effects of Leander's relic—and I even felt sorry for him, Sarathiel's prisoner in body and soul, a helpless captive to everything he had tried to prevent.

I bent and pressed my forehead to the sill.

"There was nothing you could have done differently," the revenant remarked.

"I could have stopped the Divine."

"You're mortal, nun. You aren't perfect. In fact, for a human, you make remarkably few stupid decisions. Only rarely do I want to possess you and bash your brains out against a wall."

I turned away and sank down on the pallet. "I thought you said I was the worst vessel you've ever had."

"I didn't mean that. Nun. . . ." Whatever it had started to say, it didn't seem to be able to finish. After a long pause, it said instead, *"Sarathiel still isn't at its full strength. That was why it took the priest as a vessel—it needs to hide itself as it continues to recover. It won't risk revealing itself until it has destroyed my relic."*

I lifted the shackles and let them drop against my lap, clinking. "Is there anything you can do like this?"

"I could take over your body, but only if you let me, and it wouldn't be much use. My power would still be suppressed."

I looked back at the window, at the patch of dark sky behind the bars. Clouds must have blown in, because I couldn't see any stars.

"There's one other thing," it ventured. *"Something that doesn't have to do with my power at all. Now that I've seen the altar up close, I believe I could replicate the ritual that nearly destroyed Sarathiel. But there are certain limitations,"* it went on when I didn't react. *"For a ritual that advanced to succeed, we would need a site of power—a*

place that's been prepared for Old Magic, like the altar."

"A forge to make a weapon," I said, remembering its earlier metaphor.

"Yes, precisely," it said. It sounded surprised—either because I had caught on so quickly, or because I wasn't vehemently protesting the idea. *"Unfortunately, it would take days to suitably prepare this cell. Old Magic has never been practiced here before, which is necessary for a space to withstand the energy of a powerful ritual. If we tried, I imagine the results would be quite messy."*

Mouth dry, I thought of the scorch marks on Saint Agnes's altar, and was ashamedly glad this conversation was theoretical. But my thoughts dwelled on the idea of using Old Magic nonetheless. How far would I go, if I had no other choice? I could no longer condemn those who had turned to heresy as a last resort—not now that I knew how it felt to see so many lives hanging in the balance, unable to help, the hopelessness and guilt closing in like the walls of a tomb. If there was any force that could save them . . .

It was true that the saints had committed terrible wrongs. But it was equally true that Loraille wouldn't have survived the Sorrow without relics. For each spirit imprisoned, how many innocents had been spared a terrible death? Hundreds? Thousands?

I stared at my scarred hands, my throat tight. The way I had felt as a child listening to the sisters' hymns, filled with pure, soaring, wondrous faith—I knew suddenly, with a visceral wrench of loss, that that feeling was gone forever. I could never get it back again.

"You can share these things, you know," the revenant intruded. *"You don't always have to leave everyone in agonizing suspense."*

"I can't accept it," I answered.

"Accept what?"

I wasn't certain I could put my tangled, poisonous thoughts

into words. It felt blasphemous to even try. "That—that there can be such a thing as . . . not necessary evil, because evil is never necessary—it can't be—but . . . acceptable evil. Hurt and cruelty that the Lady would allow in service to Her will. Like the goat in Naimes," I said, dimly aware that I'd never told the revenant about the goat, and it would probably think I had lost my mind. "She wouldn't make someone kick the goat."

The revenant was quiet—a careful, pained pause. *"Nun,"* it said, *"isn't that what She's done to you?"*

I heard a rattling sound, and realized I was shaking, the shackles clattering together. I wondered if I should pray. But the stars were gone, the Lady's gaze obscured. I had no sign save the hundreds of voices chanting my name outside.

TWENTY-SIX

The noise continued through the night. I slept little and ached with cold, standing frequently to look out the window. Several times I heard shouting; once I heard glass breaking, followed by screams and horses' hooves clattering across the courtyard. In the distance, something was burning, sending up a plume of orange-lit smoke.

I judged the hour near dawn when keys rattled outside the door. To my surprise, it swung open to reveal a lone orphrey, white-robed and veiled. She beckoned to me in silence.

"Where are you taking me?" I asked, but the orphrey didn't answer. I could see little of her averted face behind the veil.

"She can't answer you," the revenant said. *"She's a thrall. The spirit possessing her is acting under Sarathiel's command."* It paused as though listening. *"I can't tell for certain in this state, but I believe it's one of the blight wraiths from the square."*

I followed. She walked swiftly, remaining out of arm's reach, but paused, waiting, when I purposefully dawdled and fell behind. There was a fear and hesitation to her movements. On a whim, I asked, "Can you understand me?" But she only stared, drawing her arms protectively against her chest.

Eventually, it grew clear that she was taking me on a circuitous route to the apartments. We entered a hall I hadn't investigated the evening before. A cathedral guard stood near the lone door. He twitched as we passed, his posture stiff and his head bowed.

"Another thrall," the revenant observed. *"And another spirit inexperienced at possessing humans. Wearing that consecrated armor must be torture, but it's too afraid of Sarathiel to disobey."*

To my surprise, I felt as bad for the newly risen spirits as I did their vessels. They were like confused children, born through no fault of their own into an unforgiving world of hunger and fear. If they hurt anyone, they did so only for those reasons—not out of evil, or even malice.

As we neared the door, a conversation carried into the hall. The Divine was saying, sounding threadbare with exhaustion, "But no one at the convent will come forward. If they know anything, they aren't willing to speak. Can't we simply exorcise Rathanael from her?"

"An exorcism would merely return it to its relic," Leander's voice replied patiently. "In doing so, we would give it a chance to inhabit a new vessel. At least for now we have it contained. . . ."

While they spoke, the orphrey puzzled over the door, shrinking back several times in apparent fear before she gained the courage to touch it. The door swung open, interrupting the conversation.

The Divine was curled up in a chair in front of a window. She wasn't wearing her maquillage, and she looked pale and smudged; she clearly hadn't slept. Sarathiel stood beside her with a hand on her shoulder, which she was clasping to herself as though it were a precious relic. I wasn't sure whether it was just my imagination, or if its tranquil expression truly did betray a slight air of impatience.

It struck me, seeing the Divine so at ease with Sarathiel, that she had never favored Leander. She had kept him close to watch him—assigned him important duties merely to keep him busy. And he had played the part because he'd had no other choice, locked in a treacherous dance with his own enemy. The entire city had been fooled; so had I.

The Divine was watching me. In a rustle of silk, she rose, came to me, and drew me down to sit beside her on a cushioned settle. She tried to take my hand, but I moved it.

"Artemisia," she said earnestly. "This does not need to be painful. All you must do is tell us who has the reliquary, and then this ordeal will end. You will be better off without Rathanael."

"Why?" I asked.

A line appeared between her brows; she hadn't expected that question. "Because it's wicked."

"And Sarathiel isn't?"

Gently, she shook her head. "It was sent to me by the Lady. Perhaps you have heard . . ." She hesitated, color rising to her cheeks. I wondered if that was why she wore the maquillage. "It's true that I was not the Assembly's first choice for Divine. When I arrived in Bonsaint, I was so alone. But after countless nights of praying for guidance, uncertain of my ability to lead, the goddess gave me Sarathiel. Trust me when I say that it has spent centuries regretting its misdeeds. Lifetimes in which it has listened to the devotions, the choir, has been surrounded by the Lady's presence. It has changed— repented. Can you say the same of yours?"

The longer she spoke, the deeper my stomach sank. I too

believed that the Lady had sent me a revenant. But there was one key difference.

"No," I said, "because my revenant doesn't lie to me."

Disappointment shaded her features. She badly wanted me to believe her. "But how long have you known it? Sarathiel has been my heart's companion for many years. Of course, there are still moments when I am unsure . . . but the Lady sent me a sign," she added swiftly. "You wouldn't understand. You weren't there."

"In the cathedral?"

"You heard of it," she said breathlessly.

"The pauper's balcony. I was there."

Her eyes widened. We regarded each other at an impasse, and the world fell away in a weightless plunge as I realized that looking into her face was like gazing into a mirror. We both believed the other misguided for trusting a revenant—both thought the Lady meant us to ally ourselves with our own. One of us was right, the other wrong. A warped reflection in a glass.

A sense of unreality crept over me. Could I truly claim to know better than a Divine? What if the sign in the cathedral hadn't been for me after all? Who was I, to believe that I alone knew the Lady's will? I had based my convictions on the path of a raven's flight. The dying words of a half-insane holy woman.

Perhaps we were both wrong, both equally deluded, and it was never possible to trust a revenant.

Then the Divine shook her head. She said with quiet faith, "The sign . . . no—it was for me, I am certain of it," and the illusion cracked, a mirror fracturing.

I spoke through gritted teeth. "You have to know by now that Sarathiel's been controlling the spirits. It's the one who told you not to lower the drawbridge, isn't it?"

A sad smile crossed her face. "No. You are misinformed. Those spirits . . . they are *why* I must become Sarathiel's true vessel. Otherwise, they cannot be stopped. Sarathiel has been helping me protect the people of Bonsaint; it would not take lives."

"What about the sacristan?"

The Divine's smile turned puzzled. She turned to look at Sarathiel, who was watching us intently. "Sarathiel, why are you staying in Leander's body? When will we be together, like you promised?"

"Gabrielle," it said quietly.

She rose and went to it by the window, cupping Leander's cheek. "Perhaps you should rest. It must be taxing, inhabiting a body after so long without one."

Sarathiel turned Leander's face against her hand, closing his eyes as though seeking a momentary respite from the world. The Divine watched this with a tenderness that bordered on pain. I could tell she had been honest about her history with Sarathiel; there was a familiarity to their intimacy that spoke of countless hours in each other's company, whispered confessions exchanged in the chapel's shadows. I imagined her solitary, white-robed figure bent over the altar nightly in prayer. How pious she must have appeared—how lonely.

Suddenly her delusions made sense. Being a Divine wasn't so far off from being a saint. Sarathiel was perhaps the only being in Bonsaint who knew her not as the Divine, untouchable in her holiness, but as Gabrielle. No wonder she had fallen for it. She hadn't had anyone else.

After a moment Sarathiel drew back to look at me, seemingly unperturbed that I had witnessed the exchange. "If you tell us where the reliquary is, you will spare us a great deal of unpleasantness. We will release you unharmed, rid of Rathanael forever."

I felt a spasm of distress from the revenant.

"What do you want?" I asked. I honestly wanted to know. "Not right now, but after you destroy Saint Eugenia's relic." Remembering what Leander had said to me in the harrow, I added, "Do you even know what you want?"

In his eyes, a flicker. My breath stopped. In that instant I had thought I had seen Leander looking out at me, as though appearing in a window of the great, crumbling ruin that was Sarathiel. And then he was gone again, reclaimed by shadow.

"I want to be free," it replied without inflection, drawing a questioning look from the Divine.

Had I imagined what I had seen? My heart thumped so forcefully I could feel my pulse against every point of contact with my skin—my clothes, the cushions piled against my side. If something had just happened, Sarathiel seemed unaware of it.

"You already are," I said. "What do you plan on doing next? Killing all the humans in Loraille? Then you'll just be alone. You'll have made the world your reliquary."

"Be careful, nun," the revenant warned.

"Sarathiel?" the Divine asked.

Instead of answering, Sarathiel drew her carefully into an embrace. It pressed Leander's mouth to her curls. And then a sharp crack split the room.

At first I thought something had fallen off a shelf and broken, even though that didn't make any sense. Then I saw how limply the Divine hung in Leander's arms, the unnatural angle of her lolling head.

"I regret that the altar was destroyed," Sarathiel said, gazing over her shoulder at nothing. "It would have been a fitting way to dispose of Rathanael. Rathanael, naughty Rathanael, with its vile little obsession with Old Magic. But I will confess, I almost find it comforting that some things haven't changed. The world is so very different now than it was before."

My nerves screamed with the urge to move, to fight, to run, as Sarathiel crossed the room, the scrape of the Divine's slippers dragging across the carpet the only sound in the silent apartment. It settled on the chair opposite me, laying the Divine down so that her head was cradled against Leander's chest, almost the same way she had held it in the chapel. Her open eyes stared glassily at the ceiling. I remembered comparing her to a doll, and felt sick.

"She was starting to doubt you," I guessed.

"Indeed. Perhaps I should have tried being more like Rathanael. But I'm not certain I could stand it. I hate humans so very much, you see." Seemingly unconsciously, it placed a hand on the Divine's curls and began to stroke. "All those nights she prayed in the dark, yearning for someone to listen. How lonely she was, how uncertain. How desperate to prove herself as Divine. She required so much reassurance; it was sickening. And even then, it took me years to persuade her to trust me. How long did it take Rathanael? Days?"

I swallowed. "I didn't trust it."

"Oh, come now," it said.

"I controlled it."

The revenant winced. Leander's hand stilled. "Is that what you believe?" it asked, in what seemed like real curiosity. I wondered again how much of this Leander was experiencing: if he could see and hear and feel it all, the warmth and weight of the Divine's body, the softness of her hair, and if he were somewhere inside screaming.

"We came to an agreement," I conceded, hearing how pathetic that sounded even as the words left my mouth.

"An agreement," Sarathiel repeated, in a slightly marveling tone. "Rest assured that the moment you resort to bargaining with a revenant, you have already lost. The only reason you aren't Rathanael's thrall this very moment is because it chose not to make you one. It could have possessed you a thousand times over—every little moment that you were sleeping, injured, distracted. Quite honestly, I am surprised it didn't possess you by accident."

I remembered suddenly how it had vanished after the Battle of Bonsaint. It had nearly taken over my body, and then it had stopped. It had pulled itself back. It hadn't abandoned me after all—at least not in the way I had thought.

"Silly Rathanael," Sarathiel said, watching me through Leander's eyes. "It always did care for its human vessels."

Blood pounded in my ears. "The same way you cared about Gabrielle?" I asked.

It was as though the air had been sucked from the apartment. Sarathiel went very still. My revenant did too. The question had been a gamble, but it was increasingly obvious to me that its decision to kill the Divine hadn't been logical. She would have been the perfect vessel, far better than inhabiting Leander in every respect, yet it had chosen to remain in his body instead. And the way it was holding her; I didn't think it realized how it looked.

"Is that why you killed her?" I persisted.

"*Nun,*" the revenant warned, but now that I had started, I couldn't stop. Pieces were falling into place. I remembered the things the revenant had raved about in the tunnels beneath the city—what it had said about Saint Eugenia.

"If you'd kept her around, she might have betrayed you."

"Stop antagonizing it, you idiot. It just murdered another human in front of you." There was true panic in the revenant's voice now.

"Better to kill her than suffer her betrayal," I continued, relentless. "That makes sense. But what if she hadn't betrayed you? What if she had decided to remain your friend?"

Sarathiel still hadn't answered. It sat as though petrified, its thoughts crawling slowly behind Leander's unblinking eyes. Then it did something strange. It let out a faint gasp, as though gripped by a sudden pain, and buried Leander's head in his hands. After a long pause, it stirred to pluck one of Leander's hairs and lower it for inspection. In the candlelight, the strand shone white.

"The priest," the revenant said in surprise. *"He's resisting it. I very much doubt he has the strength to regain control, but he's trying."*

This could be my chance. The rest of the room disappeared, my focus narrowing to Sarathiel—Sarathiel, and Leander. "Or maybe you weren't worried she would betray you," I went on. "I could have had that backward. Perhaps you didn't want her to watch *you* betraying *her*."

I had no idea whether I had hit the mark. Sarathiel barely seemed to be listening. It had buried Leander's fingers in his hair, searching. It plucked out a second white strand. A third. It hissed and dug Leander's fingers against his scalp. Clenched them, as though to restore clarity through the pain.

I swallowed. It was working; I had to keep talking. "Or perhaps you just couldn't admit to yourself that you might care about a human. Is that it? You killed her to make sure you would never have a chance to find out."

That struck a nerve. It stopped and looked up at me through a cage of Leander's fingers. Deep within his devastated green eyes, I saw something familiar gazing back at me. Pleading.

"But you have found out, haven't you?" I heard the words as though they were spoken by someone else, hollow and cold. "Too late."

Sarathiel—or Leander, I couldn't tell—took one ragged, struggling breath, then another. Leander's face twisted. A sob wrenched from his chest.

I didn't dare breathe. "Leander?"

His face lifted: pale, emotionless, streaked with tears. "No."

I didn't have time to react. The Divine's body tumbled to the floor between us with a sick, heavy thump. Ignoring it, Sarathiel lunged forward to seize me, Leander's fingernails digging into the flesh of my arms. It bent his head over my shoulder, turning his face toward my ear.

"I do not need you to speak," it said, Leander's breath hot on my neck. "Rathanael will do that for you. Won't you, Rathanael? I'll put your vessel in a little dark room and see how long it takes you to go mad and scream the truth. Or perhaps I will try something else. I will carve off all your vessel's fingers, one by one. Then her nose. Her eyes. It may not make the vessel talk. But it will make you talk."

A knock came on the door. Sarathiel stopped, panting.

"What?" it inquired, still crouched over me.

"The search—the search has been successful," a voice on the other side stammered. "We've found someone willing to speak to the Divine."

Sarathiel made no visible effort to calm itself. It simply was calm, as though it had closed a pair of shutters over Leander's face. Eerily like him, it smoothed his black robes as it stood. It stepped neatly over the Divine's sprawled body on its way across the room.

"The Divine is not to be disturbed," it said. "She is resting. I will meet them in the hall."

After it had slipped out the door, I snuck over to place my ear against the wood. Outside I heard a familiar teary, quavering voice. Marguerite. She was sobbing, "I know where it is. I can take you to the reliquary."

TWENTY-SEVEN

I didn't know where we were going. Marguerite wouldn't look at me during the walk through the cathedral, her tearstained face downcast. Occasionally I heard her sniffling, and wondered if someone had hurt her. She had been taken away for questioning while I had been returned to the tower for several more hours to wait, watching the red stain of dawn bleed into the horizon beyond the window's bars, imagining her being tortured, picturing the Divine's forces converging on Saint Eugenia's reliquary and destroying it in hundreds of different ways. "Sorry," she had repeated tearfully, "I'm sorry," as they had led her away.

Now I felt as though I were on my way to an execution. The shackles weighted my wrists like millstones. Soldiers from the city guard marched around me, surrounded by a company of the heavily armored cathedral guard, their combined footsteps rapping crisply from the walls.

"Sarathiel has been busy," the revenant observed. *"All those knights are thralls."*

I snuck the cathedral guards a sideways glance. They were moving a little stiffly beneath their armor, but with their helmets on and their visors lowered, I couldn't see any sign that they were possessed. The same appeared true of the soldiers marching obliviously at their sides.

I was sure they believed they were acting on the Divine's orders. For now, her absence didn't seem suspicious. Sarathiel had spoken to the attendants and left behind the possessed orphrey so that it would seem she had company in her chambers as she slept. It had until early afternoon, perhaps, before someone grew concerned and insisted on checking on her.

The cathedral's brooding stone corridors gently yielded to morning light, which striped the floor as it spilled through the windows and filled the air with a soft, rosy glow. Sarathiel paused once to lay Leander's slender hand on a marble bench beside a window. Bathed in its radiance, his pale, finely sculpted face a contrast to the severity of his black robes, he looked like a painting, transported outside of time. I wondered if this was a place where the Divine had often sat in prayer. When Sarathiel finally turned away, I couldn't tell for certain, but I thought Leander's hair shone whiter.

We passed through the arches of the cloister and into a courtyard. The sun hadn't reached it yet, blocked by the cathedral's surrounding bulk. A damp, moldering chill pervaded, as though hundreds of dreary autumns and bitter winters lingered in the ancient stone. Ravens roosted above, dark blemishes dotting the buttresses and grotesques. They shifted restively, but didn't raise an alarm.

"Interesting," the revenant observed. *"It seems they can't easily*

sense the spirits through the knights' consecrated armor. I doubt Sarathiel planned that—it never was one of the cleverest of us revenants. Once, when we were a good deal younger, Malthas and I nearly convinced it to try possessing a duck."

I couldn't tell whether it was prattling out of nerves, or a vain attempt to cheer me up. I had spent much of the walk trying to recall how it felt to be alone inside my head. Not long ago, the quiet would have come as a blessed relief. Now the idea seemed bleak beyond imagining. Perhaps, with the Lady's mercy, the revenant and I would find each other again in the afterlife.

As we crossed the lawn, I noticed in the gloom that one of the soldiers escorting us looked familiar. He was resolutely gazing forward, his jaw set. I thought he might have been one of the soldiers from the square. Not the one who had dropped his sword, but one of the others.

Talbot, I remembered vaguely, putting a name to his face—not that it mattered. Captain Enguerrand was in prison. These weren't his men any longer. The city guard was being led by someone named Halbert, who Charles had said was loyal to the Clerisy.

Talbot happened to glance my way and accidentally met my eyes. He looked away quickly. His throat bobbed as he swallowed.

It occurred to me, almost idly, that a being like Sarathiel, who had the power to kill anyone it wanted without effort, to obliterate the population of an entire city on a whim, would never stoop to wonder whether humans were capable of outsmarting it. Certainly not a human like Marguerite.

Talbot stepped away to knock on one of the cloister's doors. An answering voice called out from the other side, and a key rattled in the lock. I looked at Marguerite more closely. She still had her head down, sniffling, her face mostly hidden behind clumps of hair, which was kinked and disheveled, coming loose from its festival braids. Her lip was swollen—someone had struck her.

Her voice came back to me. Something she had said in the infirmary. *Everyone thinks I'm just a stupid, silly little girl without a single useful thought in her head.*

I watched Talbot push open the door, revealing the knight guarding it on the other side. And I watched him slowly tip over, unconscious, landing on the ground with a boneless crash of armor.

Over him, into the courtyard, stepped Mother Dolours.

Our retinue came to a halt. Beside me, Sarathiel paused to take her in: the plain gray robes swathing her enormous girth, her eyes like gimlets above chapped, ruddy cheeks. "What is this?" Distaste crossed its features. "A nun?"

"Oh, you're about to find out," said the revenant gleefully.

The knights straightened, gripping the hilts of their swords. Before they could draw, the soldiers turned on them, unsheathing their own swords in arcs of steel that flashed blue in the shadows. The clash of blades filled the courtyard.

Mother Dolours strode through the melee, her robes billowing behind her like a ship's sails filling with wind. Swords swung past, narrowly missing her; she didn't look at them as she came. It shouldn't have been possible to hear her through the noise, but her voice echoed from the courtyard's walls, resounding. "Lady of Death, I seek Your mercy, for my enemies are many."

A soldier fell to a blow from a knight. I jerked forward, but a merciless grip closed on my arm. Sarathiel yanked me against Leander's chest, wrapping his fingers around my throat, prepared to snap my neck as easily as it had the Divine's.

Mother Dolours didn't falter. "May Your gaze fall upon them; may Your unseen hand strike them down." Her voice had become less a voice and more a roll of thunder, the tolling of a great bell. "May they cower before Your shadow. May You fill their minds with desolation."

As her prayer crashed over me, my senses sharpened to crystalline clarity: the hard warmth of Leander's chest pressing against my back, his uneven breath stirring my hair. The faint smells of soap and incense clinging to his skin. The trembling of his hand.

Sarathiel might be powerful beyond imagining, but it hadn't inhabited a human body in centuries. I expected there were some details it had forgotten. Sending a mental apology to Leander, I gathered my strength and drove my elbow against the concealed wound in his side. With a startled gasp, Sarathiel released me.

That was the only opening Mother Dolours required. She signed herself, and for a moment she seemed to transform into Mother Katherine, though the two of them looked nothing alike. Still I saw the elderly abbess framed by the opened door of the shed, my parents watching cowed behind her, their illusion of power stripped away. "By Your mercy," she boomed, "cast my enemies into darkness."

Ravens exploded cawing from the rooftops. Inside me, the revenant quailed and guttered like a candle in a winter's wind. For a terrible heartbeat I was overcome with the mindless, primordial fear of a small creature crouched in the grass, paralyzed by a hawk's shadow passing overhead. But the prayer wasn't aimed at me. In Leander's voice, Sarathiel let out a sharp, anguished cry and fell to the ground.

Amid the clashing swords, Mother Dolours turned to me. Fear lanced through my gut.

"Come, child," she said, her eyes dark as night.

I hesitated, looking down at Leander, writhing white-faced on the flagstones at my feet.

Mother Dolours said curtly, "Even if we had the time, exorcising Sarathiel from his body wouldn't help us. I can't destroy a revenant—only delay it. And not for very long."

I thought of Sarathiel's true form hovering above me in the chapel, so gargantuan that it had filled the nave. Marguerite's hand found mine. I let her drag me away. As we moved, the soldiers retreated and drew into a tight formation around us. In what seemed to be a mutual truce, the knights closed in around Leander, guarding him in turn. Light had almost reached the courtyard now, glancing from the rooftop finials and setting the uppermost windows aflame. Belatedly, it sank in that Mother Dolours had said Sarathiel's name.

Something must have shown on my face. Marguerite said in a rush, out of breath through the pounding of boots, "After you left Elaine's house and disappeared, I went to her for help. I didn't know what else to do. I told her what you told me about the page Confessor Leander took from the chambers, and she looked at a bunch of scrolls and figured out he was looking for Saint Agnes's ashes." We passed into the deeper darkness of the opposite cloister. "And then, when—when you turned up in the cathedral and got arrested—she said she sensed two revenants all the way from the convent, even though everyone else couldn't tell. It was awful—my shade was so frightened." Her blue eyes sought mine. "Is it really true? He's possessed by a revenant?"

I risked a glance over my shoulder. Between the knights, Sarathiel had rolled over and set Leander's forehead to the flagstones, fingers clenched and body arched as though in the throes of a convulsion. I swallowed. Nodded.

Then we were out a door, into the blinding light and roar of voices, the dizzying swarm of movement that filled the cathedral's square. A tide of people flooded past to slam the door shut behind us, throwing themselves against it, barricading it with their bodies.

"Artemisia! Marguerite!" This was Charles pushing into view. He had a wild look on his sweaty, grinning face, his tousled hair dusted with a coating of ash. "Jean and I freed the captain," he shouted. "Halbert almost wet himself when the guard rebelled. Look!"

I followed his pointing finger to the cathedral's front steps, onto which a group of people were shoving a wagon. Jean seemed to be doing most of the work, the muscles in his huge arms straining. He lifted one side of it and heaved; a cheer went up as it overturned with a crash against the cathedral's front doors.

Carts were being dragged toward the other doors, toppled over in piles. Furniture, barrels, and pieces of disassembled stalls joined them. Loud thumps and clatters of wood suggested that similar measures were taking place at every one of the cathedral's entrances and exits. It wasn't just civilians helping, but soldiers too. In the distance, Captain Enguerrand's hoarse voice shouted orders.

People had begun to notice me. A space was forming, a hush falling. I was met with somber face after somber face, every one of them smeared with ashes. Some were bruised and bloodied from the riots that had taken place overnight, their eyes defiant. Others clutched talismans that I recognized from the stalls—splinters of the holy arrow, scraps of cloth.

At first a number of them gazed searchingly at Marguerite, who probably looked a great deal more like the Artemisia they had expected. Then their eyes began to settle on my ungloved hand. Whispers started circulating. I couldn't hear them, but I could imagine their contents. *Look at her hand. Look at those scars.*

To my relief, an approaching figure provided a momentary

distraction as he jogged toward us through the crowd. It was Captain Enguerrand, though for a disorienting instant I didn't recognize him. It gave me a strange shock to see him dressed in ordinary clothes instead of plate armor, revealing him to be average in build, only about Charles's height and not much broader at the shoulder. Abrasions encircled his wrists where he had been tied with rope. The sword belted around his waist was his only sign of authority, but the crowd parted for him without hesitation.

"The barricades will hold for a time," he said, his tired, perceptive gaze flicking to me before settling on Mother Dolours. "How long do we have?"

Her face was grim. "Not as long as I would like. Not long enough to evacuate the city."

Marguerite's hand tightened on mine. We both knew what she meant. Overturned wagons would hold back the cathedral guard. They wouldn't contain Sarathiel.

I tried to imagine how long it would take everyone in the cathedral's square to walk to the Ghostmarch, for the drawbridge's mechanisms to be engaged and its weight let down. Then for everyone to cross, funneled across its span. I guessed that meant we only had about an hour, at best. Even if the city had a whole afternoon to evacuate, there would still be people left behind—the elderly, the less mobile, families who were sheltering in their cellars out of fear.

"Fleeing wouldn't do much good in the long run anyway," the revenant provided helpfully. *"The Sevre is annoying for a revenant to cross, but not impossible. Sarathiel will regain its full strength before these humans have gotten far."*

My skin prickled in warning, and I noticed that Mother Dolours was watching me as though she'd heard the revenant speak. Perhaps she had, I thought with a chill.

"I will strengthen our defenses with prayer," she said brusquely, leaving me none the wiser. "Captain Enguerrand, I entrust the rest to you. Don't make any fool decisions," she added, coaxing a faint smile from his tired mouth. "Lady watch over you, child."

That last part was directed at me. It occurred to me that perhaps I should say something, thank her at least, but she had already charged off, unceremoniously lowering herself to her knees on the cobbles. She bowed her head. The revenant shuddered. Inside one of the cathedral's shadowed windows, I saw the dancing flames of a candelabra go still.

I turned back around. Hundreds of anxious faces awaited my gaze. Pinned by their attention, I felt a familiar paralysis begin to creep over me. I didn't know what to do or what to say. These people had rescued me with the expectation that now that I had been freed, I would save them in turn. But the shackles had left me powerless.

Enguerrand glanced at me, then paused and looked more closely, his brow creasing. He beckoned me aside into the partial cover of a vendor's stall. Marguerite let go of my hand, but followed, dragging Charles along with her. I felt a pang of gratitude when they took up positions behind me, prepared to block anyone who tried to approach.

"I can't do anything with the shackles on," I told Enguerrand, once we had reached the awning's flapping shadow.

"I know. Mother Dolours told us." I supposed there had been enough witnesses in the cathedral for news of what had happened to have reached the convent. "We have a smith here to see about removing them, but Artemisia, before we go any farther . . ." For some reason, he looked sad. "You aren't obligated to help. I need you to understand that. If at any point you feel like you need to stop, I want you to tell me. No one will be upset with you if you can't help."

Hearing those words in his kind voice did something terrible to me that I didn't understand. My throat closed up like a fist; my heart ached as though it had been pierced. I nodded, avoiding his eyes.

He reached out as though to touch my shoulder. I flinched, and he dropped his hand. He looked at me once more with that same deep sadness, then opened the stall's flap to usher a third person inside. "This is Master Olivar, from the Blacksmiths Guild. Will you let him take a look at those cuffs?"

Master Olivar turned out to be a small, wiry man with skin as brown and wrinkled as a walnut and bright, intelligent dark eyes. To my relief, he sketched a perfunctory bow and then proceeded to ignore me almost completely in his rapt inspection of the shackles.

"I have never seen their like," he marveled, his fingers fluttering deftly over the hinges. "Extraordinary craftsmanship, extraordinary. The iron could be filed, yes, but it would take a long time, longer than you say we have. To break them open by force . . ." He shook his head. "No person has the strength. One might heat the metal first, but of course, we cannot do that without injuring young Artemisia."

His gaze hadn't lingered on my ungloved hand, but his eyes were knowing. To a blacksmith, his own arms striped with old burns, my scars had to be easily identifiable. He looked up at me keenly, questioning. "To open them, we will need the key."

If either the Divine or Sarathiel had been carrying it, I hadn't noticed. Sarathiel, I suspected, had never had any intention of releasing me. For all I knew, it could have tossed the key into the Sevre. "I don't know where it is," I answered.

In the silence that followed my admission, which I tried not to read as despairing, the worried murmurs filling the square outside intruded on the stall's fragile privacy. With the sound, my awareness of the crowd returned. I doubted many of them knew the whole truth, but they had to suspect something. Rumors must be spreading like wildfire.

My heart lurched when I glanced outside and noticed for the first time that there were children among the protestors. Even babies, cradled tightly. Their families likely thought it was safer here than at home, even with the riots. Danger had infiltrated every part of Roischal, including the streets of Bonsaint. Nowhere was safe. It wasn't the cathedral that offered a final promise of protection now—it was me. They were gathered here to be close to me.

I wondered how Saint Eugenia had felt facing the revenant on that hill in the scriptorium's tapestry—if she had been afraid, or if faith had turned her heart to iron. Or if there had never been a sunlit hill, a rearing horse, a glorious battle. Perhaps those parts had been made up, like my holy arrow. Perhaps the decisions that shaped the course of history weren't made in scenes worthy of stories and tapestries, but in ordinary places like these, driven by desperation and doubt.

Enguerrand was right, I thought with a painful twist. No one would be upset with me if I couldn't help, because they'd all be dead. The people of Roischal needed me as much as I had needed them. Even with the shackles, there was still one way I could save them.

I looked back to Captain Enguerrand and Master Olivar and said, "I need to pray."

TWENTY-EIGHT

I was left alone in the stall. To complete the illusion, I had knelt on the ground, where I had gained a view of the empty jars of pig's blood lined up along a hidden shelf. I wondered if the Lady was feeling ironic. Or perhaps the message wasn't intended for me—perhaps the stall's owner was standing outside, shaking in his boots.

If he was, I had no way of knowing. Only a few hushed voices betrayed the packed square outside, their murmurs barely louder than the stall's cloth flapping in the breeze. The news that I was praying must have spread. I felt a twinge of guilt at the lie. I was painfully aware of how little time we had and the possibility that I might be wasting it. Thus far, my conversation with the revenant hadn't been fruitful.

"So there aren't any places we could use for a ritual?" I asked in frustration, feeling as though we were talking in circles.

"No—I mean that if there are, we're unlikely to find them in time.

We would need to search the entire city. That would take days. Our best bet would be the catacombs, but I wouldn't want to risk opening any of the grates; we might as well ring a dinner bell for Sarathiel. . . ."

It continued talking, but I was only listening with half an ear, my thoughts churning. It had already explained why we couldn't create our own ritual site—the same as filing through the shackles, we didn't have time. Chewing on the inside of my cheek, I stared hard at the cobblestones under my knees. *The entire city.* Something about that phrase had stuck in my mind.

The entire city . . .

That was it. The cobbles beneath me, the stones that made up the city's walls—they were ancient. So ancient they attracted shades, just like the ruin outside my old village.

"What about Bonsaint?" I asked, the idea blossoming in my mind like a bizarre flower, wondrous to behold.

"Bonsaint? The food is average at best. Architecture, mediocre. And don't get me started on the overpopulation of nuns—"

Frowning, I interrupted, "When we first got here, you said that Bonsaint was built from the ruins of another city, one that stood during the Age of Kings." I felt its startled pause. "Old Magic must have been practiced there. And they're the same stones, used over again. That's why you think our best bet is in the catacombs, right? It's the old city down there. But the old city never went away. It's still here."

"Use an entire city as a single ritual site? That's . . . that's absolutely . . ." I could tell it wanted to say something like "ridiculous" or "mad," but it couldn't. My suggestion held a kernel of possibility.

"But would it work?" I persisted.

"No one with any real knowledge of Old Magic would ever propose

such an idea, but only because it would never occur to them to try. A ritual of that scale . . . the consequences if it failed would be astronomical." Here the revenant hesitated, and my heart plummeted. *"But nothing worse than what Sarathiel will do once it's recovered,"* it hastened to assure me, its voice slightly clipped. *"And I wouldn't get it wrong."*

"Are you sure?" I asked hoarsely, almost shaking with hope.

"Oh, I'm very sure. As I told you before, I'm no amateur. Let's see. The ritual's array would need to encompass the whole city, as though it were a very large version of the altar."

I nodded as though I were following.

"And the runes would need to be spaced at a considerable distance from each other, to avoid exerting too much force on any one location. In the absence of ritual materials, they'll need to be drawn in your blood—there needs to be an elemental force represented, and blood is one of the most potent—but we can make them small, to avoid using too much. . . ."

My hands curled. I suspected my nails were digging into my palms; I faintly sensed a dull current of pain through my scars. It was as though a fire burning in my heart, banked ever since Sarathiel had escaped, was now flaring back to life. I couldn't stay still any longer. Without meaning to, I found myself scrambling to my feet.

The revenant said quickly, *"Nun, don't get up, I'm not finished yet—"*

Too late. I had already stood and pushed aside the flap. And I couldn't turn back now: the entire square had been waiting for me to finish praying, and now that I had emerged, not defeated by a lack of answers but vital with purpose, an answering flame of hope was igniting on hundreds of faces.

For once, it wasn't hard to speak. To the assembled masses, I said, "I need something sharp. Also, can I borrow someone's horse?"

As it turned out, I didn't need the horse right away. The first rune could be drawn in the cathedral's square, since it was roughly in Bonsaint's center.

"As I was about to tell you, before you rudely interrupted me," the revenant said. *"Keep walking. We want the very oldest of the paving stones. Yes—stop—right there."*

I halted and clambered down to my knees at the spot it had indicated. Whispers followed my every movement. At first a few people had tried to touch me as I paced around the square, but Charles, Marguerite, and Jean had closed in around me like my own personal guard. I felt the revenant trying to cast its senses toward Mother Dolours, only to give up, thwarted by the shackles. *"Just keep praying, you horrible nun,"* it muttered. I pretended not to have heard.

My stomach was in knots; I was dreading what came next. I reminded myself that to everyone watching, this wouldn't look like Old Magic. It would just look like I was drawing a holy symbol. Even so, sweat began to gather beneath my chemise. I still knew that I was about to commit heresy, even if no one else did.

I couldn't lose my nerve before I even began. I had six more to go; this rune would be the first of seven, spread out to form a city-wide array.

"It will be easy," the revenant assured me. *"I can create an image of the rune inside your mind, and you only need to copy the shape. This one will probably even look familiar to you. It's a grounding rune, which is very common."*

I hesitated, glancing back at the cathedral. I could no longer see the candles glowing in the window. Scanning the ravens perched on the surrounding rooftops, I detected no hint of Trouble's white feathers. I couldn't find the words for what I wanted to ask. But I didn't need to. The revenant understood.

It said quietly, *"You don't have to be the one to do it."*

I ducked my head, trying to swallow past the lump in my throat. Unable to speak, I nodded.

"Just concentrate on relaxing. No, not like that. You have relaxed before, haven't you?" It sighed. *"On second thought, never mind. Do you remember what it felt like on the battlefield when you gave me control of your arm?"*

When that had happened, I hadn't made a conscious choice; I hadn't had time to think. It had been an instinctual act, like handing over a tool. Concentrating hard, I tried not to think, sought to find that place of blank acceptance.

When the switch occurred, it wasn't the same as in the cathedral. I didn't notice anything strange until my mouth opened and I said, "Charles, would you hand me the knife?" Except I wasn't the one asking the question. It was the revenant speaking through my mouth.

Charles had been the one to search the crowd at my request. He'd returned with a simple carving knife, its blade crude but well-honed. Now he handed it to me in silence, then solemnly stepped back. The onlookers watched eagerly to see what I would do next. I wondered in despair if the knife would end up being called the sacred dagger, its replicas sold on the streets.

Charles blanched when the revenant shrugged back my sleeve and lowered the dagger above my arm. Marguerite, less surprised, took hold of Jean's arm and firmly turned him around. I was glad

Enguerrand had left to find a horse. I had a strange feeling that if he were here, he might try to stop me.

The knife hung poised above my arm. I waited for the cut, then waited some more. Nothing happened. It was as though my body had turned to stone, the dagger frozen in midair. Light quivered on the blade; my hand was shaking.

"I can't do it," the revenant muttered at last.

It didn't mean the Old Magic, I realized in amazement. It meant that it couldn't cut me, even though it only needed a little of my blood, and the cut would barely sting. My chest tightened with unexpected sympathy. Embarrassed, the revenant quickly handed back control.

Someone in the crowd whispered, "Is she going to—" the moment before the knife's edge met my skin.

A brief flash of pain. Then a sluggish rivulet of blood traced the curve of my arm, and a single shining droplet landed on the cobbles. I hadn't cut deeply, knowing I would need to score a new wound for each rune.

I passed back control to the revenant, who immediately flung the knife aside as though repulsed by it. It dipped my fingers in the blood and began to draw.

The rune took shape in glistening dabs of red. The revenant was right; I had seen this symbol before. It was carved on one of the cornerstones of the chapel in Naimes and decorated many of the oldest tombstones in the graveyard. Novices were taught that it meant something like "peace" or "rest."

Murmurs of enlightenment spread as onlookers began to recognize the shape. I imagined the news fanning outward from the nearest bystanders like ripples in a pond, distorted to rumor by the time it lapped against the farthest corners of the square.

I hoped this wasn't going to end up on a tapestry one day: "Saint Artemisia beseeching the Lady for aid with her own heart's blood." Or worse—they had better not believe She was revealing the symbols to me like the saints of old, etched across my mind in sacred fire. At least now I understood why I had never read accounts of Old Magic being used in the War of Martyrs. If I checked again, I suspected I would see references to it everywhere, described as the Lady's miracles.

The revenant only glanced up once, bringing Charles and Marguerite into view. I hadn't explained my plan to either of them. There hadn't been time. Charles signed himself when he saw me looking. Marguerite wore a slight frown.

As the revenant finished drawing the rune, I expected a change to happen, that I would feel the Old Magic's poison seeping through my soul, or the terrible abandonment of the Lady casting me from Her sight. But I only felt slightly drained, as though a small amount of my life force had left my body along with my blood. The revenant sat up slowly, mindful of my spinning head.

As I sat there dazed, a clopping of hooves penetrated the fog. Mounted on his own black charger, Captain Enguerrand had returned with a horse—and not just any horse. Seeing the dapple–gray stallion approach, the revenant wordlessly surrendered control.

Heedless of the many onlookers, I stumbled to Priestbane and caught his bridle for balance. His hot breath gusted down my front as he nosed at my face, his whiskers tickling my cheek. He didn't seem to blame me for how hard I had ridden him after the battle. I bent to run my hands down his powerful legs, wanting to check them for signs of heat or swelling.

"He's sound. He's a good horse," Enguerrand added, a little roughly. I felt him watching me. "Can you ride?"

I wondered if I looked bad enough that he needed to ask. Before he could offer to help, I pulled myself into the saddle. I had just gotten settled when a warm, soft weight pressed against my back. Charles had boosted Marguerite up after me.

"If you're going to be cutting up your arm and bleeding all over the place, I'm coming with you," she said fiercely. "Don't argue."

I wasn't about to push her off, at least not with this many people watching. I supposed she wouldn't slow me down—Priestbane had been bred to bear a fully grown man in armor. Marguerite's extra weight wouldn't tax him on an easy ride.

The revenant was saying, *"We should start at the northwest corner of the city and draw the second rune, then work our way around. The walls would be the best place to start; they're guaranteed to be among the oldest parts of Bonsaint."*

I relayed this to Captain Enguerrand, who turned his horse to guide us, though he glanced at the patch of blood on my sleeve in concern. Priestbane impatiently mouthed the bit as our pace broke into a trot, then a canter, hoofbeats clattering loudly through the square. Marguerite yelped and clutched at my cloak until I grabbed her hands and wrapped them around my middle.

As we reached the streets, windows and doors began to open. Faces peered out, at first cautiously, and then with growing excitement. Light flushed the buildings as the sun rose higher, cresting the rooftops. Color returned to the festival banners still strung overhead.

The occasional voice calling out from a window failed to explain the hubbub at our heels. A glance over my shoulder revealed that the crowd from the square had decided to follow, the nearest people jogging to keep up, the slower trailing behind.

They accompanied us all the way to the next stop, a rugged

stretch of wall shining with moisture and thrumming with the roar of the Sevre's current. I made the cut on my arm, then passed over control to the revenant. When it looked up from drawing the second rune, I discovered that the crowd had filled the street, gaining in size as those walking at the rear began to catch up.

Onward we went. After the third rune, the Old Magic's dizzy, draining weakness lingered instead of subsiding. After the fourth, my thoughts swam. I was grateful for Marguerite behind me; otherwise I might have slid from the saddle like a sack of grain. If it weren't for the urgency of our mission, I suspected that the revenant would make me stop and rest, and probably eat some pottage.

Our journey gained a dreamlike quality. My fear of running out of time lifted away, replaced by a peaceful numbness. The people of Roischal carried me forward as though I were borne along by a tide. At one point I thought I saw Elaine beside me; I wasn't sure whether I had imagined it. Charles was there, then Jean. Another time, white petals began to rain softly over the street. I stared in bewilderment, wondering if it had started snowing, until I grew aware that onlookers were leaning from the upper windows of their houses, tossing down handfuls of Lady's tears.

It seemed that no one expected me to speak or even acknowledge them, unified with purpose merely by my presence. I distantly recalled the icon of Saint Agnes, carried during the procession beneath her fringe.

At the next stop, dozens of hands were waiting to gently draw me down from Priestbane's saddle—touches that in my exhaustion, I didn't mind. For a surreal moment, I thought they belonged to the Lady. And perhaps, in a way, they did. I thought of Enguerrand handing me his water skin after the battle. The children in the encampment offering me their scrap of bread.

I wanted to tell the revenant, *You see, here is the Lady's grace. It has been here all along. She has shown me Her grace in a drink of water when I was thirsty and bread when I was hungry and a bed when I was tired, not through miracles, but through the kindness of those who stood to gain nothing from helping me. It is through the hands of strangers that She has carried out Her will.* But I was too weary and muddle-headed to form the words aloud. By the time I had strung them together in my head, I was already being helped back onto Priestbane's saddle.

This time, to my relief, the revenant didn't relinquish control. It was good not to have to move my heavy body—to simply hand over my burdens to a friend. I watched it hold out my arm, which Marguerite was wrapping in bandages she had stripped from her chemise.

"Just one more," it said through my mouth, addressing Captain Enguerrand. "Let's head to the convent next." Then it muttered to me alone, "Stay awake, nun. They're going to need you before this is over."

Time seemed to fold in on itself. It was as though I nodded off for an instant, and then we had entered a familiar section of the city, the convent's mossy walls approaching. I braced myself to endure the scourge of the lichgate, but as we approached its iron bars, no rebukes came. A solitary voice ghosted over me, whispering softly, *"My name is Sister Anna. I pray to the goddess, though my bones are long dust. Still I pray, forever."*

Dismounted, I was led stumbling across the grounds. Marguerite held me up on one side, and Charles the other. The revenant was beginning to have difficulty controlling my body.

Beneath their worried chatter, it gasped, "I didn't predict how much of your strength this ritual would require. No one's ever attempted Old Magic on this scale before, except . . ."

It trailed off. *Except for the Raven King,* I finished numbly.

As though to banish that thought, it raised my head and called hoarsely to Captain Enguerrand, "The chapel. The final symbol needs to be drawn on the chapel's foundations."

Behind us, a scattering of screams erupted. The crowd began to flow inside more rapidly. A sister quickly scaled a ladder leaning against the wall. Looking out, she shouted down, "There are thralls coming! Knights, in armor! And"—she faltered, her face turning pale—"the confessor."

The nuns scrambled into action. The lichgate began to close on the heels of the last civilians streaming inside. The crowd had kept pace with us at the end, but the convent couldn't possibly hold everyone. I hoped the rest had fled, even though deep down I knew it didn't matter—that on this side of the lichgate or the other, there was no escape from Sarathiel.

We were passing the barnyard now. I heard a wrench of metal behind us, and realized we wouldn't reach the chapel before the thralls breached the gate. I tried to speak, and experienced a brief moment of panic before the revenant caught on. I stumbled as the weight of my body returned.

"I need to get the shackles off," I panted.

Over my head, Charles and Marguerite exchanged looks of dread. I knew what they were thinking. They had heard from Enguerrand that removing the shackles was impossible.

Then a heavy clinking sound drew everyone's attention. Jean was returning from the stable, carrying a chisel and mallet taken from the convent's small smithy, where repairs could be made to horseshoes and the wheels of the corpse-wagons. Large as the mallet was, it resembled a toy in his enormous hands.

No person has the strength, Master Olivar had said. But I wagered that he had never met Jean.

As he advanced, Charles caught Marguerite's eye. "He can do it," he insisted. "I'd bet my life on it."

Marguerite's lips parted, but no reply came. Her eyes were on the chisel. She was probably thinking that a single miscalculated swing could sever my wrist. She still hadn't let go.

"Let him," I said.

That broke the spell. They helped me to the ground. Jean set the chisel against the shackle on my left wrist. When the mallet struck, the impact reverberated through my body, humming along my bones as though my arm were the clapper inside a bell. The shackle parted, split cleanly in two.

He repositioned the chisel. Raised the mallet again. A crack, and the right shackle broke, falling away from my wrist. Power roared into my veins like a healing draught, like a river of cleansing fire. Suddenly, I found that I could stand.

A strange double vision overtook me as my eyes fell on the knights invading the convent through the breached lichgate. I felt as though I were back in Naimes, except this time, instead of watching helplessly from afar, I could stop it. I could make it so that the thralls never took another step, never raised their swords. I could do anything.

I stretched out my hand. The knights collapsed like toppled toys, the wraiths that had possessed them streaming violently from their bodies. Another wave of knights followed, and they fell in turn. The effort barely registered. I no longer felt human. I was a vessel, forged to bear the revenant's power.

The sister watching from the ladder gave a strangled cry. She clambered down, stumbling as she fled. A moment later, mist seeped over the wall, pouring down its side in a silvery curtain. At its touch, the ivy curled and browned; a sparrow dropped dead from the withered leaves. More mist crept through the open space where the gate had stood, reaching its fingers into the convent. Within, barely visible, strode a tall, black-robed figure.

On the battlefield, I hadn't dared unleash the revenant's full power near the soldiers and refugees. The same risk had held me back in the square. But now I had no choice. I had wielded the revenant's ghost-fire before in my own convent—perhaps I could control it again here.

"Revenant," I said, "attend me."

I had almost forgotten how it felt. The triumphant howl of power unleashed, the spreading of a great pair of fiery wings. My cloak and hair seemed to lift around me, weightless. Flames roared forth, tumbling over the convent's grounds. The mist evaporated in their path. The confused, roiling wraiths vanished like stars smothered behind a spreading cloud. I felt a distant twinge of regret at their loss, but it quickly faded to nothing before the towering onslaught of my hunger. The fire spread onward to engulf the city, racing through the streets, sweeping over rooftops, flooding into every window and alley and cellar.

Everywhere, souls flared to life. I could map the city by their glittering multitude alone—the rats skittering through the walls, the constellations of insects clotted around the foundations of buildings; the families huddled fearfully inside their homes, wrapped in each other's arms. But it was Sarathiel who glowed the most brightly, its brilliant light condensed into the shape of a man like molten silver poured into a mold. With distant, starved amazement, I realized that I could see the priest's soul, too—glimmers of gold drowning in Sarathiel's light.

I needed to destroy Sarathiel. This much I remembered through the consuming haze of hunger. But I couldn't devour its essence without consuming everything else—every living thing in Bonsaint, down to the worms in the graves and the weeds poking up between the cobbles.

And why not? I no longer remembered why I cared. The world was radiant. My thoughts were silver fire.

"Artemisia," pled a girl's fearful voice at my side, but I dismissed her as a mere annoyance. Once, I remembered, I had wanted to kill her. I wasn't sure why I had changed my mind.

Then I felt a waver of uncertainty. A *part* of me had wanted to kill her—but there was another side of me that hadn't. And that same side thought that I shouldn't give in to the hunger. That I should restrain myself. But if I wanted to destroy Sarathiel . . .

The golden glimmers of the priest's soul caught my attention. They were shining more brightly, spreading in patches, overtaking the silver. His body doubled over; he buried his head in his hands. Now he was more gold than silver, Sarathiel's essence pulsing furiously at the intrusion. I realized what was happening. Against all odds, the priest was resisting.

I doubted he could keep it up for long, but at the very least, he might delay Sarathiel.

And then I remembered—*the ritual*. I had to finish the ritual.

The fire snuffed out. The howling inside my head vanished. The coppery tang of blood filled my mouth and nose, and my clothes were faintly steaming.

The sisters were staring at me with their mouths open. Without the Sight, the civilians hadn't seen what had happened, but they were staring too. They had clearly sensed something, whether it was a shiver down their spines or the hairs rising on the backs of their necks—a force greater than life and death sweeping through them and sparing them all.

Marguerite's hands caught at me. She and Charles and Enguerrand were speaking to me, but I couldn't hear them. *"Go,"* the revenant snarled, its voice miserable with hunger, *"hurry,"* and then I was being bundled toward the chapel, helped along by more people than I could count.

The doors juddered open. A familiar smell of old wood, beeswax, and incense enfolded me, so unexpected that my eyes stung. It smelled exactly like the chapel in Naimes.

I blindly reached for the knife as we careened up the aisle, and found it in my hand. As soon as I had made the cut on my arm, already falling to the floor, the revenant seized control and tore the carpet before the altar aside to expose the flagstones.

The final rune began to take shape, scrawled clumsily in red. My fingers cramped. Frustrated, the revenant flexed my hand as though willing it to work. It could strengthen my body, but it couldn't help my scars.

At the periphery of my vision, I saw the sisters fail to close the chapel's door. Leander had appeared, holding it open, his arms braced wide, his white-streaked hair hanging disheveled, blood shining on his upper lip.

It wasn't Leander—it was Sarathiel.

It understood what we were doing at once. Fury and terror twisted Leander's face into a horrible mask. It moved to withdraw, but at the same time one of Leander's hands seized the doorframe. For an instant, he had regained control, and that was all it took for him to wrench himself inside.

He dropped to his knees as though in supplication. "Artemisia," he whispered, his green eyes burning into mine. "Do it."

The rune was finished. I slammed my hand down, or the revenant did, or we both did it together.

The world exploded into pain.

At first, the pain came as a shock. Then it made terrible sense. Stupid. I had been so stupid. I remembered the revenant's earlier hesitation in the stall—the moment it had realized that the ritual designed to destroy Sarathiel would also destroy itself, that there was no way to avoid this fate, that it had made the decision to sacrifice itself then and there. Not for humanity's sake, but for mine. Sarathiel wouldn't have let me live. This was the only way to save me.

Leander lay collapsed in the aisle, his features beautiful and still. He didn't seem to be breathing. Fragments of silver were tearing upward from his body like shards of broken glass, a shattered cathedral window caught in a whirlwind, the fractured panes reflecting a skeletal ribcage, a serene half-closed eye, a graceful row of pinions. Sarathiel was breaking apart—and I could feel my revenant following.

Frantically, I imagined gathering up its pieces and gripping them in my hands, clutching them against my chest, refusing to let them escape.

"*Let go,*" said the revenant. Its voice was a horrible shriek, almost unrecognizable, like a gale tearing through my mind.

Instead, I gripped it tighter.

"*You'll die!*" it howled.

Desperately, I held on.

And then the revenant was railing against me, too. The pain was so great that I could barely think. I briefly forgot my mission, only to remember again with an agony like being torn asunder. Furiously, I began to pray.

Lady, if I have served You, spare the revenant. If You are merciful, let it live. I have done what You have asked. I have suffered for You. This is the only thing I want in return.

Spare the revenant.

Please, spare the revenant . . .

My vision filled with silver light. No answer came. But She couldn't ignore me forever. If She wouldn't listen to me, I would make Her regret it.

I would die, and I would see Her soon.

EPILOGUE

I had strange dreams.

I was a child again, shoving my hands into the hearth. But this time the fire was silver and didn't burn me. The flames were standing still.

A muttered croak drew my attention. A white raven was watching me from the window, its feathers ruffled in annoyance. Its eyes were black, but as I looked closer, I realized that they weren't lightless—they glittered with thousands upon thousands of stars.

"Artemisia," it cawed, scolding me. "Artemisia!"

I startled awake in a small, whitewashed chamber, the raven's voice still ringing in my ears. At first I thought I was back in the tower where Sarathiel had imprisoned me, and had confused my dreams with waking reality. But I didn't recognize the view out the window, its shutters thrown wide: a green mountain landscape, the shadows of clouds racing over fir-covered slopes. A bell rang out the first hour of the afternoon, and when it stopped, I heard prayers being sung in deep voices. Slowly, my memories began to reorient themselves. My breathing stilled.

"Revenant?" I asked, not daring to hope.

"I'm here, nun," it said.

I shot up, the coverlet knotted in my hands, joy flooding my heart like a sunrise. I had never imagined its hideous voice would sound so welcome.

"Before you say something embarrassing, you should know that we aren't alone."

I turned to find Mother Dolours sitting in a chair in the corner of the room. My joy instantly gave way to cold, drenching terror. Marguerite had explained things to her. How much, exactly, had she explained?

By now, the abbess had to suspect my relationship with the revenant. She might even know I had used Old Magic.

Incongruously, she was darning a hole in a stocking. I got the impression that, like me, she was the kind of person who wasn't used to sitting idle. She would start going mad without a task to keep herself occupied. As though sensing my thoughts, she looked up.

"We are in the monastery of Saint Barnabas, in the far east of Roischal," she said calmly. "You could have recovered in Bonsaint, but I thought it wiser to bring you to a place where fewer casualties would result if Rathanael suddenly began to feel less cooperative. The sisters will survive without me in the meantime, I trust."

I couldn't hold back the question any longer. "What are you going to do about the revenant?" I blurted.

The chair creaked as she leaned back. She eyed me keenly. "Do I need to do something about it?" she inquired.

A shiver gripped me. I couldn't help wondering whether she had known the truth since the moment I had arrived in her convent and had been watching me the entire time. I found that I couldn't meet her eyes. I felt as though I might see something in them if I did: a fathomless night sky, glittering with stars.

"Oh, don't look so alarmed, child," she said brusquely. "We had a nice long talk while you were sleeping, Rathanael and I. The Lady spared Rathanael for a reason, and I'm not going to argue with Her about it. She and I already butt heads enough as it is. These days I find I have to pick my battles, or I would never have time for anything else."

I opened my mouth, closed it again. I suspected there was much more Mother Dolours wasn't telling me. Had the revenant possessed me at some point while I had been unconscious to talk to her? I didn't find the idea disturbing. But it struck me that Mother Dolours should have. She should have found it extremely disturbing. She should have performed an exorcism on me on the spot. What had the revenant said to her?

She had resumed darning the stocking. "Not everyone believes in wielding relics by force," she remarked. "There is power that is taken, and there is power that is freely given. I'll let you figure out what I mean by that on your own."

My eyes went to her relics. She couldn't possibly mean that she had befriended her own spirits. But it also seemed unlikely that Marguerite and I were the only ones to ever walk that path. And the way she had used her wretchling relic in the infirmary— tirelessly, effortlessly, almost as though it were cooperating with her . . .

Stunned, I watched her reach down to feel around in her darning basket. She grunted and drew out something that winked gold in the light. Crossing the room, she handed me Saint Eugenia's reliquary. The revenant's relief left me dizzy.

"If you're to keep this, they'll want you to become a vesper-tine," she said gruffly. "You'll have to put up with the robes and the duties, neither of which will suit you, I expect. You'll find out soon enough that the trappings of high office exist for no reason at all except to keep people from being too effective at their jobs, which is a great inconvenience for the Clerisy."

I looked up at her and back down at the reliquary, like a child handed a gift that might get snatched away at any moment. Then I paused, frowning, and sniffed it. "Where was it?" I asked.

She snorted. "Your friend Marguerite hid it in an empty pot of lard in the infirmary."

The revenant shuddered, but I regarded Marguerite with new appreciation. Back in Naimes, I had been instructed to rub lard on my hands every night before bed to help soften my scars, a process that she had gloomily endured with watering eyes and a wrinkled nose. I would have neglected the treatment if not for the unknown sister who had pointedly set the jar on my coverlet every evening. She had kept up the habit every night for years.

At least, I had assumed it was a sister. Suddenly, I wasn't so certain.

Mother Dolours was likely right about becoming a vespertine, but right now, getting to keep the revenant was the only thing that mattered. Turning the reliquary over in my hands, I heard her move toward the door. Belatedly, I realized that she must have found herself in a difficult position after the events in Bonsaint.

"What are you going to do now that the Divine is dead?" I asked.

Mother Dolours heaved a sigh. "Give in to everyone's demands to take her place, it seems."

I remembered what she had said about arguing with the Lady.

Not long ago, hearing that from an abbess would have shocked me, but my recent experiences had been educational. "The Lady spoke to you?"

She barked out a laugh. "Well enough, she has. I don't want to do it, which in my experience is the surest sign that I need to."

The monastery was a place of winding stone paths and windswept battlements. The wind smelled of mountain air, woodsmoke, and pine resin. When it blew from the direction of the sacred groves, I could sometimes hear the tapping of hammers as brothers drove pegs into the trees. Afterward, they returned with pails of sap to render into incense.

The monks didn't know how to react to me, which was fine, because I didn't know how to react to them, either. Theirs was a remote stronghold that received few visitors; they went about their tasks in near silence, meeting gravely for meals and prayers. The abbot was a shy, soft-spoken man with a single frostfain relic, flustered by the sudden influx of pilgrims to his domain. Thankfully, the visitors weren't allowed past the cloister, though incidents still happened. Once a man made it all the way to the refectory and prostrated himself at my feet before the apologetic brothers managed to coax him away.

I spent my days alternately resting and getting scolded by the revenant whenever I exerted myself too heavily. By its measure, this meant walking all the way down the hall by myself or climbing a few steps to see the view from the battlements. Marguerite was acting as its accomplice; as soon as I escaped my chambers, she would come hurrying, her chestnut hair flying in the wind. Often she was clutching a letter from Charles, halfway through reading it over again for the third or fourth time. Now that her identity had been uncovered, there was talk of letting her study as a curist in Chantclere. The sisters in Bonsaint were already sending references.

A week had passed before I found out that Leander had traveled to the monastery with us. No one had wanted to tell me, and by then it was nearly too late.

"He is not fit to see visitors, lady," babbled the nervous brother whom I finally managed to corner in the cloister, after hours of chasing monks around like frightened sheep. "Truthfully, I think he may have been brought here to live out his final days in peace."

Roaring filled my ears as though someone had plunged my head underwater. Distressed, and perhaps more than a little terrified, the monks hastened to escort me to the guest dormitory. I didn't remember going up the steps or down the hall; it was as though I simply appeared in the doorway to Leander's room, where I came to a sudden halt. I stood frozen, looking inside.

He lay on a bed, his slender hands resting across his stomach, as elegant and still as a marble effigy carved on a sarcophagus. He was dressed in a plain linen nightgown instead of his confessor's robes. Most startlingly of all, his hair had turned completely white. It lay curled on the pillow around his head, emphasizing his sharp cheekbones and austere brow. His pale skin held the translucency of alabaster.

"He has only woken briefly," one brother informed me, wringing his hands. "There is little that can be done for him, except to make him comfortable."

I hesitated, taking in his spectral appearance. I had assumed him dead; I had never imagined he might have survived Sarathiel's destruction, not after the torments his body had endured that day. Even now he looked as though he were lingering within the gates of Death, transforming into a spirit before my eyes.

My throat tightened. I wished he had died swiftly instead of suffering this drawn-out fate, and yet I was grateful to see him again, a feeling that startled me with its painful, punishing intensity—like swallowing a draught of water and finding that it burned instead of quenched.

Seeing my expression, the brothers made their excuses and hurried away. I found a stool and dragged it to Leander's bedside. Then I waited.

The sun slid across the floorboards and onto the wall before his eyes opened. Unsurprised by my presence, he gazed up at me with the calm fatalism of the dying. I had started to get used to his appearance by then, but it came as a new shock to see his white eyelashes against the vivid green of his eyes. They looked like they were coated in snow.

"This dream again," he murmured breathlessly. "My favorite."

"What dream is that?" My voice sounded hoarse.

"The one in which Saint Artemisia stands over me in judgment."

"I told you, I'm not a saint."

"Even in my dreams," he said softly, "you never cease arguing with me." He said this in distant wonderment, as though it were a quality he admired. "But you must realize . . . if you weren't one before . . . you are now. Not just a saint, but a high saint. One of the seven."

"Technically, he's right," the revenant commented into the void that followed this remark. *"Saint Agnes didn't destroy Sarathiel. You did."*

Leander blinked. Frowned. "Have I been praying to you? Is that why you're here?"

"This isn't a dream." My throat was dry. "You're awake."

His eyes narrowed, struggling to bring me into focus. "No," he decided. "The real Artemisia wouldn't be here."

At that, an emotion close to anger prickled hot across my skin. My chest ached. It wasn't fair of him to make me feel sorry for him. He didn't deserve my pity. "Stop dying," I told him.

A faint smile touched his lips. "Is that all?" he asked softly.

I remembered what the old curist had said in the convent, and realized there was another thing I wanted to know—especially since this might be my last chance to ask. "What happened to your brother?"

"Ah," Leander said. His eyes drifted shut. He didn't answer for so long that I thought he had lapsed back into sleep. Then he murmured, "The view from the battlements of Chantclere, overlooking the sea . . . it's a very good place to think. My favorite place, in fact. Gabriel went up there during last year's feast of Saint Theodosia. He jumped. I never found out why."

Silence reigned between us, filled with the soft rasp of Leander's breathing. I thought of the prayer book's dedication. *I'll see you soon.*

When he spoke again, I had to lean closer to hear. "In the cathedral, I meant to say . . . when I used Saint Liliane's relic on you in Naimes, to hurt you, I had only been ordained as a confessor for a few months. It was my first time using it that way. I didn't predict that it would be quite so . . ."

"Painful?" I suggested. "Cruel? I know you aren't sorry. You've used it on plenty of people since."

"I don't expect your forgiveness. In fact, it would be better if . . ." He briefly seemed to lose the thought. He turned his head aside, blinked a few times, and then picked up the thread, "As I told you, one can't like oneself in order to be a confessor."

I shook my head, disgusted. "All those people you hurt—you did it to help control the penitent?"

"When you put it that way . . . but no." Bitterness hardened his tone, turning his words as sharp and brittle as broken glass. "I did it so they wouldn't slow me down. A necessary means to an end. I believed the Lady wouldn't send anyone to help, and if I wanted to stop the disaster in Roischal, I would have to do it myself, alone. But She sent you. And you accomplished in weeks what I had been striving to accomplish for months. You succeeded where I failed."

His hand moved slightly on the coverlet. I noticed for the first time that his fingers were bare. He no longer wore the relic of Saint Liliane.

"Do you truly want my judgment?" I asked.

That caught his attention. His gaze had grown clearer, sharper. I wondered if he had realized that he was awake, but his eyes held a fevered intensity that I doubted he would let me witness if he thought this was real instead of a dream. "Yes," he answered, very quietly, so quietly I could barely hear.

"You aren't a good person, but I think you could be if you tried. So perhaps you should try."

For a long time, he didn't respond. It wasn't until I stood up to leave the room that he spoke. "Thank you," he said softly, and seemed to mean it.

Slowly, I regained my strength. I didn't visit Leander again, but I heard he had narrowly escaped death and was on his way to an astonishing recovery. I happened across a pair of monks huddled behind the refectory, discussing in hushed tones how he had begun improving immediately after my visit. "A miracle," they murmured. "A true miracle . . ."

Too busy signing themselves, they failed to notice me slipping away.

One early morning before dawn, I wrapped myself in a blanket and snuck onto the battlements. I had chosen this solitary spot for a reason. Over the past few days, the revenant had been uncharacteristically quiet, obviously working itself up to something. We wouldn't be disturbed here by Marguerite or the shy glances of brothers, their ears straining to make out the words of my frequent "prayers."

Winter had fully descended upon Roischal. Snow flurries rushed down from the black sky to land shivering on my blanket's wool; the cold numbed my ears and nose. But I didn't have to wait long. The revenant soon said, *"Nun, there's something you should know before you choose to remain my vessel."* It was silent a moment, then plunged onward. *"I'm the one who invented the binding ritual. I'm the reason why relics exist."*

My insides flipped. At first I felt sure it had made some bizarre joke, but then I thought—Traitor. Scorned One. Betrayer of its own kind.

Its vile little obsession with Old Magic.

I had never gotten a clear answer about why it was called "the Scorned."

"I didn't do it purposefully," the revenant continued. *"In fact, I never intended for the ritual to be used. I was trying to find a way to help Eugenia control my power. That particular version . . . I discarded it after realizing that Eugenia would need to sacrifice herself for it to work. But of course, being my vessel, she had helped me transcribe it. I couldn't hide its existence from her."*

I listened as though bespelled, cocooned inside the blanket's warmth. I had wanted to know more about Eugenia for so long, but I had never dared ask. Now I wondered whether I desired the truth after all.

"Later, there was a battle. She survived, but lost hundreds of soldiers—men who had followed her charge onto the battlefield. Their bodies couldn't be recovered. In the next battle came the riveners."

My chest tightened. I remembered the defeated rivener kneeling before me, struggling to rise. If there had been a chance of it being the soul of someone I had known, fought alongside— Charles, or Jean, or Enguerrand . . .

"After that, she changed. We failed to make progress on the ritual. She began praying to the Lady for hours, sometimes through the night. One morning, she blocked my voice from her mind. She went to her general and told him to find her a new vessel. She gave him the notes—the ways in which I could be controlled by a priestess after I had been bound to her bones. I fought, but she used every method at her disposal to subdue me, including the ones that I had taught her. And then came the pain, and the fire. I lived every moment as her bones burned to ash."

The snowflakes hurled themselves down, seeming to fly at me with dizzying speed until they drew closer and drifted the rest of the way like eiderdown. They landed on my cheeks in gentle puffs of cold.

"She was only fourteen," it said, *"and she died screaming to your Lady."*

I shook my head in denial, my heart aching. I could easily imagine how Eugenia must have felt, willing to make any sacrifice in her despair. "That couldn't have been what the Lady wanted her to do."

"Are you so certain? Even if you're right, it was done in Her name. In the end, for you humans, does that make so very great a difference?"

For once, I had no words to argue.

"I've told you all this because you should know that the Dead despise me as much as the living. One day we may face another revenant— one even more powerful than Sarathiel. And if we do, it isn't going to be pleased to see me."

The snow landing on my face suddenly felt like the pricks of icy needles. I pictured the melted crown of Cimeliarch the Bright, dripping down its skull. The skeletal hand of Architrave the Dim, holding its unbalanced scales. Their ancient minds twisted with resentment, grown cruel and clever and half-mad from centuries of imprisonment at human hands.

The Lady had let me keep the revenant. But what if She had done so not in answer to my prayers, but for reasons of Her own?

Before, I had compared Her plans to a game of knights and kings. Now I imagined the checkered board growing vaster, stretching far into shadow. The game piece carved into Sarathiel's likeness knocked over by an unseen hand. The shape concealed behind it gliding forward from the dark.

Something occurred to me that I had never considered before. If the Lady was playing a game, a great game, a game of life and death, then who was Her opponent?

I shivered and tried my best to banish the image from my mind.

"There's something I've been wondering," I said, eager to change the subject. "The first humans who got possessed, the ones who went on to become saints; they weren't all strong enough to control unbound spirits, were they? They couldn't have been. At least some of them must have fought with their spirits the same way I do."

"Yes," the revenant said, after a long, ancient-feeling pause. *"They were our friends."*

"Then does that mean we're—"

"You had better not push it, nun. I can possess you whenever I want. I could do far worse than make you murder someone. I could make you try on hats."

Up on the battlements, where no one could see me, I smiled.

We sat together as the sky slowly brightened to the color of milk and the flurries dwindled, revealing the monastery's thatched roofs dusted in white. Monks began to stir, dim gray shapes shuffling along with bowed heads as they attended to their morning prayers. I was considering returning to my room when I caught sight of new activity below. A pair of horses had been led into the courtyard; their reins were being handed over to a tall, hooded brother who walked with a slight limp, dressed for travel. One of the horses was white, and the other dapple-gray.

I flew down the stairs and through the twisting alley that led to the courtyard, intercepting the brother on his way to the stable. By the looks of it, he had planned to lead Priestbane to a stall before departing the monastery on his own horse. He drew to a surprised halt when I appeared, but did nothing to discourage me from laying my hand on Priestbane's neck, who turned his head, blowing hay-scented breath against my face.

I distantly noticed that the monk wasn't one of the brothers I recognized. He was too tall, too slender, his posture too elegant. Then he said, "I didn't think you would be awake," and drew back his hood.

It was the first time I had seen Leander since that day in his chamber. He looked ghostly draped in a monk's woolen robes instead of his tailored confessor's vestments, their rough weave emphasizing the cold, saintly beauty of his face and the ethereal white of his hair. He didn't appear quite real, as though he had stepped from a scene in a tapestry.

He surprised me by passing me Priestbane's reins. "I thought you might as well have him. He's already yours, as far as the masses are concerned."

"You mean—"

"I've left the contract of ownership with the brothers. You only need to sign it. I doubt you'll ever have need of it, but better to make the transaction official." Dryly, he added, "I wouldn't want anyone to accuse you of horse theft."

Words had vanished from my head like birds taking flight. I couldn't think of how to answer. I stroked Priestbane's mane, acutely aware of Leander watching. His gaze was intent, as though he was studying my face, tucking a final memory of me away.

"Why are you dressed as a monk?" I asked, hoping to jar him from his strange mood. I assumed he held monks in as much contempt as nuns; he couldn't possibly feel comfortable borrowing a Gray Brother's spare clothes.

His answer pierced me like an arrow. "I've decided to take my vows," he said. "I'm leaving Roischal to study with the brothers of Saint Severin."

It was the last answer I expected. The brothers of Saint Severin were famous for producing illuminated manuscripts of exquisite beauty, at the cost of growing stooped and half-blind before their time. I tried to picture Leander among them, leaning over a desk with his white hair glowing in the candlelight, swirls of color coming alive beneath his brush. A quiet life, one in which he would hurt no one.

During my moment of distraction, he had mounted his horse. He was already turning, a hand lifted in farewell. "Goodbye, Artemisia."

Holding Priestbane's reins, I watched him ride away between

the stone buildings, a solitary figure fading into the drifting white. When he vanished, a sense of loss struck me like an unexpected blow. I shouldn't have stood in silence; I should have said something in return.

Then an odd coincidence tickled the back of my mind. Something Sister Iris had said once, when our convent had been lent a manuscript from the brothers of Saint Severin. A minor, seemingly insignificant detail: that the brothers devotedly followed Josephine of Bissalart's techniques in the creation of their manuscripts. In my mind's eye, I saw a lantern's light glimmering over the revenants' unearthly, gilded forms.

Again, I felt the Lady's hand hovering. And in that moment I was seized by the same fierce certainty that I had felt charging into the Battle of Bonsaint—this time a certainty that Leander wasn't gone forever. One day, the Lady's plans would bring us together again.

Priestbane stamped a hoof, mouthing eagerly at the bit. Wind rushed from the valley like an invitation, lifting my hair, tugging at my robes. I took hold of Priestbane's mane and scrambled onto his bare back.

Both the monks and the revenant reacted with alarm as Priestbane charged through the monastery in a snorting clatter of hooves. *"Nun!"* "Lady, wait—" But I was already cantering away, their protests lost to the wind. A startled flock of ravens burst cawing from the walls, and among their flickering black bodies I thought I made out a familiar white shape rising into the sky, winging away toward the mountains. Filled with thoughtless joy, I turned Priestbane to follow.

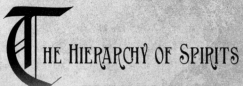

THE HIERARCHY OF SPIRITS

FIRST ORDER
THE ORDER OF THE INNOCENTS

Shade

Wisp

SECOND ORDER
SOULS LOST TO THE FORCES OF NATURE

Gaunt—*Death by famine*

Frostfain—*Death by exposure*

Undine—*Death by drowning*

Ashgrim—*Death by fire*

THIRD ORDER
SOULS LOST TO ILLNESS AND DISEASE

Feverling—*Death by fever*

Witherkin—*Death by wasting*

Wretchling—*Death by flux*

Blight wraith—*Death by blight*

Plague specter—*Death by pestilence*

FOURTH ORDER
SOULS LOST TO VIOLENCE

Rivener—*Death by battle*

Fury—*Death by murder*

Penitent—*Death by execution*

White vicar—*The spirit of a slain cleric*

FIFTH ORDER
THE SEVEN REVENANTS

Cimeliarch the Bright

Architrave the Dim

Cahethal the Mad

Oremus the Lost

Sarathiel the Obscured

Malthas the Hollow

Rathanael the Scorned

ACKNOWLEDGMENTS

I wrote this book during Covid isolation, at a time when, like many people, I felt like Artax drowning in the Swamp of Sadness, the most depressed I'd ever been in my life (which is saying something), slowly losing my facility with language, chipping away at draft after draft that read as though it had been written by a dismal AI or a committee of bewildered space aliens nervously attempting to mimic human behavior. That is to say, this book was very hard to write and I owe a considerable debt of gratitude to everyone who put up with me during it.

Firstly, I need to thank my agent, Sara Megibow, who is an eternal beacon of light and dragged me out of the swamp many times. Secondly, my wonderful editor, Karen Wojtyla, who waited with great compassion and forbearance as I crept piteously toward my deadlines like a horrible Sméagol. And all the marvelous people at S&S who work so hard normally, and had to work even harder on *Vespertine* because of our tight schedule: Nicole Fiorica, Bridget

Madsen, Elizabeth Blake-Linn, Sonia Chaghatzbanian, Irene Metaxatos, Cassie Malmo, Chantal Gersch, Emily Ritter, Anna Jarzab, Caitlin Sweeney, Nicole Russo, Mandy Veloso, Penina Lopez, and many others whose names I don't know, but who deserve a lifetime supply of gourmet chocolate for their tireless efforts behind the scenes.

Next I must thank my family and friends, who tolerated an astonishing amount of bizarre behavior as I deteriorated into a primordial ooze-like state—particularly my mom and dad, without whose support I never would have become an author, and also would have died of scurvy. And my dear friends Jes, Rachel, and Jamie, who helped me brainstorm important parts of the book, as well as Ashley Poston, for her much-needed kindness and advice.

I wouldn't be here today without the support of independent booksellers. I would like to thank everyone at my local indie Joseph-Beth, the first bookstore to feature in my childhood memories, and still my favorite bookstore today. I am also deeply grateful to bookseller Nicole Brinkley, who reached out to me at a time when I desperately needed help.

Last but not least: my profound thanks to Charlie Bowater, the phenomenally skilled artist who illustrates my covers, and hasn't yet appeared at the stroke of midnight to claim my soul, which I owe her. Truly. It's in the contract.